Doom

WILLIAM GERHARDIE was born in St Petersburg in 1895. He was educated in Russia and later at Worcester College, Oxford, where he wrote his first novel, *Futility*. During the First World War he was posted to the staff of the British Military Attaché at Petrograd, and in 1918 he went with the British Military Mission to Siberia. After two years there, he left the army with an OBE, sailing home by way of Singapore, Colombo and Port Said—a journey that forms the closing chapters of *The Polyglots*. Gerhardie wrote much of the novel at Innsbruck, completing it under difficult conditions while his father was dying.

In addition to his novels, which include *Resurrection* (1934) and *Of Mortal Love* (1936), William Gerhardie wrote several non-fiction works, among them *Anton Chekhov* (1923), written during his time at Oxford; *Memoirs of a Polyglot* (1931) and the posthumously published biographical history *God's Fifth Column* (1981). He died in London in 1977.

MICHAEL HOLROYD is well known as an author and biographer, notably of Lytton Strachey and Augustus John. He was editor, with Robert Skidelsky, of Gerhardie's *God's Fifth Column* (1981).

D0683111

Prion Lost Treasures

William Gerhardie

Doom

with a Preface by
MICHAEL HOLROYD

PRION

This edition published in 2001 by
Prion Books Limited, Imperial Works,
Perren Street, London NW5 3ED
www.prionbooks.com

First published in 1927 as *Jazz and Jasper,* as *My Sinful Earth*
in 1947 and as *Doom* in 1974
© William Gerhardie 1927
Preface © Michael Holroyd 1983

ISBN 1-85375-446-3

Printed and bound in Great Britain
by Bookmarque Limited, Croydon, Surrey

Preface

Michael Holroyd

'Dear Sir,—If it would be convenient for you to call on me here [23 St Bride Street] I should like to see you.' William Gerhardie was in Vienna when this urgent summons from Lord Beaverbrook arrived, and, in other circumstances, he might have remained there several years. However, stopping only to collect his father's urn (which he deposited on his way back at a station cloakroom in Paris), he hastened to London to hear Beaverbrook extol the excellence of his recent novel, *The Polyglots*. 'He had,' remembers Gerhardie, 'very fine judgement.' From this meeting in 1925 there grew a warm friendship, and from this friendship came *Doom*.

Over the next months Beaverbrook entertained Gerhardie very grandly, introducing him to all the smart set in London, the great and the beautiful. 'You must meet him. He's nice,' D.H. Lawrence wrote to Middleton Murry—elsewhere adding: 'He came for an hour and stayed seven.' Such heady attentions are unusual for a writer, and Gerhardie confesses that he felt flattered. If only, he sometimes reflected, he had had less genius, how Lord Beaverbrook might have helped him! After all, he seemed prepared to do almost anything for him as a journalist: he had even promised him, as a wedding present, the *Evening Standard*. But Gerhardie, who never married, was not a journalist. 'I am,' he insisted, 'an artist. Probably a great artist. It pleases me when you treat me as an artist.' So that was how Beaverbrook did treat him, tenderly, with affection, but without commercial profit. In vain he had attempted to convert *The Polyglots* into a bestseller (though not, Gerhardie noted, with quite the zeal he put into his Empire Campaign); but his real gift lay in the material he was giving Gerhardie for his next novel.

The whirl of Beaverbrook's hospitality—the yachts, the weekends, the night clubs—grew so absorbing that it precluded any actual work and before the end of 1925 Gerhardie fled abroad. By New Year's Day 1926 he had set up temporary headquarters in the South of France where, he assured Beaverbrook, 'the Muse is visiting me every morning'. Like Dickens with *Household Words*, he had agreed to write a serialized novel for the *Daily Express* and, in a burst of optimism, was soon confiding that 'I am getting lots of fun, and a fair amount of happiness, out of writing this serial, now that I am free from interruption, and I do not think you will be disappointed. Ah, if I could persuade you to become a novelist! To experience that rare feeling of walking a little outside and beside life…on the roof of No 23 St Bride Street.'

Gerhardie's correspondence with Beaverbrook at this time gives a fascinating account of the novel's development, the author's personality and his friendship with the chief character in the book. Already, by February 1926, he is admitting that his serial 'is in a bad way'. His imagination was not that of a science fiction writer, and by placing the narrative in the future he felt that he risked giving it an air of unreality. He wanted, for example, a handful of people left on a mountain top with the rest of the world disintegrated to nothing. The problem had defeated the trained scientific mind of H. G. Wells (who suggested it would have to be a dream) and it was D. H. Lawrence who, breaking out into ripples of girlish laughter at the ingenuity of his solution, gave him the metaphor of a laddered stocking, so that the world disintegrated piecemeal. It is not everyday that a world vanishes so plausibly, or with so much delicacy and charm.

But the reality which at first seemed so elusive on paper was presenting itself elsewhere in the most inconvenient ways. His house in the South of France, on which he had spent much time and whitewash, had let him down. 'The hens won't lay, the doors won't lock, the stoves won't heat,' he complained to Beaverbrook; and the maid, 'a slender girl of sixteen summers', had become, in place of his novel, the centre of all his thoughts and actions—though mainly because she suffered from constant toothache and 'wants attending to'. However, he promised, 'I will see to it that literature does not suffer.'

A further threat to the book was, he believed, supplied by Rebecca West whom Gerhardie met at Antibes and who 'curiously enough is also writing a book about you,' he wrote accusingly to Beaverbrook (14 September 1926). His dismay was shortlived. 'My sense of dissatisfaction with myself,' he explained, 'completely left me when I learnt that she had been at it for three years.' He himself had been at work now a mere year or so and was returning to the task 'with renewed interest. The fact of the matter was that when I started writing I was too close to the experiences (in London) which inspired it. I can only write in retrospect, when the irrelevant has filtered through and the essential remains in my memory; and I am now approaching this condition of mind and soul.'

During this period he received almost obtrusive encouragement from Beaverbrook. 'Will you go on with your novel now?' he asked. '...Why don't you come and see me again? You should settle in this country here for a few months. I will pay your expenses.' But wisely Gerhardie resisted the temptation. 'As for my settling down in England, your offer to pay my expenses is characteristically generous,' he replied, 'but I'd hate to come empty-handed. I think if I stay here I will produce the novel.' His confidence seemed justified, and by October he was reporting that 'the old plot has been reinforced by a new one and the newspaper proprietor is involved in a *story*, for which you won't thank me. I am really glad that I postponed it, for it is stronger and better and madder than before.'

If *Doom* is Gerhardie's maddest novel, this was partly due to the element of comic fantasy that he had by now successfully introduced into his relationship with Beaverbrook. Connoisseurs of Gerhardie have always admired the manner in which he eclipses what is actual with what is fantastic to produce his own subtle light of reality. The newspaper world was an ideal arena in which to practise this art. It was not long before he was promising, indeed threatening, with 'a flourish of the pen', to take over all policy decisions on behalf of the Beaverbrook press. For a start, on the literary side, why should they not publish plays?—he happened to have just completed one himself. Then there was the question of foreign policy. Luckily Gerhardie had a brother domiciled in Helsingfors, so there was no difficulty there. 'He is not a journalist,' Gerhardie reassured Beaverbrook, adding by way of endorsement, 'Helsingfors is not Rome.' On artistic matters generally, Gerhardie entertained far-ranging plans. 'What I really meant to ask you,' he explained to Beaverbrook (27 December 1926), 'was whether you would care to collaborate with me in writing a musical comedy...I have a good plot, and a number of unexpectedly promising melodies have occurred to me. I have a certain difficulty in writing them down as my musical education is sadly inadequate. But I could overcome this by humming them into a recording phonograph; and no doubt you could produce others, and we could get some old hack to set them down in writing and to orchestrate the thing in accordance with our wishes. You once told me that you had a great gift for jazz music, and having received could no doubt emit a fair supply of it! And you are full of stimulating ideas as I remember when discussing my novel with you.'

Under the continuous pressure of such advice, Lord Beaverbrook absconded for some time to the Upper Nile, but a stream of fantasy pursued him even to the seat of his holiday. Gerhardie himself had descended into Algeria where 'a beautiful new mistress . . . comes to see me three times a week and costs me 50 francs a time, and so I can't afford to neglect a chance of selling my article....' These Algerian adventures, which were eventually to enrich his novel *Resurrection*, could, so Gerhardie judged, be put to immediate use in the columns of the *Daily Express* for the moral benefit of its readers. 'I've been round to a number of houses of ill-fame for which Algiers is ill-famed,' he explained, 'but my instinct for self-preservation causes me, in this place, to multiply precautions so that I feel I might be in a padded overcoat. There is more comedy than lust about these places. Sex *is* a problem—for the *Daily Express* to solve. Very simple. Birth control, on the one hand; the elimination of disease on the other; and free love after that. There is no danger of overstepping the mark as some Puritans imagine; for when people have had enough they stop.'

Such commonsense fantasies were parried by Beaverbrook (the son of a rector) unsatisfactorily, until Gerhardie felt obliged to inform him (16 January 1927): 'I am very disappointed in you. I think newspaper proprietors ought to be altogether abolished and all control seized by the authors!!'

That summer, the sun slowly drove Gerhardie north—but he was no longer empty-handed. From Paris he announced (21 June 1927) the conditions for his invasion of London. 'I should like to come and show you my serial. But if you are cruising in the Mediterranean or shooting birds in remote corners of the country or otherwise not in the mood to attend to my particular literature I will stay in Paris, which city, but for your absence from it, appeals to me more than London, which, conversely, appeals to me mainly on account of your presence there.' A few days later Beaverbrook (who had just written a *Sunday Express* article about Gerhardie as a 'Splendid Failure') picked him up at Ostend in a yacht full of girls. So the extraordinary friendship continued to prosper and to fertilize Gerhardie's *Doom*.

Gerhardie was now at the height of his literary fame and this new novel, so wrote Arnold Bennett, like the *accouchement* of a political Duchess, was awaited with considerable speculation. When it appeared in April 1928 it sold better than any of the previous books and he was acknowledged, almost everywhere, to be a master of the ridiculous. The looseness of the book's structure enabled Gerhardie to combine an extravagant fantasia with a Fleet Street satire, fusing them together with poetry and wit. Yet amid the pot-pourri of comedy and manners, there is an underlying melancholy which culminates in the atomic disintegration of all but a few refugees in a hotel on a rounded mountain top isolated from the earth and now circling the sun—a token world for the vanished planet.

It is a confusing book. Evelyn Waugh, whose favourite Gerhardie novel it always remained, compared the writing to that of Ivy Compton Burnett, and elsewhere critics likened it to, among others, Beerbohm, Giraudoux, Huxley and 'the cool irresponsible dexterity of Paul Morand'. Re-reading it to-day, *Doom* seems like nothing else in the language, and the best contemporary critic was probably Arnold Bennett who wrote of its 'wild and brilliant originality'.

In his autobiography, *Memoirs of a Polyglot*, Gerhardie portrayed Beaverbrook as 'a potential great man without a mission'. It was, in the judgement of Beaverbrook's biographer A. J. P. Taylor, 'the only book known to me which gives anything like a convincing picture of Beaverbrook in middle age'. *Doom*, in many ways, is a vehicle for exploring the sensations felt within the orbit of Beaverbrook who, as Lord Ottercove, the newspaper Napoleon, is described as 'the big drum in the jazz band of our civilization' whose saving grace was that he 'suffered from an inferiority complex in the presence of Lord Beaverbrook'. Before getting to know him, Gerhardie had regarded Beaverbrook as 'less of a personality than a power', though he soon found his force and charm to be 'quite irresistible'. Yet in *Doom* Ottercove retains his power, even in dishabille. In his vest and pants he is 'still looking the part, still the unchallenged proprietor and director of the *Daily Runner*'. Gerhardie handles him with great subtlety, and with a ruthlessness which yet somehow shows both appreciation and affection. Whenever Ottercove appears on the scene the other characters take their lead from him. At one point someone suggests a celebration. 'Lord Ottercove did not reply. Lord Ottercove hated to act on other people's suggestions....If he approved of a suggestion, he said nothing; then, a few moments later, made it himself. "I'm taking you out to-night, all of you".'

For all its absurdities the book works and is largely held together by Ottercove's power, which does not dominate the other characters but draws reactions from them. His immense energy carries along a huge entourage that includes several people Gerhardie had met through Beaverbrook—Lord Castlerosse who appears as Lord de

Jones, and Arnold Bennett who, in the guise of Vernon Sprott, is described as 'a writer of talent but a merchant of genius'. Then, in the young novelist Frank Dickin, we catch an amusing glimpse of the William Gerhardie of that time, in turn anxious, elated, dismayed but always observant with a quiet authority.

Some extra confusion has been shed on this confusing novel by the multiplicity of its titles. Gerhardie had originally wanted to call it *Doom*, but his British publishers vetoed this on the ground that such reverberations of gloom would at once kill all sales. In America, even his second choice *Jazz and Jasper* (a title which hinted at the two values, social and spiritual, that in collision provide the theme of the novel) was also unacceptable. The Jazz Age, which according to Scott Fitzgerald had begun with the May Day riots of 1919, was already almost over, and Gerhardie was obliged to rename his book *Eva's Apples*. When, in 1947, the novel was republished its title was improved to *My Sinful Earth* and the title page bore an explanatory epigraph from Shakespeare's sonnet CXLVI:

> *Poor soul, the centre of my sinful earth,*
> *Fool'd by these rebel powers that thee array,*
> *Why dost thou pine within and suffer dearth,*
> *Painting thy outward walls so costly gay?*

Only some forty-five years after its first appearance, did this novel of the 1920s, that foreshadows the coming of our own era, revert to its original title *Doom* which seems, the author ventures to think, a prophetic understatement.

MICHAEL HOLROYD

1

'No, no, "Me-Too," you'd better run away now, or sit and wait here in the taxi.'

'But the taxi's so expensive, darling.' (It was not at all like Eva, he reflected, to object to his expenses.) 'I'd better come upstairs with you.'

'But no! I've an *appointment* with Lord Ottercove!'

'But I'd like to see Lord Ottercove myself.'

'But he hasn't asked to see you.'

'But he might like to—if he knew.'

'He doesn't know you.'

'He would if I came up with you.'

How she added to his difficulties!

Before the porch of a tall Fleet Street building from whose roof an electric sign proclaimed the fiery words *Daily Runner*, they argued, while the taxi-meter ticked away the aeons, and the aeons added shillings. From the pavement he gazed up at the huge inscrutable building and reflected that, located somewhere in its innermost recesses, like a spider, waiting for him, was the great Lord Ottercove, as the black hand of the hall clock moved towards the hour appointed for the interview.

Leaving Eva in the taxi, he made away with a certain unnatural kind of alacrity, a recklessly confident step, to face the braided commissionaire who listened with faint but not unhopeful surprise to the news of the visitor's claim to an appointment with his lordship. Ever jealous, however, like Peter, of his guardianship of the access to God, he provided the applicant with a form to be filled in with information of a biographical nature and outlining the general character of his business: the form to precede him to the desired destination; the aspirant to await below confirmation of the bona fides of his claim to the exalted interview. The confirmation duly forthcoming, the faithful steward handed the young visitor on to a lift-boy who, taking him up several floors, handed him on to a brother lift-boy, who presently handed him on to a third brother. Each new lift-boy to whom he was handed over looked more exclusive, had a manner at once more solemn and more deferential—the mark of one who dwells in higher altitudes, more immune from the grosser things of the earth. Up and up they went, higher and higher, till the doors of the lift opened again and he was handed out to a page altogether removed from the race of mere lift-boys. The page bade him follow him up the few remaining steps—the last golden ladder to heaven—to a landing where the page divested him of his cruder clothes of the street, took him up another three carpeted steps, and bidding him wait, knocked reverently at the door. And opened it before the visitor, who was pulling out his cuffs and adjusting his tie, was quite ready to step forward. With a jerky suddenness, not unlike that of policemen in American comic films dashing off the ground in pursuit of a criminal, he entered the room, the page shutting the door on him.

In a vast radiant space of yellow and blue, at an octagonal table surrounded by chairs, sat a slim middle-sized figure in a dark-blue suit, a negligent lock over the brow. It rose promptly, shook hands, gave the visitor one searching look with its penetrating grey eye, a guarded smile revealing white affable teeth, and sat down again to the octagonal table, bidding the visitor to do likewise but taking no further notice of him.

The visitor sat hushed and abashed, slowly taking in the surroundings, and Lord Ottercove went on with his work, going through the small pile of papers before him with record speed, while a trained lady-secretary with a coyly grave manner and a voice attuned to the requisite pitch of awed and concentrated attention received his instructions. From time to time Lord Ottercove would take up the receiver and say, 'Give me the Prime Minister,' or 'Give me the Duke of Liverpool,' and, incredible as it seemed, the Prime Minister or the Duke of Liverpool was already talking—and not from Liverpool. 'Hello, Fred,' from Lord Ottercove. 'Oh, very well and full of mischief! What? Oh, I'm bored to hell. I'm going in for a new hobby. Buying race horses. What? Let me know before you start. Good-bye to you.'

The visitor had a feeling of sharing in Lord Ottercove's multifarious activities and interests, and when he smiled—his eyes were grey and full of mischief—the visitor smiled too, involuntarily. But Lord Ottercove still took no notice of him.

And now his eyes were scanning a batch of typescript. His mouth opened. ' "Pale Primroses" by Frank Dickin,' he said and looked humorously at the visitor. 'Anything else?' he asked the secretary.

'Your spectacles.'

He stretched out his hand for them. 'Good night to you.'

And while she was gathering her papers, Lord Ottercove leaned back, his preoccupied air having deserted him, a leisurely smile having taken its place. 'Well, I am very interested to meet you, Mr. Dickin,' he said (the secretary now having retired). 'My serial editor submitted to me the beginning of a proposed novel by you with a synopsis of its general plot, and I am much intrigued by it for a reason that you won't guess. Your name— you will forgive me for saying so—was completely unknown to me. Frank Dickin did not convey anything to me in itself, you understand.'

'Frank Septimus Dickin.'

'You prefer it like that?'

'To redeem, I suppose, the plainness of the Dickin.'

'Of course, Dickin is not Dickens.' His lordship smiled indulgently.

'No, of course not.'

'Of course. Still, what attracted me—and that is chiefly why I wrote to you—are the people in your book. So real. It seemed to me I knew them.'

'Well, I do try to make them living. I think it is up to a novelist——'

'I don't mean that. I think I know the family you describe. Or, rather, their connections and appendages. A remarkable coincidence, anyway, about the names.'

Here Dickin smiled.

'So they *are* "copies"?'

'Well, yes, to a considerable extent, I am bound to confess.'

'Have you brought me the continuation as I asked you to do in my letter? If so, I will read it to-night.'

'I am afraid it is very rough manuscript. You would not feel very happy with it.'

'Then you read it to me.'

'But it's long.'

'Read it! I shall tell you when to stop.' Lord Ottercove pressed the button. The page stood in the doorway. 'Don't let any of them bother me for the next two hours. Keep them out, do you hear, and shut the door behind you!'

'Yes, m'lord.'

To Captains of Industry time is said to be money. But Generals of the Press are artists who express their sensibility in affairs. They have risen to heights beyond time and avarice and avarice in time to a condition of immanent immortality already in this world. Lord Ottercove had suddenly expressed the wish to be relieved of the blazing heat and burden of the day. For what does it profit a man to be rich if he cannot please his own moods? He was interested, satisfied: the hours he devoted to this visitor were of value to him: that was all. 'Come and sit down here, Mr. Dickin; you will get a better light.'

Dickin plunged into a delicate-looking armchair—and fell through. He started up with a look as though he thought he was going to be thrashed for it, but Lord Ottercove, with splendid unconcern for the chair, only asked: 'Have you hurt yourself?'

'On the contrary…'

'On the contrary what?'

'On the contrary: I have not hurt myself.'

'Thank God for that.'

'But I've hurt the chair.'

'Not a bit of it! Come and sit in this chair and read me your manuscript. Now then.'

'It is difficult to relate these things in their proper sequence. Some things stand out, others fade; that is all.'

'Are you talking now or reading?' asked Lord Ottercove.

'Reading.—I remember only a desultory Christmas Eve in the Tyrol. I strolled about lonely, sad, because laden with memories, through the winter streets of Innsbruck, when a small group of people emerged from a shop, arguing in Russian as to their next move. I had picked up a fair amount of Russian in captivity during the war, quartered as we were with Russian officers, and improved it later on our ill-starred mission at Archangel, which, in the order of things, left behind memories. Was it that snow called to snow? It was thawing, and the shop windows twinkling in the winter dusk were faintly reminiscent. Memory calling to memory? But I went straight up to them and, with a curt apology, expressed my pleasure at hearing the dear language. In London I would have been brought up at Marlborough Street Police Station next morning and fined five pounds for "annoying ladies in the street." In New York I would have been flung summarily into prison for attempted rape. But the Russian ladies smiled with undisguised pleasure and expectation, and talking eagerly, we immediately repaired to the Maria-Theresien-Café and exchanged experiences, attracting everyone's attention in the café by our voluble reminiscences. One lady—the fair, small, good-looking one, bubbling over with excitement—had married and divorced an Irishman, a certain Mr. Kerr whom she had met in Russia before the war, and till recently they owned a castle in Meran, but—she hinted at the Revolution, the War, the Italian annexation of South Tyrol, and, well, at their large and careless way of living. There had been debts. In fine, the castle was no more. But there were children. Four of them: two boys, two girls. Zita was the elder of the girls. She was sixteen. And, I perceived, amazingly good-looking in her bright, fair way. The younger, Eva, was at school in England. This little boy was John, the despair of her life! He simply wouldn't sit still. And, indeed, he was already fiddling with my watch chain. But she had another son, the eldest of her children, who had her eyes and loved her dearly. Raymond, the apple of her eye! He was in England. They wished he might have gone to Oxford or Cambridge. Alas, that was not possible now. He was in the motor trade. It wasn't quite the thing for him. He was more a poet at heart, melancholy, meditative, interested in bird life. But how good-looking! Raymond and Eva were the two best-looking of the family—her mother's children. They had her eyes. Now John was made for the motor trade. Let him see a wheel or a piece of wire, and he must go and touch it.

'The other lady, dark and passionate but restrained by Mrs. Kerr's volubility, was Russian too, but married to a local Austrian tram driver. She told me her story. The daughter of a landowner, like Mrs. Kerr, she met her future husband when he was a prisoner-of-war in Russia; she a Red Cross nurse. Love at first sight. She married him and helped him to escape, all very romantically. He had told her he was an engineer by education and God-knows-what besides. They came to his native Innsbruck and he resumed his duties as a tram driver. And everybody tells him he is a fool to have saddled himself with an uncongenial Russian wife and he seems to resent the marriage more than she resents his calling and has pawned the silver things she has managed to smuggle out of Russia and has been unfaithful to her and treats her brutally and she is now divorcing him because she hates him so. And yet is curious about his doings and still goes by the name of Frau König and works at a knitting establishment and is about to start work on her own— if only somebody would provide her with capital. "But I can't," immediately says Mrs. Kerr. "My husband can't give me anything. I have great hopes of getting some money from my parents in Russia, but my mother writes that she can't send us anything. They are starving practically. Life is so hard for us who have come from Russia. And our castle in Meran...It's all this awful Revolution."

'Ah, the good old days in Russia! Did I know her father, the landowner Pàvel Yàkovlevich Sabolènko? I didn't? And yet everybody who had been to Russia knew him. He owned mines, he owned railways, he owned heaven knows what not. Everybody knew him. You had only to mention the name Pàvel Yàkovlevich Sabolènko for everybody to say: "Sabolènko? Pàvel Yàkovlevich? Why, of course!" And now he said he couldn't send her a penny. It seemed a shame. But, of course, they have had a revolution. Her father was seized by his own peasants (to whom he'd been a father all his life; they even called him "our father") and was led out into the wood to be hanged, when a passing aeroplane attracted their attention and they forgot about him. But mother was seized by them on their way back, by way of afterthought, and was about to be torn limb from limb, when father butted in and shouted: "What's the good of wasting your time on an old hag like this? Get on with the Revolution!" and they all shouted, "Hear! hear! Long live the Revolution!" and elected father President of the Local Revolutionary Centre, which he was still. But the trouble was that you could never be sure with such erratic people, well-meaning but somehow not very certain of their intellectual premises. Father was a genius, of course. He had graduated at eight different universities and had written a philosophical treatise, a sort of bridge work between Plato and Schopenhauer, and had, of late, much strengthened his position in regard to the Soviets by a work on Socialism entitled "Beyond Lenin", and was regarded as an authority on mathematics. "I am telling you all this because you are a writer. You can make use of it in your books. We Sabolènkos are a most interesting, original family. One of my brothers shot himself; another got drowned..." '

'Look here,' Lord Ottercove interrupted, 'will you have a drink before you continue?'

'Thanks awfully.'

'What will you have?'

'Wine. White wine.'

'Will you have champagne?'

'Thanks, I'll have champagne. I adore it.'

Lord Ottercove rang in a special way. A butler sprang out of the floor. 'Give me the wine-list.'

The butler returned with a huge album bound in crocodile leather. 'You are looking at the binding, I notice,' said the host. 'It is the skin of a crocodile I shot myself on the Nile.' And he selected a half-bottle of the year 1895. 'According to historians,' he said, 'a magnificent vintage.'

Dickin drank the champagne and thought—because she too adored champagne—of Eva waiting for him in the taxi. But the great room with the drawn curtains and the electric radiators full on was so snug; and already the champagne was doing its care-transcending work. He hoped that Eva was very comfortable in the taxi.

'Well, go on,' said Lord Ottercove.

'It was arranged between us before we parted that we should spend that Christmas Eve together at Frau König's rooms. They had arranged to do so before they met me. I arrived shortly before midnight, laden with provisions. The Christmas-tree was lit, and John fiddling with everything that he could fiddle with, and Zita all in white and somehow marvellously seductive-looking. I marvelled at the lines of that young body. I still marvel when I think of them. It was warm and cosy in Frau König's room on account of the lit candles. Mrs. Kerr was voluble and took the words out of poor Frau König's mouth.

' "Charming!" I exclaimed. "The Real Russian Christmas!"

' "It's what I wanted!" cried Mrs. Kerr. "And I knew Frau König would be pleased to spend Christmas Eve among Russian friends. And we regard you as a Russian too."

' "As a matter of fact, I lived in Russia as a child, while my father was Secretary at the British Embassy in Petersburg, and my earliest reminiscences go back to Russia."

' "Well, there you are! I knew Frau König would appreciate a Russian Christmas Eve. And so I said to her: 'Tamara Leonidovna, you have a larger room than I have; ask us to supper, and we will spend Christmas Eve together.' And we thought of writing a little story together: 'A young brunette—Tamara Leonidovna—asked a—a young (I am not old, am I?) blonde to her Christmas-tree; and while they were thus together, there looked in on them through the window a third guest—the Moon.' "

'And, indeed, the moon looked through the tall blue pine of the forest. "Charming," I said.

' "How much will they give us for it?"

' "How do you mean?"

' "How many dollars—in an American magazine?"

' "Well—I don't know—it depends, of course——"

' "And in England? How many sterlings?"

'I am the last man to generalize about national characteristics; but there was something perennially irresponsible about Mrs. Kerr's nature. She had taken part in a £1,000 competition for a General Election forecast to be held in England on the Tuesday and arranged for a holiday tour on the following Saturday on the strength of the £1,000 which she hoped to win.'

'Ha!' laughed Lord Ottercove. 'Incredible, isn't it?'

Dickin, encouraged, continued with warmth, and without reference to the manuscript: 'The fate of these people! who had known affluent days in genial surroundings on the accustomed background of Russian life, now cast ashore in a foreign land which looks askance at them and knows them not!'

Was it the champagne which spoke in him, or a look of dissension in his listener's eye? But he grew aggressively emotional. 'They are too old to be acclimatized, too indolent to start afresh. They have dragged themselves here and cast their living carcases upon the tide of life at this great turning-point in human destiny.'

'Come, come!' said Lord Ottercove. But Dickin, dazed with the wine, was neither coming nor going. His heart was overwhelmed with love for humanity. 'They feel they dream. All familiar things by which they had learnt their values had vanished overnight. They hear a tumult outside, but they are at a loss to understand its meaning. They are no longer of the past: it is not there: it has vanished beneath their feet, and its history is not yet. They are not of the present: they do not know it, and it knows them not. They are silent, alone. They are alive, but the shadow of death has crept over them. They are dead souls with just a flicker of light on them...'

Lord Ottercove, listening, could not make out what this strange note of emotion in Dickin connoted: whether this was poetry, and if so, whether good or bad poetry. Dickin, conscious of discomfiture, felt the need to excuse himself. 'A beginning,' he said, 'in the manner of Guy de Maupassant in his more sentimental vein.' He had a feeling that the air had gained access to that air-proof compartment in him in which alone pure sentiment can thrive, and shrank at this contamination of sentimentality. 'I see I bore you.'

'Not a bit of it, my dear fellow. I cannot tell you how it all interests me—for various reasons, of which I shall tell you presently.'

'I will read on.'

'Whichever is quicker and more to the point.'

'I must read it all. It is nothing without the atmosphere.'

'I understand—about the atmosphere. Go on in your own way.'

'Both women vied to show me their photographs. Frau König took me aside surreptitiously into her small bedroom—the Christmas-tree was in the kitchen—and there showed me photographs of her father, her mother, herself and her brother, and even of the tram driver. A man with a chin and a moustachio. But when we got back into the kitchen Mrs. Kerr would not let go of me. She had brought all her photographs with her so that she might show them to me: her great genius of a father, her mother, the brother who had shot himself, and the one who was drowned. "And this is my husband."

'From the cardboard in my hand Mr. Kerr gazed at me circumspectly.

' "A handsome man, but a wicked, impossible temper. He left his people in Ireland because he could not get on with them and bought the castle in Meran and never wanted to go back. And even now, poor fellow, tries to keep up appearances—eats nothing all day but dines at night with an old friend of his, a Rittmeister, at the station restaurant."

' "Daddy's always very spick and span," said Zita.

' "So he is still about ?"

' "Oh, yes! He won't go back to Ireland while his father is alive, and he loves the Austrians."

' "Daddy is awfully stupid about learning languages," said Zita. "He's lived here all his life and can hardly speak a word of German."

' "But, of course, he can speak German," Mrs. Kerr butted in. "He always speaks German with the Rittmeister. I heard him last night."

' "Mummy, he can't, to save his life! When he orders three cups of coffee he holds out three fingers and says:'Zwei.'And in Vienna when he wanted to show us the Rathaus, he stopped a man in the street and said:'Please show me the way to the rat house.'"

' "He didn't!"

' "He did!"

' "Still, your father is a fine man, and if it hadn't been for his temper I should have never divorced him. But he used to throw things at me—a flower vase, a candelabrum, a great big jug of water. I'd have to hide in the garden all night. He was so insanely jealous!" She smiled slyly. "Perhaps not without cause."

' "This, I forgot to show you," said Frau König, "is the photograph of my fiancé."

' "Frau König," explained Mrs. Kerr, "is engaged to a very charming, intellectual young man. A Russian student in Paris."

' "To a youth?"

' "What age is he, Tamara Leonidovna?"

' "Thirty-eight or nine. This is an old photo of him, taken about twenty years ago on entering Tiflis University."

' "And what does he do?"

' "He wants to continue his course at the University in Paris in the Faculty of Philosophy. Then, eventually, he will start a factory."

' "What kind of factory?"

' "A knitting factory. We will direct it together. He is now, while pursuing his course in philosophy at the University, putting aside money for the factory by giving shorthand lessons in Paris."

' "A very active and sensible young man," commended Mrs. Kerr, "and I congratulate you, Tamara Leonidovna, with all my heart."

' "Thank you, Vera Pavlovna, I am very proud and happy———"

' "But wait, I haven't shown you the photograph of our castle," interrupted Mrs. Kerr, "our Schloss (she sighed) in Meran."

' "Oh, a very lovely old castle."

' "Here all my four children were born. Raymond and Zita upstairs; Eva and John here in the room next to the terrace. I changed my bedroom so as to be able to take shelter in the garden. But when he had calmed down there was no kinder man than my husband. This was my drawing-room—with the Japanese furniture. And they came and took everything, everything———" Tears rolled down her cheeks. "As in the *Cherry Orchard*..."

' "But why? I do not follow. Your husband is a British subject, isn't he? The Italian annexation of Süd Tirol would not affect his property."

'She nodded rapidly and sadly. "Debts..." she said. "How we lived! Horses and motor-cars. Bouts. We used to give parties which must have out-rivalled our Grand Dukes! Spent without counting! My husband—they are like that in Ireland—utterly unbusinesslike—irresponsible! And now we are punished." She looked at Zita pensively. "Yes," she said, "this Revolution has done a great deal of harm and caused untold suffering to us Russians of the cultured intellectual classes. But let us drink to Hope and a new and brighter Dawn!"

'We refilled our glasses with cognac, after which all things seemed possible. "To the factory!" I cried. "And here is to the future and an even finer, greater castle!"

' "I believe in what you say," chimed in Mrs. Kerr. " We shall be repaid for our present suffering. Even the Bible says: 'And many first shall be last, and many last first!' " '

2

The Young Girls

'They came to my *pension* the day after, Mrs. Kerr, Zita and John; and Frau König turned up afterwards and sat there like a silent reproach as Mrs. Kerr poured out her own woes, while John at once went over to my typewriter and began fiddling with the keys, and being chased away, opened a box which contained razor-blades. "John has been sent into my life as a punishment and thinks nothing of worrying his poor mummy. But Raymond is a saint and angel to me. Raymond has my eyes—the large, sorrowful eyes, you might say, of the Madonna kissing the finger-tips of her Child."

'They liked the *pension* and took a room in it. They attracted me chiefly on Zita's account. She had a wonderful way about her, as if on the brink of revealing much. "You know," she would say. "You know—it's queer how—how—you know——" And that sort of thing. And then her face had a sincere and curiously attractive, open, "you know" sort of look. She was sixteen, and wonderfully built. Men were after her, all sorts of dingy barons and counts. I took her out to dances. She seemed indifferent to her success. But I was devilishly attracted by her. I suppose she had the most perfect figure I had ever seen, and she danced adorably. Once, after dinner, when we were alone in the *pension* dining-room and she was standing warming herself against the glazed white stove in the corner, clasping it, her bosom against it, I ventured to press her from behind. She laughed and called it "artificial respiration," and I, grateful for a term, continued to interpret it, so to speak, in new terms and different forms, but calling it by the old name whenever she showed signs of deco-rous astonishment. And sneering the while at my rival, the young Count Kolberg. "Where have you picked him up?"

' "In a restaurant. He stood by the door. In a tail-coat, you know, all men look alike. Mummy called out: 'Waiter!' And he came up and introduced himself: 'Graf Kolberg.' "

' "Just like that?"

' "Yes. Clicked his heels: 'Graf Kolberg.' "

' "Fancy that!" And I gave her another little push.

' "But he is such a ninny. Twenty-eight, and hangs to his mother's apron strings. She still holds him by the hand in the street, and each year makes him a Christmas-tree."

' "Fancy that." I pushed her. For she had breasts like buffers, as though designed to break the impact with the stove.

' "But Mummy likes the old Gräfin, who is nosing everywhere to find out whether I'd be a suitable wife for him, and tries to borrow money from Mummy, thinking all English must be rich; and as she's always expecting something, Mummy's sent her a box of soap. But the old Gräfin took it in bad part. She thought it was an insinuation. I'm glad. She does look rather filthy."

' "She does," I said, and pushed her.

' "It's beastly, people thinking one has a lot of money when one hasn't any. I want to go to England and take dancing lessons," she observed, a little out of breath.

' "Whatever for?"

' "To become a professional dancer. It's a good thing."

'She was now sitting on a table and performing a sort of Müller exercise with her legs and trunk as she spoke. I began to take a more tangible interest in her formations, in the shape of her limbs, softening the crudity of my curiosity with remarks like: "Fancy this," or "Fancy that." She was in my arms, warm, flexible, enticing. Her lips searched mine. But we had eaten of some horrible cheese at the close of dinner and didn't dare to consummate the kiss. Nevertheless getting on splendidly when interrupted by the mother coming in—to talk. Babble! gabble! blabber! twaddle! twattle! and if you please, about her younger girl in England, when this one had been in my arms. The mockery of love!

' "Zita, go up and bring us Eva's letter. I should like Ferdinand Feodorovich (she always got my patronymic wrong) to read it." The letter was to her sister.

' "*We tell each other everything in our bedroom, which is private. I am called Grandmother and give advice on all subjects. Kitty is called the Babe, as she has never even believed herself in love. Marion is aged 15 and-a-half, Kitty 15. I am by age the youngest but in everything else I am considered the oldest. We had gym this afternoon. Kitty got a giggling fit and couldn't stop because Miss Hitchcock's tummy made awful noises.*

Marion's last remark was 'Oh! I'm feeling so curly in my tummy, excited like. I'm expecting some more letters to-morrow from Bonzo.' You can guess who Bonzo is, it's him for Marion."

'And so on in this strain.

' "An awful imp," was Zita's comment. "What I do, she must do too. What I have, she must have too."

' "When they were children," Mrs. Kerr explained, "Eva always said 'Me too' to everything Zita did—' Me too.' And so we all nicknamed her 'Me-Too.' "

' "I'd like to meet her when I go to England," I said.

' "She'd want to," Zita said, "if she knows I've met you."

' "Well, why not?" said Mrs. Kerr. "I will write to her. Frederick Konstantinovich (again she got my patronymic wrong), a very charming, intellectual young man, a friend of ours. I am sure she'll be very pleased."

' "She will!" said Zita sardonically.

'When I was in England I wrote to Eva and we engaged in some correspondence, exchanging photographs, before I was able to go down to meet her. She could not understand this long delay and wondered what might be the cause of it; and Marion, it seemed, scrutinized my photo through a magnifying glass to see if perchance I hadn't spots on my face which might well account for my reserve. And Eva wrote to me:

' *"Even if you have spots on your face, show yourself."*

'We met. She was lovely. Unbelievably so. And she wrote to Marion, who had gone home for the vacation:

' *"He has no spots, is tall, not elegant, but clean looking. And says he loves me five times more than before. Am I not a lucky girl?"*

'When I went abroad she continued writing to me, mostly about Marion and Kitty. *"Marion, Kitty and I are sleeping together like last term. I like Marion and Kitty. We have arranged that we are going to have a house in Canada together, as we are afraid we are going to be old maids. If one of us marries she is going to stay in Canada sometimes. We are also all thinking of becoming missionaries. Marion is too funny. She thinks she is in love!! but she still thinks she will be an old maid. Marion, Kitty and I are making rules for a Committee. We are the Members of the Committee. We have agreed that everything is secret, but that I can tell you, and Marion can tell her brother. We have to tell each other everything except our worst sin. It sounds funny, but we are all very wicked and have each done something we couldn't tell other people. So we have agreed that we haven't got to tell that. You may know mine, but I'm not sure. There are lots of By-Laws besides. I will give you further perticulers later. All matters must be discussed in privacy. All members are equal in all affairs. T.C. (password) must only be used on urgent occasions. Any member wishing to leave the Committee can do so if her word of honour is given to remain silent consurning all matters discussed in the aforesaid Committee. If remaining members agree that a certain Member has broken a rule, that Member must pay a penalty fine of 2d. and also if a Member has lost her rules. Those are the rules. I think it's a very good Committee, don't you? I've been informed by Miss Hitchcock that I've got to go in for Junior Cambridge exam next. I don't think I will. I think I should get brain fever, my brain being already weak. It's ever so hot to-day—more so than userlay. I had to undo my coat coming out. In the garden there are lots of snowdrops, crocuses, primroses, tulips and hyasinths out. I hope you apprechiate this lengthy episel.—Your Eva."*

' *"P.S.—Mummy writes that Count Kolberg is still after Zita who cannot bear his soppiness."*

'In the winter I was in Innsbruck. They were expecting Eva, who had left school as they could not afford to pay her fees. We all went to meet her. Even now I can see the long Paris train steaming into Innsbruck Station, and Eva alighting, rather more the young lady than when I had last seen her in England. When Zita that evening showed me her albums with snaps, "Me-Too" insisted on doing likewise. Their mother, encouraged by the thought of the economy made in sparing Eva's future school fees, deemed it well to celebrate the release in terms of midnight frolics—"Making a night of it," she called it. She got us all to join some dancing class of a certain Fräulein Stube, and Count Kolberg came along too, and brought his cousins and friends along. Eva danced with all the counts and barons and smiled into their eyes. And Zita, you could see, hated that smile. She knew her

"Me-Too" inside out. But the barons adored it; and Zita, who had not cared for Kolberg and the barons, now that Eva deflected them, grew visibly jealous. "I don't want to be seen about with this lump!" (Eva's legs were ripening fast.) "I'll make her get up and take exercise," and like remarks. And she never called her Eva, but "Me-Too," with a certain venom of intonation. But Eva, coy, continued smiling at the barons, who were like flies round her.

'New Year's Eve we spent at the Maria-Theresien Restaurant. A huge brass band from the public park installed in the dining-room—deafening music. The room crowded to overflowing. Men prowling about in the hope of stealing a chair. Some Johnny actually seizing one of ours: "May I?" I open my mouth to say "Indeed not!" but that moment the band crashes into martial vehemence—and my words are lost. Mrs. Kerr happy, her lost château, lost income, debts, all forgotten in the excitement of the moment, sits near me, praises all and everybody: "Ah, that dancing mistress Fräulein Stube! A charming, intellectual young woman. So nice! so educated! speaks English like a native!" Presently I dance with the said Fräulein Stube and ask her in explicit English:

' "What is this dance?"
' "Please?" says Fräulein Stube.
' "What is this dance? A fox-trot?"
' "Please?"
' "Is this a fox-trot?"
' "No, de Schimmey," she replies.
' "In England we dance differently," I say to her after a while.
' "Please?"
' "We dance differently in England."
' "Please?"
'In the effort I stepped on to her toe. "I beg your pardon," I stammered.
' "Please?"
' "I beg your pardon."
' "Yes, dis de Schimmey," she said.

'And then again I am in the midst of Mrs. Kerr's amazing volubility, praising all and everybody: "You dance so gracefully, so elegantly. And Fräulein Stube, such a really nice and cultured, intellectual woman! So pleasant, well brought-up, and educated! Knows languages, talks English like a native." Suddenly all rise, holding up mugs of beer. "Prosit! Prosit! Prosit!" And, indeed, the hand of the big clock points midnight. The band crashes on for a full two minutes. And stops. Noise and confusion. Friends and strangers alike are drinking *Bruderschaft*. From the table next to ours a man rises (he is unshaven, but in a sort of dinner suit with a reddish velvet waistcoat), and introduces himself: "Lieutenant-Colonel von Wiesendorf"; then introduces his daughter. We rise and introduce ourselves and one another. They drag up their table to ours, and we are one large party. The Colonel says he can speak English, his object in hooking himself on to us being either to show off or to practise our language, which, he says, he picked up in Africa.

' "In the Foreign Legion?" I ask.

' "Pfui Teufel, no!" he says. "Only desperadoes serve in the Foreign Legion."

'Evidently a *faux pas*.

' "*Bruderschaft!*—Hoch! Hoch! Hoch!" And the Colonel and myself are linked in brotherhood and call each other "thou." Mrs. Kerr and Fräulein von Wiesendorf drink *Bruderschaft* and become inseparable. Zita and Eva, in their turn, drink *Bruderschaft* with Fräulein von Wiesendorf. Finally Graf Kolberg with the Colonel. The band now crashes with unheard-of vehemence. All drink.'

Here Frank Dickin stopped reading and helped himself to more champagne; then continued with unction:

'Fräulein von Wiesendorf, whose great virtue, according to herself, is that she is very jolly: "I'm so jolly!" she squeals, and kicks her heels up, becomes a bosom friend of Mrs. Kerr. "Ah, Ferdinand Vassilievich," she says (getting me wrong again), "you have no idea what a sincere, cultured, jolly, well-informed and intellectual girl she is! Her father, in his position of Comptroller of Public Morals, cannot take her out to all the cabarets and night clubs, and she hasn't even been to the Austria-Bar or the Odeon! But I will chaperon her and take her everywhere, and she's so pleased!"

'And together, they drag us to a cellar-restaurant, the barons like hounds on Eva's scent—Zita neglected, forgotten. And the Colonel, the Comptroller of Public Morals, scratches his head, says "Na! the New Year is not all the year, nor New Year's Day every day," and comes along too, Fräulein von Wiesendorf kicking her heels up with joy. In the cellar-restaurant the goings-on have been going on five or six nights running, ever since Christmas Eve. Shaky waiters with small, red, sleepy eyes. The head waiter—it is the third night he hasn't closed his eyes—propped up with drink, sings along with the band and, as a special favour, right into my ear, occasionally spluttering on my cheek and forehead:

> ' "*Da sprach der Tut-An-Kamen:*
> ' *Tun sich die Leut' nicht schamen?*' "

And we eat and we drink and we revel, till the music grows plaintive and sorrowful, and I dance with Zita, while the band complains:

> ' "*Wenn ich dich seh,*
>   *Da will ich weinen.*"

And she, poor girl, looked it. Eva had robbed her of all her admirers, including Count Kolberg. Melancholy music breeds melancholy thoughts. As we return to the table I overhear Mrs. Kerr complaining to the Colonel: "We cultured Russians of the intellectual class have suffered badly in the Revolution." And there she was, pessimistic about life, pessimistic about the outcome of their law-suit, no money, no home, lawyers mostly frauds.

' "Stop that music!" cries the Comptroller.

'The music stops. "What will you have instead?" the head waiter and bandmaster ask readily.

' "*O Katerina!*"

'And Mrs. Kerr shuffles along in the clumsy Colonel's arms to the ragamuffin beat.

' "A very nice, sincere, understanding man, and a deep thinker," was her comment as, bowed out by the band and the waiters, we come out into the early morning frost.

' "Zita, dear, what is the matter with you?"

'She did not answer. I walked home beside her, not then aware of what she thought and felt; but afterwards she told me. Ever since she was a child she had a sort of psychic complex: she thought that she was mad and that everybody was hiding it from her. Her old grandfather in Ireland could not see Zita, who had golden hair, without tears, for her flaming hair recalled to him her dead grandmother. Whereas Zita thought that Grandpapa cried because he knew that she was mad. Her stern old grandfather, who thought nothing of saying to his guests sitting out on the stairs during a ball, "The stairs were made to walk on, not to sit on. Get up!" crying at the thought of her affliction! And now she knew that she was mad, ghastly, desperately mad, and that they were all hiding it from her. She thought, thought, thought of it, and all to no purpose. She knew an uncanny lot without thinking; but when she *thought* she knew nothing at all. And she decided that she was uncommonly dull—that was it: mad, mad beyond hope and repair!

'The sudden cessation of attention on the part of Graf Kolberg and the barons was due to her madness. Somebody must have blurted it out. Clearly they shunned her. Going over, in a body, to "Me-Too." How awful. This was the end of all things.

'There are moments when we positively seek humiliation. "Me-Too" had taken all her partners from her, had left her destitute and lonely. But she felt, in her extremity, the need to propitiate the victor by an admission of her helplessness, her complete prostration, put all her cards before him, make him responsible for her next move, the invading enemy who must assume responsibility for the welfare of the population in the area he has occupied. Take it, curse you, my last rag of self-respect and exult in the completeness of your victory! This is the spirit in which, on reaching home, Zita must have faced her younger sister. She confessed that she was mad and that she knew that they were hiding it from her. She stood ashamed, expectant, with head bent, as if to say, "Now there! What can you think of it?" while "Me-Too," half undressed, lay on the bed, and pondered. She pondered a long time over this doleful piece of news, with insight, a profound and melancholy understanding. "I think," she said at last, "I think we are both mad."

' "You're *crazy*!" Zita cried.

'Suddenly she felt sane, terrifyingly, devastatingly sane.'

3

'Ha!' said Lord Ottercove.—'Was it like that?'

'I keep pretty close to life where I can,' answered Dickin.

'Well, go on. What happened to the woman, Mrs. Kerr?'

'They could not afford to stay on at the *pension*, and they took a room and a kitchen in town, for the four of them. But she would not cut out the dances.

' "You know, Frederick Fyodorovich, what I'll tell you. I am disappointed in Tamara Leonidovna. As you know, all our things have been confiscated by the bailiff. Everything, everything! But I managed to smuggle through a bedroom carpet to a friend of mine at Bozen, and I gave Tamara Leonidovna 500,000 Kronen, over thirty shillings, to go to Bozen and bring the carpet. But my friend in Bozen, when she saw her, got positively frightened of Tamara Leonidovna, who really looks forbidding. A dark-haired, dark-eyed woman, just like a gipsy. Those lips, those consuming eyes. She is terribly sensual, you know."

' "Is she?"

' "You don't mean to say that you haven't noticed it?"

' "I haven't."

' "Hasn't she made any advances to you?"

' "No."

'Mrs. Kerr thought for a space. "Well, all the more honour to her, then. Because, you can see by her face and whole figure how hard it is for her to bridle her passions. The tram driver, Herr König, won't have her come near him now that they're divorced. He has another woman. And poor Tamara Leonidovna, who has been used to a married life, doesn't know what to do with herself. But she leads, I think, an exemplary life. And all the more honour to her, I say—but it's not good, it's a strain on her. Well, the lady got such a fright when she saw Tamara Leonidovna that she would not give the carpet. And Tamara Leonidovna got so scared of the lady being scared to death of her that when the lady did offer to give her the carpet Tamara Leonidovna wouldn't take it. And her German, as you know, is not up to much.

' " 'Why didn't you take the carpet when she offered it,

Tamara Leonidovna?' I cried, when she returned here on Saturday, empty-handed—just as I am waving my hair to go to the Hôtel d'Europe ball. Imagine my position: I hadn't a Krone left. The last went to pay for the entrance tickets, for I was counting on Tamara Leonidovna returning with the bedroom carpet. And my hair already waved. And here she stands and says: 'She wouldn't give the carpet.' And looks at me like that—uncertainly, and adds: 'Besides, I was afraid of the Customs.'

' " 'The Customs?' I say. 'Then you *did* have a chance to get the carpet from her?'

' " 'I had a chance,' she says, uncertainly.

' " 'Then why—why—why (I was so angry that I shook the curling-tongs at her) tell me—otherwise?' I wanted to say 'a lie,' but restrained myself.

' " 'Ah, if that's the way you talk to me, after all my kindness to you, good-bye to you,' she said, and slammed the door behind her.

' "I rushed off to the station restaurant, where my husband always dines with the Rittmeister. 'Charles!' I cried, 'that woman has come back without the carpet! What am I to do now? I am dressed for the ball and I've ordered the table and I've no money to pay for the champagne supper! What *am* I to do, Charles ?' "

' "And what did he do?"

' "He cursed me, Fyodor Ferdinandovich. Cursed me, cursed me, cursed me—oh, *terrible*! He never talks to me now—only curses."

' "And the Rittmeister?"

' "The Rittmeister laughed."

'The Rittmeister must have laughed very contagiously, for, remembering how he laughed, Mrs. Kerr began to laugh too, at first quietly, then louder and louder, till her laughter became riotous. "What a life!" she sighed, wiping the tears that had come to her eyes from laughing so heartily. "I have ceased to take myself, or my clothes, or my life, or my fate, seriously. I only look and laugh, look in wonder, in astonishment—and laugh. But as I tell you, I am disappointed in Tamara Leonidovna. And what language she uses! Like a cab driver. I am grateful to God that my children do not know Russian. And that poor student she wants to marry!"

' "Why 'poor'?" '

' "She will consume him. She is fire." '

' "Daddy ought to know her," from Zita. '

' "He knows her." '

' "But more closely." '

'However, they went to the Hôtel d'Europe ball and there they met Lord de Jones, who knew them. And I presume he paid for the champagne supper.'

'Look here,' said Lord Ottercove, looking worried, 'now you are actually using real names. Well-known names.'

Frank smiled.

'I have kept all the original names deliberately so as to attract your attention. I knew I would have to change them for publication. But this is a small matter.'

Lord Ottercove smiled, then leaned back and laughed.

'That was clever of you! I must confess that but for the names my serial editor might have easily passed it over.——So de Jones paid, did he?' Lord Ottercove looked pensive.

'I presume so.'

'But actually you know who pays?'

'Who?'

Lord Ottercove pointed a forefinger at his own chest.

Frank Dickin looked at him with dull amazement, but as Lord Ottercove looked morose, did not press for explanation. 'The silly woman rather advertised her connexion with Lord de Jones and told me, as though she were giving me a hundred pounds, that she was going to introduce me to the noble lord! I hadn't the slightest interest to meet him. A pretty big fool, I imagine, to judge by his tastes in women.'

'He has married my niece,' said Lord Ottercove.

'No!—I say, this is rather a brick I've let fall.'

'You mean to say you didn't know it?'

'Well—how shall I say?—I did and I didn't. I thought it would help to keep up your flagging interest in my serial if I introduced into it Hidden Hand bits from the back-door life of your relative. Not that I know much about him. We novelists have to rely largely on our own imagination. Though I remember now that Lord and Lady de Jones were on their honeymoon and put up at the Tirolerhof in Innsbruck.'

'That's a bigger brick than the first.'

'I am so sorry.'

'Not a bit of it. I don't think you realize that what interests me most in your serial is not what de Jones does but why he does it. What it is that attracts him so in Mrs. Kerr. It must be nearly twenty years now since he first met her, I believe, in Russia. Or was she already married? And now I realize. You have conveyed her character wonderfully well. I think it is that extraordinary irresponsibility, that—that—that something else. It's there, I feel it, though I can't for the moment describe the peculiar fascination. What else can it be? Is she still so good-looking?'

'Good-looking, no, but attractive. Her daughters have it from her.'

'He always goes back to her. It is the second time he is married. My niece should never have married him. But there is genius in him. He could have been a second Newton if he had wanted to. As it is, he is a Genius of the Untried. They are all like that, the whole family. I have a great affection for him. But Eleonor is determined to divorce him. He'll be quite penniless unless I find him something to do. But go on. What happened to the woman?'

'I lost sight of them soon after that dance, and Frau König told me they had gone off to Abbazia, while Lord de Jones had returned to England. I enquired about her own affairs. "Everything now depends on the knitting machine, which is due to arrive in March."

' "And your fiancé in Paris?"

' "He is saving money for the factory. But imagine!" she exclaimed, "in his last letter—so pathetic—he writes that the franc, owing to the political machinations of the Cartel des Gauches, has all gone to pieces and reduced the potential capital of our knitting factory."

'We spoke of Mrs. Kerr. "Your Mrs. Kerr," said Tamara Leonidovna, "is a goose. Just a Great Big Goose.——What a fool that woman is! Not a cent in her pocket, not an idea in her top storey beyond dancing and pleasing men—at her age! A newly married man, too—just because he is a lord! Openly, before her daughters! What matter that she is divorced? I, too, am divorced and six years younger than she is, but I keep myself back." A look of strain came into her face. "I don't let myself go." She set her jaw, clenched her fists. "I try to keep myself in check. I have more pride, more self-respect than—than——When he comes back from Paris then—then—then yes." '

'Go on,' said Lord Ottercove.

4

DOGS AND NIGHTINGALES

'I saw nothing of them till the spring, when I had a surprise visit from Mrs. Kerr, looking considerably dilapidated. "Ach, Ferdinand Ferdinandovich, you won't believe what I have been through in these two months! If I were a writer like you I would write a novel in the *genre* of Dostoevski, so true, and yet incredible, so poignant! I have begun a diary. I will bring it to you this afternoon. You can make use of it for your books.

' "Lord de Jones lent me some money to go and have a thorough change and rest, and so Zita, Eva, John and I went to Abbazia. A lovely coast. Blue sea; sunshine; casino, roulette, chemin de fer, baccarat. A real change and rest for the nerves. All day we gamble, and at night dancing, flirtations. Both girls passionate gamblers, also John. But luck went against us and we found we had no more money to go on with. I pawned some of my things and we lived very comfortably for a time at the Grand Hotel—dancing, music, sea bathing twice a day and getting to know lots of very agreeable young men on the beach, and at night moonlight walks in the wood—in couples: Zita with the Italian boy; Eva with the young Dane; and I with the Spaniard Rodrigo. Or to the cinema—always in couples, Rodrigo looking at me with great passionate eyes. Very delightful and charming. When the money was exhausted, I found a post as housekeeper in a small *pension* overlooking the sea—very artistically situated; and Zita, Eva and John were taken in by a lady friend of Rodrigo's, a very nice, quiet, well-read woman. I would be busy all day in the kitchen which gives out into the garden, and the children, looking so gay and fresh in their white summer things, would be coming to see me all the time. And I'd say to them, 'Go and play in the garden,' and I would give them things through the window, as the lady friend of Rodrigo's could not provide them with food. 'There you are, children, take this and this and this,' and I'd give them cakes, coffee, sugar, sweets, dainties, pastry, everything, and they'd take it home and eat it and come back for more. And I'd give them more through the window, all kinds of preserved meats and provisions: 'Here you are, children,' and they never went short of anything while I was housekeeper there. But—but would you believe it, Fyodor Frederickovich? The landlady, seeing me give nourishment to my children, gave me the sack. If it had been for myself, I'd understand, but for the children! I have noticed a strange insensibility in those people, a hardness, a general—how shall I say?—unfeelingness. No love, no understanding of children. I just looked at her like that—I could say nothing. I could not have expressed what was in my heart. A feeling of sorrow, not of anger. And as I took my things and passed her on the doorstep I just turned my head to her: 'In Russia this could not have been,' and went without a word.

' "Outside in the street, the children around me, I stop and ask: 'All-wise and loving God,' I ask, 'why dost Thou punish me so? *Why*?'

' "From there I got into the Grand Hotel as 'Kaffee-Köchin,' and all day long I had to boil coffee, first for the clients, then for the hotel staff—all day long boil coffee and nothing but coffee. They gave me a tiny little room on the roof, overlooking an unfinished church, and at night dogs would come to sleep in that church and howl hungrily—dogs; and up in the trees, nightingales. I opened the window. Below in the square, lilac shrubs in bloom. The scent of lilac. And thoughts, like a bevy of bees, stung my heart. I remembered our dear Russia when I was a young girl, my mother a young woman, my father, my two brothers, and how I felt and how I hoped. It all came back—Pushkin, Lermontov, Tolstoy, Turgenev, Dostoevski—and hot tears streamed down my cheeks. 'Dear God,' I said, 'to think what was once! and what is now! Come back, days of youth, of my innocence, and hot faith in the divinity of Thy Creation, Thy Love! Vague dreams of my heart, virgin and untouched, of my unsullied soul, come back, come back!'——The breath of spring. Dogs, an unfinished church, you know…and those nightingales, all the night through. Dogs and nightingales.

' "All day long I boiled coffee. I went by the name of 'Frau Kaffeeköchin,' for I alone in the whole hotel was to boil coffee and I wasn't to do anything else. From six in the morning till ten at night I boiled coffee. But at half-past ten I would put on my yellow-satin gown and sit out on the Casino terrace, order a vermouth, light a cigarette, and never in a thousand years would it occur to anyone that the smart elegantly gowned, romantic-looking woman sitting out on the Casino terrace and looking, you might say, like a Queen of the Steppes, was the Frau Kaffeeköchin of the Grand Hotel. And one night, as I sit there, an old beggar, sick, filthy, stenchy, all in rags, and barefoot, comes up to me. 'Here, beggar,' I give him a copper, and he holds out his hand and introduces himself: 'Captain of the Imperial Russian Navy, Nobleman Khan Balalykin.' Yes, Khan Balalykin—a Tartar Prince! And, do you know, Ferdinand Ferdinandovich, he fell in love with me? What am I to do? Where I go he follows me. 'No,' he says, 'I cannot live without you,' and looks at me with soft, lovelorn eyes. And also calls me 'My Queen of the Steppes.' Or quotes a lyric from Lermontov. Well, we made a night of it, and spoke of Russia. Next morning I return to the hotel to work; he after me, right into the kitchen. 'Sit down, Captain,' I say; 'here is meat, bread, cheese, butter, beer. Eat and drink, it will do you good, restore your strength a bit. He tucked in, oblivious of everything, poor old man, he looked so starved; but here the head cook, a huge great man, comes in—a great big animal with a short, thick neck, just like an ox—horrible!—an obnoxious big bully, the real cave man. And, would you believe it, Ferdinand Fyodorovich, begins to remonstrate with Captain Khan Balalykin, who is peacefully tucking in at the table? But I wasn't going to be bullied by this ox of a man. 'Don't you dare shout at me,' I screamed, 'I'm not afraid of you. I care that much for your being head cook. In Russia at one time one used to beat one's cook when one wasn't satisfied with him, and I, the daughter of Pàvel Yàkovlevich Sabolènko, won't stand any of your nonsense, I can tell you!' Well, I thought this would pacify him a little. But no! The ox shouts and storms more than ever and begins to insult Captain Khan Balalykin. Well, I wasn't going to have my guest reviled and insulted. He may look dirty and all that, which is not surprising in his sphere as a beggar, but he is a real gentleman of the old school, a captain of the Russian Navy, graduated with Honours at the Imperial Naval Academy, and the bully is a common ignorant Austrian cook. I took the big brass pan with the potatoes and crashed it to the ground: I was so angry. Well, he begins shouting madder than ever and kicks Captain Khan Balalykin out of the kitchen and then fetches in the manager and points at me and the potatoes on the floor and screams: 'It's she!' And the pair of them begin to scream at me together, though I can scream as loud as they together. 'No—it's *he!*— *he!—he!*' I scream, and go for both of them with my fists. Insulting a distinguished Russian officer, an old nobleman Khan Balalykin, a graduate of the Imperial Naval Academy: I *was* so wild!

' "Well, do you know, Fyodor Ferdinandovich, the manager, being hand-in-glove with the head cook, gave me the sack. I pawned my last ruby ring and we all came back this morning. In Milan we ran across Fräulein von Wiesendorf, and we all came back together."

' "And how is she?" I asked.

' "Well, it seems from all the drinking bouts during the *Fasching* and the late hours, Fräulein von Wiesendorf got the colics and a sort of nervous breakdown. Her father, who is Comptroller of Public Morals, alarmed at his daughter's condition, called in the doctor, who examined Fräulein von Wiesendorf and found symptoms of the beginnings of consumption, and ordered her *immediately*, without a moment's loss or hesitation, at railway speed to Italy. 'As fast as the train will carry you!' he said. Fräulein von Weisendorf throws a few odd things into a bag and darts off, helter-skelter, to Italy, and arrives, holus-bolus, in Genoa, and as she has no means, takes a post as governess to children. Nine children of assorted ages. She has to teach and feed and wash for them and take them out for walks, and the children all veritable devils, real Machiavellis, cruel, mischievous, teasing her, and the parents exigent and stingy. In a month poor Fräulein von Wiesendorf was worn to a shadow;

a doctor was called in, examined her, and— 'Back home!' he said, 'at full tilt! As fast as you can fly!' She arrived in hot haste this morning. Tomorrow night we are making a last night of it, and the day after I am off to Abbazia."

' "What! again!"

' "To get the ruby ring back from the pawn-shop. I've borrowed some money here on the strength of my caracole coat."

' "And how are Zita, Eva and John?"

' "The children are so happy. As we had no quarters to go to on arrival we went and sat in the Hofpark, and we've chummed up with four Bulgarian students: two small ones, a thin one, and a big one. The two small ones have fallen in love with Zita and Eva, the thin one with Fräulein von Wiesendorf, and the big one with me. I must be off now to look for a room for the children, and don't forget to ask them for my diary." '

5

PALE PRIMROSES THAT DIE UNMARRIED

'I met Zita, Eva and John a few days later, crossing the Maria-Theresienstrasse on their way to their sparse meal at the cheap restaurant under the arch. They were rather short of money, but full of enthusiasm on account of the Bulgarian students. "We spend all our time with them in the Hofpark," they told me. Later I saw them home to their room—a poor room tucked away behind someone else's kitchen; one narrow bed for the two girls and a little sofa for John. "And doesn't your father bother about you?" I asked.

' "Daddy's gone back to Ireland."

'We decided, in the absence of the mother, to make a climbing expedition to the top of the Patscherkofl mountain, and arranged to meet at four o'clock next morning. It was still dark as we set out, clad in the appropriate mountaineering fashion: alpenstock and rucksack; the girls in Tyrolese peasant dress: short skirt, tight waist; John and I in blue coat and leather shorts, and leaving the still somnolent streets of the town behind us, began the ascent. At Igls we halted and breakfasted, then continued the steep, winding climb through the pine woods, as the red sun rose to meet us. John ran in front and behind, and Zita and Eva walked sprightly on either side of me, and we spoke of how nice it would be to make a hut in the pine woods or live in a cave. And to all Zita's "I's" Eva said "we." By midday we reached Heiligwasser, famed for the miraculous cure of the sick, and unpacked our rucksacks for lunch; then continued the winding ascent. The Inn Vale now stretched deep beneath us. More mountains, like ghost ships on an uncharted sea, loomed into sight as we climbed the spiral grass-edged path, encountering more flowers on our way: snowdrops, buttercups, daisies, bluebells, primulas, violets, while little brooks skurried down head-over-heels to announce that spring was already come. An hour's distance from our goal, we spread out our mantles on the green slope of a sheltered warm valley where daffodils grew in profusion by the side of a brook, and stretched our limbs and dozed rapturously in the sun.

'Profusion is not a good thing. So I mused, watching the two sisters, each so exquisite in her own way that at once when you began to focus your attention on the one, you were diverted from her by the other. They thus neutralized each other's charm to a great extent and dissipated your affection. And lying with them in the sun, I watched them lustless, in benignant peace. How beautiful life could be for a space!

'Rising, we set out on the last but one stage in our journey, climbing hills without paths, cutting across pastures where frisky young cows, turned irresponsible on these heights, jumped over the moon; now clearing gurgling brooks which still ran hurry-skurry down to the valleys to tell the glad tidings; now stooping to drink the cool water. By two we reached the top of the shaggy mountain slope: above loomed the gleaming naked dead rock of the summit. A separate journey, after an hour's repose.

'At the Gasthaus we drank beer and booked accommodation for the night; then lay on the edge of a plateau projecting peri-lously over the void and looked down at Innsbruck, miniature as on a map, the river Inn bedded in the soft, green folds of the valley, the parcelled fields, the dotted villages, the spired churches, all lucent and serene in the spring sun. Leaving John asleep in the tavern, we climbed the steep rocky way to the peak, clinging to loose stones and sending them rolling a mile or two till they rebounded with a heavy earthen thud in the abyss. No more shrubs or alpine roses; nor a human habitation any-where. The last was the Gasthaus, which is now lost to sight. On we climb till, in the first dusk, we reach the flat rocky mountain-top: there is nowhere higher to go. The girls frolic and gambol like frisky gazelles: the air is amazingly light. But I sat away on a rock, struck speechless by the mighty spectacle. The neighbour-ing mountain-peaks, all level now and grandly equal, looked on into the gathering dusk, heavy with unspoken utterance.

'Where, the veil lifted, have I seen the tints and shadows of the unimaginable day?'

'But as the rocky summits, like ghostly dreadnoughts anchored in doom's waters, closed their eyes in the ensuing gloom, we hastened to retrace our steps towards the Gasthaus. Zita was in a hurry to get back to John. The paths diverged on every side of us. We were afraid lest darkness should overtake us before we reached the Gasthaus, and, all agreeing on the neces-sity for haste, disagreed as to which path we ought to follow. Zita thought she knew a shorter way to the inn than the one we had come by, which I doubted. So Eva and I stuck to the old path, or what we imagined to be the old path, which led us unto-wardly down the steep edge of the mountain, as Zita quickly vanished on the other side. When you look at a hill from below, it all seems perfectly easy and simple: you either walk up or else you walk down, according to whether you wish to find yourself at the top or the bottom. But as you begin to descend you find that the hill has a trick of breaking into new hills, new valleys, new precipices; that having at length reached the foot of your hill, you are still at the top of another, and rounding it to get into the valley, you are thwarted by another precipice. Once Zita appeared far away, it seemed on the edge of a fourth hill; then vanished. We shouted as loud as our voices would carry; the wind took our words but brought us none back. Dusk fell upon us rapidly, and stones rolled dangerously beneath our feet, as we felt our way down the slippery steep rock. Soon it was too dark to move at all. We sat down on a stony slope, and Eva cried. I could have done so myself, with the exhaustion and nervous tension and vexation of it all; but her tears accomplished the trick for me. We were even too tired to eat. It was fresh in the dark, but not cold. We thought that Zita was back now and asleep with John at the inn. We spread our mantles and, sooner than we knew, we slept.

'In the night there was a storm, and we ran hand-in-hand down the slippery stones in search of shelter; and then hid ourselves under a rock.

'At dawn we were up, and having eaten of the contents of our rucksacks, we set afoot in search of the path, keeping together for fear of worse things. When a moving dot of a figure appeared across the wide gulf that separated us from another chain of rocks, we shouted and waved, and the figure waved back. Thinking it must be a man from the Gasthaus, we waved again and shouted ourselves hoarse. Manoeuvring, the figure and ourselves came nearer; we could dimly hear it shouting to us, presumably explaining the direction. Then, as it neared, we recognized Zita's scarf flying in the wind, and then her voice asking the way. We began a mad rush to reach each other, ran across fields and brooks, climbed trackless slopes of naked rock, till, meeting on neutral ground in a small valley, she told us of the fearful night she had spent alone, and burst into tears. With breaks for food, we continued our search, all keeping together, till the sun sank behind the mountains and the shadows crept up and, once again, it was night.

'We slept huddled together, and thought of John alone at the inn. Still, the Wirt would take care of him, and, compared with us, he was comfortable.

'In the course of next day we reconnoitred all round the summit and found ourselves trapped: very evidently the one pass connecting the rock with the main body of the hill had fallen away. We were cut off from the rest of the world, isolated on the naked rock which, like a tooth, sloped down at an angle we could not hope to descend without being swept into the precipice by the stones which barely piled on its steep sides and every now and then rolled off into the abyss. This was, we guessed, what must have happened to the one connecting link by which we had climbed to the peak of the mountain, now clearly inaccessible except possibly by air.

'We began to ration our supplies and wait for relief. Surely the people at the Gasthaus where John still waited for us would do something? By the following day we began to doubt whether our provisions could last out another day. Doubtless the Gasthaus people were searching for us; but how would they reach us with the pass missing? Where could they get an aeroplane? Munich was the nearest centre. Or perhaps John, quicksilver that he was, had left soon after us and the people at the inn concluded that we had all returned to Innsbruck.

'The day after was glorious and hot, and towards midday we had cleared our last supplies. We lay on the ground and felt very still and odd. I watched Zita lying on her belly, her long legs stretched out and apart. The sun was beating on us. Luckily there was no lack of water. How long could one last out on water? And would the rescue party come at all? We did not say it to one another. We seemed to know and feel it that the other understood. They were young; it was a pity. For it looked, though the weather was so beautiful, uncommonly like the end. The spring, and they so young. And death yawning to claim our bones. Somehow, as I lay there watching them, these lines from Shakespeare swung back into my mind:

' "*Pale primroses,*
　　that die unmarried, ere
　　they can behold
　Bright Phoebus in his strength,
　　a malady
　Most incident to maids…"

'At that moment Zita turned a look, molten gold from the sun, upon me. Why should she?

'We kissed under the hot rays of the sun, taking the last it had to offer us before it withdrew its beams to shine on us no more.

'And then it was that Eva, whom I had forgotten, caught my look and said:

' "Me too." '

Lord Ottercove interrupted the reading with an astonished 'Ha!' sprang up with that agility which testified to his success, went over to the sideboard and mixed himself some whisky. Frank must have discerned disapproval in the gurgling notes of the whisky as it poured down into his lordship's cavity, for, 'The sun,' he protested, 'spring, death crouching at you, the end of life in time, and these pale primroses to die unmarried———'

'Are you—I don't quite understand—defending the book or your conduct?'

' That is———'

'Yes?' The noble lord now looked like a magistrate.

'I don't think this is a fair question.'

'I agree.—Go on.'

'Reading?'

'Of course.'

'I think I've read enough.'

'My dear fellow, you can't stop like that. I am dying to know what happened.'

'What happened? Is a fellow to blame for getting saved?'

'All saved?'

'All. They came and found us the day after. A picnic party from Innsbruck. The pass had not been destroyed as we imagined, and indeed there were several passes. We'd made a mistake. I am not very clever at mountaineering, you know. Nor the girls either. John, as suspected, had slipped down to Innsbruck almost immediately on waking, thinking we had gone back to town. So all's well that ends well.'

'Rather terrible that, what?' said Lord Ottercove.

'I appeal to your idealism. Yawning death. Pale primroses to die unmarried. No escape. I tell you we thought we were for ever lost.'

'Didn't you think so too readily?'

'I deprecate this attempt to abuse the autonomy of a work of literature.'

'So it is merely literature?'

'I don't think it's fair to my characters of you to ask.'

'Read on!' laughed Lord Ottercove.

6

'In the autumn I was in Vienna. One day as I returned from a walk the maid in the *pension* told me that two ladies were waiting for me in my room. Who but Mrs. Kerr and Eva! My first thought was: Does the mother know? But from her ebullient flow I soon perceived that all was well.

'A long tale. She had come back with the ruby ring, and for some time at all events they lived quite comfortably on the proceeds. When they had spent their last, "I went," she said, "and threw myself on the charity of the police authorities, who were very kind and sent the three of us, John, Eva and myself, by goods train to Vienna. An English lady had taken Zita back to England with her as a companion. Arrived in Vienna, I went straight to the policeman on the platform and said: 'Here we are—destitute, without means. What do you propose to do with us?' It's always better to be downright: no good doing things by half. Once destitute, throw all responsibility on the police. He looked very worried and said: 'Follow me,' and took us to the gendarme, who told us to wait in the waiting-room. We waited three or four hours. Meanwhile, the first policeman came back, with a confused look and something clenched in his fist. 'I am not a rich man,' he said, opening his fist, 'but please accept that.' I was touched. 30,000 Kronen—almost two shillings. The gendarme came to invite us into his chief's office. A nice grey-haired old gentleman. He had tears in his eyes as he looked at the children, and was all milk and honey when I related to him of our Schloss in Meran, now in the hands of the Italians, and said softly: *'Sic transit gloria mundi!'*

' "Anyhow, they took John off my hands. They put him in an orphanage. You won't believe how nice it is for him there. Never been so happy before! Warm and cosy and plenty of boys of his own age to play with. And, do you know, he heckles them all and fights them. We visited him the next day, Eva and I. He was at his midday meal. Very good food. But he said, 'Mummy, what is the matter with this meat? It chews and chews and doesn't eat up.' Made them all laugh.

' " 'Me-Too' and I were conveyed to the workhouse. And, fancy, crossing the Landstrasse-Hauptstrasse, we saw two of the Bulgarian students—the thin one and one of the small ones. Eva shouted to them across the street, but they couldn't hear. The workhouse—not too bad, only no privacy. A huge barrack-like room and lots of low, fallen women who use dreadful language. I don't like it on Eva's account. Yesterday, when 'Me-Too' came in and left the door open, there was such a volley of abuse from an old hag that I shut my ears so as not to hear. But Eva said never a word, only looked at her like that. You could see the race in her.

' "We found out your address through police records—they are really so well organized in this town—and, well, we've come to see you and to ask if you won't take us out to some dance or other to-night. We are so tired of the regulation workhouse meals. I still have my smart yellow-satin gown in which Khan Balalykin admired me so much and thought I looked like a Queen of the Steppes. And 'Me-Too' still has her orange crêpe-de-Chine dress. She hid it in her purse—it folds ever so small—when the bailiffs came into our Schloss in Meran and took everything away from us."

'I expressed my willingness, my pleasure. I asked her tactfully if I could not lend her a little money. She took the note with charming simplicity "on condition," she said, "that you will let me pay it back later—when things mend up in Russia."

'At the cabaret, the "Nachtlokal" which she had selected as being the most elegant according to her husband when in the affluent old days he used to take her to Vienna for the season, she nevertheless complained of the general inferiority and paucity of Vienna night life as compared with that of Petrograd or Moscow, and that brought her back again to Russia. "Ach, Russia! We upper classes in Russia have been thrown in the dirt and trampled on with the muddy feet of the coarse proletariat." It would have been heartless of me to remind her of the complete independence of her personal misfortunes of the fate of Russia, heartless and uncalled for. "But we shall go back and find, I truly expect and believe, our reward in riches and pleasures as yet undreamt of, and then when you come and visit us there, Fyodor Ferdinandovich, we shall have such a binge together as will outshine anything previously known in that line."

' "Of course we will," I said tenderly, laying my hand on her own.

' "I believe in it!" she cried, "hotly and passionately! In the face of all the calamities and disasters falling upon me, it shall not be said that I have lost faith!" She looked passionately at the orchestra.

'I filled her champagne glass. The band played doleful music. She touched my arm. "But I do not regret these experiences. The kind hearts, the interesting people one comes to meet. That policeman. The grey-haired Colonel's tears." Her eyes filled; and, indeed, she looked that moment like "the Madonna kissing the finger-tips of her Child." "And, you know, even the workhouse women. That old hag who shouted so at 'Me-Too' —well, I've chummed up with her. Not a bad woman at heart. She has had a hard life. A great beauty. An early seduction..."

'She sighed. "We have no luck. Imagine, my mother has managed to get out of Russia at last and even smuggle through some jewellery, so Eva and I both wrote to her to be quick and send us some money till the authorities can find us situations. But she is in Monte Carlo, gambling heavily, it seems, and writes back: 'I can't. I am bust.' "

'Eva, while her mother talked to me, flirted with me over her mother's head. "Come and talk to me," her look seemed to say.

'It was cruel after the dance-supper to take them back in a taxi to the workhouse. But what could I do? I was, after paying for the supper, stony broke myself. I could not have arranged to keep them at an hotel indefinitely, and the authorities who were charged with finding work for them would have discontinued their efforts on their leaving the workhouse.

'A week later, she came in to me, jubilant. They had both got positions, Eva as nurse to small children, Mrs. Kerr as housekeeper to a solitary Austrian Colonel. "An intellectual, original man. We read Dostoevski together, and I am keeping a journal which eventually I hope to develop into a novel. We are both of us so happy, Ferdinand Fyodorovich———"

' "Fomitch," I corrected. "My father was called Tom—Fomà, in Russian."

' "—Ferdinand Fomitch, that we want you to take us out this evening, make a night of it. The other night 'Me-Too' and I went

out to a night club together, to celebrate our release from the
workhouse and our good fortune in getting situations so soon,
and we struck up an acquaintance with two Russian gentlemen:
Ivan Andrèiech Zshikov, and the other: Fyodor Yàkovlevich
Suhomlinski. Suhomlinski fell in love at first sight with 'Me-Too';
and Zshikov with me. Zshikov has long almond eyes and looks
like that into mine all the time. Jokes, little flirtations. Very delight-
ful and charming. From there we went together to another
cabaret. In the street some other unknown men fell into step with
us, and we all went along together to an underground tavern—
like the one in Innsbruck, only larger and gayer. And all the men
in love—either with Eva or me. All Russians in exile, huddled
together, helping one another to bear up. Very charming and
touching. The Hussar Kòlenka Shavèlenkov; Olèg Aleksèiech
Pevtsòff, disappointed in love and seeking a meaning in life; and
Captain of Lancers, Rotmister von Bologovski. Yes, calls himself
'von'—'von Bologovski.' All intellectual, original people. We
revel till three in the morning, and, do you know, when Eva had
to go back to her charges the mistress made quite a scene, in
spite of 'Me-Too' explaining to her that she had been out with
her mother; and nearly dismissed her. It was her first day there,
you see. But I slipped in noiselessly with my latch key; my old
Diogenes of a Colonel was still snoring, and there are no servants.
He leaves early and does not come back till six. So I give little
parties when he is away. I try to make a kind of Russian intellectual centre, to attract interesting, original people, a sort of nucleus
of the Russian Colony in Vienna. A large dining-room. I give them
tea with lemon. They feel very pleased. All interesting, well-read
people of unconventional views. Zshikov came, and Suhomlinski
(to see Eva, who slips in with her elder charges when she can),
and also Kòlenka Shavèlenkov, and Olèg Aleksèiech Pevtsòff, the
disappointed, and the Lancer Rotmister von Bologovski; all came,
drank tea and smoked and argued, very sincerely and passionately
about politics and art. I was very pleased on Eva's account. Very
beneficial and instructive for her. I was sorry Zita wasn't there. But
she writes this morning that she has left the English lady and has
taken a post as professional dancing partner, at a dancing place
in Hammersmith. She is very pleased, for the lady she was
companion to she says was a stuffy old thing." '

7

'Well, I went to one or two of her intellectual tea parties, and once I just missed Lord de Jones by a hair's-breadth: he had left a minute or so before my arrival.'

'De Jones! You don't say so!' exclaimed Lord Ottercove. 'Ha!' And he shook his head.

'And how,' he asked after a pause, pulling out his watch and looking at it with mild alarm, 'do you finish your serial? Does your hero marry both sisters and serve his time for bigamy?'

'No. I will read it to you.'

'Don't: it suffices that I have your word for it. Shall *I* tell you what becomes of your characters?'

'Do.'

'Shall I tell you where they are?'

'Where?'

'Here. In London.'

'I know.'

'But do you know who got them to come over?'

'I can guess.'

'You're good at guessing, are you? And can you guess why he got them over?'

'I think I have shown through the pages of my serial that I am not insensible to his interest in the mother.'

'Or in the daughter.'

'In the daughter?'

'The younger daughter.'

'Eva? Great heavens!'

'I am happy,' said Lord Ottercove, 'to be able to introduce into your serial this little touch of suspense. Indeed, if there is an element lacking in your story it is this element of suspense. Between you and me, it is an element entirely unimportant and one which, I have always found, interferes with the peaceful enjoyment of a story as it tells itself through the growth and actions of the characters. But it is, nevertheless, an element upon which serial editors insist as a matter of tradition. But I am going to change all that. I am, perhaps you have noticed, changing the tradition of journalism in this country.'

'For the better,' said Frank.

'What?'

'For the better,' said Frank.

'Now I like your story. I think it is a corking tale. I accept it for my newspapers, and, what is more, I will pay for it. Yes! I will. Now what do you want for it?'

Frank hesitated only a moment. Better men than he owed their fortune to a bold word put in in the proper accent at the proper moment. Big men act big, so that their gestures may go down to history. And what did Shakespeare say? ' There is a tide in the affairs of men, which, taken at the flood, leads on to fortune; omitted, all the voyage of their life is bound in shallows and in miseries.'

He closed his eyes. 'Ten thousand pounds,' he said.

Now, despite the opening given him, Lord Ottercove did not avail himself of the immortal gesture. Or, perhaps, he could not recognize a tide in the affairs of another man.

'Ha!' he said, and leaned back. 'If I—if I gave you—gave you—' (the sum seemed to stick in his throat), 'gave you ten thousand pounds my staff would think I'd gone right off my chump; and I should have, of course.'

He took up the receiver and said: 'I want Mr. Wilson.' And turning back to the visitor: 'I can't do these things over the head of my serial editor. I can't do these things over the heads of my editors,' he repeated; and again: 'I can't do these things———' to fill the interval of time it took Mr. Wilson to reach the office. And now Mr. Wilson, with eyes and crown discreetly lustrous, was shown in by the page.

'This, Mr. Wilson, is Mr. Dickin, from whom I want to buy a serial. I asked him to name a price, and he said ten thousand pounds, which is, of course, preposterous.'

Mr. Wilson inclined his head a little, thus discreetly suggesting that it was preposterous.

'Mr. Dickin,' continued Lord Ottercove, 'is not acquainted with the prices of serials paid by newspapers. Obviously so, to judge by the figure he named. What do you think we ought to pay him?'

'Well———' said Mr. Wilson. The situation was one warranting discretion. 'The prices vary.' It was not wise to say more.

Lord Ottercove looked sad and troubled at having to be so.

'According to the serial and the author,' Mr. Wilson added.

'I suppose,' Lord Ottercove said doubtfully, 'you are a fairly good author?'

'I suppose so,' Frank said gloomily.

'Has Vernon Sprott read any of your novels?' Vernon Sprott was the foreman of British fiction, proud of purse and dexterous with the pen.

'I don't know.'

'We'll ask him.—Give me Vernon Sprott.—Vernon, old boy, how are you?' Frank had a feeling that he was at the centre of all things, in the very signal-box from which all the wires were pulled and the signals flashed the wide world over. 'Vernon, I say, have you read any of Frank Dickin's novels? You have? Well, what do you think of them? What? They're all right? Vernon, good evening to you!' He put down the receiver. 'He says they're all right.'

'That's good.'

'Well——' said Lord Ottercove, still far from making history. But the next moment, as a cat is reputed nearly always to fall on its feet, he slipped into history. 'Are you,' he said, 'at all ready to leave it all to me?'

'To no one more!' Dickin said passionately, feeling that he was now treading a pivot on which fortunes turn, and henceforward fly round, multiplying incessantly.

'I'll tell you what I will do for you. I'll let you draw on my account.'

'On your account?'

'Yuh!'

'To—to what extent?'

'Without limit.'

'But how do you mean?'

'As much as you need.'

Frank, flushed, his scalp tingling, punctuated the air with words of embarrassed and bewildered gratitude. '—incredible—incomprehensible.'

Lord Ottercove, as in an alternating duet, kept up with: 'Not a bit. I like doing it.'

'I cannot believe it.'

'My dear fellow, it's a pleasure to me.'

'I'm staggered.'

'It shall be done!'

'Speechless.—It's a dream.'

'Which is your bank?'

'Barclays.'

He took up the receiver. 'I want Mrs. Hannibal.'

Mrs. Hannibal was Lord Ottercove's Secretary-in-Chief. This was, as she entered, already apparent from her general demeanour, from her outward calm and ease and the smiles and little graces she was able to bestow on visitors: that somewhat frozen smile of a lion tamer who, while smiling thus his careless smile at the fascinated audience, is yet, you notice by a certain pink light in the corner of his eye, not unaware of the gravity of the task in hand, of the fearful perils of the open cage with the unaccountable big lion.

'Mrs. Hannibal, will you arrange for Mr. Dickin to draw on my account at Barclays Bank to an unlimited extent, till further notice.'

Mrs. Hannibal had trained herself never to look astonished. 'Yes,' she said, making a shorthand note of it in her pad, and vanished with ease to complete it in practice. At that moment another visitor—a strange man in large ungainly boots—was ushered into the vast gay room.

'Hullo, Chris!' Lord Ottercove exclaimed.

'How are you, Rex?'

'Oh—bored to hell. Mr. Dickin has just been reading me his serial.' And without any further introduction, he rose and took the visitor across to the large blue sofa at the far end of the room, and both men sat down and engaged in a silent conversation in which the movements of their lips alone were perceptible (as so often happens on the stage). After a while they rose and sauntered towards Frank.

'Have you, Mr. Dickin, ever heard of a man who can grow two blades of grass for every one? You haven't? Well, Lord de Jones is the man to do it, and, moreover, I am the man to get him to do it. You know Mr. Dickin, Chris?'

'No,' said Lord de Jones, holding out a bony hand. 'How do you do?'

'But he knows *you*, Chris. He's put you into his blooming book!'

Lord de Jones smiled, revealing a row of shark-like teeth. There was something, Frank felt, uncanny and incalculable about him. Lord de Jones could be most suitably described as 'a strange man.'

'Lord de Jones,' explained the host, 'is a religious scientist. He belongs to the Adventist sect. His argument, if you make bold to disagree with him, is that any one unwilling to be converted to his faith is prevented from doing so by the Devil.'

'I believe,' said Lord de Jones earnestly, 'that the world is approaching its prophesied end——'

'Creaking under the burden of his abominations,' laughed his wife's uncle.

'It may be for that reason,' rejoined Lord de Jones, 'that I have been chosen as His instrument to bring about an end.'

'It may be. But before you are instrumental in so doing you will be good enough to carry out your plan of increasing the crop-growing capacity and general fecundity of this lazy mother earth by closing all the craters in the world.'

'Oh?' said Dickin. 'Is that a fact? I mean is it a fact that the closing of craters would inevitably have that effect?'

'Yuh,' said Lord Ottercove.

'Are you sure? Is it good science?'

'It's good politics, anyway. The only thing to give old Joe a leg up. The Liberal Party has no platform. Never had one since the Great War. But this crop-increasing stunt will appeal to all sections of the community, and will be the saving of the party. It appeals to me on two grounds. It's sound economics—at least on the face of it; it's got a Liberal smack about it: "International Good Will. Live and Let Live. Bread for the People." Why, it will simply swing him back into the saddle!—But you will exercise discretion, won't you?' he turned to Frank. 'I hope you don't transcribe everything into your books, do you?'

'Everything,' said Frank.

For a while the three of them sat silent round the octagonal table. Lord Ottercove looked kind and a little fatigued; Lord de Jones silent and pensive. Frank looked at the great newspaper proprietor, who was obviously tired but still genial and kind, and his heart swelled with gratitude and a love for Ottercove, and the world that he graced and illumined. 'I think,' he said, 'I am really taking up too much of your time.'

'Not at all. Do stay. And will you dine with me on Friday night at half-past eight at my house?'

The intimate warmth of the great room, the political confidences exchanged in his presence, all this filled Frank Dickin with a sense of loyal elation. At last he rose.

'I hope to see you several times before Friday,' said Lord Ottercove, rising and proffering a strong, sensitive hand. 'Don't forget to give your address to my Secretary, and come and see me any time you like. Good-bye to you. And mind the step.'

On the landing, Mrs. Hannibal caught him and gave him a special cheque-book. 'This will be all right,' she said. 'I have advised them.'

In the glass in the lift he saw red patches on his cheeks. He thought that unless he steadied his thoughts he might have a stroke. His heart ebbed and swelled and he walked unsteadily on his feet past the braided commissionaire into the lighted street.

8

EVA

Eva did not reproach him for his inordinately long absence. And the taxi-driver, whatever he may have looked like before, now looked resigned, as if hoping for the best. 'I stopped him ticking after a time,' she said, 'and I told him you would pay him well. So he looked quite pleased and stopped ticking.'

'I know it was a long time. It must have seemed a terribly long time.'

'Oh, it seemed ages and ages and ages! I thought perhaps you had had a stroke or that Lord Ottercove had strangled you. And then I simply ceased worrying and fell asleep.'

'And the taxi-driver?'

'He fell asleep too. I told him it would be all right.'

'And yet,' said Frank, looking at his watch, 'I haven't been away three hours!'

'And I dreamt that it was a big mystery case, and that they dragged out your body and hanged Lord Ottercove for instigating the affair and——'

'I've been reading my book to him.'

'Your book?'

'About you, darling.'

'Oh, darling!'

As the taxi-driver, who had by now outgrown the faculty of astonishment, asked for a clue, Frank directed him, provisionally, to Piccadilly Circus. Alone, Eva at once pressed herself to his side and brought her mouth to his for kissing, before he was really ready for it; for he had drunk too much champagne and had read aloud so long and now was hiccupping all the time.

'Stop hiccupping,' she said.

The day had been rich in new impressions to allow him to savour his happiness. That morning, after a long absence, he had come back from Paris. The Calais boat sidling to the Dover pier. British porters, big, sturdy ruffians, elbowing, like a football team, by the gang-plank; suddenly charging the decks, making away with your boxes and bags. Then the bright shining boat-train gliding away and racing along through the dim countryside, London-ward, without stop. Victoria at last. The vast hideous metropolis blinking through the milky mist. And Eva's letter in his pocket-book:

'Darling Blue Eyes.—So sorry you are ill. And here I'm waiting for you all alone in London Town.'

He had not understood the secret pleading of these words, till, following up the girl's address to a dingy lodging-house off the Edgware Road, the landlady related to him how Eva, waiting for him, had held out three weeks, but that her sister Zita tracked her down through the police and took her home with her where, ever since, she was kept under surveillance but was allowed to take the terrier out for daily exercise in the adjoining Park. Eva, said the landlady, was a nice girl; owed rent, but all the time while waiting for him at the lodging-house sat piously at home, retired early to her bed to read a novel and eat chocolates.

She had waited, perilously, for him all these weeks, running up a debt, while he idled away in Paris on the pretext of sickness and postponed indefinitely his arrival! She had no money; but had not reproached him, had only written: 'Come as soon as you are better. Perhaps it's selfish of me to ask you to get better quickly. But I am *waiting* for you, Ferdinand,' etc. His name was Frank, but she did not like the plainness of it, and so called him Ferdinand. The landlady, who told him she had in her day eloped romantically and married secretly and very, very happily, exhorted him to be the knight-errant who should, like her own late husband, free his Eva from her intolerable captivity; while he rather wished she would mind her own business and let him do as he saw fit. And then, having pursued all the terriers in Hyde Park in vain, and equally so in Kensington Gardens, he had halted for a moment by Whiteley's window in Queen's Road and somebody sidled up to him, and before he turned to look he could feel the warmth of her delighted gaze. 'Eva! And I had lost all hope of ever finding you!'

They lunched together hurriedly and then took a taxi to his appointed interview with Ottercove.

' "Me-Too" Darling! And how did Zita find you?'

'Through Scotland Yard.'

'And she came and took you away, did she?'

'Yes; she broke in and cried: "You've got a man here!" and began opening all the cupboards and looking under the bed. But I was alone, in bed, reading a novel and eating chocolates and waiting.'

'Waiting?'

'For you, darling.'

'Oh, darling!'

'And who paid?'

'She paid.'

'Rather generous of her.'

'But she took it all out of my savings bank at the post office.'

'Oh! how mean! how cruel!'

'And she took me home with her and locked me up, and got Mr. Pilling to lecture to me on morals.'

'But what is Mr. Pilling to you!'

'He is our guardian while Mummy is away in Ireland.'

'He has guarded you well,' Frank said, not without bitterness. 'What about Zita?'

'He's taken a fancy to Zita—long ago at the Arcadia Ball Rooms where he's a professional with her.'

'A fine guardian! What is their relation?'

'What do you mean?'

'You know quite well what I mean.' He looked bluntly into her eyes. 'Yes——?'

'Yes,' she nodded.

'And so he's taken you both under his wing?'

'Yes. And Mr. Pilling said I was not to go out except to take the terrier out for exercise. And I took him every morning out into the Park and wandered all over Kensington Gardens, hoping I might come across you suddenly.'

'And you did!'

'And I did!'

'Darling Eva!' He pressed her to his side.

The taxi-cab had reached the bottom of the Strand and was rounding Nelson's Column. 'I must think of a hotel,' he said. 'I daresay I shall find a room at the Madrid Palace.'

'No, no,' she said, 'that is not a smart hotel. Mr. Pilling will say it isn't smart.'

'Hang Mr. Pilling! Besides, why can't you tell him I am staying at the Ritz?'

She thought a while. 'I didn't think of it. Yes, I will tell him you are staying at the Ritz.'

He gave directions to the driver; ran up the steps into the hotel, ordered a room, and came back to her. 'Darling, what do you want to do now?'

'Let us get out, darling, and walk and think. I am so tired of living in this taxi.'

He dismissed the man, after paying the full penalty of his caprice, and they walked on into Piccadilly and inadvertently turned into Old Bond Street. 'What do you want to do?' he asked again. 'You are surely not going back to your sister's to-night, are you?'

'No, no, I am not!'

Her reassurance weakened his resolve. 'But if she searches for you; if she goes to Scotland Yard?' he asked uneasily.

'I don't care, darling. I want to be with you.'

'We'll dine.'

'Yes, and after dinner go to a dance.'

'All right,' he said, unenthusiastically. 'What your mother used to call "make a night of it!" '

'Mummy writes that she is very dull in Ireland.'

'What is she doing there?'

'She's gone to visit daddy's people to see what they can do for us. I'd like,' she added, 'to go to the Kiss-Lick Club.—It isn't really expensive.'

'No. All right.'

'But I——'

'But you——?'

'But I haven't an evening dress. The old Meran orange crêpe-de-Chine one is an old rag now.'

'We'll get one.'

'But, darling, are you rich enough?'

'Just enough,' he said, not wishing to encourage her in her extravagance.

Now she was already standing at a shop window, trying to decide between two equally attractive dresses. But as they went in, the choice, and with it the difficulty of selection, and the perils of subsequent remorse, multiplied alarmingly. Seated, like a royal pair, in luxurious armchairs, the mannequins parading with studied step before them, they displayed, in return for the united efforts of the selling staff, an increasingly dispersed appreciation. From time to time, Eva disappeared behind a screen to emerge from it as an exhibit, to the venal praises of the saleswoman, who, anxious to bring matters to a head, gradually narrowed down the field of choice to two expensive evening dresses.

'I really can't make up my mind which I should take.'

'Both,' he said.

The saleswoman looked up at him in a way which made him feel that he had risen in her estimation.

'But are you sure——?'

'I think I can just do it.' To-morrow he would draw a cheque on Ottercove. It seemed scarcely credible. The affair smacked of the fairy godfather type of Christmas tale in an all-fiction magazine for juveniles. Yet Ottercove, his cheque-book, and his bank balance were presumably realities. In the midst of life we're in a dream, he mused. As they were being bowed out into the street, Eva suddenly remembered that she really had no shoes to match the dresses, and he took her into the nearest shop, where she selected competently, while asking him: 'Are you quite sure——?' the best the shop could offer.

'I think I'll manage,' he replied, more by way of secret loyalty to Ottercove, who, he recalled, had said, 'As much as *you* need.'

The shops were just closing; but, of his own accord, he suggested that she indulge in lingerie, and here, despite the closing hour, Eva's fancy ran adrift, while his new-born tenderness for her prevented him from curbing her desires.

But he did not himself indulge in any purchases that evening, as an ascetic act of abstinence before the pure image of the kindly Ottercove which, like an ikon illumined by a candle, always shone before him. Nevertheless the devil tempted him from time to time. Suppose, he thought, Lord Ottercove had gone mad. It was not impossible. He could then gradually appropriate all his property. Till the executors stopped him. If so, was that not a cause for hurry? And Eva's impulse was right? But it would never do to tell her. Not even if Lord Ottercove was mad.

He whispered in her ear as they pushed through the revolving door into the hall of the hotel, and she signed her name—with a, to unsuspecting eyes surely imperceptible, hesitation—'Nancy Dickin.' As they ascended in the lift, he was tendering excuses:

'It's a poor room, you know.'

'Is,' she asked, 'my room as poor as yours?'

'It's the same,' he said.

Forgetting to kiss him, she immediately began to inspect her purchases, till he suggested it was time she put them on.

'It's cold.' She twitched her shoulders.

'There's a gas fire.'

'Yes, yes. Darling, ring the bell for me.'

And to the maid, in a commanding, knowing tone:

'Put on the gas fire at eleven o'clock so it should be warm when we return. My husband likes it warm.'

'Yes, ma'am.'

At the Kiss-Lick she beamed all the time. While they danced she talked to him of himself. 'Pilling said—Zita said—I said to Pilling: "Mr. Dickin doesn't care a rap for your opinions! He wouldn't look at you——" ' Or suddenly, without preliminary introduction, she would volunteer such isolated bits of information as: 'He hurt me with my teeth. I cried.'

'Who? Pilling?'

'No, the dentist. And the man in the Tube thought I was a

little Russian girl because I had a grey fur cap and was reading the translation of a Russian novel.'

Eva, he noticed, was very observant and ironic about Mr. Pilling. 'He tries to speak French to Zita, because he thinks it's grand. Pilling thinks she has influence.'

'With whom?'

'With Lord Ottercove. Through Lord de Jones, you know, who is Mummy's friend. He is very funny.'

'Who? Pilling?'

'No, Lord de Jones. He goes about muttering funny things to me about wanting to blow up the earth. I think he is not quite all there. But Pilling would like Lord Ottercove to finance him.'

'Whom? Lord de Jones?'

'No, Pilling. He'd like to open out on his own. A dancing place, a night club like this one. Only he says he wants Lord Ottercove or somebody to finance him, because it will cost a lot of money. Pilling is very high class. He has bought a cottage at Marlow and called it "Villa Esperanza." '

'Full of hope, evidently!'

'And he makes up to a man there because he is a member of the motor-boat club, and Pilling can't be a member of the motor-boat club because he has no motor-boat. And he says he only needs Lord Ottercove to finance him to buy himself a motor-boat. That is why I wanted to meet Lord Ottercove this afternoon; and you wouldn't let me.'

'You wanted to speak to Lord Ottercove to—to——' he stammered with incredulity.

'To ask him if he'd like to finance Pilling.'

'But why?'

'I thought it would please Pilling.'

While they supped, her legs touched his and he had but one thought and one desire: to return with her to the hotel, to grasp her, clutch her, smother and devour her just as she was now with her wistful violet eyes and her thoughts of Pilling. She sipped her champagne. She was silent, completely content. Her large eyes were bright dewy flowers.

Ensconced in a taxi, she at once fell over him and brought her mouth to his for kissing. But kissing, by this time, was nothing new to him. He wanted new vistas of experience.

Then they were back, alone. He clutched her in his arms. 'Come, come, come,' he pleaded. She had quickly slipped into bed before he returned to the room, and looked at him doubtfully.

'Ah!' he cried in the accents of the primitive man.

But she had turned her back to him. 'Darling———' she murmured.

'What!' he cried.

'Yes,' she said, ' it isn't always easy to be a woman, darling.'

He looked at her blankly. 'Where is my revolver?'

'Your revolver?'

'Or I shall go out and hang myself———'

'What do you mean?'

'On the nearest lamp-post.'

After pacing the room up and down for a space, he lay down. But he could not sleep. At last he dressed and, to the astonishment of the night porter, went out and, incurring the suspicion of a lone policeman, loitered in empty Piccadilly Circus. He had calmed down, and his thoughts turned back to his miraculous acquaintance with Lord Ottercove and his unlimited offer of money, so generous that he could hardly force himself to take advantage of it. He would sooner assassinate his old grandmother for the meagre contents of her purse than overdraw Lord Ottercove's account. Wandering aimlessly about the quiet streets, tears dimmed his eyes as he reflected on the essential goodness of human nature. His look was moist, peculiarly naïve, and if a confidence trickster had that moment come up to him he would have been inclined to accept his offer, convinced that he would and could not harm him.

Eva was not asleep when he came back. Where had he seen it? Ah, she reminded him of that picture of a kitten tucked away in a big bed, with one paw over the quilt, one eye closed, the other open and looking at the world. In the dark they talked across the bedside table which separated their two beds, and she told him of all that had happened to her since he saw her last in Vienna. 'Lord de Jones got Mummy to put me into a Secretarial College as he said he would need a secretary to go on his mission with him round the world to close all the craters and Mount Vesuvius and such for which Lord Ottercove is financing him for propaganda and such like purposes, and that he could see from the colour of my eyes that he could trust me. Mummy wants to go with Lord de Jones on his mission all round the world because she says she hasn't been round the world and would like to see it as his private secretary, but Lord de Jones says he'd rather I went with him, much rather than Mummy. And so he put me into this Secretarial College to learn shorthand and typewriting, and the Principal was making up to him, because he was Viscount de Jones. He was making up to me.'

'Who? The Principal? Or Lord de Jones?'

'The Principal. And Lord de Jones. But I don't mind Lord de Jones because he is an old friend of Mummy's. But the Principal was a real rotter. He had a sort of conservatory behind his study where he used to receive visitors, and there was a palm tree there and an aquarium with goldfish, and he said to me when I said I was leaving him because he was a fool, " We had better kiss and be friends," and he tried to kiss me there among the goldfish.'

'No!'

'He did! And he used to pay his teaching staff at the end of the week in silver money. Three or four half-crowns, not more. They all stood huddled together at the end of the room and he'd recline in his chair at the desk and call out: "Jones!" "Ferguson!" "Gould!" (Never "Mrs. Ferguson," or "Miss Gould!") "Here!" and give them three or four half-crowns each. And the typewriting mistress, Miss Gould, only got two half-crowns and a shilling.'

'And they seemed pleased?'

'No, not pleased, but kind of dumb, cowed, hungry-looking. And when Mummy was behind with the payment because Lord de Jones had quarrelled with his wife and she wouldn't let him have any more money, Mr. Bumphill got very ratty and said I had a bad character. I asked him what I had done; and he said: "You are lazy, and where is your loyalty to the College? Have you ever recommended it to a single human being?" '

' "I have," I said.

'He suddenly looked very interested. "And to whom, pray?" said he.

' "To Mr. Gorilla," said I, "a Spanish young gentleman."

' "Oh, indeed! I am interested to hear it," says he. "Take his name down, Miss Frazer.—H'm! And what is his address?"

' "The Zoological Gardens," said I.'

'And then?'

'Then I left his Secretarial College. Mr. Pilling thought I should study to become a nurse.'

'And why must you listen to Mr. Pilling?'

'I told you he is our guardian.'

'A fine guardian!' said Frank bitterly. 'I'd like to bash his head for his treatment of Zita.'

'But what about yourself?' she asked, it seemed to him rather tactlessly.

'That was different. That was on a hill.'

'It was lovely. And Zita too thought it was lovely. But she said she could never tell Pilling about it. She doesn't know what he'd do to you if he knew.'

'No need for him to know,' Frank said, gloomily. And then: 'I say, is he...Pilling a great reader of novels?'

'I don't know, darling. I don't remember having seen any of yours in their flat, though Pilling once said about you, "He is very clever. I wish I had his brains. I would not be a professional, nor Zita either." '

'Why don't they marry?'

'Pilling told her from the start that he couldn't marry her as he was already married, but separated from his wife, but Zita being always business-like and practically minded asked Pilling to guarantee to her on paper that he would remain true and loyal to her all his life. But Pilling said he couldn't do such a thing as a man can never trust himself. Zita then met a doctor—an old consumptive fellow, full of gout and ischias and sciatica and heart disease—who fell in love with her and wanted her to be his own eternally and everlastingly, and as he also could not marry her he gave her the guarantee she asked in writing that he would be true to her during all his lifetime and even had it stamped at Somerset House; and then she became just like his wife. But he died in a week—from heart failure.'

'And what did Zita say?'

'She said: "I could have murdered him for it." '

'Poor thing! And now?'

'Now she has gone back to Pilling unconditionally. She did ask him for a guarantee, but he only laughed at her. She still warns me about men. But I also laugh at her.'

'Yet she controls your movements?'

'Yes, she does. Once, when I got so tired of sitting at home with Zita and Pilling and went for a walk by myself, and a fat gentleman I met on the station platform at Victoria took me to a dance, Zita gave me an awful hiding and told Pilling to give me a dressing-down and then slapped me.'

'Really slapped you hard?'

'Yes, darling, I haven't had an easy kind of life, I can tell you.'

'And so Pilling sent you to the hospital to study to become a nurse, did he?'

'He did. I had to cram my poor brains with so much anatomy. And the things they made us look at, the operations and things. Once I fainted; then I got used to it.'

'And do you really know something about it?'

'I know every little bone in your body.'

'Really?'

'There was a doctor there, an Irishman. He used to help me with my examinations and kiss me.'

'You let him?'

'He loved me, he said. And it was spring like that time on the hill, and so stuffy at night, and the text-books so difficult, and he so clever!'

'And then?'

'And then I ran away. I didn't come back after my annual leave. I went to London to Mrs. White's boarding-house.'

'Why?'

'Because you wrote to me from Paris that you wanted me to meet you in London, and so I came to London from Colchester and waited for you—weeks and weeks, till my sister came—the matron at the hospital had started a hue and cry—and took me away.'

'And then?'

'Then Pilling said I must go back to hospital, but I said I'd rather die than go back to hospital, so I had a row with Pilling. He was furious, and I was furious, and so I went away to Mother Martha's boarding-house and took a room, but I had no money, so had to look for a situation.'

'You all alone in London looking for a situation! while I was lounging lazily in Paris!'

'Yes. I went to the shops asking for a job, and I didn't know where I could get a reference. The managers were all the same. They said: "You have intriguing eyes." Or, "If you'll be nice and friendly with me, I'll give you a good cushy job." I had a good job in a draper's shop in Holborn; I got twenty-five shillings a week. But as they began to reduce their staff and I was the last-comer I was the first to go. Then I got a job as part cashier, part waitress in a teashop in the City. It was quite interesting. Business men would come up and talk to me and promise me a job. They said I had intriguing eyes. One man said: "You have eyes like violets." They would come up to the counter and we'd discuss together City topics. And one fat man asked me if I knew what Nero was doing while Rome was burning, and I said I didn't know, and he said: "Fiddling." And we'd all burst laughing. It was quite intriguing.'

His heart ached for her. Poor child, all alone, men like vultures, ready to pounce on her: forgetting that men, old and young, common and cultivated, were to her a navigable ocean whereon indeed she was an A 1 skipper.

'Then I lost my job as part cashier because the manageress said I added up all wrong and she couldn't make head or tail whether the shop was making profits or losses, and I said she had better add up herself to make sure, and I went back to Mother Martha's boarding-house and waited, waited for you, while Mother Martha swilled whisky by herself upstairs. And when the Irish doctor from the hospital came to see me, Mother Martha, who was full of whisky, said I had a lover in my room and that she'd write and tell my father in Ireland. But I said: "I shall inform my solicitor: False Accusation," and she got scared like a rabbit and crawled upstairs to swill down some more whisky.'

'And then?'

'Then I went to see what Zita and Pilling were doing and left Mother Martha severely alone.'

'Do you know what time it is? It's four o'clock!'

'Good-night, darling.'

'Good-night, darling.'

9

Leaving the hotel next morning, they passed the gauntlet of waiting menials and tipped their way through to the door to the total price of their freedom, while the door porter waved his arms in the middle of the street in an ostentatious display to arrest a taxi for them, and a page boy craned his neck at the glass door to see if it was coming, to receive, for looking interested, another sixpence.

At the bank he cashed, without any trouble, a cheque for one hundred pounds, and indulged in some purchases for himself. Unlike Edith Wharton's American heroes and heroines, he did not buy a grand piano, a motor-car, or a steam yacht, but invested in shirts, waistcoats, a new pair of pyjamas, a bathing-suit and an opera hat. At a bookstall he bought a booklet in a bright yellow jacket entitled *Dictators of the Press* and a recent volume of *Who's Who*, and at lunch, having tired a little of Eva's conversation, devoted himself to the literature he had purchased.

Who's Who, laconic but informative, recorded:

'Ottercove, Rex Victor Alexander Green, P.C., 1st Baron Ottercove of Ottercove, *b*. Ottercove, New Zealand; unmarried; *heiress*: niece, Eleonor, Viscountess de Jones; *recreation*: controlling public opinion; *address*: Bourne Abbey, Kent; Stonedge House, S.W.1.'

He read it out aloud to Eva, who said that Pilling would approve of the address.

The little yellow booklet related in a racy style the facts which were more or less common knowledge to the public, but re-dressed them with gay ribbons of fancy and let them scurry down the ebullient river of facile imagination. Frank learnt that Lord Ottercove was probably the greatest political and financial force operating in the England of the twentieth century—greater than Lord Northcliffe, greater than Lord Beaverbrook. Yes, greater! History records (said the little yellow book) that if the latter two had chosen to pull together there was nothing in the realm of the material universe that those two peers could not accomplish. Now what they could do if they pulled together, Lord Ottercove, it seemed, could do alone. If you took the trouble to turn up in the *Encyclopaedia Britannica* the rubric recording the development of journalism in the last half-century, you would learn that just as Lord Northcliffe's advent opens a new page, and Lord Beaverbrook's another, so the arrival of Lord Ottercove in Fleet Street definitely marks a third and, possibly, last, stage.

He was born (the booklet said) of English missionary stock in New Zealand, who, after working for the furtherance of what they regarded as the Christian Cause, in heathen lands, retired to that Commonwealth upon whose soil our hero first saw light. Human meteors had been known to exist before: but never one quite so swift, so bright, so deft, so certain. By seventeen, Rex Green controlled the major part of the New Zealand industries. By the time he was nineteen he exhausted all Colonial possibilities and went to the United States and captured Wall Street. At twenty-four he accumulated such a fortune that, from sheer revulsion, he stopped making money (except for such as rolled in on its own momentum), came to England and plunged into home politics. He unmade two Prime Ministers, made a third, buried a fourth, and, tired of the game of politics, accepted a peerage, buying a controlling share in the *Universal Press of the United Kingdom Syndicate*. He bought fifty-one per cent. of the shares of a daily newspaper, arranging that this newspaper should purchase fifty-one per cent. of the shares of another newspaper, which second newspaper he instructed to buy fifty-one per cent. of the shares of a third newspaper, continuing the application of this principle till, controlling the first newspaper, he automatically controlled all the worthwhile newspapers in the United Kingdom.

Yet, despite his meteoric sweep, Rex Green was a man of strong attachments. So when, with the offer of a peerage, the time arrived for choosing a new name, and all the county, town, village, street and railway names in England lay before him, the great man remembered the little village in New Zealand that had been the landing-stage where he alighted we know not whence upon the Realm of Matter, and decided by adopting its name to distinguish the village. 'In Ottercove I was born, and as Ottercove I will die,' he was reported to have said at the banquet given in his honour by the Ottercove inhabitants during his visit there soon after his creation, thereby drawing tears from their eyes; a banquet followed by a tour of inspection round the village, small, and with a railroad station so embryonic that you could not even buy a ticket there, but picturesque in its simple rustic way, quite a dear little place full of coves, creeks, and little brooks with beavers and otters, quite domesticated, it seemed, and almost eating out of your hand. The guest of honour, it is reported, beamed with pleasure as he beheld the place of his birth, and is said to have added to his foregoing remark at the banquet: 'And in Ottercove I wish to be buried,' thereby drawing renewed tears from the onlookers' eyes.

'Well,' said Frank, closing the book and leaning back luxuriously, 'it seems we've struck oil this time!'

'But why don't you get Lord Ottercove to give you some money, darling?'

'I have,' he said.

'How much?'

'Well, I don't know. He said "without limit." ' It was out before he had meant it to be.

'Without limit,' she said. 'But that means that you can buy yourself everything, darling, horses and houses with grounds all over England and Scotland and——'

'No, no——'

'But yes, darling. "Without limit" means everything.'

'But, no——'

'But it does, darling. Everything, everything without limit.'

He was sorry he had said it.

'We must tell Mummy,' she said.

'Great heavens, no! Why tell her?'

'She will be pleased.'

'Now then,' he said, rising and helping her with her coat and then taking *Who's Who* under his arm. 'No. I shall make the restaurant a gift of it.'

'No, darling, don't. Pilling would love to have it.'

'What does he want with a copy of *Who's Who*?'

'He'd read and read it days and nights.'

'Whatever for?'

'To find out who is who.'

'But how will you get it over to him?'

'In a taxi.'

'Well, look here, you had better take a taxi and go straight to

Pilling with it.' There were moments, after prolonged social intercourse with people, when his soul positively shrieked to be left alone.

'I shall ring you up at your club,' she said, as she drove away with the book.

10

At the club he found a message from Mrs. Hannibal that Lord Ottercove expected him to tea at five o'clock at his house. Frank, who was late, having failed by sheer strength of will to accelerate the movement of the train in the Inner Circle, jumped into a taxi at Dover Street, imploring the driver to make a dash for Stonedge House. But the vehicle, freighted with his dismay and anxiety, got jammed in a mesh of other vehicles. A march through London by the Unemployed, the taxi-driver put him wise: a call to Direct Action. Not for the first time. Frank jumped out, paid the fare, and made a dash through the crowd. A cordon of policemen barred his way into the square. Gaping suspiciously at him, they none the less let him pass through to Stonedge House.

The butler informed him that his lordship was expecting him, but had not yet come in from his walk, and conducted him into a great bare lounge with windows overlooking the Park, a huge marble chimney-piece, as in a club room, with an oil portrait of a member of the Royal family hung over it, and a lady sitting by the log fire. She smiled to him and said Lord Ottercove had asked her to meet him so that she might write an article about him for one of Lord Ottercove's newspapers, probably the *Evening Ensign*. They had barely exchanged a few words when Lord Ottercove strolled in sombrely across the soft carpet with a cloud on his face.

Frank wondered whether the cause of it was not his cashing forthwith one hundred pounds of Lord Ottercove's money. 'Why aren't you having any tea?' asked the host, and rang for the butler. 'Well, have you talked it over?' he asked rather wearily.

'Mr. Dickin has only just come,' said the lady, thus giving her partner away, Frank felt, rather cruelly.

Lord Ottercove gave his visitor a searching look, as though he thought this was a bad beginning. 'They wouldn't let me pass through the crowd,' Frank proffered his excuses.

'Nor would they let me,' said Lord Ottercove.

'A bewildering procession of the Unemployed,' the lady journalist remarked. 'More ominous than the last one.'

'Yes. I don't know what is going to happen. Processions are indelicate manifestations and are best discouraged by indifference. But an idle curiosity sends everyone out into the streets to see what is happening and swells the ranks of the dissatisfied. It is the same with revolutions. Mankind is periodically beset by mass dissatisfaction when, at some obscure, unmeaning signal, men suddenly begin to air their private grievances in a mass—as though that could possibly help them; and then, growing hearty, and with that corporate look in their eyes, they are ready to track down the Evil in their life to any handy bogey—the capitalist, the Jew, the profiteer, the Bolshevik, or any foreigner. It used to be religion—the Jesuit, the Pope, the Turk, or the Freemason—but that is now out of fashion. I do not see that anything is likely to side-track their present agitation saving some big stunt which would appeal to their imagination—such as the increased crop-growing scheme which Lord de Jones and myself have in mind. Miss Henderson, will you make a note of that for your Sunday article? Lord de Jones, who is a scientist by training, and myself, under the auspices of the re-dressed and re-bandaged Liberal Party (with Joe pleased as Punch at last to have a party policy), are travelling round the world to agitate public opinion in the countries concerned in favour of the closing of craters, wherever such are known to exist, to increase the crop-growing capacity of weary Mother Earth, for the general benefit of the human race, irrespective of class or nationality. The policy is to be launched in the broadest Liberal terms, and I want my newspapers to give it the widest possible publicity.'

'When do you hope to start on your journey, Lord Ottercove?'

'I cannot tell you. We have to time it with the General Election. It wouldn't do to have it all behind us before the General Election begins. A policy is only a policy if it is a promise. A difficulty is only a difficulty if it needs overcoming. A difficulty overcome is like your last year's birthday present. You cannot talk of it with any credit to yourself. And in politics you must boast in order to get credit, and, though you cannot boast of what you have done, you can boast of what you will do, if they let you do it for them.'

'Do you expect any difficulties ahead of you?'

'Our difficulty is that there will not be any to enable us to overcome them with glory. But I expect we shall be able to overcome that difficulty by creating a few difficulties of the spectacular order we require to swing old Joe back into the saddle at the next General Election, which cannot now be long delayed.'

'Is it an established scientific fact,' Frank ventured, 'that the closing of the craters *would* increase the crop?'

Lord Ottercove frowned. 'You've asked me that before. I cannot tell you. It's a journalistic fact, anyhow.' He paused. 'But I have no reason to doubt it. It stands to reason, if you reflect. More heat, more pressure from the bowels of the earth, and the quicker the blades pushed to the surface. That's how I read the scientific aspect of it. But de Jones ought to know; he is a scientist.'

'Rather a genius by the looks of him,' said Frank, in order to hear Lord Ottercove reply with deliberation:

'A Genius of the Untried.'

'I see,' said Frank, 'you will leave nothing untried, not even questionable science, if you may thereby alleviate the lot of the people.'

'I am a man of the people,' said Lord Ottercove, 'and my sympathies are with the people. But here it is not a case of alleviating the lot of the people. Increased crop will cheapen bread, undoubtedly, but only to lower wages. I know my capitalists!'

'But there are socialist weapons for that.'

'Strikes,' said Lord Ottercove. 'Direct action. Revolutions.'

Frank was not so much disarmed as submerged by the intensity of Lord Ottercove's self-assurance.

'No,' said Lord Ottercove. 'My aim is somewhat different. In ancient Rome the people were given bread and shows. They will have their bread and plenty of it, the Lord and Lord de Jones willing; but I am out to give them shows, grip their attention, side-track the vicious trend of idle minds—or I am not a journalist.'

He paused to give both listeners an opportunity to survey the boldness and originality of his vision.

'I am a journalist, and I love my newspapers. You, Miss Henderson, and you, Mr. Dickin, must have known love in the course of your lives; my love is akin to yours, but rather than being wasted on a mistress' (he looked at Dickin) 'or on a lover' (he looked at Miss Henderson enquiringly), 'it is lavished on my newspapers. I love my newspapers.' Tears stood in his eyes as he spoke, and Miss Henderson and Frank lowered their heads as though they were in church. 'I am amazed, with a sweet amazement, when I suddenly look into my heart and discover the depth of my love for these journals of mine.' Miss Henderson and Frank suspended their breath and continued suspending it so far as this is possible. 'They were nothing. I witnessed and sponsored their birth; guarded their adolescence; tended their youth; exulted in their maturity.'—He paused, as if having revealed too much of his heart.

'There is also an intellectual side to it,' he said at last, as if to prove that such things were not foreign to him. 'I have slowly come to the realization that things, the ordinary common things we see and grip, *are* not: they only seem. They are phantoms, dreams of some one great Dreamer who has dreamt us and presently awakes to congratulate himself.'

'And are we the dream or the dreamer?'

'Well,' said Lord Ottercove, pensively, 'I haven't so far rounded off my philosophy, though now that you have put this question it is already clear to me that two courses of enquiry are feasible.'

'I mean, are we included in the congratulation?'

'Well,' said Lord Ottercove, 'my original thesis was in the negative. But now I have come to think that, for a series of Sunday articles in which I want to incorporate my philosophy, the notion that we are the Dreamer and everything unpleasant in life the dream, about to be dissolved in the reality of our awakening, is rather more cheerful and more suitable from a journalistic point of view, and I will pursue the Dreamer as against the Dream course.'

'But is that a ground?'

'Certainly. A journalistic ground.'

'But I thought you were going to write philosophy.'

'Journalism, as I was going to explain, is philosophy. Life is a dream, according to my philosophy, a dream of illusions. And this faculty of creating illusions in a world of appearances is, I claim, the function of the journalist.'

'Make-belief?'

'If you like to—to put it so crudely,' said Lord Ottercove, evidently hurt. It seemed strange to see this rich, successful, powerful, middle-aged, newspaper magnate, once Cabinet Minister, hurt. So it seemed he was vulnerable?

Miss Henderson rose, and her employer and host, in his double capacity, saw her out into the hall, murmuring, 'So you have grasped the trend of the Wheat-Growing Story?'—completing his instructions in an undertone: 'And will you do a story on Mr. Dickin? Dwell on the strange similarity of his name to another famous novelist.'

'Which one, Lord Ottercove?'

'Dickens, my girl. Author of *David Copperfield*, *The Pickwick Papers*, *Oliver Twist*, *The Tale of Two Cities*. You might work Mr. Dickin into these tales. Perhaps suggest a common ancestry. Here's a title for you: "Is Genius Hereditary?: The Unpublished Story of the Dickens Issue." You might add that modesty, a fastidious dislike to shine in the blinding light of his grandparent, caused this shy, blinking, unassuming-looking youth, who, nevertheless, in the course of years is groping after the crown of his illustrious forebear, to drop the "s" in his name and substitute "i" for "e".'

'I see.'

'Well, I've given you two stories. Write them to-night and send them in to me before breakfast to-morrow. I will read them in bed directly on waking. Good-bye to you.'

Frank was about to follow Miss Henderson, and rose; but 'Don't go,' said the host, and each sank back into an enormous leather chair, Lord Ottercove opening his mouth to pose a question—perhaps why Frank had cashed so much money—when the butler strode in, announcing:

'Mr. Atkinson, my lord.'

'Come in! Come in, Atkinson!' roared Lord Ottercove. 'You bloody ruffian—come right in. Well, how's New Zealand? Gone to hell, I suppose, since I left it, what? This is Mr. Dickin. You've read his books, of course. *The Tale of Two Cities. David Copperfield.*'

'Of course, of course.'

'Bloody liar, you've read nothing.'

'Too busy, too busy,' murmured Mr. Atkinson.

'How would you like turning out twenty motor-cars a day, Mr. Dickin? This man here earns more money in an hour of his sleep by growing fat than you with all your artistry and intelligence and talent can earn in a year!'

'I assure you,' Mr. Atkinson protested, 'there is great artistry in designing a new model. And the machinery, too, trickish—devilishly trickish. At least Archie thinks so. But then Archie——'

'Is a liar,' supplied Lord Ottercove, looking humorously at Frank, who, not knowing Archie, smiled at them both non-committally.

'Did I tell you Archie's latest?' asked the guest.

'No.'

'He'd gone out hunting lions in East Africa. "I advance," he says, "under cover, and straight before me sits a lion. I aim—and bang! down goes the lion. But there, a few paces off, if you please, sits a second lion. Bang! And down he goes. I shoulder my gun and advance under cover, and there, just in front, sits the third lion——" '

The telephone at Lord Ottercove's feet rang discreetly, and taking it up, 'Of course,' he said. 'Use your judgment. What's the use of my having a great editor like you if I am to do all the work? Quite. In the question of National Defence I am supporting the Admiralty against the Air Force. All you need know. Good-bye to you.'

The motor-car manufacturer was evidently only waiting for the host to put down the receiver, for:

' "And there to the side of me was the fourth lion," ' he said, beaming all over.

Lord Ottercove looked pensive. 'Excuse me,' he said, and taking up the telephone from the floor, spoke, 'Give me Lady de Jones. How are you, Eleonor? Look here, you'd better have Admiral Battersea to your right and the Emir to your left to-morrow night. I want to mark my support of the Admiralty. What? You would rather I gave you the £30,000 necklace for your birthday? You're welcome to it, of course. But I advise you against it. Why? I don't think it will do you any good having it. Why? It would not make you happy. Why not? The remorse at imposing on your uncle. Not a bit, you are welcome to it, my dear; it is only advice. Good day to you.'

' "And there," ' said Mr. Atkinson, watching his friend put down the telephone, "was the fifth lion." '

'Excuse me,' said the host, and he warbled a strange wood-note like a bird's (which he must have learnt when as a boy he tended to spend his school hours in the wood behind Ottercove); in answer to which vocal sign Mrs. Hannibal came into his presence. 'Tell Franklin,' said Lord Ottercove, completing his instructions in an undertone with an almost silent movement of his robust lips. The instructions were so long and explicit that the car manufacturer, despairing of securing Lord Ottercove's attention, button-holed Frank Dickin, and was saying to him in a tone hushed to a level likely not to interfere with their host's business conversation but adequately forceful and dramatic:

' "And there," says he, "to either side of me were the sixth and seventh lions. Bang! Bang! Down they went." '

'What's that?' Lord Ottercove questioned, Mrs. Hannibal having gone to execute his instructions.

' "Down they went..." '

'Who?'

'The sixth and the seventh lion.'

'H'm.'

' "And there," he says, " bang in front of me—was—the eighth lion!" '

Here the car manufacturer paused for appreciation, a little tardy in coming: and then, not waiting for it and holding his curved sides to prevent them from splitting, burst out into a Homeric roar.

'Well,' he said, cheerily, linking this his leave-taking to the humorous anecdote, but his face growing serious, 'Thank you for your hospitality. What message have you for me to take back with me to New Zealand? Is the old country all right? Will keep the flag flying? Eh? What?'

'Sure!' from Lord Ottercove, more forced than spontaneous.

'If,' said the car manufacturer, 'you can keep Labour down and their wages you'll be all right in this old country yet.'

'This is a point,' Lord Ottercove said coldly, 'on which I differ from you,' looking to Frank for recognition of this sympathetic attitude to the workers.

'But ain't we both of us Conservatives?'

'In New Zealand, yes, but not in this country, Atkinson.'

'How so?' the dull, bloodshot look of an uncomprehending bull coming into the manufacturer's face.

'In so far as I wish to conserve the liberties won by the Liberals in the past, I am a Conservative; but in as much as I would gain new liberties worth the conservation, I am a Liberal.'

He paused, and added:

'I stand for tolerance—for the complete toleration of everything short of the intolerable.'

The car manufacturer, shaking his head at the brainy madcapness that overtakes some successful business men, made for the door, followed cheerily by Ottercove, who, to prolong his pleasurable reflections on his own intellectual success, expatiated on it by proffering, with subversive gusto, advice to a man he knew incapable of following it. 'Atkinson, you should stop making money and go in for Thought.'

'Why should I, if it keeps me occupied?'

'It's a vice. A man should stop when he has made enough. I've stopped.'

Frank made a mental picture of Lord Ottercove stopping. 'You don't make any more money, Lord Ottercove?' he asked.

'No. Except for such as makes itself. Of course, every year I am called upon to invest fresh capital. But that is not for want of any facility of imagination in the art of spending it.'

Lord Ottercove followed Mr. Atkinson into the hall, and as he waited for his host's return Frank Dickin's mind sang and tingled at the thought of money. Money! Money! Money! How did Lord Ottercove make so much money? 'Business ability,' was the saying. But what was it? Frank's ideas were vague and nebulous. Lord Ottercove, he thought, bought consols, sold them at valuation, at contango, and depreciation; bought debentures at quotation; accumulated stock, multiplied it by going into liquidation—and made a fortune. Frank believed High Finance to be closely allied with Mysticism. It was ineffable and inutterable: it could be revealed, but not explained; its priests were inspired. As Lord Ottercove returned to him, with a smile, he blessed Lord Ottercove's entire organization for the kindly light that emanated from him. Lord Ottercove's bias, he was pleased to note, was artistic. He turned his turnovers like a virtuoso, delighting in what he could do with so little effort. His friend-ships, his natural disposition, were all for artists. His collar and negligent tie bore witness to it. Whenever Frank was about to rise, Lord Ottercove would say, 'Don't go.' And when at last the guest, feeling the indecency of lingering any longer, rose con-vincingly, Lord Ottercove reminded him that he was dining with him on the morrow.

'I am afraid for my own sake,' said the visitor, 'that the more you see of me, the sooner will the reaction in you, to borrow the language of critics, make itself felt.'

'My dear fellow,' said Lord Ottercove, 'you don't know how all this delights me. Are you,' he asked in the hushed tones of a doctor who enquires if your stomach is in order, 'drawing all the money you want?'

'Yes. Thanks awfully.'

'Good-bye to you!'

11

When at half-past eight next evening Frank arrived at Stonedge House, and the footman, divesting him, with critical thoughtful-ness, of his street clothes, ushered him into the inner rooms, a lady, regally resplendent, came out to meet him, and greeting him with spontaneous affability, took him upstairs to the drawing-room, saying, 'I can't drag Uncle Rex from the roasting fire in his room. He is always miserably cold.' But already Lord Ottercove, festal in his immaculate tail-coat and pumps, was slowly coming up the steps behind them, and— 'How are you?' he asked.

A question to which it is difficult to say anything but, 'Oh, very well.'

They had not been in the blue, mirrored drawing-room many

moments when the butler flung open the doors and announced:

'His Majesty the Emir of Turkestania.'

A tall ample man, with a protruding shirt front, blew in like a whirlwind and immediately began to register a vocal admiration for the hostess's sparkling sea-green dress. 'The result of your Paris season I can see, Lady de Jones,' he boomed in tones of teasing gallantry.

'As I know to my cost,' said her uncle. 'This is Mr. Frank Dickin, your Majesty. You've read his novels, of course.'

' Who hasn't read them!' exclaimed the Emir, and, turning to the hostess: 'A most artistic, subversively provocative dress!' when the butler again appeared at the door on the landing and announced:

'Admiral Lord Battersea.'

Up the red carpeted steps came a corpulent figure with a face familiar to the readers of the picture press in a large-rimmed naval cap tilted at a rakish angle over a wind-beaten sea-dog face: now projecting out of a prosaic but discreetly confident tail-coat.

From time to time the butler appeared on the threshold, announcing the guests as they came up the steps; and presently he ceased announcing, and at a sign they all trooped down again to dinner. As the footman pushed up the chair behind him, Frank began to take his dispositions. In a moment of periodical unemployment when both his partners were engaged in conversations, he would prick his ears—for he was curious about his fellow men—and listen. Admiral Battersea was saying in his hoarse, sea-grunting way to the pretty, dark-eyed woman at his side:

'The Prince of Wales, I hear, kept very fit during the trip by taking a great deal of exercise.'

He found Lord de Jones at his side peculiarly congenial. Did he know the Kerrs? Didn't he! Eva? 'The darling!' said de Jones. And Mrs. Kerr?

Lord de Jones's silence seemed to hold a lot.

'She craved for impossible things,' Dickin suggested.

'And she got them,' said de Jones.

'What she wanted.'

'Exactly what she wanted. They were Impossible.'

They covered many a familiar plane—Russia, Vienna, the Tyrol. 'Did you know her father?' asked de Jones. 'I went out to Russia as a young man. I was taken to their country place by him. She had just got married. Lovely. She was lovely then; really lovely. Just like Eva now. If I'd known her three days earlier she wouldn't have married Kerr.' He was pensive. 'Eva might have been my daughter.' He stopped, as if realizing the superfluity of his reflections. 'It doesn't matter now. Nothing matters now. A journey with her round the world. And then—the *coup de grâce*! It is finished...' The butler was removing his plate. He looked ironically at Frank. 'It is finished,' he said, a strange light in his greenish eyes.

'Would you mind it awfully?' he asked Frank.

'What?'

'If I were to end it all.'

'How do you mean?'

'At a stroke. The world and its suffering.'

'But I thought you were concerned to grow more wheat.'

'Wheat!' said de Jones, drinking lugubriously. 'Wheat!'

When the ladies had left them to their smoke and smirky wit, Frank found himself side by side with Admiral Battersea, who, he reflected, was surely the extreme opposite of his own type, so much so that if Lord Battersea had read his books, he would, given the chance, have gladly got him shot and considered it a service to the community. Lord Ottercove must have read his thoughts, for, 'Admiral,' he said, 'come and sit by my side.' The conversation turned upon whisky, which was described as a good thing; at which the Emir protested. 'Wine,' he said, 'is a good thing; but whisky——!'

'*Good* whisky, your Majesty.'

'Ah, good whisky!'

Good whisky, it was agreed, was a good thing.

From whisky they switched on to politicians who drank whisky and from politicians to politics. 'Ah, Joe,' said Lord Ottercove. 'There's nobody like him. Just you wait till he is again in the saddle.'

'He is a long way off it,' grunted Lord Battersea.

'But he wants it'—there was a glint in Ottercove's eye—'he wants it with all his heart. When a man day and night thinks of the one thing he wants, he gets it.'

'He has oratory, inspiration, energy; he only lacks one thing: a goal, an objective,' said another guest.

'What can you do?' said the host. 'Liberals have had no policy since the war. But now we have something. I am off myself
with Chris'—he nodded towards Lord de Jones— 'on this stunt
of ours, and I hope'—he dropped his voice to a whisper and his
lips moved inaudibly— 'to identify the party with it.'

Upstairs in the ball-room, where chairs had been spread in
rows, a dark, passionate man was already singing and some guests
had seated themselves and were listening, while Lord Ottercove
walked about, with a long fat cigar in his mouth, looking
pleased. Frank found the pretty girl on his left, now looking
beautiful, with melodious eyes. She closed her eyes at him in
bliss and said that passionate music stirred people's passions. To
his right, leaning back leisurely, was Lord Battersea, puffing away
at his cigar, while the baritone squeezed the juice of tears out of
the 'Lotusblume.' And when the song was done, the British
Admiral, who had measured his strength on the high seas with
von Scheer, each, on his own admission, emerging the victor,
now with eyes dim with beatitude murmured ecstatically:

'*Die Lotusblume... Die Lotusblume...*'

12

Next morning Frank telephoned to Eva and arranged to take
her out to lunch. He waited for her half an hour in the Victoria
Arcade and suddenly caught sight of her mouse-grey cap and
mouse-grey fur mounting the Underground stairs (Eva looked
down when she walked), and she was at his side, and she was in
the taxi, and at once she was kissing.

'Why so late?'

'Shopping,' she said.

'Mummy has come back with John from Ireland,' she told
him over lunch, 'and absolutely wants me to bring you to tea.'

'Where?'

'At home. I mean at Pilling's flat in Maida Vale.'

As they were half-way through and waiting for the sweet, she
passed him, with a smile but without a word, an account, he
perceived, for £203 10s.

'What's this?'

'Furniture,' she said. 'A dining-room suite for Zita. It's her birthday, you know.'

'You bought her that?'

'I've had it sent this morning with a visiting card— "With Miss Eva Kerr's compliments." '

'Oh. And who is going to pay for it?'

'I thought it would be nothing to you, darling, now that you can draw on Lord Ottercove without limit. And it would take me years and years to pay it out of my secretarial funds.'

'God Almighty!' he said; and then again, after a pause: 'God Almighty!'

'What's the matter, darling?'

He grasped his head with both hands and shook it savagely. 'God Almighty!' he said.

'You are an awful old miser,' she said.

'But why did you do such a thing?'

'I thought Pilling would look pleased.'

'But why couldn't you *ask*?'

'But you haven't seen the furniture! It isn't at all expensive for what it is: it's real lemon-wood.'

'But whatever made you buy such a thing?'

'Because they already have a bedroom suite and are paying off for it; but not a dining-room suite. They can't afford a dining-room suite.'

'But what is that to me?'

'But I've *told* you: it's her birthday, darling, and it's nothing to you.'

'But to run up to such a figure! Are you mad?'

'But you haven't seen it!' she cried impatiently. 'Wait till you've seen it. What's the use of arguing before you've seen it!'

'I'll stop it!' he said, rising.

'It's been delivered this morning, darling.'

'I'll get them to take it back.'

'You can't do such a thing; it's a birthday gift.'

'I shall apply for facilities of payment, and Pilling can pay it off within the next hundred years.'

'You can't, darling. It would look so shabby. And Pilling wouldn't think you were a gentleman. Besides, I said to them at the shop this morning: "There will be no trouble: Lord Ottercove, you know." And they looked like understanding.'

'This morning?'

'That's why I was late, darling.'

He felt that he had nothing further to say.

They took a taxi-cab and went straight to the Pillings'. They found the family, except for Raymond, in full strength. Pilling, a strong, wiry man with crisp, curly black hair, frivolous on the surface but really with 'no nonsense about him,' was almost fulsomely flattering and trying to speak French to Mrs. Kerr.

'He speaks it remarkably fluently for an Englishman,' was Mrs. Kerr's comment as she turned to Frank. 'I was just telling Mr. Pilling that my father who had graduated at eight different faculties and universities could speak twelve languages like a native.'

'I envy him,' said Pilling, with a little bow which he thought continental ideas of good breeding exacted. 'If I had his abilities and, I understand, wealth, all the doors would be open to me. As it is I try to keep up my French whenever the opportunity presents itself.'

'In buses and trains,' added Zita. 'Morty's such a bore!'

'Well, French is an amiable language,' said Frank, 'but I find it difficult to scintillate in it—even more difficult than in any other language!'

He expected the natural retort: 'The difficulty would seem to lie in your scintillation rather than in any particular language.' But that also seemed to be their own difficulty. Pilling replied: 'My own idea, though you may correct me, is that nothing so helps the study of foreign languages as travel, and as I hope, with the financing of my project, presently to come into some money, my dear Zita and myself propose to undertake an extensive European trip to improve our linguistic equipment and to broaden our general outlook.'

'If you go to Abbazia,' cried Mrs. Kerr, eagerly, 'I can give you an introduction to the lady friend of the Spaniard Rodrigo. A very nice, quiet, well-read woman.'

'Yes, yes!' Eva cried.

'Or if you pass through Innsbruck, you must absolutely look up my friend Fräulein von Wiesendorf, and I am sure she would be very glad to give you German lessons.'

'I am very much indebted to you for this information,' Pilling bowed, 'and if you allow me I will make a note of their addresses.' He produced out of his waistcoat pocket a neat leather-bound pocket-book and pencil, and their two heads mingled as he recorded: 'Fräulein von Wiesendorf, in the care of Herr Oberst von Wiesendorf, Comptroller of Public Morals, Innsbruck, Tyrol, Austria.'

'And what about Tamara Leonidovna?' said Eva.

'Frau König? No, no, she is too fiery; she would consume him.'

Passing into the dining-room, Frank perceived a striking suite of bright polished furniture. As he stood gaping at it, Eva in the doorway slightly pinched his arm, and her look seemed to say: 'Now what did I tell you?'

'I congratulate you,' Mrs. Kerr turned to Frank, 'on your very good taste.'

'It's "Me-Too's" choice,' said Zita.

'But it's Ferdinand Fyodorovich's—how shall I say?—inspiration.'

'The Power-behind-the-Throne! Ha! ha! ha!' laughed Pilling—rather like a horse.

'I've heard of your prosperity. Very charming and touching.'

'Dam' fine fibre in this wood,' said Pilling knowingly.

'What did I tell you, darling?' Eva said.

'And not at all expensive,' added Mrs. Kerr. 'When I come to think what we paid for our Japanese suite in our Meran Schloss——'

'I told you it's a bargain,' Eva said.

'Dirt cheap, considering,' Pilling explained, 'the *finesse* of the fibre.'

'I suppose it is,' Frank sighed.

'Good value,' said Eva.

'Only the colour is wrong,' Zita quietly remarked.

They all turned to her enquiringly.

'The wall-paper,' she pointed by way of explanation.

'Still, it's very nice and sweet. And now let us all sit down to tea.'

'There is a Russian saying,' laughed Mrs. Kerr: ' "You don't look into the mouth of a gift horse." '

'I wish I knew Russian,' said Pilling.

'You must come and stay with us,' said Mrs. Kerr, 'when things mend in Russia.'

The door opened and a lanky, awkward boy on the verge of youth walked timidly into the room.

'Hello, John!' said Zita.

'Is that John?' Frank cried. 'To think it's John who fiddled with my razor blades way back in the Tyrol! How he's pushed up!'

John giggled bashfully.

'Come up, John,' from Eva.

'John, say how do you do,' from Zita.

A tremulous leaf of a lad, at that awkward age bordering on adolescence when one is neither fish nor flesh nor good red herring, came up lankily and shook hands with a shy grin. And that nervous youth had once been a dare-devil child!

'Hello, John,' from Pilling.

'John is so shy,' from Eva.

'Come and have tea, John,' from his mother.

Pilling looked him over, up and down. 'Cheer up, John!'

John giggled bashfully.

'John is so shy,' Zita said.

'You'll be all right on the farm, John,' from Eva.

'John is going on the farm when we go back to Ireland,' Mrs. Kerr explained.

'To our cousins in Ireland,' said Eva.

'With Daddy,' said Zita.

'Cheer up, John!' from Pilling.

'John is so shy,' from Zita.

'Don't be shy, John,' from Eva.

'This is a real family reunion to-day,' observed Mrs. Kerr. 'Very charming and touching. I am sorry Raymond couldn't come, or we would have all been together.'

'I have a real feeling for family,' Pilling remarked, 'and consider Zita's people like my own.'

'It's very delightful and homely. And I hope we shall have a rattling good holiday together before Eva starts on her tour with Lord de Jones, and John and I return to Ireland.'

'Lord de Jones asked me to come with him as his private

secretary because he likes me very much and I remind him, he says, of Mummy. We start for Paris end of this month.'

'My husband can't hear the name of de Jones,' Mrs. Kerr explained, 'without a thirst for violence seizing him. I suppose it is because Lord de Jones came into my life almost immediately on our getting married. And, curiously enough, I loved him for the same reason that I loved my husband. Both had wandered away from their families, seeking something remote and romantic, and both had alighted on me! I called them "my lost dogs." And Lord de Jones—he was then the Honourable Christopher Mosquito—was also called "Werther." Only, unlike Werther, he was not a poet, but a scientist, with queer, sombre ideas about the end of the world and his mission. Very romantic and charming. And my husband was Kestner, the *fiancé*, you know. Only they were not friends, as in *Werther*, but enemies. They used to go out with my father bear-shooting on sleighs, but really trying to kill each other. I waited at home, wondering which of them would come back. Very exciting and thrilling.'

'Lord de Jones telephoned to me,' said Eva, 'to come and see him on business, and as he was ill in bed he asked me to sit down beside him and hold his hand, as he said it did him good, as I reminded him of Mummy.'

'When I was a young girl like Eva,' Mrs. Kerr pursued with a look of tender reminiscence, 'I used to visit a young student, who lived in an attic and who was terribly in love with me, and sit on his bed, while he looked into my eyes and wept.'

'But Mr. Bumphill thinks it's he who got me a secretarial post—but I said to him: "Confound your impudence! We want no introductions to anybody," I said, "we are well known. My *fiancé*——" '

'Who's your *fiancé*?' asked Zita eagerly.

'Him,' said Eva, with a casual nod at Frank. ' "My *fiancé*," I said, "secured admission to Lord Ottercove by merely putting us into a story." '

Pilling looked at Frank enquiringly.

'That's true,' said Frank.

'I congratulate you,' Pilling said. And then, not without emotion: 'I sincerely congratulate you. You are a made man.'

' "And as for Lord de Jones," I said, "he's Mummy's friend," I said, "and no admirer of yours." So Mr. Bumphill looked very thoughtfully at the goldfishes and said at last: "Come, let us kiss and be friends." '

'Now I was thinking,' said Pilling, as he shifted his look from Eva to Frank, 'of starting'—he looked for approval to his paramour—'with the expert assistance of my dear Zita, a West End dancing establishment of my own, if Lord Ottercove saw fit to finance the project.'

Eva sat facing Frank across the long tea-table, staring at him with her large violet eyes, as if to take him in properly, and now as Pilling spoke a faint look of irony came into them that made them ripple with light. As Frank passed her in a narrow passage she pinched his arm.

'What's all this nonsense about your going away with de Jones?' he asked, and noticed that she had spied in the briskness of his tone the nervous jealousy that prompted it. 'You're not going, really, are you?'

'No.'

'Will you, darling, dine with me to-night? and we might go to the theatre afterwards.'

'If Zita lets me.'

'She surely will.'

'If Pilling lets her.'

'Oh, hang Pilling!'

'Hang Pilling!' she echoed.

'I do want you to come to the theatre with me to-night.'

'To something funny,' she said.

'We'll go to the Opera. I want you to hear the *Walküre*.'

'Is it a funny thing?'

'Oh, screamingly funny!'

But she missed his intonation. 'We saw, Baby and I, when she was here last month, *The Constant Nymph*. Rather good.'

'Who is Baby?'

'My little Irish cousin. She is back again in County Clare. And there was a man on my right who said I was like Tony. "Pardon me," he said, "but you are just like my conception of Antonia." "I have a nobler soul," I said: "I am more like Tessa." And he called me "The Nymph." Quite amusing.'

But she did not find it very amusing; she sat still, listening with an attentive but unreceiving look, like a good little girl in church.

In the taxi she sighed and said, 'Another three weeks, and you won't see me any more. Perhaps never again.'

'But what do you mean?'

'De Jones,' she said and nodded gravely.

'But you said No. I asked you this afternoon and you said No, you weren't going.'

'I didn't want to disappoint you,' she said.

On nearing home she asked the taxi-driver to make a noise— and the obliging man pressed the accelerator— 'to make Zita jealous,' she explained. 'Now that they live together Pilling never takes her out, and if he does, once in a blue moon, they go by bus; never in a taxi.'

'I've noticed she has grown bitter.'

'Bitter. Bitter. That's the right word for her. You have hit on the right word, darling. Bitter. I must tell her.—Louder!' she called to the taxi-driver.

The man was forcing his machine to convey the illusion of machine-gun fire.

'Still louder!' said Eva.

At last a window raised itself at the top and a head, dim and nebulous in the gloom, thrust out under it. 'Oh, it's you, Eva?' came Zita's voice.

'Arrived,' answered Eva.

13

THE SPIDER

In the vast cream-and-blue office all the lamps were discreetly shaded and cast a mild, steady light; the electric radiators exuded an even, purified warmth. Lord Ottercove seemed to go on with his work unencumbered, nay, stimulated by Frank's presence. Frank would arrive at any time after six o'clock in the evening, and the braided commissionaire who confronted applicants with questionnaires would at once call out to the lift-boy: 'Mr. Dickin to see his lordship.' And Frank would be taken straight up, without relays on the way, and handed by the original lift-boy to the topmost page, who, without a second's hesitation, announced him to his master: 'Mr. Dickin, m'lord,' immediately followed by a 'Show him in.' He would saunter in noiselessly across the polished floor, Lord Ottercove taking no notice of him, and lounge luxuriously in one of the enormous blue chairs, and dream. Now visitors would be shown in, and Frank would listen, wonder and learn. Learn of the enormous net of activities controlled by Lord Ottercove. Now the page would announce that the editors of Lord Ottercove's newspapers, whom he had called for a conference, were on the landing, and indeed one could already hear the shuffling of editorial feet. But Lord Ottercove might be settling a point with Frank as to the relative value of Buddha's philosophy in the light of Einsteinian physics, or the historic veracity of the Immaculate Conception, and he would call out to the page: 'Don't let them in, unless it be over your dead body!' And the page, flattered by the momentous responsibility thrust on his slender shoulders, leaned zealously against the door behind which editorial feet were still shuffling, till the great chief, the historic or philosophic point settled, shouted: 'Let 'em in!' They entered in a thin file, men of assorted girths, sizes and physiognomies, and Lord Ottercove, as he beheld them, would call out to Frank, with the leer of a Nero: 'How do you like them, Dickin? eh? Aren't they a gang of bloody ruffians, what?' while the editors with solemn mien and stately port settled round the octagonal table, Lord Ottercove among them but eminently presiding. And now for matters of high policy! 'Damn John Knox,' Lord Ottercove would say. 'These interminable Sunday articles about him! I am sick to death of him. Let us have something new and fresh.' And gradually he would expand into a living message and tell them what it was he wanted his newspapers to say; his hands would rise, his fingers spread and come together, till they held the extracted substance, the salt, the Bovril-like quintessence of the meaning he wished to have conveyed to the waiting world outside. Fascinated, his editors watched him, fascinated and mesmerized, while he, like a conductor of orchestra, played on their heart-strings, till even the sulky and backward ones melted.

They rose, the conference being over. Tired he sat there, his hand over his brow.

'To get them to pull in a team. Not so easy,' he said.

'I don't think your staff like me very much,' said Dickin. 'They think I have wormed myself into your heart and become an evil influence. A sort of Rasputin.'

'Ha, ha, ha!' laughed Ottercove. He rose, pressed the bell, ordered dinner.

The butler sprang out of the floor, the octagonal table was cleared of papers and fittings. Chicken, caviare took their place. And champagne bottles.

They sat down to dinner. The host, who had had the telephone placed at his elbow, would every now and then take up the receiver and communicate with the editors of his newspapers, or the editors would themselves telephone to ask for instructions, when he would say: 'I am supporting the Air Force against the Admiralty. All you need know.'

'But last Friday when I had tea with you at your house you were supporting the Admiralty against the Air Force,' Frank said.

'Getting too cocky,' Lord Ottercove explained.

'I suppose they are.'

'Besides, it doesn't do for a newspaper proprietor to be one-sided. He must steer the middle course.'

'I suppose he must.'

To be alone with a man who has wrecked more than one Ministry, and register his sigh cumulative of a strenuous day's work, to feel the contact of power! By no means a negligible experience. Frank felt he would like to incite Lord Ottercove to further action. But what action? Something big, something shattering, something gigantic. Wreck the Celestial Empire? Establish a Kingdom of Jewdom? a Negro Republic? Imbue the Fascisti with Socialist sense?

His heart swelled at the thought, and he looked at his host tenderly. 'I should like to write—to describe—all this.'

'Well,' said Lord Ottercove, 'and why not?'

14

When Frank called on him again at his office, Lord Ottercove was lying on the sofa, covered by a luxurious Eastern rug, the telephone on the floor by his side and two electric radiators turned full on to him, dictating to a pretty stenographer discreetly seated on the edge of a chair beside him. He looked enquiringly at Frank as if to ask: 'Now isn't that good enough copy for you?'

Frank looked hot and more than usually perplexed and embarrassed. He had experienced some difficulty in getting dressed for dinner. He had broken his collar stud, then torn his collar. He found the shirt studs would not go through the boiled shirt, while the new collar stud would not keep open. He discovered that he had no clean tie and that the waistcoats, except for one which had no buckle at the back, were all in the wash, and the one without the buckle had, moreover, shrunk so much that he could not get the buttons through it. He lost his temper, and his hat, and then, unable to secure a taxi, dashed off to the nearest Underground station and got into the wrong train. Emerging at the other end, he trod on to some slippery nastiness on the pavement and nearly broke his neck. He realized that he was over two hours late for dinner and he felt deeply distressed and unhappy. Lord Ottercove, on the other hand, looked harassed. Perhaps the news of the dining-room suite had reached him. Or perhaps he thought Frank wasn't drawing nearly enough. But whenever now he met Lord Ottercove, Frank read a meaning into his look. Lord Ottercove looked sad, dubious, alarmed; or was trying not to look dubious, alarmed or sad. The uncertainty of Lord Ottercove's reactions to the scale of Frank's financial manipulations began to tell on the latter's nerves. 'As much as you need,' Lord Ottercove had said. But his needs had grown with his wants, and alarmed him. And he was as much pained by the thought of exceeding Lord Ottercove's generosity (Lord Ottercove's watchful generosity) as he was by the possibility of erring quite needlessly on the side of financial timidity and reluctance to use his good fortune. There was no kind of security in this arrangement, and suddenly he felt he couldn't stand it. It was already in his throat. 'I want to ask you to——'

'I've had a man in here just now playing' ——Lord Ottercove pointed at the piano— 'Rimsky-Korsakoff. That lovely bit from his opera. Oh, what's the name? It's on my lips——'

'I want to ask you to turn off that financial arrangement,' Frank said. 'It's too upsetting. I——'

Lord Ottercove had pressed the bell button.

'Stop that banking arrangement Mr. Dickin has with me,' he said, as Mrs. Hannibal entered the room.

Frank gasped.

Mrs. Hannibal made a shorthand note of it and retired.

'It's on my lips,' said Lord Ottercove. 'I know the opera well. Lord! now what *is* the name?' He pulled out his watch and looked up at Frank.

'I know I'm late. An evening of misadventures culminating' (he was going to say 'in your stopping my principal source of income,' but pulled up in time) 'in my nearly breaking my neck as I stepped on to some slippery nastiness on the pavement.' His sense of social injustice provoked by Lord Ottercove's action, who, after depriving him of the principal means to a comfortable existence, remained lying on the sofa calmly stroking his pekingese, vented itself through a side outlet. 'Confound these dogs and their owners! They should be made to respect the integrity of pavements. Pavements were made for men, not for dogs. But in this country it's all topsy-turvy. If I were the Prime Minister of England I should exterminate the breed.'

Lord Ottercove suddenly jumped off the sofa and, without a word, went over to the octagonal table in the middle of the room and made a note. Then, rising, 'I will act on your suggestion,' he said.

'What? exterminate the breed of dogs?'

'Not I. The Prime Minister.'

'Hardly a popular task you are giving him?'

'Give him just enough rope to hang himself on,' said Lord Ottercove. He rang the bell, ordered a journalist to write an obituary article on a world-famous novelist about to be operated upon for appendicitis, and instructed a reporter to spend all night outside the house of a man remanded on bail on the chance of his committing suicide; then leaned back and said: 'As you are too late for dinner, I am taking you to-night to sup at the Kiss–Lick Club.'

'Are you really?'

Lord Ottercove began taking off his boots. Frank watched him, and was moved. There is something moving in seeing a great newspaper magnate and owner of several score million pounds removing his boots like any other citizen of the Western portion of the British Empire. One cannot assist at such a spectacle without an inward feeling that this should not be so. It should not be so, when a somebody-and-nobody in the Eastern part of the same Empire has his sandals removed for him by servile wives or servants. And yet, resent it as you may, there was something fine, unquestionably right and noble in seeing Lord Ottercove remove his boots, in a quick, breezy manner, as though he thought this the most natural thing in the world.

And he did more than remove his boots. He disappeared into the bathroom and returned from there in his vest and pants—just as any other man might do—and yet still looking the part, still the unchallenged proprietor and director of the *Daily Runner*. He slipped into pumps and a boiled shirt prepared for him by his valet Gilbert, into the black braided trousers, tacked on the stiff white collar—so tortuous a task for most men—quite effortlessly, and presently was tying his white bow-tie. And now he emerged in an exquisite tail-coat, spruce and tight like a glove.

In the historic lift they descended to the ground and got into the great motor, Mimi, the decadent and undogly pekingese, with them. A crowd of *Daily Runner* hands had gathered at the corner of the building, and Lord Ottercove touched his brow with his forefinger on the chance of their having saluted him. 'They're awfully disappointed, I guess, that I am not emerging from that office with a woman.' The huge propellered car ran swiftly and imperiously down the deserted Fleet Street and, suddenly, spread out wings in front and behind and left the ground, clearing the roofs of Fleet Street houses, flying Piccadilly-ward. Frank gasped with surprise.

'You didn't expect that, now, did you?' said Lord Ottercove.

'I did not.'

'This is, in fact, the first model of a "Winged Chariot" to reach this country. But I guess I won't be long the only one to have a chariot.'

'Winged chariots!' mused Frank. 'If, in addition, we could have winged love, a winged life, I would not refuse eternity at that.'

'If you had the refusal of it!' grunted Lord Ottercove, from the depth of the car, hatless as usual.

'You talk like a publisher,' Frank laughed; and presently asked: 'Do you believe in immortality, Lord Ottercove?'

'Not a bit of it.'

'As Lord Balfour once said, "If there is no life after this, then life is a miserable joke. And whose joke?" '

'When did he say that and to whom?'

'He is reported by Lady Oxford to have said it to her.' Lord Ottercove took out a pocket-book and pencil and made a note of it. For a while he looked pensive.

'You are thinking——?' Frank said.

'Of Rimsky-Korsakoff's opera. What the hell is the name?'

'After love, music is the best thing in the world.'

'Love,' said Lord Ottercove, 'is an inconvenience.'

'You mean sexual love?'

'No, love. Sexual love is a nuisance.'

Waiters were falling prostrate before Lord Ottercove at the Kiss-Lick Club and (in a manner of exaggeration) were committing hara-kiri before him. But he gathered them round him and said: 'Can any of you tell me the name of Rimsky-Korsakoff's famous opera?'

They couldn't.

He called the head waiter: who couldn't. He called the manager; the director and his sleeping partner; they summoned the bandmaster, who returned to his band and conferred with the musicians and came back, shrugging his shoulders. Lord Ottercove looked sad and perplexed. 'There is no solution,' he said at last, 'but to get hold of Rimsky-Korsakoff in Leningrad or Moscow.'

'He is dead,' said Frank.

'Really!' Lord Ottercove shook his head. 'Betrayed again,' he muttered. He ate gloomily for a time, and watching him, Frank wondered how even the rich in this world could not evade the anguish of thwarted longings! The two men ate in silence. When the meal was drawing to its close, Lord Ottercove looked up at

Frank. 'Don't worry,' he said. 'I will telegraph the name to you to-morrow morning.'

'You are very kind,' said Frank. 'You cannot imagine how that relieves me.'

'Now this,' said Lord Ottercove more cheerily, 'is instructive for you to see as a novelist. A real Michael Arlen atmosphere!'

'Ah!'

Frank did not tell Ottercove that he had already been to the Kiss-Lick with Eva a few nights before. He perceived that Ottercove liked to astonish him, and so he adopted the attitude of a newly-fledged chicken and to everything that was pointed out to him he said: 'Ah!'

'Do you see that young man over there sitting at the side of my niece?' said the host. 'Now it is my turn to continue your serial. That is Raymond Kerr.'

'Raymond Kerr!'

'Raymond Kerr.'

'Raymond Kerr! Her favourite boy? The one she used always to talk of. "Raymond has my eyes." Raymond this. Raymond that.'

'There is only one Raymond. And there is Chris de Jones.'

'I know him.'

'But you don't know that the two are related.'

'How related?'

'Quite spontaneously. Chris is his dad—his "Papa." '

'It never occurred to me! Yet, of course. There is a sort of resemblance.'

'A very marked resemblance.'

'Though Raymond is good-looking.'

'His mother's boy.'

'And de Jones looks saintly but hideous.'

'He looks the part. A man with a mission. An ominous mission. Wait and he will tell you that he is the new Messiah. He came out with it once under chloroform; said his mission was to blow us all up.'

'I think,' said Frank, 'that it is quite conceivable that the end of the world might come about in some such casual way. A fanatic like that...Suppose he blows up the earth instead of increasing the crop?'

'I wish he did,' said Ottercove.

'Is he mad?'

'Mad as a hatter! But a genius.'

'Of the untried,' said Frank.

Lord Ottercove looked at him first circumspectly, then quizzically.

'Hullo, hullo, Mr. Kerr!'

'How do you do, Lord Ottercove.'

'This is Mr. Dickin, the novelist, you know him?'

Mr. Kerr, an extremely foolish-looking man, fixed a suspicious pair of eyes on Frank. 'How do you do?'

'And you are happy on your farm in Ireland?'

Mr. Kerr took Lord Ottercove by the arm to where Lady de Jones and Raymond were sitting amorously together, and said in a significant undertone:

'This is my revenge.'

Then, as significantly, he walked away.

Lord Ottercove took Frank Dickin by the arm and led him towards Eleonor and Raymond Kerr. 'This,' he observed, 'is really getting to be more and more of a Michael Arlen atmosphere, of great help to you as a novelist, I daresay.—Well, Eleonor, how are you? Hullo, Raymond. Enjoying your fame as a prospective co-respondent, what? Some men win battles and get fame; others write lyrics; others, again, well,—do as you do. This is Mr. Dickin, the novelist. You know my niece? Kerr, do you know Mr. Dickin? You don't? But he knows all about you. You will see that he does as soon as you read his serial. Eleonor, how is your divorce getting on?'

'I expect it will be all right, Uncle Rex, but the difficulty is you never know just when it will be over, and with the baby coming——' She looked at Dickin fearlessly. She was a modern woman.

'Yes,' said her uncle, 'you cannot time these things.'

'The divorce?'

'I mean the baby.'

'The baby is a deliberate protest on my part against Chris's deserting me for Raymond's mother.'

'Quite. I appreciate your motive. But you should have timed him for a little later. As it is, the baby will land between two stools. And as for Chris, he is at present more interested in

Raymond's sister than Raymond's mother.'

'I cannot have the baby landing between two stools. Chris must acknowledge the baby as his son. It's bad enough that Raymond has been tricked by him out of his heritage, and, as Raymond's son, the baby is a de Jones by blood, and ought to have the name, too. Mr. Dickin, you are a psychologist. Don't you think I am right?'

'You are quite right, Lady de Jones.'

'I see your point,' said her uncle. 'Chris may deny the paternity of the baby: but he cannot deny its grand-parentage. So he might as well not deny anything. And Raymond will not press his parental claims.'

'No. You see, he feels that he will thus be getting something of his own back, if not for himself, at least for his son.'

'If it is a son.'

'I hope it is.'

'Oh, here is Chris. We'll speak to him about it. Hullo, Chris.'

'Hello, Rex.'

'Now look here, Chris. Eleonor wants to marry Raymond. I don't mind. But—' (his lips moved silently), 'she's used to a great name; she'll feel chilly, naked, don't you know, as plain Mrs. Raymond Kerr.'

'I'm very sorry. But what can I do? I'd gladly sell him my name.'

'No—no, it's all very simple. It's all perfectly simple. You adopt Raymond as your son and heir. When you die he will be Viscount de Jones, and while you still potter about he'll be— what will he be?'

'The Honourable Raymond Mosquito.'

'Well, that's better than nothing. Here, Eleonor, I propose that'—his lips moved silently—'Chris adopts Raymond straightaway. Then the baby'll be born a de Jones, and no need for Chris to adopt the baby. Kills two birds with one stone.'

Raymond seemed very pleased.

'But the baby's nearly due.'

'Oh, well, in that case, Chris, you'll have to acknowledge it as your own child, for, you know, it won't fit into its proper time.'

'I don't mind,' said Chris.

'What will he be?'

'Depends on what you call him.'

' What will you call him, Eleonor?'

'If it's a boy, I'll call him Robert.'

'The Honourable Robert Mosquito.'

'Now that's all right. All perfectly in order. When can you do it?'

'What?'

'Adopt Raymond.'

'Not till after the divorce, of course.'

'Why, Chris?'

'I can't adopt my co-respondent, can I?'

'But what nonsense, Chris!' cried Eleonor. 'Raymond doesn't come into the divorce at all. It's his mother who is the co-respondent.'

'I thought it was Raymond's sister,' said Lord Ottercove.

'It was the mother at the time we started the proceedings, and let us stick to her or we shall never get divorced,' said Eleonor irritably. 'You have no memory, Chris. You forget you are taking the blame on yourself.'

'I don't mind.'

'Still,' Lord Ottercove observed, 'I doubt the wisdom of adopting Raymond till after the divorce. It might prejudice the case. The difference, as I envisage the situation, is whether Raymond is to be Chris's elder or younger son. For if the baby is born before Raymond is adopted, Raymond will be the younger brother of the baby.'

'What! the younger brother of his own son!' Eleonor exclaimed. 'I understand nothing.'

'That's right. The baby'll be the elder brother of his own father. And why not?' said her uncle.

'I'd rather,' she said, 'he was what he is: the son of his father and mother.'

'Well,' said Lord Ottercove, 'it's all very simple. It's all perfectly simple. All you have to do is to adopt the baby, and he will be Raymond's son again—the Honourable Robert Mosquito.'

'No, he won't,' said de Jones.

'What will he be, Chris?'

'Master Robert Mosquito.'

'Well, all this will right itself,' said Lord Ottercove, 'the moment Chris dies.'

They all looked at de Jones expectantly.

'But, of course, the baby may turn out to be a girl,' he said.

'Quite conceivably she may.'

On the way home, in the taxi, Frank once more reviewed the matrimonial situation unfolded before him at the Kiss-Lick Club and found that he could not improve on the harmony of Ottercove's solution.

At the club he found a telegram from Eva, dispatched from Dublin:

'Wire money at once. Love. Eva.'

15

He was wakened at his club by an attendant who brought in his morning mail and a telegram. The telegram ran:

'The name of Rimsky-Korsakoff's opera is quote Sadko unquote. Ottercove.'

So it was!

It was a 'reply paid' telegram, and Frank scribbled back:

'Congratulations. Much relieved. Unspeakably happy. Dickin.'

Among the morning mail was a letter from Eva, bearing an Irish post-mark.

'*I am sending you,*' she wrote, '*all my beautiful love, and please send me some money as quick as ever you can. Will tell you reason for it afterwards. Am leaving with de J. for Paris and Rome, etc., end of next week. If you really wish to see me alone we could meet at Holyhead, as I am afraid to come to London on account of Daddy and his people, who are stuffy and churchy old birds and would get suspicious, darling, if I stayed away too long with you, don't you see, and if you came to Holyhead I could pretend you see, I only went to see Aunt Jane, etc., in Dublin, don't you see. Can't write any more as Postman is outside and screeching for my letter—"Country Post!" Accept all my Beautiful Love, etc. Also I have a little cat and I call him Ferdinand. And don't forget to meet me Tuesday midnight on the landing-stage at Holyhead and arrange everything for our Honeymoon. —Eva.*'

Frank, who hated the idea of arriving empty-handed, but, since the sudden stoppage of the Ottercove source, did not dispose of the necessary sums, shrank at the thought of Eva's extravagance. By a happy chance he heard of a draper and milliner in the Edgware Road who was selling out her business and he went and bought up most of her remaining stock, thinking Eva would be glad to have it. The box he brought with him to Holyhead comprised a corset, eight pairs of crisp calico knickers, a number of strong cotton stockings, a skirt, and a couple of hats. He left the box containing these treasures in the room at the hotel and went out to the pier to meet the boat which, at midnight, a lighted shell out of the dark, suddenly swam up towards him; and on board, waving to him, already stood Eva.

She alighted with a portmanteau, and the boat train took them back into Holyhead Town. 'I thought something was sure to happen, and you wouldn't come,' he said.

'All the village boys,' she said, 'came to see me off at the station. "Ah!" they said, "here's Miss Kerr going off to London!" '

'Did they now?'

'They did.'

'I've brought you a present,' he said.

'Where is it?' she asked quickly.

'It's in the room at the hotel.'

'Is it a ring?'

'No, it's not a ring.'

'Is it—I mean—jewellery?'

'No—it's clothes.'

'Clothes?'

'Clothes.'

'I thought you'd like to have them,' he said, opening the box at the hotel.

She took out the things one by one and laid them out on the bed. 'H'm! H'm!' she said. 'Of course, darling, they're old, very old.'

'Never been worn,' Frank said, a little stiffly.

'I don't mean that. I mean old-fashioned. Those two hats, for instance. Nobody wears such hats nowadays.'

'I am sure you'd look very well in them.'

'It's the fashion when Mummy was a young girl or even earlier.'

'Still,' he said, 'they look strong. I don't see why you shouldn't wear them.'

'And these stockings—cotton, you know.'

'They look very neat and strong,' he said.

'These knickers'—she held them out—'calico—they scratch.'

'Well,' he said, a little ruffled, 'I only wished to please you.'

'I know. But——'

'This bodice,' he said. 'I am sure it's very nice.'

'No one wears corsets now, darling.'

'Well,' he said, evidently hurt, 'I am sure I haven't bought it for myself, and if you don't want to wear it——'

He went away and lay sulking on his bed. 'Gratitude!' he thought. For all his trouble and expense...

'I'll wear them,' she said, coming up to him tenderly. 'You know I'd do anything to please you, darling. Let us have no more quarrelling about these clothes, darling; they aren't worth it.'

'Oh, aren't they?' he said, rolling over and turning his back to her.

But she came up to him, tenderly, sauntered up to him, lovingly, on tiptoe, and overtook him on the other side. 'You look funny,' she said.

'Funny?'

'Kind of puzzled.'

'I've poured some beer into a glass containing peroxide of hydrogen.' He stood up and looked at her: 'Most unusual beer.'

'Your skin, darling.'

'Yes.'

'Against my skin.'

'Is that,' he asked, 'why they say that love is only skin deep?'

'Never mind what they say.'

'I don't mind,' he said, and drew her passionately to himself.

'I like,' she said, 'when you begin suddenly to breathe like that—like a steam engine.' A strange look of prepared abandonment came on to her face as she drew herself up to him and closed her eyes.

'Eva, you looked like that then—on that hill.'

They were awed, breathless. Standing behind her, he clasped her with his sinewy arms, his hands like travelling flames. She threw her head back as his mouth pressed into the warm hollow of her shoulder, burnt her through and through. He lifted her and carried her, with a simulation of ease, across the room. 'There.—And the village boys in Ireland all mad on you. And Ferdinand has all this—and this—and this—all to himself.'

'All for you,' she said.

In the morning he woke up to a mood of warning and sat up. 'Ottercove——'

'Yes, darling?'

'Has stopped all my money.'

'He hasn't!' she cried. And also sat up.

'He has.'

'I wouldn't have wired to you for money had I known, darling, of Ottercove's action. He is a walking mountain of impudence!'

'But you needed it all the same for your journey.'

'No, it wasn't the journey. It was for charity.'

'Charity?'

'You see, I was asked to go about getting subscriptions for a life-boat saving fund or something and got all sorts of people to put down their names, but neglected to collect the money from them. About twenty pounds in all. So I thought it would be simpler to wire to you for it, don't you see?'

'I see.'

'Couldn't remember their addresses.'

'So you had no money for the journey?'

'A French lady called Thérèse Lapin who lives in Dublin gave me money to go to London with.'

'Whatever for?'

'On a tour of inspection. She has a daughter in London, and Madame Lapin has heard in a roundabout way that her daughter is living with a married man. So she wants me to take some eggs and butter to her daughter and report to her on my way back whether the daughter lives with a married man or whether she is straight and the rumour has been spread through malice.'

'So you want to go to London?'

'Darling, I must, for I wouldn't know what to do with the eggs and butter. They're in the portmanteau.'

The sun now looked into the room, and Eva, sitting up in bed, delicately sipped her chocolate. 'And all the time while I

was away in Ireland I talked about you to my little cousin Baby,
and I said, every time there was a noise outside, that it must be
you arriving, and Baby ran out to look and there was no one
there. And on Sunday mornings I would say to her: "Now if you
come to church with me you will see him, for he is surely there,
sitting in his pew." And, together, we'd tear off to church, talking
all the way of your sitting there already, and Baby's cheeks—she
is only twelve, you know—glowing with excitement. "Now," I'd
say to her, "you are going to see him." And we would both get
so excited that I'd forget myself that I was only teasing her.'

'What is your cousin Baby like? Is she nice?'

'She's like me, only her hair isn't a bit curly, but quite straight,
and she has brown eyes instead of violet ones.'

In the afternoon they sat not far from the sea, and Frank was
beginning to snooze. Eva had got him to buy picture postcards
and stamps and, sitting beside him, scribbled innumerable postcards.

'To whom all this, Eva?'

'Village friends.'

'Let me see.' Nearly all recipients were men, addressed as
'Esquires.' One was a 'Mr.' 'Hello,' he said, 'why is this one a
"Mr." while all the others are "Esquires"?'

'Oh,' she said, 'it's good enough for him.'

'It isn't fair, you know; it's vulgar to discriminate in these
things.'

'But if I write "Esquire" to him he'll go round showing it to
all the people in the village, and Daddy might find out I am in
Holyhead with you. You don't know the frightful danger I am
in. I must be so very careful, darling, on account of Daddy and
his people in Ireland who are very strict on morals and things.
It is a village, and everything, you know, goes round like wild-
fire. And I only told them I was going down to Dublin to see
Aunt Jane and would be back the same day.'

'What awful busybodies!'

'And on board there was a register for anyone who cared to
sign his name in it. And I couldn't help myself, you know, and I
signed my name: Miss Eva Kerr. Destination: London, viâ
Holyhead.'

'Whatever did you do that for?'

'I couldn't help myself, darling. Because the register is reprinted in all the local Irish newspapers, you see, and I thought it would be so nice to have all the old fogeys in the village, don't you see, read it in their evening papers: "Ah," they'd say: "Here is Miss Eva Kerr off to London viâ Holyhead." Rather nice, you know, if you know what I mean.'

'Well, here we are in Holyhead. And aren't we pleased! Or what is your idea of perfect bliss?'

'I like to eat chocolates and as I eat them to think of you, Ferdinand.'

' "But I feel," said Byron, "and I feel it bitterly—that a man should not consume his life at the side and on the bosom of a woman, and a stranger; that even the recompense, and it is much, is not enough, and that this Cicisbean existence is to be condemned." '

'What's the matter?'

'Don't know. Don't feel very well. But you are a nurse; you ought to be able to tell me what is the matter.'

Eva looked very enigmatic. 'H'm…Yes, yes.'

And then, hard up for an answer, she kissed him. She kissed him again and again, and, it seemed, would not stop.

To kiss and to be conscious of conferring a favour, to feel ashamed of it, and to wonder when, where, *your* satisfaction came in—was now his melancholy lot. She was, he felt, shy of him, had always been, fundamentally, shy of him. Only in the taxi on their long drive back to the hotel she let herself go. She wanted that love which he could only feel when he had lost her. Women want it there and then, and men cannot give it till it is too late.

The railway porter, carrying her box of clothes to the London train next morning, looked as though he did not think much of them, anyhow. Frank bought himself a copy of *The Nation and Athenaeum*, and Eva, asked what she wanted to read, said, with some hesitation: 'Buy me…*Home Chat*.' It gave him a pang—a twist of the heart.

She read it stealthily and looked up at him. All the way to London Eva attracted every one's attention on account of her unusual hat and dowdy skirt coming down nearly to her heels, and keeping off, Frank thought, possible lewd glances at her legs.

Arrived in London, she went straight away to the Dublin

lady's daughter. She had a rattling good time with them, went off for the week-end with them in a big car to picnics, races, shows and theatres, attracting great attention by her extraordinary new clothes and the enormous plumed and fruit-clad hats (the married man who shared a flat with Mlle Lapin visibly seduced by Eva's charms), and, on passing home through Dublin, she reported nothing to the mother; only said she had forgotten to deliver the eggs and butter, but otherwise had had a rattling good time.

Lord de Jones, whom she had met in London, had given her money to go on a learned errand for him to Edinburgh University in connexion with their forthcoming mission to the Continent. But, after lunching with her lover, she decided she had better spend the day with him.

The day was bright. The shops beckoned invitingly.

'Buy me——'

'You know Lord Ottercove has stopped all my money?'

'Buy me all the same a little book of poetry.'

'What poetry?'

'Any poetry. A little book—to read in bed. It mustn't be heavy, you know.'

'Well—yes.'

'I saw a nice little book in blue leather in a shop window the other day. I am sure it's poetry. Buy me that.'

'Anything else?'

'Chocolates. To read in bed and eat and think of you, Ferdinand.'

'Yes.'

'And do send me roses for my birthday.'

'Yes. The fifteenth of this month. I won't forget.'

She saw him off at the station, but left before the train went to meet de Jones, who had telephoned for her that morning.

'Remember: *roses*. All other flowers, Pilling says, are vulgar.'

She waved to him at the corner, and was gone.

16

The Farewell

'Mummy was surprised,' she wrote to Frank from Ireland a few days later, *'at the many underclothes you've given me. But when I said it was a parting gift on account of my going away to Rome and Paris with de Jones, she said it was all right. As for de Jones, Darling, I am Furious: I told him all. And He is Furious. I told him all the Truth that I never went on his errand to Edinburgh University but spent the day with you in London as well as the money He'd given me for Travelling Expenses on sweets and things. And He says he is going to dismiss me. Never mind, if I'll flirt with Him he won't dismiss me. And I said to him that you bought me a box of chocolates before you left, and a little book of poems to read in bed. "Oh," says He, "that is a Consolation!" I shall be in London all next week, packing. We leave on Friday morning. Shall wait for you on Thursday at Paddington at Eleven Sharp. It will be our last day together.*

'Your Eva.'

But she was not there at eleven. She was not there at twelve. As he paced up and down he was conscious that all the porters and the waiting taxi-cab drivers looked at him with interest. Shameless flag vendors button-holed him with pertinacity. He paced on, angry and exhausted, his thick, heavy overcoat on his arm, and a small fly flew straight into his ear; and pacing up and down vehemently he stepped again on to some slippery nastiness on the pavement. 'Must tell Ottercove,' he made a mental note of it. 'Have this scandal ventilated in the House.' At one o'clock he went into the station bar and drank a glass of beer on an empty stomach, and suddenly he took courage, ceased to be concerned about the formidable mass opinion of the porters on the subject of himself, saw them as mere independent, ignorant at that, individuals. The movement of the traffic, the sight of a girl stepping into a coach and revealing a ripening, silk-stockinged leg—such sights and sounds began to work on him, till his mind, with the beer and the oxygen inhaled, hummed like music, and saw God.

'Well!——' he said; and then again: 'Well——?'

'Why, darling, what has happened?'

The presence of John emphasized her crime and irritated him unspeakably. 'You ask me: you—you—you ask me——' He could not continue. He cast an accusing look at the brother, who giggled bashfully.

'Zita said I must take John about with me and show him London, for he is so shy and it's his last day, you know. To-morrow he is going on a farm in Ireland. "And," says she, "you've only one young brother." '

'And what about her? It's our last day together.'

'Exactly! But she wants to be alone with Pilling all the time. How she loves Pilling!'

'And why aren't you wearing the nice new clothes I gave you?'

'Child: it won't do.'

'It won't do?'

'No, child.'

While John was looking into a shop window, Frank pleaded with her whether they could not really spend this last day alone.

'I will telephone to her,' said Eva, as if struck by a brain-wave, 'and see what she says.'

She vanished in a telephone booth, and Frank and John watched her mute lips through the glass door assiduously explaining into the telephone what looked a difficult, and at the other end an uncongenial, proposition.

'No,' she said, emerging from the booth, 'she says John must come with us, because he is so shy and would lose himself alone in London. "You have only one little brother," she said.'

'This is damnable,' thought Frank. 'At any rate let us go and have lunch somewhere,' he said aloud, 'and think it over.'

They lunched in embarrassed silence, broken here and there by an embarrassed question. 'You crossed over when?'

'Tuesday. Arrived in London very late, so went to a hotel. Travelled with nine Catholic priests,' she said, 'so all went to the same hotel, and to the cinema together, and we all held hands.'

'Nine Catholic priests, and you in the middle?'

'No, at one end. Father Michael and I holding hands, and all the other eight, too, in a chain. Very intriguing.'

'Must have been.'

After lunch, as they were sauntering along, an idea occurred to Frank. 'John,' he said, 'would you like to go to a theatre—by yourself?'

'Fancy! all by yourself like a grown-up man!' said Eva.

John giggled nervously.

'To a show of Maskelyne and Devant's?'

'Fancy!' said Eva. 'Acrobats, John! Acrobats and things. Eh? John?'

'I don't mind,' said John.

They jumped into a taxi, and Frank bought a stall ticket, and John, accepting it with a kind of nervous misgiving, was ushered into the darkness (the performance having already begun), the attendant like a gaoler on his heels. 'Tell him, tell him to look after John, who is so shy!' Eva cried. But John and his gaoler had vanished in the dark.

Freedom at last! They were free, free, free; free of all but the exigence of their freedom. He avoided the shops with her, but she must have a bottle of scent and let him buy all that the saleswoman insinuated. She gave in completely to the saleswoman's idea of what was the proper thing for her. The saleswoman seemed to have no doubt, and appreciating Frank's secret loathing of her and her sex, made it a point of honour for him to comply with Eva's tutored wishes.

'And I just want to look at these dresses.'

'Better come out and look at Nature. A lovely day!'

'I'd like that dress.'

'No doubt. I'd like a new suit.'

'Must have another dress to go about with de Jones, you know. In Paris and Rome.'

'I got old Ottercove to stop his payments too soon, it would seem. Too soon, too damned soon!'

'Couldn't you borrow, perhaps?'

'Couldn't I!—Women will sell their bodies and souls for a vivid rag,' he said bitterly.

He looked at her and read her thoughts. With a melancholy twinge, she reflected that she had evidently sold hers without any such extenuating material compensation. 'You are an awful old miser,' she said.

He suffered hell. Damn it all, she seemed to have no idea

about the value of money! She did not know that the number
of pounds in his pocket-book was strictly limited.

Through the park they drifted into Kensington Gardens, and
walked across the grass towards the Serpentine. Eva wouldn't let
him take her arm.

'Bad form,' she explained.

They hired a boat, and as he rowed he watched her steer. She
steered intently but very badly, zigzagging needlessly all the way,
while he puffed and sweated at the oars; which provoked him
into biting sarcasm.

'Crooked again!'

'Why don't you put it straight with the oars?'

'Can't you see me,' he said, puffing, 'otherwise employed?'

'Now don't get ratty, darling, or you will feel sorry afterwards.'

'Why sorry?'

'When you think of it—remember, I mean.'

By the time they had rowed back, it was time, she judged, to
go and fetch John from the matinée. 'If we are not there, he
won't know where to turn to: he is so shy,' she said. 'And Zita
said to me, "Take care of John; you won't always have your little
brother with you." '

This solicitude on behalf of John angered him. 'Damn it all,
we thought nothing of leaving him alone at the inn.'

'What inn, darling?'

'On the top of the Patscherkofl mountain in the Tyrol. Don't
you remember?'

Her eyes darkened and lightened again. 'I remember, darling,
I remember.'

'And it's our last day together.'

'I am thinking——'

'What?'

'I have no real travelling costume for my Continental trip.'

'I have no proper overcoat, damn you.' Oh, why were there
no girls as beautiful as the latest film star and as intelligent as
Henry James!

'Well, John, did you enjoy the performance?'

'Great fun,' stammered John.

'Tell us all about it, John.'

'There was a man,' said John, 'and a ring, and another man on the ring——'

'That will do, John. Wait till we are settled down in the café,' she said.

'Now, then, John.'

'There was a ring and a man held on to the ring and a girl held on to the man and——'

'Wait, John.—I was just thinking, if Zita asks me all about the performance I must tell the same story as John.'

'All the more reason why John should be allowed to disclose his impressions,' said Frank.

'Yes. Go on, John.'

'There was a man,' said John, 'and a ring——'

'What will you have, John,' she asked, 'tea or chocolate?'

On the way home, John talked of the performance. 'There was a man,' he would say, 'with a ring, and a girl held on to the man.'

'Shut up, John. That will do.'

She went in with John, and Frank said he would wait for her in Kensington Gardens to take her out to dinner. He was tired and glad to be alone. He sat down on a bench, and an ugly, repulsive girl of ten disengaged herself from a group of urchins and sat down between him and an old lady and began to tease him, pointing at him with her dirty forefinger. 'You funny-looking bloke, you. Now why don't you smile?' And all the other urchins crowded round and giggled at him. 'Come on! Let's see a smile!' the girl went on, encouraged.

The old lady at his side saw fit to intervene. 'Behave yourself,' she said, 'or go away and leave the gentleman alone.'

'It's 'im I'm torking to, not yer; you 'old yer tongue.'

'Disgraceful girl!' said the old lady. But the little girl went on at Frank:

'Come, show us you can smile. Now then!'

'Shut up, will you!' suddenly he roared at her.

The girl went red and shrivelled up on the bench. 'It's 'er,' she said tearfully, pointing at the old lady, 'not me. None of 'er bloomin' business.'

One of those nasty winter fogs was descending on to London when Eva, late by an hour, appeared at the gate.

''Is sweet'eart!' jeered the girl, and all the urchins giggled with her.

'Well,' he said, rising, 'I *have* had a time, waiting for you.'

'Zita and Pilling kept me back with their nonsense about my getting de Jones to talk to Ottercove about Pilling's dancing place. I told them I'd be late and keep you waiting, but Pilling said: "Ferdinand will wait." '

They were rattling along in a taxi, and he was telling her all about the cheeky girl in Kensington Gardens.

'Darling, I am not interested.'

'In anything that happens to me.'

'That isn't true, darling. When I am away from you I always talk about you. This evening, for example, while you were waiting for me. I asked them if they thought you were very beautiful, but Pilling said: "I shouldn't say he was beautiful to look at, but he is very clever. I wish I had his brains." '

To Frank, who for years had been regarded as the fool of the family, this universal discovery of his brains was stimulating and refreshing.

At dinner Eva was crotchety because he would not take her out to the Savoy to dance. 'It isn't really at all expensive, darling. It really isn't. I only want to go so as to tell Zita how you don't mind throwing away money on me. Because Pilling is so careful, and she hates it so. Only to be able to tell her, you see.'

'Well, tell her.'

'What!'

'Anything you like.'

'H'm. That's an idea. I never thought of that.'

'Tell her we dined with their Majesties.'

'Zita,' she confessed to him, 'doesn't seem to like you much. She said, "The one good thing about him is that he has pots of money." '

'Pots! Barrels full! Brains and money. Beauty, too! Oh, what a lucky man am I! But why is it that I feel I'd like to go and blow my brains out?'

'If you don't stop quarrelling,' she said, 'I will leave immediately, and you will be sorry all your life.'

'Then we shall leave together.'

On their way back he stopped the taxi-cab a few doors away from Pilling's house and walked on with her into a more deserted lane. They walked in silence. Suddenly it came to him that he might be seeing her for the last time. And what was it that she resented? That he had so far omitted to say the fateful word? He guided her to a sort of blind door in the masonry of a house, and took her in his arms. But a policeman hove in sight and said, 'Move on, please. You're not allowed to stand here.'

They went on and turned into another lane. She hurried him, saying that Pilling and Zita were surely anxious that she was not yet home. It angered him, and at the thought of the last inadequate hours together, full of bickerings and vexations, tears flooded his eyes as he suddenly kissed her good-bye. He stood in the darkness, watching her as she walked to the end of the lane and, without turning to him, disappeared round the corner.

He walked away at an accelerated pace. He said: 'No. Never again. It's finished as if it had never been! I am glad, and nothing that may come will wipe out the memory of my saying here, deliberately, immediately on parting, that I am glad I did not say the word.' He walked the length of Bayswater Road into Oxford Street and all the way to his club, and on entering his room pulled out his diary and wrote:

'...I put it down on record——'

17

It was thus that soon after Eva's departure with the mystical de Jones, Frank found himself one afternoon strolling vacantly down Regent Street. A crowd of people. Bustling, frolicking folk. Women, gay, charming, so beautiful, so tender, whose arms, if they could guess, might open for the kiss—and who passed him without a look! Flitting by on what was the latest in footwear, thin ankles, swelling into glossy silken calves—oh, rapture! oh, seduction! How lonely one could be in a crowd. For it wasn't—he reflected—that there was any one cohesive and receptive sensibility in that crowd, which frolicked and enjoyed life while he suffered, into which he could have merged with any profit. Groups of laughing young voices. Why could he not talk to them without causing them to feel they had been slighted, or landing himself at Marlborough Street Police Station? Why could he not join them without very soon being bored? There they were, groups on the face of it, but really solitary, yearning, suffering souls like himself. There was no sort of one central well in all this diffused, accidentally accumulated hilarity from which one could draw. All came out to look at the feast—and all looked without being filled.

He saw rich men in furs and motor-cars, and wished them joy of it; he read the New Year's Honours list, and sensed no pang; he watched old colleagues overtake him on the road to fame, and felt no jealousy; he had seen his father's fortune blown to smithereens, without a blink: but that every woman whom he looked at twice did not immediately yield herself to him was something he found hard to bear, harder to forgive. To possess all the comely women in the world, the female portion of the universe, in a sort of cumulative, consummative kiss—it was his dream. For—indisputably— one woman was not like another; and how? how enjoy them all? While lying, as he thought appeased, in one woman's arms, the thought that there must be another in some particular different from his own would at once renew his restlessness and send him searching, searching round the globe. Content as last, content and happy at Port Said, the thought of what he must be missing in Calcutta was sufficient to uproot him and send him on his onward quest over plain and mountain, dune and sea, continent and ocean, till, with ever greater frequency, he would rebound in London, in Piccadilly Circus, the reputed centre of the world, with his heart still burning, with hot tears in his parched throat. 'I can't bear it,' he said, looking with a kind of stupor at the fountain he had seen before. 'I will kill myself.'

A practical man inessentially, Frank was impractical in essentials. He had a kind of vague idea that the whole universe and all that it held could, under favourable conditions, be embraced in a woman's kiss. The consummation—*das Welt-Alles*! The All-in-all. There was a critic just then who wrote copiously in the *Adelphi* about the One and the Many. Yes, perhaps the One was to be realized most clearly in one of the many. 'Very likely,' he said, 'very likely.' Was he already beginning to regret his Eva's absence? No, he had weighed her kisses in the balance and had found them wanting. Except for that first virgin kiss upon the mountain-top when she came up close, close to him, took a long breath and closed her eyes...

He turned into Piccadilly, steadied his thoughts, and continued in a Tolstoyan mood of honest self-analysis: 'Then what am I to do? Renounce the flesh and turn saint? Difficult. Difficult and uncongenial. Essentially the world is good and one ought to know how to be happy. But happiness is a strange thing: it is in two parts and is conditioned by an inner equilibrium. On the surface I oscillate in a kind of twilight, through black night into the dawn and back: but within, my soul sings like a lark and it is morning. And all is well and beyond implication. I knew it long ago. Yet I cannot sit down in the cool quiet of a pillared cathedral as I would by choice, with all my passions and lusts raging in me, raging in me! Essentially all is well. Certainly. Certainly. But that does not do away with the surface things being all wrong. Mere pin-pricks. Perhaps. But the skin is a sensitive tissue.'

Tired out, he sat down on a bench in the Green Park and pulled out his *Times*. How it assumed that all was well and orderly in the world. With what propriety it examined and relegated to the requisite sections and columns the haphazard irrelevance of life. But how sane, how quiet and dignified and, withal, informed. Under a rubric headed 'Science,' he read:

'...In the course of the year Jeans had explored the problem further, and has reached conclusions of immense significance in our conceptions of the universe. These are, in short, that the chemical elements of which we have knowledge are only one end of an indefinite series and that end a degeneration from an indefinitely more complex set of atoms in the distant stars and nebulae. The conditions in which life is possible are an extreme case, possibly unique, and came about by a destruction of matter through countless aeons of time. The primary physical process of the universe is the conversion of matter into radiation, a process not even suspected until 1904. The primary matter of the universe consists of highly complex atoms, dissociated and incapable of association inasmuch as they change their make-up millions of times in a second.'

He stopped reading and pondered. 'Dissociated and incapable of association.' Significant. Significant and suggestive. 'The primary matter of the universe...consists of atoms incapable of association...inasmuch as they change their make-up millions of times in a second.' 'Like me,' he thought. And came to the conclusion that he was, his salvation lay, in the primary matter of the universe.

Calmed down, appeased by a distant hope of merging into the primary matter of the universe and finding peace in changing his make-up with it millions of times in a second with more inward profit than heretofore and more pleasure than he found in his already frequent reboundings in London, he strolled on across the Park and called in to see Lord Ottercove.

Lord Ottercove, as he saw him, looked as though he had no wish to change his make-up millions of times in a second, but was indeed perfectly content with his make-up, such as it was, and moreover, dissociated himself from the primary matter of the universe, being content to dwell within that end of the indefinite series of chemical elements which had come about by a destruction of matter through countless aeons of time and described in the paragraph of *The Times* as an extreme, possibly unique, case in which life (and journalistic activity) was possible.

'Forgive me for not rising,' he said. 'But all these things will fall off my lap if I do.'

'What need for me to forgive you,' thought Frank, 'since you have already forgiven yourself?'

There was an air about Lord Ottercove as though he knew what a rich and splendid type he was for the imaginative novelist—and he was always ready to help the young and striving artist—but could scarcely comprehend the blindness of established novelists to the riches lying at their feet. Now that he knew Frank had conceived him as the hero of his new novel he not only proved a willing sitter, but lent his own imagination towards bettering Frank's plot. And this he did in a way that tended to enhance the prestige and lovableness of the hero by placing him in more favourable situations than those envisaged by the author. Frank, in relating the plot of his new novel, might say: 'And here the scientist gets the better of the hero by an ingenious use of the latter's newspapers to an end the hero cannot at this stage foresee.'

'Quite,' Lord Ottercove would say. 'But by pretending not to see the scientist's game the newspaper proprietor outwits him in the following chapter.'

Frank was grateful to Lord Ottercove for the privilege of seeing him in all his multifarious attitudes from every angle and aspect: in his beautifully fitting tail-coats (there were several of them in the office and in every one of his town and country houses); in his silk pyjamas; in the heroic act of jumping out of bed; sitting on the edge of it in pensive mood with his bare feet dangling meditatively; in dishabille; in dressing-gown and *en pantoufles*; or shaving in his vest and pants: in all attitudes and from all angles Lord Ottercove, Frank could but remark, was unequivocally great. It seemed as if Lord Ottercove in his unfailing thoughtfulness provided him with these opportunities to study him at all hours and in all attitudes. If Frank had not, as yet, had the opportunity of studying his lordship *au naturel*, it was because such study, for descriptive purposes in a work of fiction, was, he willingly recognized, in advance of current customs and usages.

'Well, how are you?' said Lord Ottercove. 'How are your sales?'

In the first week of January, having run through some twenty issues of one of Ottercove's newspapers, 'Pale Primroses,' by Frank Septimus Dickin, in a pale jacket liberally sprinkled with flowers of the title, made its appearance on the bookstalls; yet enjoying but a melancholy sale, which, with rumours of a new European imbroglio, dropped like the jaw of one astonished. 'Completely and utterly stopped,' said Frank.

'Look here,' said Lord Ottercove, 'you should get married.'

'Gladly. But who will marry me with my sales stopped. My publisher's wife's aunt died the other day, and he said to me over the telephone: "I think it only right to close down the office for a week to commemorate our respect for the dead woman." '

Lord Ottercove thought deeply, and said:

'You should get married.'

'To whom?'

'I'll introduce you. A peach of a girl. A beautiful face. I can look at it for hours at a stretch without getting bored. The trouble with her is that she's got—too much money.'

'But will she marry me?'

'She would if I gave you—gave you as a wedding present— the *Evening Ensign*.'

There was a pause. 'It's a pity,' Frank flutingly addressed the upper air, 'that I don't know her.'

'I will introduce you.'

'When?'

'Come and dine with me to-morrow night at my house.'

18

THE COTTAGE

Not unnaturally cottagers are apt to dream of palaces, while it is well known that princes eat their hearts out for being denied the joy of dwelling in a cottage. 'The Cottage,' situated in a shrubby garden high up in the Finchley Road, was Lord Ottercove's unofficial home, whither he retired whenever he felt like swinging a loose leg. Owning a great house in the West End of London, and several castles and country houses, he naturally preferred to dwell in the seclusion of 'The Cottage' in the Finchley Road. The ground floor had but two rooms: a dining and a sitting-room, and here at the after-theatre hour he was that night dispensing supper to a bevy of chorus girls escorted by a number of young lords.

Lord Ottercove was a success. Whatever he touched, flowered: whatever he left, withered—and died of its own rottenness. He stood in the doorway now, in his exquisite tail-coat, one hand thrust in his trouser-pocket, indolently tapping his heel and looking on with that intelligent, bright look which seemed to say: 'I have long since reached my goal in life without much effort: what could I possibly do next?'

'Come in, Freddie, come in, now don't be shy!' he cried to a young actor hesitating on the threshold. 'My love, my sweetheart, my honeysuckle, how are you?'—to a bevy of beauties, as they sidled in, twitching their nude shoulders.

'Freezing, darling Rex,' they twittered.

'Rita,' to a leading lady, 'do you love me?'

'You are Christ to me!'

And then, panting slightly (by the end of the night Frank loved her panting, and by the end of the month he hated it), in sauntered a, Frank perceived, conspicuously good-looking girl in red, and by his host's eager introduction: 'This is Mr. Dickin. Miss Cynthia Wellington,' Frank understood that she indeed must be his proffered prize.

If so, she didn't seem to understand her mission. Her face certainly, as Ottercove had said, could be contemplated for hours at a stretch, indeed with cumulative pleasure. She had been placed beside him and she was mildly interested in what Frank could contrive to tell her. But supper over and the host having taken her aside for a few moments, she came back another woman, and Frank found he had no difficulty now in riveting her attention. The other guests, numbering a princess of the blood, a starving Russian diplomat, exquisitely arrayed, and the cream of Theatreland, sustained a strenuous conversation of unmeaning levity till it was late enough for all to go without pronouncing the party a failure. Lord Ottercove's attitude—Frank read the question in his look—was:

'Amusing dogs—or are they not amusing? Have you been used to something more amusing?'

The dogs were not amusing.

He kept Frank and Cynthia back till all the other guests had gone, and then told the butler to wake up the chauffeur, and sent them home in the winged chariot.

Frank had not been long in the car with her when he discovered that Cynthia was desirable. As the chariot, after a good, long run down the Finchley Road, suddenly took wing and Cynthia panted, he grasped her hand as though to reassure her, and having grasped her (good old Ottercove to provide him with this opportunity!), he did not let go. When Cynthia panted again, it was a different kind of panting.

The view that all women are alike seemed to Frank, as a piece of thinking, to err on the inadequate side. They were indeed all different. But in one particular all women were alike, and that was in their uniform desire to be different; and in their cheap fear of seeming cheap. Seized by the idea of making her his wife and eager to anticipate the marriage ceremony, he was prepared to hear her say that no doubt he thought her just like any other woman, and he replied that, on the contrary, she seemed to him peculiarly, uniquely different from them all; after which assurance she behaved like all the other women, and then said:

'Now, I wonder what you'll think of me after that.'

He had not thought anything of her to start with and did not think any the worse of her now.

'Now,' he said, 'we simply *must* get married.'

The winged chariot and his thoughts, descending from the air at a slope, touched ground at the same time. The car ran forward. His thoughts ran on. 'The day after to-morrow.'

'I suppose we might,' Cynthia said quietly. 'Are you rich enough?'

Didn't want to hurt his feelings, evidently. Let him think he was the breadwinner. A girl of exquisite sensibility. Are you rich enough, indeed! He had ten pounds in his breast-pocket; and beyond that he might yet have something in his trouser-pockets. Probably a shilling piece.

'I've more than you think,' he said. 'Ottercove has promised me, in case of marriage with you, the *Evening Ensign* as a wedding present.'

At that she sat up. 'Very nice.'

Before the car pulled up at her door, she said:

'Come and have tea with me to-morrow.'

'I will have tea with you to-morrow—Sunday, and marry you the following Monday.'

He gave Lord Ottercove's flying chauffeur ten pounds, and undressing for bed, emptied his trouser-pocket of the shilling.

19

Out of the shilling he purchased next day a ticket on the Metropolitan Railway and rang at the bell of Cynthia's door, in Half-Moon Street. When the door yielded under his vehement onslaught he strode like a fighting-cock past the door-porter, for he was burning with love. But the door-porter, an elderly man, called him back and said:

'Kindly wipe your feet, sir, on the mat outside; this is an expensive carpet and belongs to the first-floor people.'

'But isn't Miss Wellington on the first floor?'

'No, sir, she lives in the attic.'

He crawled upstairs, up innumerable flights of stairs, and the higher he climbed the lower his spirits descended. Strange, he reflected, that a girl whose trouble Ottercove had said was money should live in an attic. But there it was! Millionaires elected to do things for pleasure that other folks were paid to do.

Wasn't the late Emperor of All the Russias' favourite recreation chopping wood in the palace yard?

A maid responded to his summons, and he entered a neatly-appointed apartment. He had scarcely had time to smile at Cynthia when the maid announced:

'Mr. Mortimer Pilling.'

And the delicate room held the strong, wiry man with the crisp, curly black hair. ''Pon my word! Dickin, of all people! Had no idea you knew him, Cynthia. You never let on!'

'How could I! I only know him since last night.'

'Oh, really?' Pilling looked enquiringly at Frank.

'It seems as if I had known you all my life—even earlier in a pre-terrestrial existence. But, in point of fact, we only met last night. Where was it? Ah, yes, at Ottercove's,' said Frank.

'A man,' said Pilling, 'I always wished to meet. A most delight-ful man, by all accounts, and one who could be useful to me in a thousand little ways and particularly in a little enterprise I have in mind.'

'You must meet him, Mortimer,' said Cynthia, as the bell rang at the front door. There was a sigh of exhaustion in the hall, and when Cynthia returned, she was followed in by a new guest.

'Mr. Mortimer Pilling. Lord Ottercove.'

Lord Ottercove gave Pilling one searching long look with his penetrating grey eye and shook hands. Mortimer Pilling looked as though his day had arrived. But Lord Ottercove turned to Frank: 'Well, how did you enjoy yourself last night?'

'By all accounts,' said Pilling, following Lord Ottercove round the room, 'he enjoyed himself very much. Ha! ha! ha!'

'It was dull,' said Ottercove to Frank, and not looking at Pilling.

'You need Mrs. Kerr,' said Pilling, looking from Frank to Ottercove, 'to brighten up a party. You remember, Dickin, our tea-party together last month?'

' What?—Yes,' said Frank.

Lord Ottercove sat down heavily in a big chair and never once looked up at Pilling. Never had Frank Dickin seen him so impressive. The Sovereign of Fleet Street had surreptitiously climbed up eight flights of stairs (he who said he suffered from his heart) and now sat still in a great armchair and wouldn't look at Pilling. Never, Frank, reflected, is a great man more surely a great man than in a low-ceilinged attic, at the side of a Pilling. For, but for the Pillings, no one might know that Lord Ottercove was a great man.

'How are de Jones and Eva?' Frank enquired.

'Very well,' said Ottercove.

'I am very fond of Eva,' put in Pilling.

'Nearly done with Paris and going on to Rome. I am off myself to join them at Nice at the end of the month. Will you come with me?'

'Well,' said Frank, looking anxiously at Cynthia, who returned a look which he interpreted as a sign not to reveal to Ottercove the secret of their forthcoming marriage.

'Have you seen the papers?' Lord Ottercove asked, confining his enquiry to Frank and Cynthia, while Pilling quickly said: 'About the General Election?'

'How old Joe's already shouting,' Ottercove continued, oblivious of Pilling's question, 'about the bursting granaries that would be ours if we back the Liberals to put an end to international bickerings and jealousies and push on with the Lord de Jones Scheme. And his Hackney speech!' Lord Ottercove assumed the pose of a public speaker: ' "And we shall ask, By what right whether human or divine, some men's tummies digest more bread and butter in one hour of their sleep than you, O Toiling Masses, can earn by the sweat of your brow in a week?" '

' " 'Ear, 'ear! Good old Joe!" ' Pilling supplied.

'But he silences them with a gesture; his hand again shoots out: "*And we shall ask——*" Grand fellow!'

'A great orator,' exclaimed Pilling.

Lord Ottercove's eyes dimmed. 'Joe,' he said, 'is a giant.'

'He is,' said Pilling, looking from Lord Ottercove to Frank.

Lord Ottercove did not look at him. 'And the news that de Jones has been received with acclamation by the Paris mob. Good sign that. Cheaper bread for the common people! And old Joe knows how to give it the right ring. Grand fellow! We'll beat the Conservatives at the poll this time, you'll see. It'll do them good to be beaten.'

'Why?'

'Conservatism is a subversive habit of conserving the liberties won in the past by their opponents. If Conservatism is to be alive to-morrow, let Liberals have their way to-day.' He rose, and turning to Frank, said:

'Come and see me to-morrow at five.'

Frank looked significantly at Cynthia. 'Can't at five;—six.'

Pilling left soon after Lord Ottercove.

Frank and Cynthia left a considerable time after Pilling.

20

When Frank called on Lord Ottercove at six o'clock on Monday, Lord Ottercove was standing at a window in his office, gazing pensively at the dissolving outlines of St. Paul's steadily devoured by the dusk. Lord Ottercove's pose reminded Frank of Napoleon looking at burning Moscow, and of Kerenski, in imitation of Napoleon, gazing from a window in the Winter Palace at the burning theatre 'Bouffe,' and Frank felt that the situation called for a fitting and pregnant remark on the man of action by the man of letters: 'A man of letters puts into letters what he cannot put into action.' But Lord Ottercove, who had soared above mean human endeavour and now only pondered upon it, considered himself a man of thought, and did not look pleased.

'I was thinking,' he said, 'of youth and the glory of struggle. How I envy you young men. The future belongs to you.'

'Why envy us, since the present belongs to you? The future is but a deferred present.'

'All the good the present is to us is that it helps us to forget that we have no future.'

'Mankind has not yet learnt,' said Frank, 'to live in and for each moment. That is the poetry of life. And that is why I have just gone and got married: as an emphatic way of living in the present.'

'Got married?' said Lord Ottercove, knitting his brows. 'To whom?'

'To Cynthia Wellington.'

Lord Ottercove walked up and down several times. 'Incredible,' he said. 'It amazes me. Why, she'll be the ruin of you.

An extravagant girl like that, and you have no money.'

'But she has, hasn't she?'

'Too much!—by the way she goes about it. That's the trouble with her. Tends to give the impression of having what she hasn't got.'

'But you said so.'

'Ironically. You should study the inflexion when I speak; it is all-important. As important as punctuation. Ever heard of King Charles?'

'Yes.'

> ' "*King Charles walked and talked*
> *Half an hour after his head was cut off.*"

That doesn't seem to make sense.'

'No. How indeed could a man walk and talk half an hour after his head was cut off?'

'Precisely. Even King Charles couldn't do it. But put a full stop after "talked" and it makes perfect sense. You may have heard of treaties being wrecked by a comma out of place. And what punctuation is for the written speech, intonation is for the spoken language. You should have listened for it.'

'I have heard of treaties wrecked by faulty punctuation,' Frank said bitterly; 'but this is my first experience of two human lives ruined by an ambiguous intonation.'

'Obviously you married under a misapprehension. But she! I am surprised she didn't know any better. I am rather concerned about the matter. I knew her mother well. What was she thinking? Marrying a man like you without a farthing to bless himself with!'

'I told her you would give me the *Evening Ensign* as a wedding present.'

Lord Ottercove frowned.

'You said so.'

'I cannot,' said Lord Ottercove, 'give you the *Evening Ensign* as a wedding present. It is my principal evening paper. It has the best tone of all the evening papers; it is read by the cream of the capital. But look here, I'll tell you what I'll do for you.'

Frank looked up at him hopefully.

'I'll take an article from you. I'll pay you' —he blew hard while considering the sum— 'twenty pounds for it. You know, when I like a fellow there's nothing that I wouldn't do for him! I am like that—can't help myself. My staff consider me wildly extravagant.'

'Is there any valid objection to paying me even more?'

'Well, look here,' said Lord Ottercove, 'you must make a name for yourself, and I will pay you more.'

'All very well, but how? How?'

'Well, we must bring your personality before the public. I am sure that if your personality is brought before the public, the public will begin to get curious about your personality and begin to want to buy your books.'

Frank meditated for a minute. 'There is nothing in my life of any interest to anybody, except perhaps that I was born at the time my father was First Secretary at our Embassy in St. Petersburg, and——'

'Well, that's interesting enough. Couldn't you develop the situation?'

'How? Perhaps suggest that the Tsar eloped with my mother?'

'Of course. That would immediately reflect on your paternity and bring into question your legitimacy.'

'A marked resemblance to the late Emperor—what?'

'Certainly. It will make them talk.' He took up the receiver. 'Send up Miss Sherwood to me, will you. I want her to write up a story about Mr. Dickin who is in my office.'

Frank learnt that 'stories' was the journalistic term for articles; whereas real stories—he suggested writing a short story for Lord Ottercove for £100—were called 'articles.'

'All right,' said Lord Ottercove. 'Write it to-night and let me have your article by six o'clock to-morrow morning. I will read it in bed before breakfast.' He leaned back in his chair and stretched his arms to the ceiling. 'Oh God, I'm bored to hell,' he said, and yawned voluptuously.

'Now, Miss Sherwood, you know Mr. Dickin, the famous novelist. Don't say you haven't read his books. That would sound uneducated. Now I want you to write a story about him that would reach the wider public which lives in ignorance of him only because they haven't heard of him. I am convinced that he

has a great future before him, a future of fame and felicity. He
has already taken the first step towards it: he has gone and got
married to-day. But I feel that the public wants to know personal details about him. There is, in the first place, his birth,
under mysterious circumstances, in Russia. His mother was an
intimate of the Imperial family. It is delicate ground we are
treading upon here, but I know you are a clever woman and I
have every confidence in your address and discretion. Your treatment of my niece's divorce case confirms my opinion. You could
begin by giving a pen-portrait of the late Tsar by projecting, so
to speak, on to the screen of your story salient points of the
amorous life of the late Emperor. Go to the British Museum and
see if you find something, or look through the works of William
Le Queux. I remember reading something about spies in Russia
or somewhere—sure to be something about Rasputin or somebody. Well, here is Dickin's mother...' Lord Ottercove's tone grew
inaudible; he took her across to the blue sofa. His robust lips
moved silently. 'You understand...' Dickin heard, '...more than
the lad cares to admit.'

'It's a fine story,' nodded Miss Sherwood.

Lord Ottercove looked radiant. 'Creating illusions,' he murmured, 'in a world of appearances. The essential function of the
journalist. Mrs. Hannibal,' he said in a loud, clear voice, 'have that
hung up as my motto all over the building.'

Mrs. Hannibal, making a shorthand note of it, retired to execute his instructions.

'Well,' said Lord Ottercove, stretching his hands to heaven, but
restraining a yawn.

Miss Sherwood and Frank understood that the séance was at
an end.

After the door had closed on them, Lord Ottercove vented
his yawn, looked at his watch, and jumped up.

21

'On the banks of the River Neva stands the city of St.
Petersburg, in the Empire of Russia.'

Thus, illustrated by a picture of the Fortress of Peter and Paul, the *Sunday Runner* started off Miss Sherwood's article. Frank read it out aloud in bed to his wife as they woke up on Sunday in her (now their) attic flat in Half-Moon Street. 'It is not perhaps generally known that Mr. Frank Septimus Dickin, the novelist, was born in Petrograd—or as he prefers to call it, St. Petersburg—his father at the time being Naval Attaché to our Embassy. This austerely beautiful city has changed its name twice since its inception by Peter the Great, who christened it in the Swedish idiom after himself. The late war changed the idiom to Russian, while maintaining the name, and the revolution changed the name to that of Lenin, while preserving the Russian idiom. In truth, a romantic city. (A corner picture showed the Winter Palace and the Quay.) Here Peter once walked. Here the last tragic emperor dwelt in fear and misgiving, while Lenin stormed the citadel by word of mouth and word of print—the capital which was soon to bear his name! Mr. Dickin, who loves this granite city of private palaces, built by Peter and sung by the great poet Pushkin and haunted by the spirit of Rasputin, claims to be connected with it by ties of blood of the Romanov strain. It is a romantic story which, perhaps, some day he will give us in full: the love of the last and most tragic of Romanovs for the novelist's beautiful mother. There are things in life that are hurt by indelicate scrutiny, things which shrink before the too-eager curiosity of the sensational mind, when the biographer must withdraw or stand aside and linger in reverence.'

Ensconced in a single bed with his wife, Frank felt more like an adjunct than a husband, and the reading of the article he thought might rehabilitate his dwindling prestige with Cynthia. If he had no money, he had at least, it seemed, imperial blood. When, on discovering his financial infecundity, she had said: 'What are we to do?' he had replied: 'Don't you bother. Live on as you've been doing and take no notice of me.' Hence the single bed. She was to go on sleeping in it as before and ignore his presence in it.

Their married life was enriched by a stream of press-cuttings which trickled in with every post. Miss Sherwood's article was reprinted by some of the provincial newspapers, and Frank's Press-Cutting Agency had no difficulty in supplying him with paragraphs of a biographical interest.

'Imperial Claim,' was the heading in an American journal.

'We understand that among the claimants to the dubious throne of Russia is a young English novelist, Mr. Dickin, who claims the parentage of the Czar and a connection with the capital way back to Peter the Great.'

Another cutting, headed, 'Descendant of the Tsars,' read:

'Mr. Dickin's family has sprung from a branch of Peter the Great, and Mr. Dickin himself, as is perhaps not generally known, is the son of the Emperor Nicholas II. by a morganatic marriage— the last of the Romanovs, whose reign has been brought to destruction by the Rasputin régime and consummated by Lenin.'

A new cutting read:

'Claiming to be the son of Rasputin, Mr. Dickin's connection with the Russian Court goes back, through his mother, to Peter the Great, and, indeed, earlier, to the first Romanov, in whose time a relative of Mrs. Dickin was Mayor of Moscow. Mr. Dickin thus is well immersed in Russian atmosphere. He is also the author of "Pale Primroses" (Sender: 7s. 6d.).'

As time went on, the press-notices became more involved and informative. 'Mr. Dickin's mother,' read a notice, 'which may not be generally known, was a governess at the Imperial Russian Court who became the Czar's mistress and later that of Lenin, and his fame reposes on these twin tragic pillars of Czardom and Communism.'

A further cutting, from a Liverpool paper, read:

'Illegitimate Son of Rasputin and Lenin. Mr. Dickin's mother, whose son's novel, "Pale Primroses" (Sender: 7s. 6d.) we reviewed in this column last week, was among the victims at the seizure of the Winter Palace, where she had been housed by her friend Kerensky during his all too abortive régime, after being for years the governess of the heir to the throne and an intimate friend of the Emperor—a mere puppet, as will be recalled, in the hands of the sinister Rasputin; and it was her fate, with the surrender of the Women's Battalion which defended the Palace, to fall into the unregenerate hands of Lenin. Mr. Dickin's parentage, on his own admission, like that of many a great poet born in time of stress, may be said to be in jeopardy and, we feel, will lead many a scholar of the future into that fascinating country and furnish him with matter for research.'

A Dundee paper reprinted this identically, up to the words 'Woman's Battalion,' after which it had added: 'of which she was the leader.'

'Well,' said Frank. 'We seem to have had a good run for our money!'

'If it helps to sell the book,' said Cynthia.

'Bound to do! And now that we are comfortably settled in our own abode, don't you think, my dear, that we ought to give a party?'

'Whom could we ask?'

'I mean return hospitality to Ottercove before he goes abroad.'

'But he is so difficult about food.'

'I know. Always gets poisoned. It's uncanny the way some people have a gift for getting poisoned in the most innocuous circumstances. I can't conceive of getting poisoned short of going to an apothecary's and asking for a bottle of poison. But Ottercove can't swallow an egg without dropping his napkin on the floor and groaning: "Poisoned!" '

'But what does he eat?'

'We might write to his butler to find out.'

'Well, if you like, write to the butler,' she said warily.

'I don't remember his name.'

'What does that matter?'

'It doesn't, of course.' He sat down to Cynthia's (now his) writing-table and began to write to the butler, reading aloud to his wife as he did so, feeling that, in matrimony, a man cedes one half of his thoughts to his mate:

' "My Dear Friend——" '

'You don't address a butler as My Dear Friend. Frank! Really!'

'It is perhaps a little pushing.'

'You simply write: To Mr. So-and-So.'

'Every day of my life with you, my dear, I am learning something!'

And he wrote: 'To Mr.———, Butler to Lord Ottercove. Conceiving the idea of entertaining your lord at dinner, I appeal to you in all sincerity and friendship to supply me with a list of his lordship's favourite dishes.'

'Leave out "appeal in all sincerity and friendship."'

'All right. "Request in all earnestness."'

'No, leave that out, too.'

Cynthia's intellect was not, he perceived, penetrating. She always meant what she said and thought that others said what they meant.

'Then we might ask—whom?'

'Whom?'

'The Foreign Secretary. The difficulty is how to begin my letter to him. "Signor, I would esteem it a privilege———"'

'Frank! Really! Don't you know that only foreigners, I mean Italians, are addressed "Signor"?'

'I thought the Foreign Secretary was a foreigner.'

'Frank! Really! Don't you know any better?'

'But why then is he called the Foreign Secretary?'

'Because he has to deal with foreigners—with other foreign secretaries!'

'Ah!—that's why!—But are they, *too*, called foreign because they deal with foreigners?'

'Of course.'

'A world, I see, populated by foreigners.'

'Foreign to us. We foreign to them.'

'Every day of my life with you I learn something!'

A reply came next day from the butler of Lord Ottercove.

'Sir,' he wrote, 'My lord is fond of cold chicken, ham, plaice, salmon, a mutton chop (well done) with mashed potatoes, curry and rice, roast beef (hot), and strawberries. His lordship's favourite drink is whisky.—Your obedient servant, T. Wilkins.

'P.S.—Taking the liberty to show your kind letter to his lordship, my lord desires me to say that he would prefer a hard-boiled egg.'

At half-past seven Lord Ottercove's winged chariot came to a halt, grandly yet sensitively, at their door in Half-Moon Street, and, not bothering to wipe his feet, Lord Ottercove climbed up the expensive carpet and the remaining seven flights to their comfortable attic flat, panting dreadfully.

Frank took him at once into the dining-room. 'Since there is no cook on the premises, Cynthia is attending to the egg. And a great big fine egg it is too; you will see for yourself.'

'Fine,' said Lord Ottercove.

'Cynthia, bring forth the golden egg!'

Cynthia came in, with a plate in her hands.

'There,' cried Frank, 'there you have it. There it is. A real egg.'

'Great—grand——' said Lord Ottercove.

'Sit down. There's no one else to wait for. We invited the Foreign Secretary. But he couldn't come. Either couldn't or wouldn't. Anyway, didn't. Tuck in, Lord Ottercove.'

'Great——' said Lord Ottercove, eating. 'Grand——'

'And a drop of port,' said Frank, 'to gulp it down with.'

'Grand fellow——'

'The meal's finished!' peremptorily.

'Yes, I must be off. I am speaking at the House of Lords to-night.' The guest rose. 'Grand fellow!' to Frank. 'Well, darling,' to Cynthia, 'happy? eh?'

'Quite, Rex,' she said, doubtfully. And paused, as if to say, in the confidential way a woman has with a man worth confiding in: 'Rex dear, what about the *Evening Ensign*?' But Lord Ottercove, who was endowed with extraordinary powers of divination into human motive, accelerated his steps downstairs. His conscience, owing to the hospitality partaken of, or, perhaps, because of its lamentable inadequacy and the implications therefrom arising, pricked him on the third step down, and he turned his head to say to Frank:

'Look here, I'll take another article from you.'

But Frank's gestures, to the visible annoyance of his wife, had now become quite Eastern in their obsequiousness. 'Good, my lord,' he salaamed. 'Kind, my lord.'

Cynthia stood on the doorstep, while Frank went out into the street and stroked the car. The chauffeur and Gilbert had both jumped out and were assisting their master into its soft and spacious confines. Frank stood at the door of the winged chariot, smug and nimble with its wings tucked under its shining sides, and commented aloud:

'Tuck in his lordship's feet. Look after him well, Gilbert.'

'Yessir.'

Lord Ottercove was pleased. The source of human pleasure is a hidden well: for one reason or another Lord Ottercove looked pleased. 'Great!—Grand!—' he kept muttering.

'Evenberry, faithful steward,' Frank was addressing the chauffeur, 'drive his lordship carefully. Avoid sharp corners. Keep well within the speed limit.'

'Yes, sir.'

'Now then, Gilbert, I rely on you.'

'Yessir.'

'Good master you have. Take good care of him.'

'Yessir.'

'Good man, Gilbert,' said Lord Ottercove benignantly, as to a horse. 'Good man. Good servant.'

'Gilbert, enter into the joy of your lord.'

Cynthia stood, shivering a little, on the doorstep.

As the car moved off, Lord Ottercove, as always hatless, waved an indulgent hand. 'Good-bye, sweetie!'

'Good-bye, Rex.'

The car, owing to the lack of space, did not take wing but prosaically turned the corner.

'If your hospitality is scant,' said Frank, 'nothing like enlarging on your guest's preserves.' He ran into the house, kicking the cat on the way, and, wiping his shoes on the mat, to spare the first-floor people's carpet, climbed upstairs.

'A joke's a joke,' remarked his lordship to himself, since there was no one else to say it to, 'but a fellow can't make a decent speech on an empty stomach.' He took up the communication tube and said to the chauffeur:

'Call in at the Kiss-Lick Club.'

22

'Well, how are your sales?' cried Lord Ottercove as Frank crossed the threshold into his office.

'Seven copies a day.'

'Low average,' observed the press baron.

'I know why it doesn't sell.'

'Why?'

'It's a poor novel. That's why. Poor stuff.'

'Damn' poor stuff,' agreed Lord Ottercove. 'That's why I am interested in it.'

The author looked up at him in surprise.

'Any fool can sell a good novel. But it takes genius to sell a poor book. That's why I like pushing it.'

'That is why I come to see you, hoping you may succeed in pushing it.'

'When I like a fellow,' the baron said in loud, robust tones, his light-grey eyes glinting jovially, 'there is nothing that I wouldn't do for him! You saw the boy who was in my office when you came in? You know who he is?'

'Who?'

'The business-manager of all my newspapers.'

'That boy?'

'That boy. He's seventeen. You heard our business conversation?'

'It was like machine-gun fire.'

'That's how I do my business!' said Lord Ottercove. 'That boy, the business-manager of all my newspapers, was a page, what they call a bell boy out there, at the Metropole in San Francisco four months ago. He took my luggage up, switched on the light, drew the curtains, unstrapped my suitcase, took out the slippers. I had forgotten Gilbert on the road, and this solicitude and efficiency in the bell boy touched me to the heart. "Good boy," I said. "Good heart. Kind soul."

' "I have a reason for it, sir," he said.

' "What reason?"

' "I want a job from you."

' "Well, look here," I said, "you come to England one of these days, into my office, and I will give you a job."

'He came a month after, worked his passage, you know, and found his way into my office. "I've come for that job, sir."

' "Well, look here," I said, "I want a business-manager who can manage all the business of all my newspapers. Can you manage it? If you can't manage it I will make you a lift-boy."

' "I'll manage it," he said. And, by George, he does! You've heard our conversation?'

'Like rapid fire.'

'That's how I do my business!'

'You don't let them climb up?'

'No. I put a good boy up. And if he isn't any good I pull him down.'

'I'd like to get as much out of you as that bell boy.'

'And why not? I am a man of money, and I am bored to hell, and your rotten book amuses me.'

'Quite. But you've a personality so charming and magnetic and you like to talk about yourself and you do it so engagingly that as a rule one forgets about one's ulterior motives and becomes disinterested!'

'Well, look here,' said Lord Ottercove, 'we must do something about that book of yours. We'll have to advertise it. As a rotten book. The rottenest book of the century. What do you say to that?'

'Might take on.'

'Sure to do!'

The success of this stratagem, however, proved social rather than financial. A few nights later, Lord Ottercove, after talking to Frank of himself till midnight, suddenly rose and said: 'I am taking you to-night to a ball.'

'Are you really! Had I better ring up Cynthia and ask her to come along too?'

'Oh, no! You'll be bored to death with her. She's all right for love and that sort of thing. But never take her out with you. She used to bore me stiff before she married you. Now let us go.'

As the chariot was turning into a side lane, the baron suddenly leaned over to his companion. 'I must tell you before the chariot comes to a stop, for it may interest you as a novelist, that where I am taking you now is Society. Not quite the real society, but the lighter Mayfair Michael Arlen sort, somewhat polluted with actors and such. Bohemian and the like, and chorus girls. I am doing this to help you with atmosphere and local colour—invaluable for you, as a recorder of contemporary morals and customs, to get first-hand and red hot.'

'You are too kind.'

They had scarcely had their coats removed from them when the hostess appeared at the door and quickly whispered something to

Lord Ottercove, who, acting on the hint, said to Frank in a hushed undertone: 'Whiz like mad across the hall!'

Frank did as he was bid, and, rejoining him in the drawing-room, 'You see,' Lord Ottercove explained, 'we tried to get you safely past Lady Kennan and Mrs. Ashton, who, having heard of your being acclaimed the author of the rottenest novel of the century, had come out into the hall to snap you up on your arrival. It's the sort of rare distinction that they are all out to secure for their salons. There are three great literary hostesses in London: Lady Kennan, Mrs. Ashton, and Lady Isabel Croft, where you are to-night. The three hostesses tend to frequent one another's parties and they stand out in the hall to snatch away a literary novelty before the hostess has had time to warn and welcome him, and your being acclaimed the rottenest author of our time was something quite unusual; they are all mad to have you. Now go and talk to them.'

Lord Ottercove was borne away by a couple of hearty men, while Lady Isabel, a tall, excited woman, came up to Frank and welcomed him effusively. 'I've put the two there off the scent, said you hadn't arrived yet, so they are waiting in the hall. I am so glad you've come. Rex rang me up this afternoon. "Shall I bring you a literary prodigy, a man who's written the rottenest book of our time and century?" "Actually *the* rottenest? Oh, do, Rex darling, do!" I said, "and see that he isn't kidnapped at the door." But you've escaped their claws beautifully. That was a gallant dash across the hall. Now come and have something to eat; you deserve it.' And she pressed champagne and caviare sandwiches upon him, and then led him into another room full of over-powdered, over-painted, over-talkative women here and there dotted by a white-black figure of a man, and she made him sit beside her on the floor very uncomfortably so that he was afraid that his shirt front, having blown out, would next blow open and the studs fly out on to the parquet. And she introduced him to an ex-Chancellor of the Exchequer: 'Johnny, this is Mr. Dickin, who wrote the rottenest novel of our time.'

The ex-Chancellor of the Exchequer beamed with delight, and shaking Frank, who had jumped up from the floor, heartily by the hand, said: 'Have you written the rottenest book of our time? Excellent! Haw! haw! haw!'

'Come,' said the hostess, 'I'll introduce you to my daughters. I have two lovely daughters. They've heard all about you and are thrilled at the idea of meeting you. Pamela, this is Mr. Dickin.'

Pamela was blonde and serious and interested in literature. 'Now are you the rottenest novelist?' she asked. 'Because this afternoon I met a man who said that he was even more rotten than you.'

'I can't believe it,' said Frank.

'Now what do you want to do?' asked the hostess. 'Do you want to eat or drink or smoke or dance or——?'

'Dance.'

'Pamela, take him upstairs and dance with him.'

Pamela took him upstairs into the music-room, and on the way thither introduced him to people sitting out on the steps.

'This is Eleonor de Jones.'

'Oh, but we know him!' Eleonor exclaimed.

'Mr. Dickin. Mr. Raymond Mosquito.'

'Have you written the rottenest novel?' Eleonor asked.

'I must have done.'

'How splendid!' And she wrung from him before she let him go the promise to attend her baby's christening.

'Raymond's been adopted, then?' he asked Pamela as they danced upstairs.

'Yes. They will be married very soon now. Have you seen the baby?'

'A boy?'

'A boy. The image of Raymond. Isn't he beautiful?'

'He has Eva's eyes.' While he danced on with Pamela, who was blonde, Maisy, her younger sister, even more blonde, talked to him all the time, while dancing with another. 'Who are you?' she kept asking him, and he would not tell.

As he was going, she held him back by the hand. 'Don't go,' she said. 'Oh, don't go. I've found out who you are,' she looked into his eyes long and intently. 'It couldn't be better.'

23

In matrimony, Frank and Cynthia both proved themselves to be inveterate individualists; they would be untrue to each other several times every day, so that when, exhausted and full of champagne, they returned to their flat in the morning, they could but stare and feebly giggle at each other. Thus far their partnership was a success.

Frank, whose mind began to run on the rails of publicity which he discovered to be an unparalleled art, sometimes, when her condition made it possible, discoursed on it before his wife. 'There are,' he would say, striding about in his dressing-gown out of which he rarely emerged before dusk, 'no end of ways of advertising oneself.'

'For example?' she questioned.

'For example, thanking prominent people extravagantly in the press for the least little thing they may have done for you. It's a graceful and lucrative self-advertisement. If, for example, the Duke of Bamboo should happen to nod to you on a dark day, having mistaken you for someone else, write to *The Times* that you have been unspeakably touched by the kind and thoughtful attitude of his Royal Highness to yourself and your works. Next day other newspapers, with the befuddled inaccuracy of the daily press, will comment on the incident under some such headlines: "Novelist Discovered and Helped by the Duke of Bamboo. His Royal Highness as Reader and Critic." Furthermore, the Duke, seeing it, might feel really flattered and demand to see the actual book, and, old and of infirm memory, might think that it's some other book that he has seen before, and—who knows?—may create a sensation by what must be, for Royalty, an unprecedented reference to a printed volume. If he but sneezes over it, all other British subjects will follow suit. And you are made.'

But his sales, despite all his philosophy, fell below his least sanguine expectations. He complained bitterly to Lord Ottercove, who indulged in some detached speculation. 'You must shed,' he said, 'your old personality, and assume a new individuality. I am

convinced that if the public hears you have shed your old personality they will get curious about your new individuality and
will begin to want to read your books.'

'I think,' said Frank, 'that if I shed my clothes with my personality, they would be more curious still.'

'You would make a real impression on the public.'

'You seriously mean it?'

'They would see you were serious. The public doesn't like to
be trifled with. As a serious artist you must be prepared to suffer for your art.'

'Have I not suffered enough?'

'I will get some one to interview you on your attitude.'

'What attitude?'

'Towards nudeness. Mrs. Prologue would be the right woman
for you, I daresay.' He looked at Dickin as if measuring his
stature, and took up the receiver. 'Send Mrs. Prologue up to me.'

'But she won't expect me to—' Frank blushed. 'She won't, I
hope——'

'No, no, of course not. What the hell do you think my office
is? A house of convenience? It is enough if she reports it.'

'But how will she know?'

'Well, you've got to tackle her yourself.'

'Mrs. Prologue, m'lord,' announced the page.

'Show her in.—This, Mrs. Prologue, is Mr. Dickin, the novelist.
No, not Dickens. He is—how shall I say?—morbid, perverse,
threatens to go about—well—you are a married woman, Mrs.
Prologue, and I needn't paraphrase these things for you—naked,
in a word. It's—how shall I say?—it's——'

'A complex,' helped out Mrs. Prologue.

'That's right. A complex.'

Frank was afraid that this spectacled and earnest-looking lady
might 'dare' him; but she was quiet and sensible, and did not
insist. 'Is it'—she fixed a pair of competent eyes upon him—
'your conviction that we should——'

'He, not we,' corrected her employer.

'That you should go about—in that state?'

'It's more—it's a belief—a sort of religion,' said Frank.

'I see. *Nacktkultur*. I've been reading a story recently by Paul
Morand, who very amusingly deals with a club up in Norway

devoted to the practising of these theories——'

'That's right! That's right! You've hit on it, Mrs. Prologue. You'll be able to write a story about Mr. Dickin. You may say in fact, that he has, while performing the cult of this *Kultur* or that, been surprised by a visit from—we'll have to think of some name—to the roof of his house where he performs it. I leave him to you.'

Frank returned to Half-Moon Street, which Cynthia, by the way, it occurred to him had deserted some days ago, in more buoyant spirits. He did not resent her disappearance. A man who had failed to provide his horse with a stable, the stable with a manger, the manger with fodder, would, indeed, be unreasonable to object to his horse's grazing outside in the field. And in this harsh and difficult world Frank was not unreasonable. He watched, contentedly, her grazing on the greenest and most flourishing fields of London, Paris, and New York. He walked about in the flat, inspecting the shelves in the kitchen containing things in tins bought with her money; and in applying them to their uses drew on his common sense and such powers of divination as he possessed; and reflected that man's needs were few, and woman's less. He even attempted, with a certain misgiving, to boil himself an egg on the 'Primus' stove, unable to foretell under what circumstances it might explode. How sweet it was to exist alone and owe nothing to anybody!

The post brought him a batch of press-notices. 'The author of "Pale Primroses," ' read a cutting, '(who, it will be remembered, turned up naked at a recent literary gathering), is greatly in vogue and is, in fact, quite the lion of the moment.'

Also he seemed to be getting more and more homage from Liverpool, whereas the city of Glasgow appeared to despise him, and he conceived in his heart a warm sympathy for Liverpool, and a shy distaste for Glasgow salved his wounded self-esteem. (But, when, a month later, he had occasion to arrive in Liverpool he was ignored; whereas at Glasgow straight away he hit it off with a Scotch lassie, and they stepped it to swing music and she was more than kissed by him forthwith. And a different notion of the relative hospitality of Liverpool and Glasgow now took shape in his receptive mind.)

Mrs. Prologue's article bore fruit. A week later he was able to inform Lord Ottercove that his sales were enormous. 'Enormous!'

'Good!' said the baron, thinking. 'Change the title to "The Diary of a Naked Man." '

'There is nothing naked in it.'

'Tell them that there will be in Part II.'

'But I'm not writing a Part II. It's complete.'

'I guess you'll have to,' said Lord Ottercove.

'What else? Perhaps also change my name?' Frank's tone was ironic.

'Your name?' Lord Ottercove reflected. 'Your christian name.'

'My christian name?'

'Couldn't you call yourself Charles?'

'I could call myself Jesus if necessary.'

'No, not Jesus. Charles. It goes well with your surname.'

'Well—I might, of course. It may help.'

'Bound to do! I am off to Nice to-morrow. But call me up each day to tell me how you are selling. Good-bye to you! And mind the step.'

With a little training one could move, Frank felt, about the modern world with ease and felicity and face with equanimity the deadliest of situations. He would find himself making ambiguous statements to reporters who interviewed him relative to his parentage.

'Are you the son of the late Nicholas II?'

'I do not propose at this juncture of events to say anything which might render the position of certain parties and persons involved more difficult than it is already.'

'Do you claim the imperial throne?'

'I do not consider the present moment propitious for the making of any definite statement bearing on this thorny and delicate question, which, moreover, may easily be misinterpreted. I follow the development of the political situation in Russia with equanimity, firm in the belief that when the time for expressing their choice is at hand the people of Russia will not fail in their wisdom, loyalty and courage.'

In all his public utterances Frank displayed unfailing moderation and restraint in reference to the situation that had spun itself into a web around him, and when a Russian Grand Duke in the Kiss-Lick Club heckled him in the vestibule and even hit

him on the ear with an immaculately folded umbrella and otherwise tried to make himself disagreeable to him, with a view to
consummating the quarrel in assassination, Frank did not lose his
head, but tried to avoid him so as not to be involved too early
in the Russian imbroglio. When a reporter interviewed him on
the regrettable incident in the Kiss-Lick Club, Frank said:

'I feel—and I say it earnestly—that we who love Russia
should know how to merge our petty differences in a common
devotion to a holy cause, and, awaiting the grand moment,
remember the magnitude of our responsibilities and the dignity
imposed upon us by a great and noble heritage.'

The restraint and moderation of his utterances won him a following among the anglicized Russian émigrés in London, who,
distrusting the qualities of their own race, had learnt to admire
British parliamentary language as reported in the newspapers. But
in proportion to his success as a pretender, he became increasingly
aware of being watched by Chesham House, of being followed on
his daily strolls by individuals who looked suspiciously like agents
of the Tcheka. He applied, on the advice of friends, to Scotland
Yard, and two plain-clothed policemen were assigned to accom-
pany him on his walks and protect him from (a) those zealous
puritans who wanted to destroy him so as to put an end to what
they understood from certain references to the quality of his
books to be his propagation of foul literature; (b) rival claimants to
the throne of Russia; and (c) the Bolshevist agents of the Tcheka
who resented his imperialism. His fame reached its apotheosis
when the Soviet Foreign Minister, in reply to the now hackneyed
British accusation of their spreading Bolshevist propaganda in the
British Empire, cited Mr. Dickin in the Soviet note to Downing
Street as an active instance of the fostering of an imperialistic
movement by the British and their intervention in the domestic
politics of Russia, and the British Foreign Secretary in the House
of Commons disclaimed, while deprecating Mr. Dickin's activities, responsibility for his acts and dissociated what he described to
be the private views of a novelist from the considered policy of
the Foreign Office. By that time Frank had sold over one hundred
and twenty thousand copies of 'Pale Primroses,' alias 'The Diary of
a Naked Man,' to say nothing of American rights, film rights, dramatic rights, translation rights, and second, third, and fourth

British Empire (excluding Canada) serial rights. The resulting publicity procured him a lucrative commission for a series of articles in an American magazine, a lost relative, and three offers of marriage.

24

NICE

The day after the christening of the Kerr—de Jones baby, Frank, having received a telegram from Ottercove inviting him to come to Nice, went abroad. His wife was grazing somewhere—he didn't know where.

He didn't bother about Cynthia. He didn't see why he should bother about her. He could have divorced her, or she could have divorced him, but he didn't see why he should go to the bother of divorcing her. He simply didn't bother about her. And, moreover, she didn't bother about him.

Mrs. Kerr, he recalled, had been conspicuous at the christening of the Honourable Richard Mosquito, and Pilling had been loud in extolling, some felt rather indiscreetly, the Kerr strain in the baby. Raymond, hastily adopted by de Jones, officiated in the absence of his father at the side of Eleonor. He looked very red and hot and embarrassed at the arrival of his little son-brother, and resented Pilling's *faux pas*, who, conscious of his blunder, and anxious to agree that the baby was the image of de Jones, added inadvertently: 'But of course! The image of his grandfather,' while Mr. Kerr walked about sardonically, as if saying: 'This is my revenge.'

'Can't stand that man Pilling,' Raymond said bitterly.

'I, on the contrary,' rejoined his mother, 'find him a very charming, intellectual young man.'

'Why doesn't he marry Zita?'

'My dear, he can't. He is already married.'

'Then why doesn't he leave her to marry another man?'

'They live together—just the same as if they were married. That is a common custom nowadays among the more intellectual classes. Already in my youth it was accepted. You even find it in Turgenev and Dostoevski.'

In parting on the kerb, Frank overheard Mrs. Kerr thanking her son. 'Chris can give me nothing now. And if he could, he would give it all to Eva.'

'Eleonor,' said Raymond, 'has no banking account of her own. But she has a cheque-book and draws on her uncle's account to an unlimited extent.'

'A very nice, well-read, original young woman, and I am very fond of her,' was Mrs. Kerr's reply.

Smiling thus over these insistent memories of yesterday, Frank pulled open the blinds in the morning: the Blue train was touching the south coast of France.

Nice. The most beautiful thing about Nice is its name, full of a delicious springtide fragrance. Apart from the name, it may be questioned, Frank thought, whether there was anything else particularly beautiful about the town, that somewhat hard and heartless courtesan *de luxe* organized for the sale of dubious pleasure.

Already from the window of your carriage you behold the long train bending like a serpent as it races up the coast carrying dutifully its load of passengers who had dribbled from the four corners of the world, congregating towards Paris, rushed in the night through northern wet and wind and bleakness, to turn the corner at Marseilles at day-break, and now gaily down the sunny Côte d'Azur, past all the pink and cream and white of basking villas, towards Nice.

In another three hours, Frank reflected, he would see Eva, and the benignant luxury of the scenery illustrated his anticipation. The train curved amid the rocky hills and flowery valleys, past the rose-white garden villas perched above the blue, blue sea— all swiftly whirling by.

Nice.

'His lordship is lunching in the restaurant and asks you to come in, sir.'

Entering the huge dining-room, Frank instantly perceived Lord Ottercove's steel-grey eye peering at him in its essential hardness, but softened as it were by an air of bonhomie. There was about the baron's face something at once fine and comic, stern and pantaloonish, Jehovahian and George Robian. His glinting eyes blazed with a righteous blue fire, while his tilted nose protruded a naïve, peeping curiosity about human affairs, and his noble brow frowned olympically. When he closed one eye at you to glint with double force with the other, he looked a satyr. At one side of him was Eva, gay and spring-like in appearance; at the other, Lord de Jones, more shark-like than ever. No one could look less a peer than de Jones.

'Why won't you take off your coat and come and have lunch?' said Ottercove, genially. The three of them looked as though they had been revelling considerably.

'You do all look washed out,' said Frank.

'We've decided to make a halt here before going on to Rome,' said Ottercove. 'I must recuperate my forces before I tackle Mussolini over the craters.'

'Do you expect any serious opposition?'

'Yuh. I guess they'll want heavy compensation. The Vesuvius, alone, they argue, is a steady source of revenue, attracting hordes of tourists.'

'But he must see the international side of it if he has any goodwill in him.'

'The goodwill among men,' said the baron, 'is a moral support physically precarious for any man to lean on. But all the better for us. We are in no hurry since the General Election is again delayed. We must give the illusion of warring, of desperately battling with evil and sinister forces—of David fighting Goliath.'

'Well, you certainly look exhausted.'

'Don't look at Chris,' said Eva. 'He is always dirty-looking, he can't help it. I mean he's clean, but dirty-looking. There are such people. And there are others, who are dirty and always look quite clean.'

' You wise little girl, Eva,' said Ottercove tenderly.

'Lord Ottercove, have you read Ferdinand's novel?' she asked.

'I've read it twice.'

'H'm. I must read it again,' she said.

After lunch, Lord Ottercove took them up to his suite. On the table in the drawing-room copies of his newspapers were spread out invitingly. 'I can't,' said Frank, fingering the *Evening Ensign*, 'behold this newspaper without an inward pang.'

Lord Ottercove frowned. He did not like to be reminded of it. Instead, and in pursuance of a certain association of ideas, he asked:

'What have you done to Cynthia?'

'Alas! Alack!' said Frank, who, in the absence of his host's material interest in their marriage, did not see himself compelled to satisfy the baron's idle curiosity.

Learning from Frank that he had put up at another hotel and would not move over to this for fear of being ruined, 'Stay with me two or three weeks,' said Lord Ottercove. 'You don't know what pleasure it gives me.' His words were so warm and inviting. 'Gilbert,' he said softly, 'go and see if there are any more rooms on this floor.'

'Yes, m'lord.'

Gilbert returned to say that there was the choice of a suite and a room. Which of the two did his lordship wish him to reserve for Mr. Dickin?

'Mr. Dickin will see and choose for himself,' said Lord Ottercove. 'And now I will jump into bed. I shall see the three of you, I hope, at dinner and take you to the Opera at Monte Carlo.'

'Agreed!'

25

When, dressed, that night he joined them in Ottercove's private drawing-room, Frank was amazed by the new, modern aspect of Eva. How was it that he had never been so struck with her before? What ease! what grace! withal, what beauty!

They dined at the Nigresco in Nice and then hurried at a dangerous speed in a hired Rolls-Royce to Monte Carlo, and again, in Ottercove's box, alone with three men, Eva's charm was conspicuous, as on the stage the melancholy chime of Kremlin bells determined the slow but steady ruin of a conscience-stricken man.

On the way back to Nice, they were thoughtful. *Boris Godounov* had made a deep impression on the baron, who never missed a performance. 'Fine man Moussorgski!' he muttered. 'A great and wonderful genius! To have written that!' He paused. 'If he were alive, to-day, I would have made him a duke, or editor-in-chief of all my newspapers.'

'Or given him the *Evening Ensign* as a wedding present,' added Frank.

Lord Ottercove closed one eye and glared at Frank with the other, and then closed it too and went to sleep in the depth of the car.

In the night, Frank could not sleep for jealousy. Why was she so intimate with de Jones and Ottercove? Why?

At three, he crept to her door and knocked gently. She opened the door.

He went in.

'Darling!' he said.

'Darling!' she answered, and came into his arms.

'I am wretched,' he said, covering his face with his hands.

'Darling,' she watched him tenderly, 'you are getting very thin. Your corner tooth is losing colour.' She looked at that thin individual with scanty hair, and thought, without pressing the thought home to her: 'Is that thing the thing on which I have spent all my beautiful love?—Never mind, such as he is, he is mine.'

'It is tragic,' Frank said, 'to grow ugly without ever having been beautiful.'

She gave him a long kiss. And they were silent, and the silence seemed pregnant with memories. 'Do you remember?' it seemed to say.

And for him there was fear and foreboding of loss in that kiss. He held her breathless and exulted in the thought that her naked heart beat against his.

She looked into his eyes. 'Do with me what you like.'

How could he have ever parted with her? How could he ever part with her?

26

All next day they spent with Ottercove. Lord Ottercove habitually put up at Nice, with the sole purpose, it would seem, of dining at Monte Carlo. He came to the Riviera to relax after the strenuous social life of London. And his relaxation, by the force of habit, took the form of whizzing up and down the curved and much frequented road of the Côte d'Azur to lunch at Cannes, to dine at Mentone, or hurrying off to play golf, hurrying to get into bed and sleep hurriedly, to be wakened by Gilbert to dress and hurry along to dine at Rapallo. After a month of such relaxation, he would hurry back to London to rush from house to house (mysteriously preceded by Mrs. Hannibal and his telephone operator) and write hurried articles and print newspapers, and the newsboys were already hurrying out of the building carrying batches of them and selling them at a run. Lord Ottercove privately claimed that since his descent on London he had 'gingered up' the public life of Great Britain. His success was evidenced by his peerage; which is no guarantee of anything more than success.

His own personality and the effect it produced on his time and surroundings interested and stimulated him beyond all else. An American reporter in Nice had referred in the local press to Lord Ottercove's having the head of a musician, and he instantly sent out Gilbert to buy an album with the portraits of all the notable composers, and left it in his private drawing-room, and his friends (who had read the notice) said: 'Rex, that chap Beethoven has your head to a T.' And another said, 'Rex, upon my word, you have mistaken your profession and we enjoin you, ere too late, to turn musical. Then, in a few years they will be saying: "Ottercove— Now, let me see, who is Ottercove?"—"Oh, the man who wrote the Symphony in B flat." '

He smiled indulgently. He went down the steps (forgetting the existence of the lift) whistling to himself and wondering— really if—and *if really*—how nice.

In the car, since the question had been jarringly dropped as it seemed to him, he turned to Eva.

'Eva, do you think,' he said from his reclining, hatless attitude in the depth of the great car, 'I look like a composer?'

'You look like an angel, Rex,' she said.

'Thank you, darling.'

'You're not as beautiful as Ferdinand,' she added, 'but you are very clever.'

'Thank you, darling; thank you, dear; that's comforting.'

'Chris,' said Ottercove, 'how is your work getting on? Is it true I hear you mean to blow us all up?'

'If I didn't, others would. Ideas like these never come singly. There must be half a dozen men at least now harbouring this amiable idea.'

Lord Ottercove glanced at Frank and Eva. 'I told you he was a lunatic.'

'It's you who are lunatics. Anyone, I tell you, could do it and talk about doing it, for no one would believe him, everyone would think he was a lunatic.' De Jones looked away, detached.

'Let us change the conversation,' Eva said.

They were hurrying in the direction of Cagnes—a destination which at all times that it is mentioned is accompanied by a sort of footnote that it is a place other than, and therefore not to be confused with, Cannes. 'You speak, French,' said Ottercove. 'Tell him to go to Cagnes. Cagnes, not Cannes.'

Frank took up the telephone tube and said to the chauffeur: 'Cagnes.'

'Cagnes,' repeated Lord Ottercove. 'Not Cannes.'

'Cagnes,' said Frank into the tube. 'Not Cannes.'

'I understand perfectly,' said the chauffeur.

It seemed that the distinction was more familiar than generally supposed. Still, the similarity was unfortunate, and many a passenger for Cagnes must have found himself, unwittingly, in Cannes. And many a passenger for Cannes must have discovered himself, with inward qualms and bitter questionings, in Cagnes. But there it was, and even Ottercove could not change this state of things.

They alighted on the green hillside by the sea, and Ottercove, perennially the host, opened the picnic basket. 'Damn!' he said. 'That jackass Gilbert has forgotten the glasses.' Inwardly they all cursed Gilbert. 'You speak French,' said Ottercove to Frank. 'Go and ask that peasant woman on the top of that hill to lend us a few glasses. Here——' He held out a batch of notes.

'I've got some money.'

'Here, give her this.'

The old peasant woman, who was sitting on the ground beside her donkey, could produce but two doubtful-looking glasses, and Frank thrust the batch of bank notes—some four hundred francs in all—into her hand.

'But, monsieur!' she cried, bewildered. 'All this for a couple of glasses! No, no——'

They washed the glasses in champagne, drinking what was left of it and eating delectable sandwiches delicately prepared by a luxurious hotel. Then Lord Ottercove took his Bible out of his side-pocket and began to read:

' "And I beheld when he had opened the sixth seal, and, lo, there was a great earthquake; and the sun became black as sackcloth of hair, and the moon became as blood;

' "And the stars of heaven fell unto the earth, even as a fig tree casteth her untimely figs, when she is shaken of a mighty wind.

' "And the heaven departed as a scroll when it is rolled together; and every mountain and island were moved out of their places.

' "And the kings of the earth, and the great men, and the rich men, and the chief captains, and the mighty men, and every bondman, and every free man, hid themselves in the dens and in the rocks of the mountains;

' "And said to the mountains and rocks, Fall on us, and hide us from the face of him that sitteth on the throne, and from the wrath of the Lamb:

' "For the great day of his wrath is come; and who shall be able to stand?" '

He shut the book, and for a while there was silence. De Jones took off his glasses and wiped them pensively with his handkerchief; then quoted softly:

' "And God shall wipe away all tears from their eyes; and there shall be no more death, neither sorrow, nor crying, neither shall there be any more pain: for the former things are passed away." '

Frank waved away the flies. 'If I were God I would consign all flies to the lake which burneth with fire and brimstone. For don't tell me that they know not what they do!'

Eva looked at him reproachfully. 'You are so stupid, darling. You wave and shout at the flies.'

'But they do go away.'

'It's not because you shout, but because you wave that they go away.'

'H'm, that's possible. I never thought of that. I admit I am impractical.'

The secret of a successful picnic, in view of its invariable discomfort, is that it should be as short as possible. They—all of them towny people—discovered this very soon and rose as if by mutual consent.

'You speak French,' said Ottercove to Frank. 'Go and take these glasses back to the old woman on the hill and tell her she can have all the sandwiches and fruit and champagne——'

'Bottles,' qualified de Jones.

'Bottles—all we've left, in fact.'

Frank did as he was bid.

They got back into the hired Rolls-Royce, and as they drove away, this time in the direction of Cannes, on the hillside, by the side of an old donkey, stood an old wrinkled woman who looked in their direction till they were lost to sight.

In the depth of the car, three men and a girl leaned back as far as it is possible for three men and a girl to do so in a car. Lord Ottercove was dozing. Eva gently playing the ukulele.

'I didn't know you played the ukulele,' Frank remarked.

'There are things, Ferdinand, you do not know,' she said.

Ottercove opened one eye. 'You are right, sweetie,' he said. 'He is no good: I'm the man for you.'

' "I'm the man! I'm the man!" This is from Candida,' chimed in de Jones. 'Let me quote, on my behalf, from the same work: "All the love in the world is waiting to speak: but it is shy—shy—shy." '

'Eva,' said Frank. 'Eva.'

'What?'

'Eyes as blue as the Mediterranean...'

'Now, Eva, you must choose,' said Ottercove, 'between this decrepit Genius of the Untried who claims he can push up the grass but is only fit to push up the daisies; the dubious heir to a, if possible, more dubious throne; and a half-demented peer. Now come on, my love, and choose your prize. Spot the winner.'

Eva smiled and played the ukulele dreamily. And the music

seemed to say, Why choose? when you are snug, at ease, sprawling in the depth of a great car rushing softly by the edge of the blue sea.

27

Returned, Eva vanished mysteriously and came back with a book and asked them to write in her album.

'All these your admirers, Eva?' Ottercove scanned the pages wearily. 'Hello, what's this?

> ' "*O Eva, O Eva,*
>   *I love you so mighty,*
>   *I wish my pyjama was*
>   *Next to your nighty.*"

Whoever wrote this, Eva?'

'A little schoolboy in Ireland.'

'Shame!'

'He loved me.'

'That's something.'

Frank the while was scanning the pages of the *Sunday Runner*, Ottercove's youngest and favourite offspring. 'Rotten newspaper,' he said, as if to himself, but loud enough for Ottercove to hear him. 'Nothing of me in it.'

'I am taking you to-night to Maxim's. And now,' said Lord Ottercove, 'I'll jump into bed. Good-night to you.'

And, to precipitate their going, he was already removing his tie and collar.

That night at Maxim's Eva looked exquisite. She had not, Frank felt, before now released her more expensive potentialities. Now she looked like really releasing them. And Lord Ottercove looked very much like encouraging her to release them. She was a plant that suddenly flowered when put in a vase of champagne. The competition for her on the part of the three men developed into rapid fire. 'Now then, Eva, why this hesitation?' Ottercove demanded. 'I am a man of brains. I am a man of money. I am a man of love.'

'Do you love me, Rex?'

He smote the table. 'With all my heart.'

'Truly?'

'I swear by my love for my newspapers, or may God strike me dead!'

'And you, Ferdinand?'

'Can you ask? What of my courage? Am I not setting out alone against all his newspapers, with possibly the other newspaper lord at the back of him—in fact, the whole of the more sinister Press of Great Britain against me!'

Lord Ottercove, gripping his knife and fork in his two fists— he was in high spirits to-night—leaned back and laughed. There was in his gesture all the self-confidence and abandon of men who had climbed to the top of the ladder. On the top of the ladder one is apt to let oneself go. (Which, by no means, applies to all ladders. One's solicitude for one's fate on most ladders is never so keen as on the last rung. But—let us be perfectly clear —it is a solicitude different in kind from that which is experienced by people passing *under* a ladder.)

'And you, Chris?' she asked. 'Will you love me all your life?'

'All my life and fifty years after.'

'You might be Mr. Solberg, the Registrar of Copyrights at Washington,' said Frank.

'Isn't Ferdinand beautiful?'

'As beautiful as my nose.'

Lord Ottercove was getting cheerier and cheerier, and he danced less steadily than he was wont to do. 'Now, Chris, don't you make love to Eva. Hands off! you married men! You haven't been divorced a month. I at least am a bachelor and can marry her to-morrow—if the fancy takes us. Can't I, Eva? I'll stop that crater mission of yours if you don't take yourself away in time.' He looked at Eva. 'I've got to blow him up a bit from time to time, or he gets too cocky, you know.'

'It's me who'll do it,' said Chris.

'Do what?'

'Blow you all up.'

Lord Ottercove called the waiter and paid. While they were putting on their coats and pushing through the door into the street, Chris and Frank lingering behind, Lord Ottercove jumped into the car after Eva, slammed the door and drove off.

28

THE REVELATION

'Well,' said Lord de Jones, taking Frank by the arm and leading him into a similar establishment almost next door, 'if they are off we shall continue by ourselves.' And he ordered more champagne and more chicken. The hour was far advanced into the morning and the last revellers were leaving the premises. The band played on sulkily for the two new visitors and looked appealingly at the waiters. 'Look here, Frank,' de Jones said, rather thickly, 'you're a jolly good sort and I am awful fond of you.'

'I, too, I really am, very fond of you, more than I can say.'

The wine had done its noble work: they lived in a world of mutual and uncritical esteem.

'By Jove, you're a fine fellow, Frank, that's what you are! A fine fellow. A *fine fellow*. And a damn good writer too!'

Frank remembered through his dim but blissful state that Chris could never be persuaded to read a book of any sort, let alone Frank's novels, but now this fact did not detract but rather added value to the sincerity of the noble lord's appreciation. And when, with swelling heart, Frank answered, 'And I feel, Chris, you're first among contemporary scientists!' he really felt it. As the waiter opened a new bottle of champagne, Lord de Jones lapsed into reminiscence. 'Why do I love that girl? Traits of her mother? As a young man I did not care for women, and they did not care for me. You see what I look like. A Frenchwoman once described my appearance as "*ignoble*"! But that one when I saw her first in Russia! Now, of course, she is nothing much to look at. But at that time she was extraordinarily good-looking—better than her daughter. I was constrained by her husband and was half blind to her suggestive looks. I wouldn't listen. Till one day as I was leaving her she fell before me on the floor. That somehow got hold of my senses. Raymond dates back to that incident, I believe. The vision of her prostrate on the floor haunted me always. It made me come back to her. I always went back. And now she's too old... I am drunk, or I wouldn't be telling you this.'

He was silent awhile. 'Eva——' he said. 'He abducted her, but we two can go on loving her more than *he* will ever understand.'

Dickin's eyes filled. 'We love her,' he said. 'We all love her. Perhaps Rex also loves her. Why can't we all love her and love one another?'

'Don't I know my excellent uncle Lord O.! Have you seen him sign himself "O."? A tremendous O. Nevertheless, the numerical symbol.'

'You are hard on the baron.'

'Am I? I like his boyishness, his prodigious vitality. He is Hannibal playing quoits with the world. Not, I regret to say, because he loves the world, but because he loves playing quoits. But a rather lovable *enfant terrible*, all the same. He could have helped me. But he would back out of it next day. He has no large plan of action; but he conceals this very cleverly by dramatizing every little situation on the spur of the moment, improvising campaigns at the turn of an effective phrase, and making you think that his least bit of whim is the component part of a large premeditated whole.'

'I know. A sort of second inspiration known to dramatists, more clever but more freakish than the main idea.'

'Exactly. But he has no main idea, unless it is a certain feeling for caution, which, coupled with his second inspiration in which he is a virtuoso, determines his success. He may turn into a great peace-maker to-morrow, and the day after find himself uttering: "It is not peace I have brought, but a sword," and side with the forces of war; and in turn, prove successful in each. I am bitter because I cannot get him to help me in my mission without resorting to subterfuge, which maddens me. This idiotic crop-growing scheme! He was quick enough to seize it for his own journalistic ends without bothering to probe the scientific aspect. If I could make him understand my real motive I might fire his imagination for a day; but he would sleep on it (he always sleeps on all important questions and telephones his decision in the morning), sleep on it and ring me up at dawn: "Look here, Chris. It is a brilliant idea. But I advise you against it. Why? It would not do you any good. Good-bye to you," and hang up the receiver. "Do you no good." Not him, no! No advertising possibilities. Actors and audience simultaneously reduced to smithereens!

'Why should we regret it? Schopenhauer could not understand how it was that man, in the teeth of all this pain and hell of life, had not the sense and pluck to end it. Wherever I look, in every moment there is pain. The pain of memory, the pain of anxiety, the pain of sheer dullness, the pain of regret. You cannot think either backwards or forwards for ten minutes without a pang of pain. Then why should we be sorry to quit it, to take ourselves away to where pain cannot reach us?

' *"Who breathes must suffer and who thinks must mourn,*
   And he alone is blest who ne'er was born."

'It's a poor life, Frank. The more successful, the more multifarious and sensitive, the more painful. We are, from our birth, caught in a vice and cannot away. You don't believe in the devil. But I do. The brain is the devil. A malignant cancerous growth. It's a mockery from start to finish. We are simply made to chase after our own tail, and Satan stands by and laughs: "Let us see whether they have sense and pluck enough to end it." The mundane life is a blind avenue we have strayed into while nobody was looking. We must get out. There is no other course. We do not belong here. Do not the eyes of humans and beasts alike tell you that we do not belong here! We must quit *en masse*, get away.

'The cruelty and pain of this world. The pain and cruelty. Donkeys and mules goaded with a stick; the resigned suffering in their eyes. The Arabs cut their donkeys and then prod the wound: "Go on, damn you." And, in the same way, we are all goaded. On the raw, or we won't move. Goaded by desire, remorse, love, hope, despair. Hourly, minute by minute.

'This is not an age that believes in the coming of a new Messiah. It believes, foolishly, in what it can touch and see. What will you say, Frank, when I tell you that already as a youth I had intimations of a mission, of being a—don't laugh—a new Messiah, clad not in fine raiment, nor born in a manger, but, in the fashion of the age, scientifically equipped! Christ showed the way, but lacked the mechanical means. He said this visible world had to be completely and utterly destroyed: he waited for the miracle; but none came. Christ had love, but no dynamite.

'But not for ever shall mankind be mocked. My friends, the

hour of deliverance is at hand. How is it: "I am the Resurrection and the life." The Resurrection and the life.' Suddenly his eyes were moist. He wept.

As they walked back it was light and the birds were twittering in the square.

29

When Frank knocked at Eva's door there was no answer. As he flung himself into bed, the sun already pressed itself through the curtain.

The glowing earth swam in a silver sky. It swam and swam. And a shark came out and followed it, wanting to devour it. The poor earth had but two fins and swam helplessly out of the reach of de Jones's jaws. There she was with all her cities and towns labouring to get away, panting dreadfully; how hard he pushed her and how ineffectively. That was because he was a passenger upon her, as helpless as a man endeavouring to accelerate the motion of a train. In his office on the top of the roof, from the captain's bridge, Ottercove shouted orders through a megaphone: 'Faster! faster! faster!' he cried. And the capitalists whipped up the slaves and made them row faster. But a Trade Union strike was just on, and the miners and rowing men quitted tools. And the Prime Minister, as he urged the policemen to hearten them up with their bayonet points, appealed to the galley slaves' sense of duty and patriotism, and called on them 'by a supreme effort, their loyalty and solidarity in the cause of Humanity, to save this planet, our Mother Earth, the common heritage of all our race, from the treacherous jaws of that monster,' while Ottercove from the bridge whence there opened a limitless view of the world, including Ludgate Hill and St. Paul's, shouted at them through the megaphone: 'Faster, damn you! Still faster!' Already de Jones's huge lower jaw dropped and took water as he swam up very close, and Frank's heart stopped beating. The shark's jaws opened quite wide about to swallow the earth, with London and Paris and Vienna and all, and the men in the fields and the women and animals and the suffering; and Ottercove from the bridge (pushing aside the Prime

Minister) encouraged the rowing men with a long, big stick, as de Jones's sharp teeth fastened upon the green flanks of the earth— an enormous stick like the trunk of a tree: Bang! bang! bang! The knocking grew louder.

Frank opened his eyes. 'Come in,' he said.

The door opened admitting Gilbert's tremulous frame. 'Sorry to waken you, sir, but his lordship asks if you will take breakfast with him in his bedroom.'

He threw on his dressing-gown and followed the valet into his master's apartment, where he found the baron in bed, which was littered with newspapers. 'Well,' said Lord Ottercove genially, 'I've got away with the goods.' The balcony door was wide open. The blue Mediterranean stretched out its paws and basked in the sun.

De Jones came in, and at the same time Eva, in her pink dressing-gown and red-heeled slippers, sidled in from the adjoining room. 'Gilbert,' she said, 'please wrap these up for me.'

' Yes, my lady.'

'Let me introduce you to my wife,' said Ottercove.

'Your wife——?'

'We went and got married last night,' she explained.

'A brain-wave,' said Ottercove. 'I get such brain-waves some-times.'

'A happy thought,' said Eva.

'The second inspiration,' de Jones looked at Frank.

'Anyway I got the better of you two there,' said Ottercove uncertainly.

'You did,' said Eva. 'It never occurred to them to do it. And I am sure I gave you plenty of opportunities, Ferdinand.' Her tone was meek and propitiating. 'So it's not my fault.'

'No, of course not. Still—it's a blow. One is never so keen on a thing as when one has just lost it.'

Lord Ottercove smiled pleasantly. The assertion seemed to rehabilitate his doubting judgment as to whether he had acted wisely overnight. 'Of course,' he said, 'she's a nice girl and wanted encouraging with marriage to a man of brains and money, who can do something with her. I felt all along it would have been sheer waste throwing her away on either of you. Casting pearls before swine, though I don't, of course, mean anything personal. Will you both lunch with us?'

At lunch Lord Ottercove was subdued. All competition had suddenly ceased with his acclaim as the winner; yet he did not look at all as though he had won the Derby. He looked as he must have felt: as if he had rolled head over heels in his best trousers and torn a hole in the seat, and that instead of everyone laughing and clapping they merely said to him, 'Go and change.' In passing things during lunch and helping himself he looked a little shame-faced, and the three men were all glad when the meal was over and they could go for a drive. Each wanted to be sure that Eva took the ukulele with her to help them slide over the blank minutes. Frank enjoyed riding about with Lord Ottercove in powerful motor-cars, rapidly, rapidly, with a purposeful air, to no particular destination. It was somehow, he felt, symbolical of Ottercove's whole person. 'Now, Chris, shut up and let us hear what Frank has to say.' And after listening, 'Now, Frank, shut up. You've said enough. Chris, let's hear you.' Then: 'Well, neither of you seems to have anything very illuminating to say. I had better think it out myself.'

'You're a genius,' said Frank. 'A genius of God-knows-what: but a genius!'

'Yes,' concurred de Jones, 'there is no doubt at all about your greatness: there may be some doubt about the quality of your greatness, but no doubt about the greatness.'

'Yes, when you are without your spectacles, Rex, you look a genius,' said Eva. 'But the moment you put them on, you look like a doctor or a harassed business man, or a clergyman who says, "How are we this morning?"'

'My heart,' said Lord Ottercove, 'very jumpy to-day.'

'I think it's the stomach,' said Eva.

'I think it's the stomach,' said Ottercove gravely, but reassured.

'I think so,' said Frank. 'Complete stoppage of the bowels.'

'Better go back and telephone for the doctor,' said Eva.

Lord Ottercove was touched if you chanced to ask about his health, and now at Eva's solicitude his eyes brimmed with tears. He took her hand and stroked it. He was so moved by her attitude that he could not speak, and only swallowed several times, and looked away. His health was not too good. His boiler would suddenly demur in the midst of festivities and pursue a mood of its own. And looking at the baron's shining nose, as he reclined hatless in the depth of the limousine, Dickin wondered if the centre of his lordship's mind was not—his expression suggested it—superintending the issues fought within him.

'No wonder,' Eva said, 'your nose is red and shiny with all this whizzing up and down in motor-cars and not a moment's quietness.'

He stroked her hand and went to sleep.

Frank looked a long time at Eva, reproachfully, before he asked in a whisper: 'Why, why did you marry him? Why?'

'I thought it would please Pilling.'

'And I am forgotten! It didn't take long.'

'But you are married yourself.'

'True—I'd forgotten.'

'Rex telegraphed last night after we had got married, for Mummy and Zita and Pilling and Raymond and all to come out. "Let 'em all come out, the whole bag o' tricks!" he said. And we were married by a funny-looking parson; Rex had to pull him out of bed to marry us. He gave him five minutes to slip into some clothes and a hundred pounds of money, and he married us in the sitting-room without any trouble; said it would be all right. I was so pleased it was definite. But Rex looked puzzled and worried, and talked to himself all the time, and when we were back in the car he said he must have walked upstairs to the clergyman's flat in his sleep, and wondered whether what he had just done could not be undone perhaps by the Pope if he said he was a sleep-walker. But I said the law was sacred and definite for better and worse. And when we were all alone in the car, and I began kissing him because he was my husband and expected him to behave like a bridegroom, he was so scared and looked through the window as though he wanted to jump out. And I held him back and tried to calm him down, and he kept saying: "My God! My God!" And he asked me what had happened on the hill then? And I said, "Read Ferdinand's serial." And he said, " Did it happen as in the serial?" I said, "Read the serial and never mind what happened." And so he looked as though he'd gone and paid a huge price for something he'd bought at a shop and then got home and found it was quite rotten.'

'You may be his wife, Eva,' de Jones said, 'but first and foremost you are my secretary. And you shall remain with me for the duration of my mission.'

'Yes, I will do my best, Chris, to help you grow wheat.'

He laughed. 'They will believe anything—anything. But if ever you conceive something really terrible, nobody will hinder you, but they will let you blow them up into smithereens with the sympathetic assistance of the Ottercoves and such who will believe the first cock-and-bull story that you choose to tell them.'

Lord Ottercove opened one eye and glared with it at de Jones; then closed it.

'Let us change the conversation,' Eva said.

Pointing at a pillared villa, 'I like that pillared thing,' Frank said. 'It asserts itself on the surrounding landscape. It's a yea-saying to life! None of your snivelling English houses looking like half-built factories of red brick, hiding their faces as if ashamed of themselves.'

'Buy it, Rex, just for the two of us,' said Eva.

'I'll buy it,' said the baron.

They got out and bought it, and then motored back to Nice in time for tea.

After tea, de Jones took Frank by the arm and marched him up and down the deserted, wind-swept Promenade des Anglais. 'Why did he marry that girl, Frank? He had no notion of it when he left us at Maxim's last night. Just to be able to say to us in the morning: "I've got away with the goods." For the love of the phrase. And mind you, he didn't seduce her—no fun in that, no advertisement! altogether too ordinary—but he married her to do something more striking that may arouse comment. He just felt that he owed it to himself and his brains and his money and all to afford a real piece of folly.'

'No, Chris, it is we who are the fools for not having married her. His second inspiration has not failed him. It never does. He has enriched the rest of his life. Her sheer livingness is inexhaustible, and—I can see it in your eyes, hear it in your voice— you love her; as I do, more and more—to my dismay. All art is the translation of the subjective into an object. Thus, I prefer Eva to earnest women who can talk of Pessimism and Buddhism but have no living and spontaneous form themselves. When an object like Eva shows no visible sign of containing a subject but appeals beyond all analysis, it means that the divine spirit has found in her a happy home.'

'You are right, Frank. What some please to call the divided soul is the taste of a spiritual epicure whose crime and curse is that he does not care for preserved food. My excellent uncle, Lord O., must always have everything of the best.'

'Oh, the memory of that first kiss! How she came into my arms, pliable like a young plant. The hot sun, the menace of our end, and the longing not to die unmarried. Chris, I can't believe that I have lost her. She will have all his houses and horses and servants to play with.'

'But not all the King's horses, not all the King's men, can put Humpty-Dumpty together again.'

When in the evening Frank returned to his rooms, he found a gold watch on his table. The watch was studded with large diamonds and inside was the engraved inscription:

'From Eva Ottercove,
With love.'

When he entered the Ottercoves' suite and lingered in the drawing-room, he was startled by the animated conversation which reached him from the adjoining bedroom. 'Now, don't you think,' said a grieved, perhaps somewhat sarcastic voice, unmistakably the baron's, 'you should have taken me into your counsels instead of first disposing of the watch and then sending the jeweller to me for the money?'

'But you haven't seen it!' the baroness rejoined impatiently. 'It's not at all expensive for what it is; it's all in diamonds. What's the use of your saying anything when you haven't *seen* it?'

'Just so. Don't you think I should have seen it, in view of your youth and inexperience, instead of laying yourself out to be swindled?'

'It's nothing to you even to be swindled, so why make any bones about it?'

This seemed to disarm the other for a space. 'Why do you do these things?' he then asked sadly.

'I wanted to please him.'

'But you could have waited a little, or asked.'

'You are an awful old miser,' she said, 'and I am sorry I ever married you.'

'I see that I shall have to engage a governess to go about with you and chaperon you for a bit.'

'You are a walking mountain of impudence!' said the baroness, 'and I don't know what God was about when he made you!'

30

Eva's comment was not lost on Lord Ottercove. When next morning they drove to the Beau-Site in Cannes, Lord Ottercove wore a more becoming pair of horn-rimmed spectacles.

'Just gone and settled their affairs,' he said, coming out on to the sunny terrace, where Eva's relatives awaited him against the background of an ornamental garden and tennis courts, on which rich Americans and English exercised their limbs all day.

'Very charming and touching,' said Mrs. Kerr. 'But you should not have put yourself out, Lord Ottercove. Raymond would have settled my bill, I am sure. He is his mother's boy.'

'Mummy, you are too silly for words!' Zita flared up. 'Where does Raymond get his money?'

'From Eleonor of course.'

'And Eleonor?'

'From her uncle.'

'Well?'

'But I give it all to Chris.'

'Mummy is so stupid. She always draws wrong conclusions from everything. There she goes about with that "Please trample on me" look, smoking cigarettes all day, agreeing with everybody. She takes Italian lessons at five shillings an hour, and in order to make up for it, gives golfing lessons at five shillings an hour, and then takes her pupils out to tea, and spends ten shillings; or has her portrait done in the café; always invites everybody, stands drinks and cigarettes all round, pays for everybody; speaks to everybody in the restaurants—Italians, Germans, Scandinavians.'

'She is a white woman,' muttered Lord Ottercove.

'You know what I'll tell you, Lord Ottercove! I am disappointed in Fyodor Ferdinandovitch. I knew nothing—nothing about it, till I read it in "Pale Primroses." Naturally I asked the girls, and it all came out.'

'I know.'

'But both! *Both*!'

'He didn't wish to leave either out, for fear of offending the other, I guess.'

'Mrs. Kerr,' said Frank, 'I appeal to your idealism and good sense. In the severity of your indignation you did not sufficiently allow for the circumstances in which, if I may put it thus, the drama was enacted. Picture the scene. All around us, an epic panorama, and I alone with two girls. Lovely girls. The mountain spring—certain death—and Shakespeare's immortal lines:

> ' "*O Proserpina!*
> *For the flowers now that frighted thou let'st fall*
> *From Dis's wagon! daffodils,*
> *That come before the swallow dares, and take*
> *The winds of March with beauty; violets dim,*
> *But sweeter than the lids of Juno's eyes*
> *Or Cytherea's breath; pale primroses,*
> *That die unmarried, ere they can behold*
> *Bright Phoebus in his strength, a malady*
> *Most incident to maids; bold oxlips and*
> *The crown imperial; lilies of all kinds,*
> *The flower-de-luce being one. O! these I lack*
> *To make you garlands of, and my sweet friend,*
> *To strew him o'er and o'er!*"

These loyal girls!' He placed a hand on either sister's shoulder, and drew them to him. 'These splendid girls!'

'Whom you have dishonoured!'

'Tut–tut, Mummy!' said Zita. 'You mustn't blurt these things out! Morty will murder Frank if he knows.'

'Well,' said Lord Ottercove, 'I have made an honest woman—of one of them at any rate.'

'I do not understand you, Lord Ottercove.'

'I have made an honest woman of Eva.'

'Explain it to me, please. I don't understand.'

'I have married her.'

There was a pause. Mrs. Kerr looked round at them all, and satisfied herself that the statement was bona fide.

'Well—I am very pleased. I must say that you have chosen well and wisely. She will make a good wife for you. I congratulate you both.'

'I hope, Mrs. Kerr,' Frank said, 'that your grudge against me is over. I trust that you will rejoice in your daughter's happiness, and will ever remember that the assignation of unworthy motives never helps but always weakens an argument.'

'Frank talks rot, but always with conviction. He would make a good lawyer,' said Ottercove.

'Yes, or a great priest,' said Frank, strangely pleased with himself.

'Now let's make a night of it!' proposed Mrs. Kerr.

Lord Ottercove did not reply. Lord Ottercove hated to act on other people's suggestions and as a rule 'advised them against it,' and if pressed for his reasons, produced arguments so cynically free from plausibility that he seemed himself amused by their bewildering effect on his opponent. If he approved of a suggestion, he said nothing; then, a few moments later, made it himself.

'I am taking you out to-night, all of you,' he said.

Pilling took Frank by the arm and marched him ahead, while the others followed behind at a distance.

'Glad you done it,' he said. 'I thought it was me. My conscience sort of worried me. It's a dirty thing to do. Thank heaven, it was you.'

'Damn it all, Pilling. It was a hill. Spring! Sunshine! You know those lines from Shakespeare?

> ' "*O Proserpina!*
> *For the flowers now that frighted*——" '

'Shut up, Frank!'

'I tell you we thought it was the end——'

'*Force majeure.* I realize. That whitewashes it a bit. An Act of God. Otherwise I doubt, you know, whether you would be eligible for the best clubs.'

'Still, I am disappointed in Ferdinand Fyodorovitch,' chided Mrs. Kerr, coming up from behind.

'I appeal to your idealism,' Frank uttered automatically. 'As I said, the sun, the mountain spring—and those immortal lines—"O Proserpina!" '

They would not let him go on. Strange: it seemed as if they regarded his appeals to Shakespeare as in bad taste. The moment he began to quote those lovely lines, they would look sullen or get angry and ask him to 'shut up.' 'It would really seem that my great crime consisted in getting saved!'

Eleonor, after some consultation with Raymond, came up to her uncle and took him aside. 'It's all very well,' she said, 'Chris having adopted Raymond. But suppose Chris marries again and has a child of his own?'

'Then we must get him married at once.'

'Married! That is just what we are anxious to prevent, for fear it might result in a male child.'

'Married, of course, to somebody who is beyond hope of bearing children,' said Ottercove.

'But who?'

'To his old love, of course—Mrs. Kerr.'

'But how do you know she can't have a child?'

'Her doctor told me in confidence.'

'But he will refuse!'

'We must bring pressure to bear on him.'

'How?'

'Chris is ruined, and he's used to spending money. He knows I won't give him a penny, and, in fact, he wouldn't take it from me. He likes to feel independent of me. But, of course, it's only natural that Raymond, married to my niece, who draws on my account to an unlimited extent, can't help, good and loving son that he is, helping his mother. And Chris, married to her, will be all right.'

'Raymond and I want to marry next week in Paris,' said Eleonor.

Lord Ottercove's lips moved almost silently. 'Why not marry here? I know a chap—a parson—most obliging. Pulled him out of bed the other night to marry us. Read the marriage ceremony unruffled.'

'Yes, most obliging,' Eva concurred.

'And you, Chris? And you, Mrs. Kerr?'

'What's that?'

'Why don't you get married?'

'I don't know that it's very safe to attach me to her with the tape of a spent passion.'

'Look here, I've got hold of a fellow—a pastor of some obscure denomination. Very accommodating. He will remarry you all. What d'you think of it?'

'I am very glad, Chris, to be of use. You are a genius——'

'Of the untried,' said Ottercove.

'A real genius in science. And I want to help you in your discoveries. Yes, I do. Take the case of the Curies.'

'You mean Monsieur and Madame Curie?'

'Yes, I do. You will instruct me in your science and we will make new discoveries together, you and I, Christopher!'

'Help us!' Turning to Frank, he whispered: 'They think they have got the better of me there. But the boot's on the other foot! What do I care whether I am blown up—single or married?'

'So, in the end, all are satisfied,' said Ottercove.

'Except my poor ancestors,' murmured de Jones.

'Who are dead.'

'Who are dead.'

Pilling seemed pleased and impressed. 'Lord Ottercove,' he remarked, as if out of the baron's hearing, but loud enough for the baron to hear, 'is a man of wide sympathies.'

'He is a live wire,' from de Jones.

That night, dashing off to Monte Carlo, where Lord Ottercove was entertaining them, Pilling was seen to get into the baron's car, who not only did not seem to resent this intrusion, but actually welcomed him with a smile. 'I have, as you say, wide sympathies. When I see a man struggling in the water, I can't resist a helping hand. It is my nature,' he was heard to say, stepping out of the car.

And, stepping again into the car with Pilling close on his heels, on the way back to Nice, he was heard to say: 'I have an interest in a number of hotels which brings me in—er—about—er—three hundred thousand pounds a year, and I'll finance you in your undertaking,' and slam the door behind him.

Next day, Mrs. Kerr, who liked to show off her offspring, called her new husband into the bathroom where John was shaving. 'Look, look!' she said. 'What a huge sponge John has!' But Christopher looked as though he could wish the sponge had been smaller and the dowry larger.

The same day Frank picked up, in the lounge of the hotel, a newspaper, which informed him:

'Among the arrivals at the Hotel Mauresco are Lord and Lady Ottercove, Viscount and Viscountess de Jones, Mr. Frank Dickin, the novelist, and the Honourable Raymond and Mrs. Mosquito.'

31

Since the wedding had taken place in Nice, the bride and bridegroom felt that they had to 'get away' for their honeymoon, and elected a voyage by yacht. 'I have got away with the goods,' Lord Ottercove had said, 'and I must get them away.'

'I must leave at once,' said de Jones.

'I agree,' from Ottercove.

But as de Jones would not part with his secretary, and the new Lady de Jones would not part with her husband, they all left together, Frank as a supernumerary.

Perhaps, as a result of his marriage to Mrs. Kerr, Lord de Jones found delight in concentrating on his missionary work, dictating for hours and hours to Eva, who complained of 'her poor brains.' He dictated to her, and made her read aloud her shorthand, and every time it seemed to him anew a mystery and a miracle. He could not make himself believe that anyone was really capable of deciphering those puzzled and bewildered little signs they made.

He was in love with her, and every word she typed seemed to him a romance. He scanned her typescript, and saw a letter she had erased with her own darling fingers so as to insert the right one: his heart filled with tears.

Frank conceived it his duty to warn her. 'This dictating is all very well, but it's not the end of the business. It's unwholesome to be alone with that man. He can——'

'He can do nothing.'

'He can seduce you.'

'You have.'

'I'd forgotten.'

She looked at him quizzically.

'You know—yes, I might as well say it plainly—well, about Chris and your mother.'

'They are married.'

'Now they are. Raymond is a living indictment of their relations.'

'Raymond never cared for his father. But I don't mind Chris loving me, because he is a friend of Mummy's.'

'I have nothing further to say.'

'Thank goodness for that!'

But he would come back with more.

'You shouldn't make yourself so cheap, Eva!'

'It gives him so much pleasure, and me so little trouble.'

'You leave my girl-wife alone!' said Ottercove, coming upon Chris and Eva suddenly in the seclusion of the Captain's bridge. 'Why don't you leave the girl alone?'

De Jones blinked at him. ' "There is a divinity," ' he said, ' "that shapes our ends, rough-hew them as we may." '

'You've got your wife, Chris. What do you want with mine?'

'She reminds me of her mother,' said de Jones, after reflection.

'Ha! Not so bad!'

'She's more like her mother was than her mother is.'

'But I've got away with the goods!' He strolled up and down several times, and then stopped, peering at the horizon. 'Oh, my heart!'

'I think it's the stomach,' said Chris.

'Yes, I think it's the stomach,' said Ottercove.

'Poor darling!' from Eva.

At that, tears came to his eyes, and he turned away to hide his emotion.

32

Fliesse, fliesse, lieber Fluss!
Nimmer werd' ich froh;
So verrauschte Scherz und Kuss
Und die Treue so.
                    GOETHE.

Everything went wrong with Frank; he could succeed in nothing. He had no luck in anything—but he won steadily at ping-pong. He was rapidly losing his hair. But on that score he was optimistic. As his hair fell out more and more, he lost neither courage nor faith, but interpreted this as a process preparatory to new growth. The new hair which was to make its appearance must, he argued, have room; and the old hair was making room for it—with alacrity. When, after a time, it had entirely disappeared, he judged that now at last the field was clear for a fresh crop. And, as if to compensate him for his premature bereavement on the top, unbiased nature encouraged a particularly bristling, pushful growth out of his nostrils. Even so, his faith in the value of human striving had not deserted him. All other remedies having failed, he determined to grow hair by sheer strength of will. And he was succeeding—succeeding...

Lord Ottercove devoted more and more time to reading. He had always been a great reader, but now, since his marriage to Eva, he spent the clock round with her reading a book to himself. He had always been bored, but now, married to her, he seemed more bored than ever before.

The haze and hurry, the dreamy unreality of modern life. Frank was bewildered rather than bored with it. He was thrown like flotsam into the stream and was carried along. But he would get out—and life would be timeless. He could not tell how passionately he craved to get out of life in time, while he was with de Jones, Mrs. Kerr and Ottercove.

The scrambling on the part of the three men for Eva's favours, as the yacht ploughed its way towards Naples, was too much for Frank, and he left them at Genoa, travelling north by rail.

And now, as he looked back, the bleak hours he once spent with Eva seemed coloured beads wetted in light and translucent with a meaning. The actual giving at the time was crude and like a pain. The remembrance of it, as it grew more distant, was as the faint perfume of roses, a romance far off. Dead, perhaps, we see these things completely. He remembered how in that first kiss she had pressed herself, a pliant plant, against him, and closed her eyes, as if to shut in the vision: there was something in her movement half instinctive which thrilled him in one so young; half naïve, as though she had only read of it in books and now, for the first time, was tasting love, and staging it, in actual life! He remembered how at his dentist's one day, they had sat together side by side on the narrow sofa in the waiting-room, and as the attendant turned his back on them, he had touched her thigh and knee (oh, thigh! oh, knee!), and at once when they were out, and in the taxi, she had kissed him on his dentisted mouth. He remembered, too, how she had written to him once about a Cambridge 'student,' alleged to have given her circumstantial proof of his, Ferdinand's, unfaithfulness; and when he wrote to her, demanding that she substantiate the charge, and challenged her to identify the Cambridge 'student,' her writing back: 'Let us drop the subject, as the matter is muddling.' Or how, after saying to him: 'You must absolutely send me roses for my birthday to-morrow, Ferdinand!' she telegraphed next day: 'Please don't send flowers;' and the basket of flowers he sent her in gallant disregard of her wire, crossed her letter to him containing a bill for £5 for a suit she could not resist acquiring, and which she lent forthwith to a friend who did not come back with it. At the time he resented this overture. Now, in retrospect, it moved him: did it not show a touching solicitude not to lead him into needless expense in the face of an existing debt—when she might so easily have asked for both! He now thought of her feelings when one day he had spoken to her like a boor, and barely tried to conceal his tedium in her presence. He remembered the moistened look in her eye, the curve of her brow, the twitch of her lashes. And these metaphors of love stirred and racked his soul.

In Milan, cold, sparse, and unfriendly, where at nightfall woeful figures dotted the wide, deserted, wind-swept streets, his heart, mellowed by distance, constricted in sombre anguish. 'Poor women!' he thought.

Getting into the Vienna express at midnight, into a *coupé* in which the blinds were drawn and the passengers asleep, his mood darkened and deepened. A siren at his side, opening her eyes at his intrusion, resumed a desultory conversation with another, a pale coughing girl, with whom she was travelling north where 'trade' was deemed to be better. 'On arrival,' she flustered, 'I must buy myself some new hair, and then you will wait for me downstairs while I go up and see Francesca about giving us a room.' The girl close to him addressed him in Italian. 'I do not speak Italian,' Frank said. 'Do you speak English?'

'Yes,' she said, articulating deliberately: 'we have no b-hananas; we have no b-hananas to—day.'

Was that all she knew of English? No, there were other words she knew. 'Love'—'kiss'—'cheque-book.' Did he have a cheque-book? Englishmen, she said, always had a cheque-book. It was, she thought, their distinguishing characteristic.—Where were they going? To Budapest—where they had once lived with their parents. 'At the time when we were still honest,' she added.

'Fallen women! Lost women! Poor lost women!'

'In this world we are all lost men and women,' echoed a voice in him to the shattering rhythm of the train.

All lost men and women. Lost. Some more luxuriously lost than others, but all, all lost. Lost and damned. No escape!

He closed his eyes. Lost, lost, lost—lost, lost, lost...

A long, wide, endless road stretched before him. He is walking down that road, the road to Purgatory. What is the crowd outside that house? He stops and watches. They are carrying out an open coffin with a young girl in it. The old harpies in the crowd shake their heads. 'She took her life.'—'What, took her life?'—'She has been betrayed by a young good-for-nothing.'—'No, she died in childbirth.'

'Let me! Let me!' He rushes to her. 'I was the first to cause her fall. Oh, wait! Don't close the lid! O, Eva! Dearest heart. She died for love...like Fräulein Else.'

He sheds hot tears as he kneels on her cold tomb which hides her and her young white purity. But as he rises and leaves the cemetery, she follows silently behind him to the gate, where, sensing something, he turns round. 'Eva!'

'I don't want to be buried. I am yours,' she says, coming to him in her long white shroud. 'Take me away with you.'

They kiss. He is forgiven.

'What's this?' He opens his eyes, heavy with tears.

'Verona. A stop of forty minutes,' imparts his *vis-à-vis*, 'and there is a cold buffet.'

Another dream, another life!

33

He found himself, largely against his intention, writing long letters to Eva. But Eva never wrote—only cabled. He had cables from Stockholm and Moscow, Pekin and Buenos Ayres. It was not until they were nearing home that Frank had a letter from her. Christopher de Jones, she wrote, was madly in love with her. *'He said he wanted me to be his entirely and everlastingly, if you know what I mean. I let him have his way because he says he is quite serious about blowing up the world, and I think if he had a little baby of his own, shurely he wouldn't do such a thing. But Rex does not agree with me. I told him all the truth about Christopher and He says He is going to divorce me. I am furious, and He is Furious. Never mind, Darling, if I flirt with him he won't divorce me.'*

Frank planned to stay abroad for a long time to come. He would not return to England, perhaps for years. One morning, however, he received advice from Victoria Station that his cloakroom expenses in respect of a trunk he had forwarded to his address in London, and which could not be cleared by the Customs as he had not sent them the key, were piling up by arithmetical progression, rising hourly, minute by minute. The news shocked him out of his resolution to stay away from England. Hiring a car, he rushed headlong to the station and caught the express train to Boulogne, to learn, on his arrival at Victoria, that his cloak-room expenses amounted to seventeen shillings and ninepence. Arrived in England, he made up his mind to stay there. A month later, he recorded in his journal:

'There is nothing left remarkable beneath the visiting moon. The magnetic O. usurps more and more of my interest. Late at night we dash into the country, spending the night at his resplendent country house, and rush back to town in the morning.

Feverish activity. Articles are written, printed, and forgotten; to-day's paper lights tomorrow's fire. It goes on—dances and enter-tainments; the dinners and drinks of today are washed away into the ocean tomorrow. "Tomorrow and tomorrow, and tomorrow, creeps in this petty pace from day to day, till the last syllable of recorded time, and all our yesterdays have lighted fools the way to dusty death." O, if only this were all to end, change soon, this vexatious, unavailing life in time! Don't make it long, O Lord!

'Yesterday I visited Bourne Abbey (Ottercove's country house) with O. and Eva. As we went upstairs I sniffed the air; there seemed to be a queer musty smell. I asked O. what it was. "I am sorry, Frank," he said. "I am very sorry that there should be a smell." Eva seemed quite at home; no trace of self-consciousness —a perfect hostess.

'Last week Christopher de Jones came to see me. The electric light had failed, and his face looked worn and secretive by candle-light, like a monk's. The lines round his mouth had deepened, too. We talked of the end of the world; his voice and general attitude were apocalyptic. He ended up by making a confession. "You know why I always come here. It is because you know her. I come to you so as to talk of her. You love her. And I—I—I——"

'I should welcome the change foreshadowed in the Apocalypse. For time is a cheat, and life a snare. It is the curse of life in time that it can only give us one thing at a time, while a latent memory of Eden in us longs for all things all the time; "and nothing," says Shakespeare (meaning not-being) "brings me all things." "Abwarten" (abide, or perhaps better: mark time) was Goethe's motto in the wisdom of old age. But while conscious of the mirage of love and freedom (for here again, while all the world seems open to you, you must needs trail a narrow path, zigzag it as you will), I have not the strength of will to forgo their piece-meal felicities with their fickle promise of what life was before the fall. And so it is that though I expect nothing from life (and thus have agreeable surprises), I shall live it (as one would say of read-ing an unpromising manuscript) with interest, till we are changed, in a moment, in the twinkling of an eye, at the last trump.

'And, aye, there is hope! Lord de Jones has bought a penny trumpet and threatens to shatter us all into dust. Well, we shall see. Or, rather, we shall not see. Cease seeing. I wonder which...'

34

Lord de Jones put down the newspaper, and closed his eyes. After the reading of a newspaper, particularly a Sunday newspaper, he generally experienced an acute feeling of nausea, as though he had eaten a fruit salad of the very worst kind. And indeed there was enough in it to-day to disconcert a sensitive reader. There was the 'Dog Election' in England; the Fundamentalist-Evolutionist feud in America growing into what looked very like a civil war; and a European imbroglio most likely to develop into a new world war overnight. Yet in all three cases the initial cause of contention had been so slight that but for the gravity of the consequences he would have dismissed it all as unreal.

The 'Dog Election,' which had shaken the country in the second half of April, had its origin, he recalled, in Frank Dickin's, on a previous evening, as he was hurrying to keep an appointment with Lord Ottercove, slipping on the pavement and, in his indignation, recommending to his host the wholesale extermination of the breed of dogs. Lord Ottercove, who had made a note of it at the time, caused it to be described in his newspapers as a public nuisance which the Government should put a speedy end to, and when, a week later, a prominent member of Parliament slipped and broke his leg, Lord Ottercove's newspapers rose *en masse* against dogs. In a hundred years' time, one of his papers affirmed, historians would note with horror that in the first half of the twentieth century dogs were allowed complete licence of behaviour in the public thoroughfares. An altogether unexpected outburst of support from readers, thousands of whom had apparently been storing up for many years a somewhat unmanly resentment against the dog race, emboldened Lord Ottercove to push the matter to extremities. DOGS MUST GO—his posters cried in unison. Now the Prime Minister, a man of inconspicuous curiosity and an overwhelming sense of right and wrong, read these articles. A country squire, who had been persuaded to shoulder the burden of government much against his inclination, he was a confirmed dog lover. The thought of exterminating our dumb and loyal friends was repugnant to him. But his conscience told him that pavements erected with the tax-payers' money were being abused by caninity; accidents were accumulating, deaths might ensue any day. The dogs were in the wrong; yes, the dogs must go. It was his duty to carry out the policy however unpopular, if he thought it a matter of duty that the policy should be carried out. And he was a man of duty. 'Exterminate the dog breed!' became the slogan and policy (though largely against the advice of elder statesmen) of the Conservative Party. The Liberal Party, it would seem, had only been waiting for this. Assisted and advised by Lord Ottercove, they made 'The Preservation and Protection of Our Friend the Dog' the chief item of their party programme. 'Joe' (as he was called by his intimates), the Liberal leader, temperamentally repelled by dogs, had been photographed sitting in a basket chair, a grave-eyed poodle with his front legs across the Liberal leader's knees. 'The heart of England is sound,' they said, stealing the Tory touch, 'so long as she remains a dog-loving Nation.' And again: 'Do away with the dogs: and the country will assuredly go to them!'

'Where will it go?' from a heckler (put there by the Liberal candidate himself).

'To the dogs, sir!' blandly and crushingly.

Loud laughter.

The Labour Party unfortunately split itself over the issue. The more responsible section sympathized with the socializing efforts of the Conservative Prime Minister; the other half resented the adoption on the part of the reactionaries of what by the look and sound of it should have been a Socialist programme, and they were helped by the lovers of whippets and rabbit coursing, and the gamblers who flocked to the dog races. The controversy grew in passion; something not unlike a civil war loomed behind this sinister antagonism; a St. Bartholomew Night threatened from day to day, a pogrom with extensive dog massacres having been organized by the more energetic Die-hard section of the Tory Party who did not believe in half measures, distrusted the Prime Minister's tendency to conciliation and compromise and were anxious to check his retreat and, by forcing his hand, oblige him to take a firm stand. Till the *Nation*, commenting in a leading article upon the situation that had arisen over the 'Right of Dog' question, pointed out with characteristic pertinence and good sense that in the heat of passion the main issue had been overlooked, as usual, namely, whether there was not a possibility of doing away with the indubitable nuisance caused by dogs who are wrongly granted the freedom of the pavement without necessarily doing away with the dogs themselves. The *New Statesman* and the *Spectator* raised the same question in their individual voices. But nobody cared to listen to them. The Conservative Government resigned on a vote of confidence, and in the General Election which ensued the Liberals carried everything before them.

In America, Lord de Jones read, there was a growing feud between Fundamentalists and Evolutionists. An Evolutionist had declared that he was ready to appear at a Fundamentalist meeting and 'dare' God to smite him dead. An ardent Fundamentalist disciple, believing that he was serving his cause, connected the steel platform on which the Evolutionist was speaking by a wire with the main electric current of the premises, thereby electrocuting the Evolutionist in the very act of his challenge. Details, however, leaked out by and by, resulting in what threatened to become a religious war between the two faiths hardly to be paralleled since the Wars of the Crusades, if then. The Fundamentalist declared at his trial that in so far as God Himself had put the idea into his head, it was the hand of God that had struck down the blasphemer; and in his summing-up the judge directed the jury to determine just how far it was God and how far devilry. The jury were reluctant to pass a verdict of 'guilty' against so almighty a being, and counsel at a subsequent trial conceded so much to the scientific bias of the day as to declare that the electrocution of the Evolutionist was in the nature of a miracle intended to create and sustain faith, elevating an otherwise unimportant mechanical trick into the realms of the supernatural. The Fundamentalist was acquitted; and in the ensuing riots directed by outraged Free Thinkers and Revolutionaries against the headquarters of the Fundamentalists in Massachusetts, the responsible leaders of the faith, though admitting the uncalled-for action and excessive zeal of their feather-brained disciple, who, while wishing to assist their cause, had unwittingly damaged it, yet claimed that a little trick like that could not implicate the essential wisdom of their faith nor undermine the foundations of Fundamentalism.

All over the world, Lord de Jones knew, and particularly in England, the struggle between capital and labour grew more bitter and, as time went on, threatened to develop into a general revolution; to side-track which the respective Governments agreed to have a war. A *casus belli* was looked for; and was found. A Russian Tsarist 'Government' living in exile in Paris had published its claims on Eastern Prussia, which once upon a time was Slav; inasmuch as Petrograd (though this they were reluctant to admit) had once been Finnish soil, and was now being claimed by a Fascist Government in Helsingfors whose motto was 'A Greater Finland!' Germany, while admitting the justice of the Finnish claims, disputed those of Russia; and Russia, while disputing the Finnish claims, insisted on its own to Eastern Prussia. The new war was broadly (and amicably) conceived on these lines, and the British Government, declaring that it could not countenance another war in Europe, plunged into it—so as to prevent it.

Lord Ottercove hailed the prospect of war (in lieu of revolution) with mixed feelings of journalistic felicity and human discomfiture. As the probability—and later the unavoidability—of war became more certain, the humane resistance in him yielded to patriotic excitement, and he wrote himself the leading article, heading it: 'The Nation Demands——' And the nation, reading it at breakfast next morning, felt that, yes, it was in them to demand, and they demanded and would not sheathe the sword until they had fought to utter exhaustion. And young men from the public schools were already training in bayonet drill on the lawns of Kensington Gardens under sergeants whose dictum, oft repeated, was that the war was to be won by saluting by numbers. Grey-haired City men were forming fours everywhere, and, as a relaxation from it, forming two deep. Once again there was 'A Cause.'

When, to forget the war, Lord de Jones turned in to a music-hall matinée, a comedian was singing:

'I joined the Army yesterday,

> *So the Army of to-day*
> *'S all right;'*

and a stoutish prima donna replied in mezzo-soprano:

> *'I didn't like you, John,*
> *Before you joined the Army, John;*
> *I like you now*
> *You've got your khaki on!'*

and displayed her fat legs in a whirl.

35

One afternoon in early spring, when the streets of London resounded with bugles and drums calling the manhood of Britain to rise in arms in defence of Russia's menaced right to Petrograd and Germany's ownership of Eastern Prussia, a hazel-eyed girl with dark curls rang the bell of Stonedge House and asked for Lady Ottercove, who a moment later greeted the visitor with astonished delight.

'Baby!' she exclaimed and threw her arms around her neck. She dragged Baby by the hand into the drawing-room, and from the drawing-room into the second drawing-room, and from there into the ball-room, and then up to her beautiful bedroom; and in all the rooms Baby displayed astonished rapture. 'I have another house,' Eva said, 'in the country, and Rex has another small house in town where we go when we wish to be alone with nobody to bother us, and I have a villa near Nice and a Rolls and lots of servants and everything, and more money than I know what to do with.'

'Not really!'

'Oh yes! And Rex is very pleased with me, he says, and very proud.'

And, indeed, every one of Lord Ottercove's friends could testify that Lady Ottercove proved an admirable hostess. She seemed to carry out her duties with easy grace and without self-consciousness; she had learnt the essentials of the game from hearsay; and there was something so fresh, so naïve, so spontaneous about her nature that men found her irresistible. And women she did not trouble about.

'Aren't you terribly, *terribly* happy?' Baby asked.

Eva suddenly looked grave and sad. 'Can you,' she said, 'keep a secret?'

Baby said she could.

'If you can, I will do something for you.'

'Really? What?'

'Save your life.'

'No?'

'Yes. I will tell you if you promise never, *never* to say a word to anyone. It's about Christopher de Jones. All these years he has been wanting to blow up the earth with all the people, etcetera, on it, and when we were in Greece and he descended into a deep, deep crater which he said was the deepest crater of them all, going right down into the bowels of the earth, he said to me that he had only to disintegrate one single atom in it to blow up all the earth with all the people on it into smithereens. But I said that this was very, very wicked of him, so he said that suffering humanity had suffered long enough, and that if he blew it up it would no longer suffer pain, and so on, but that as he loved me more than anything else on earth he wished to spend the last few hours with me, holding hands, etcetera, and one day he came to me all radiant in the face and happy, and said he'd done it. "Done what?" I said. "Split the atom," he said, and that we were all doomed and done for. "But, Chris," I said, "how could you have done such a thing!"

' "It's all right," he said. "You needn't worry; it's all quite respectable, and there is no noise or explosion. I have only disintegrated the atom, and now all matter, the whole of the world is slowly disintegrating, too, peeling away into nothing. Soon nothing will be left of our planet."

' "But, oh, Chris!" I said.

' "It's all right," he said. "There is no pain, no suffering, no inconvenience or discomfort. People just soften, disintegrate atom by atom, turn into whiffs of steam, a sort of mist, and vanish like smoke up the chimney. All is over in a few seconds."

' "Chris," I said, "I don't understand."

' "It's—how shall I say—as if people ate themselves up," he said.

' "But they can't quite, Chris. There'll be crumbs left after them."

' "No, crumbs and all."

' "But the mouth will be left, Chris; when the mouth has eaten everything there will still be the mouth left to eat."

' "And the mouth will eat it," he said.

' "I see. Chris, I want to tell you something," I said.

' "What?" he said.

' "I am going to have a baby," I said.

' "Oh!" he said. "Whose baby?"

'I looked soft and tender, as if it might be his. "Chris," I said, "can you not save yourself and the baby—and me, too, perhaps?"

' "I would do anything," he said, "to save you and the baby, but I've laddered the world. You know what happens when you've laddered a silk stocking."

' "You've got to buy a new pair," I said.

' "Exactly," he said.

' "You can't buy a—a new world?" I said.

' "I'll have to see if I can mend the old one," he said.

' "Can you?"

'He said he didn't know. He said he would have to look into it, think about it. He might be able, he said, to isolate a bit of earth somewhere—a mountain-top or something, where we three could be saved.

' "Yes, yes!" I said. "We three and all our friends. Just a little house-party!"

' "No house-parties, by God!" he said. "Just you and I and the baby—you and I and the baby." '

Eva paused. Baby looked at her long and sadly, modestly, too, as if reluctant to press her own claims to survival.

'But if you keep quiet about it,' said Eva, 'I shall tell you where to go. You will just hide in the cellar or somewhere, lie low for a day or two, and then creep out when I tell you to. I will make it all right with Chris.'

For a long while the two cousins chattered together of matters irrelevant to the coming apocalypse; but presently they were back in the future. 'And Rex, and Ferdinand, and one or two others,' said Eva. 'I will manage it so that Chris doesn't know.'

'And your mother, and Zita, and Pilling, I suppose?'

'No, no! We mustn't have a crowd. You see, there will be very little to eat on the top of a hill. But we'll have a good time, all the same.'

36

THE LAST SUPPER

Thursday was the opening night of the 'New Babylon,' Pilling's new night club. The butler had been announcing arrivals:

'Lord and Lady de Jones.

'Mr. and Mrs. Raymond Mosquito.

'Mrs. Frank Dickin.'

Then, flinging open the doors, the butler made a last belated appearance: 'Mr. Kerr, m'lord.'

'Now this is very, very nice. Come right in, Mr. Kerr!' from Lord Ottercove.

At the long table presided over by Ottercove, Frank found himself sitting by the side of his own wife. After the long absence, she was a vision of enchantment, and her presence, new yet familiar, breaking the crust of ice in his heart, released rivers of rapture; and outside it was spring, drowsed with desires, and here was she, his lovely mate...

And yet? And yet? Considered objectively, enquired into dispassionately, was marriage really a solution of one's difficulties? Be honest now, he said to himself. One wife was at once too much and not enough. Fifty wives, renewable like water in a swimming pool, would have been better. He would have sat there, all lust gone, among them, a man of action turned philosopher, passing a weary hand over this lock or that brow, seeking solace from repletion in intellectual intercourse—yes, with a man, a man who agreed that life was wanting! 'What?' he was roused from his reverie, and, not hearing the question, replied: 'Rather!'

Indisputably, Cynthia was enchanting, and even Lord Ottercove singled her out after dinner. 'Are you the prettiest girl in London, Cynthia?' He kissed her full on the mouth.

'No, Rex, no!'

An actress, jealous of Cynthia's success, flung her champagne over her. Cynthia, shocked beyond words, and followed by all her admirers, retired to another room, where she was presently joined by the actress, who lavished profuse apologies on her: 'I am so frightfully sorry, darling!'

'It's quite all right, darling.'

And all the women who hated each other, called the other thus: 'darling.'

It was, to all appearance, a brilliant party. Vernon Sprott was there—Vernon Sprott, the foreman of British fiction, whose novel entitled *The New Babylon Hotel & Restaurant* had provided the name for Pilling's night club, in consideration of which Mr. Sprott received a royalty on the gross profits of the New Babylon Club of 0.0000002 per cent. free of income tax and payable to him after deduction of a commission of ten per cent. by Mr. Sprott's Literary Agent. And both he and his literary agent (who was there) could not take their eyes off Cynthia, by common consent the special, the most distinctive ornament of the evening. She looked a little pale, dream-like, ravishing, romantic; and as she danced, her eyes seemed to say: 'Do you remember?' and Frank could scarcely wait for the end of the party to elope with his wife, to carry her away…away…She said what Juliet had said before her: that it was too sudden!

Only Christopher de Jones seemed glum. He sat and watched how Eva danced with an intent young man whose cleverness was in his feet; danced confidentially, *giving* him her pliable young body, every movement of which seemed to say: 'I am thine, thine…' For such is the language of pleading melody. He could read, it seemed to him, the souls of all the men and women, guests, musicians, waiters, and divine what the head waiter, the orchestra men, each suffering unit thought to himself: how each only languished and inwardly moaned. Another little while, he thought, and it would all be over…

37

A Pair of Bare Legs

Baby, who had been sent out by her cousin to ascertain the local conditions in the Austrian Alps, having, after a lapse of two weeks, only reported that dogs were not allowed in the public parks of Innsbruck and that persons doing damage to the flower-beds would be prosecuted, Frank, the next candidate scheduled for salvation, was dispatched in Baby's wake.

He found her at the top of a mountain towering above the Inn valley, playing chess with a handsome young bank clerk from Vienna, on his annual holiday in the Tyrol. Neither knew a word of the other's language, and they made love with the aid of a dictionary. He found the words and passed her the dictionary. *Liebe—Wonne—Verlangen.* She read the English equivalent—love—bliss—desire—and purred.

Frank deemed the *pension* and the hill in every way an adequate *pied-à-terre*, worthy of preservation and, so far as he could judge, eminently suitable for isolation from the atomic disintegration about to overtake the world; and he gave Eva all the available information as to victuals, trains, etc., warning her, among other things, not to pull the communication cord while the train was in motion unless there was genuine need for it; and even gave the Italian of it: '*Tirare la maniglia solo in caso di pericolo. Ogni abuso verrà punito!*'

The Pension Kogl stood alone on the mountain-top, and gazing down from his balcony in the morning Frank saw an old Habsburg Schloss stretched out beneath him, which looked like the London Regent Palace Hotel. Breakfast, perhaps, was a little on the short side, and on the bedside-table on which it was laid there was a tablecloth with the words embroidered in red Gothic letters '*Wenig aber von Herzen.*' Below, under Frank's windows, the proprietress' husband, the Wirt, looking very like Gogol's Taras Boulba, paced the yard in a skull cap at six o'clock in the morning. He was a bad sleeper, essentially fitted, he thought, to see to it that the sleepy servant girls did not oversleep themselves. He was up and on the look-out for defaulters, like a sergeant-major waiting in the barrack yard. In a bungalow annexe across lived an old apoplectic little baron who, early each morning, about the time of mine host's appearance, popped out his head through the window, whereon the ensuing conversation could be overheard:

'Good morning, Herr Baron! Have you slept well? The weather—well, I think—or I should say, it *seems* to me—that the sky might clear up, in which case it is possible—I say, it is *possible*—yes, possible that we may have good weather to-day. Yes, yes, I am hopeful, Herr Baron.'

Herr Kogl stood close to the Baron's window and spat on the ground. The Herr Baron, out of a feeling of fellowship, spat out of the window: 'Kh–kh–kh–Kh—hhhrrr—Khhh!' they spat.

'Hey! Where you off to!' the host would suddenly yell out at the young farm hand setting out for town in the milk cart.

'To town.'

'Off you go!' shouting angrily. 'Hurry up, you rascal! Overslept again, you lazy bounder! Whip up, young scoundrel, you!—Youth,' he would add tenderly, turning back to the Baron.

Till nine o'clock in the morning he would thus stroll up and down the yard, his hands behind his back; and then serve himself his first Schnaps.

Herr Kogl's distinction was that he was credited with a strong will. Frau Kogl's mother, who had bought the *pension* on her Alsatian savings, had long hoped for just such a man for her daughter, whom indeed she did not consult in the matter, though once, in an unusually tender and communicative mood, she had in fact asked her: 'What sort of a man would you like for a husband, Anny?' Anny had lowered her lashes and said: 'With a strong will.' Herr Kogl was chosen without hesitation as the embodiment of a will that would take care of his wife's property; and now, living up to his reputation, he would bawl at her from time to time: 'Hey, there! Anna!—I have called: "*Anna!*" '—and she obeyed.

Their son, who had a smooth voice, quiet manners, and a cast in one eye, knew on which side his bread was buttered, and though a little fearful of his father, clung to his moneyed mother, and disdained the assumed authority of his father, who, to bear out his own reputation, bawled at him occasionally: 'Hey, there! Herbert! I said: "*Herbert!*" ' when his son half turned a reluctant ear to him. Frau Kogl herself had moods when she liked to assert her authority; but they were intermittent and brief. She could never decide anything. Her mother was right in choosing for her a husband who bawled at her. Frau Kogl had no illusions about his general usefulness, and secretly thought him a rogue. But she needed someone to bawl at her. When he bawled, his authority in her eyes was restored; and she loved him.

The nip in the air of an early mountain spring morning! Old forgotten feelings flooded his being. As Frank went down the stairs, he passed the bare-legged scullery maid, who was washing the steps. He looked round, and she smiled. And when later in the morning she helped carry up his large trunk, he could not take away his gaze from those healthy white legs.

'Good morning, Herr Dickin,' the host greeted him. 'I am hoping that if the clouds disperse—I am hoping, I say, that if they disperse, we may be having—we may be having, I say— having fine weather to-day. But I regret to say it is Saint Peter'— he pointed to the skies— 'who is in charge of the winds, and our petition—our petition, I say, must be addressed to him up there in the heavens, oh yes.'

Dickin laughed amiably, and on passing the bar he heard Frau Kogl upbraiding her husband:

'You shouldn't tell such silly jokes to the foreign guests; they will think you're dotty.'

'It may be a silly joke,' Herr Kogl agreed, 'or it may not be a silly joke, but he laughs: so anything seems good enough for him.'

'Why, no; he is a clever man, a poet,' retorted Frau Kogl.

'I am a poet myself,' answered Herr Kogl.

'You're a fat, dotty old man, that's what you are,' said Frau Kogl. 'What have you done with the glasses? Don't stand there like that——'

'Shut up, will you!' he bawled, and banged his fist on the counter.

She quailed before the man with the strong will.

From his balcony Frank could see the scullery girl swish with her bare legs through the wet grass, and come back with a bas- ket laden with fruit. He cut across to meet her. He had a terrible longing to speak to her, but he could not find words. Because she was desirable, even though her face was objectionable, she seemed to him (as women do seem when they are desirable) to be endowed with a critical and sensitive intelligence which might resent a clumsy overture, or an approach that was not plausible. And so he walked towards her with a casual and indifferent air. But when she smiled at him his shyness left him and he asked her what the joke was.

'Ach, to-day,' she said, 'I must laugh, because I look so funny in these boots.' How ugly her face was. And yet how desirable that body.

Herr Kogl, at the door, found words to say to him. Herr Kogl always found words to say to everybody. It was his sole occupation. When he wasn't either eating or drinking, he stood in the yard and exchanged comments with visitors and casual passers-by. No one had ever seen him take a drop of wine in public, and he affected to disdain it, though he had bloodshot, oily eyes that betrayed him, and a belly quivering like jelly. 'Wine? Why, there's nothing in it,' he would say. 'I—never—have—any.' But every time he went down into the cellar to fill the decanter, he first filled himself and then the decanter.

Now he stood in the doorway, red and obese, and addressed a small, fluffy old dog of a nondescript breed and an incredible filthiness. 'Rags has been and had a puppy—a little ragamuffin like herself, what! Rags, you bad thing! Rags, you dirty tyke! Rags, you immoral old bitch! For shame! I shouldn't have thought it of you, at your age!' And he dug his crooked forefinger into Dickin's chest, as he was wont to do when emphasising a point; especially in moments of hilarious recollection, as when he might say: 'Oh, *that* thing! Well, of *course*!' At such moments he would dig even a little lower than the ribs, because the joke addressed itself to a more central part of you—the abdominal part, wherein all jokes are seated; or so at least we must suppose, because when men laugh too heartily they protect and support these, their boilers, from bursting.

Again, as he stood there, Frank caught a glimpse of the scullery maid's bare legs, as she went out to hang out some linen. 'What are you smiling for?' he asked, overtaking her, Herr Kogl now having turned in.

'Ach! Herr Dickin,' she said, 'when you speak to me I must

always laugh. I don't know why.'

He looked round. There was no one about. 'When do you finish your work?'

'I go to bed at half-past ten.'

'Won't you come and see me before going to bed?'

'Where?' she asked.

'In my room.'

'What shall I do in your room?'

His blood coursed feverishly through his veins, his brain was on fire, at the thought of what they could not do in his room. 'Keep me company,' he said.

She nodded assent, and went in with the dry linen. Returning, he ran into Herr Kogl, who came out of the cellar with the decanter, licking and smacking his thick ruby lips. 'Herr Kogl, will you have a glass of wine with me?'

Herr Kogl shook his head slowly, closing his eyes.

'I—never—have—wine.   I—consider—that—there—is—nothing—in—it. Oh yes.' His diction was distinct, correct, precise, deliberate, and slow.

'Well, you are certainly setting an edifying example to your boy, aren't you, Herr Kogl?'

'My boy,' said Herr Kogl, 'is all right.'

With a mystic, an unearthly look, Herr Kogl retired to the safe behind the counter, and came back with a large sheet of parchment in his big, shaking red hands. 'His college certificate,' he said, turning away to hide his emotion and to give the visitor the opportunity of ascertaining for himself the high standard of Herbert's scholastic achievements:

> Calligraphy—proficient;
> Arithmetic—good;
> Cooking—very satisfactory;
> Slaughtering—praiseworthy;
> Waiting at the table—very good;
> Deportment—excellent;
> General conduct—excellent.

'Eminently satisfactory,' said Dickin, returning the document.

'He is at the Hotel and Restaurant Institute in Vienna,' the father said proudly, 'and I afford him practical opportunities for perfecting his studies when he is here for his summer vacation by allowing him to wait at table. Of course, under my supervision,' he added.

'You ought to be very proud of him.'

'Proud? Why?'

'Of course you ought to be! You *are* proud.'

'Well, of course—proud—why not? You wouldn't think, would you, eh? A Tyrolese poodle like him, now, would you?…attain such distinction in Vienna itself!' And two large beads stood in Herr Kogl's jaundiced bloodshot eyes.

At lunch, in the large panelled room looking out on the old archducal Schloss beneath, steeped in the foliage of its enormous and forsaken park, Frank found himself seated facing a Lutheran pastor from Germany, who had large sad eyes, a quiet, melancholy voice, and helped himself without cease to the *Kalter Aufschnitt*. He thought the world was all right, the church all right, and nothing wanted changing. Among the guests was a Russian Grand Duke who turned out to be the cousin of Frank's one-time opponent who had hit him on the ear with an umbrella at the Kiss-Lick Club. The Grand Duke's cousin was killed in a motor smash in Poland. His own brother was assassinated elsewhere. An uncle died in mysterious circumstances. It seemed, of the old guard, there remained only Frank and he, and over a decanter of Tyrolese wine, consumed together, they relinquished their claim to the throne of Russia in each other's favour.

'Ah! You are a writer!' the Grand Duke exclaimed happily. 'You write in English? Ah, well! I've my own theories about English literature. I am obstinate in the belief that in the portrayal of Dorian Gray, Oscar Wilde did not mean to depict his own personality, so to speak.'

Frank sounded the Grand Duke as to his further opinions. Wordsworth? No, he hadn't heard of Wordsworth. Keats?—No: who was he? No, he preferred the moderns. There was one modern writer—German, he believed—who amused him. Bernhard Schau.—Oh, he was British? How interesting! He had bought quite a number of his works in Berlin, and enjoyed dipping into them—he liked him for the wit salted with cynicism. Did his Highness read any other English authors? The Grand Duke considered for a moment, wrinkling his brow.—Of

course—Byron! Who did not love that tremendous, that stupen-
dous, unbelievable genius, the greatest the world has yet seen?
'Childe Harold.'—Ah! The Grand Duke thought he himself was
a little like that—like Byron and Lermontov—romantic, re-
bellious, you know, seeking something (he made a gesture to the
heavens)—dissatisfied with his surroundings—that's it, dissatisfied with his surroundings and seeking a meaning in life. Yes, he
was a lover of literature—though he preferred sport—riding and
hunting; drinking, too, he was not averse to. He considered, as if
struck by a sudden idea. 'Have a drink,' he said.

They passed into the lounge, into which Herr Kogl burst periodically, to explain the working of the electric stove, which could
be switched on at will but must not be, he cautioned, switched off
without a preliminary intimation to Herbert, in charge of the
electric supply station, because a sudden superfluity of electricity
sent the dynamo into commotion. Here Frank perceived a dark-
haired, dark-eyed woman, looking like a gipsy. 'Frau König!' he
exclaimed. 'By heaven! This is unexpected!'

Frau König, on the other hand, did not appear to regard this
meeting as unexpected, but at once proceeded to recount her
life at the point at which his knowledge of it had been interrupted. 'My fiancé, alas, has failed again in his examinations at
the University, and that has put us back for another couple of
years and deferred our hope of establishing the knitting factory.
He says the Paris professors have been prejudiced against him on
account of his Russian nationality and vented on him their bitterness over the Russian State Bonds they had acquired and lost
in the Revolution, and agreed to plough him.' And she introduced him to Frau Professor Koch, who occupied the room
next to his and owned a dachshund, on whose account she felt
concerned and diffident, for, 'He has inflammation of the lungs,'
she said; 'his cough is terrible!'

It rained. By the electric stove, Baby played chess with the
bank clerk, whose holiday was up and who that night was going
back to Vienna. During lunch, when Baby had anxiously eyed
him, he had talked to the table at large, explaining how the new
divorce law was operating in Vienna—he talked of divorce,
while she wanted to be united to him for the rest of existence!
She had better, now that time was getting short, try and talk to

him—difficult though it was—in French. What had she better say to him? How draw him? How tell him? She thought hard.

'Do you ski in Austria with a horse?' she asked at last.

He did not understand.

The rain poured down straightly and beautifully, shooting through those myriad trees on the mountain sides. The bank clerk saw in Frank his natural successor, and hated him. The company constrained him.

But a quarter of an hour before he was driven down to the station in the little red car, they ran away hand in hand into the Schloss park, and came back dripping with wet. She stood at the window and waved to him shyly: 'Good-bye,' as the little red motor buzzed off.

Good-bye! Good-bye!

How grey, how monotonous mountain scenery looked in the rain! 'Well, Baby, how do you like this place?'

She turned round and looked absently at Frank. She loved it, but complained that there were fleas in her bed. Frau Kogl, to whom the complaint was made, said that it was '*ausgeschlossen*'—quite out of the question. '*Das gibt es nicht*'—it isn't done. But the 'boots' with the green apron was philosophical. Fleas—well, what about it? They existed. There were fleas in the carpet—fleas everywhere—between bedclothes—in a word, in nature. Fleas, he implied, were in the scheme of things. God had so ordained it. The 'boots'' attitude, like that of the modern philosophers, was one of acceptance; he accepted all evil and all good in life with equal grace. Herr Kogl ordered him to go to the chemist and buy a preparation notoriously fatal to fleas, and the 'boots' came back carefully carrying a small bottle, in whose efficacy he did not believe.

At dinner, Frank found himself seated among a group of German tourists. Herr Nikulitsch, despite his Czech name, was a German—corpulent, spectacled, with a large, square, short-cropped blond head; in fact so typical a German that had he had the luck to be in England between the years 1914 and 1918 he would have been arrested without provocation. His wife had eyes which were so queerly adjusted that when she talked to you she seemed to be looking at someone else. Frank was faced by this cow of a woman who could only understand the German point of view about the war; and two Scottish old maids who could only understand the British point of view about the war; neither of whom could understand the other. The Scottish old maids complained derisively about the *Kalter Aufschnitt*: 'The idea of giving you cheese without biscuits! Ha!' They shook their heads and smiled malignantly. They marvelled at these 'foreigners'! The more they saw of them, the more they marvelled!

'The Germans,' said Frau Nikulitsch, 'are good people. We are good people at heart. Anyone of goodwill will admit that we are good people. But the French are a nation of sadists.'

'Yes,' said the Frau Pastor, 'we are a thoroughly good people, devoid of all guile. We haven't an ungracious thought.'

Baby listened politely. It was not what she had read in the *Daily Mail*. 'Tricking Huns. Once a German, always a German. Blond beasts,' were phrases that occurred to her. Frank was talking to the Frau Pastor now, and because he wanted to be sympathetic, and to show off his own broad-mindedness and the tolerant, liberal spirit of his countrymen, he told her, with a smile (as if making light of it), that our own royalty was mostly German; and he felt that it was strange that she thought nothing of it, a little churlish of her even—it was as though she made light of his kindness and that of his countrymen who bore this alien taint with good grace. The Frau Pastor seemed to think England was rather lucky.

And why, she asked, was England supporting the Russian claim to Eastern Prussia, and simultaneously supporting the Finnish claim to Northern Russia?

It was, said Frank, in pursuance of an ideal to keep alive the feeble flame of patriotism in the face of a growing international revolution. Men were losing interest in their countries, so you had to tread on their toes to keep up their national pride.

'And the English,' said the Frau Pastor (living up to the ideal), 'behaved worst of all in the last war.'

Frank thought of showing her a 1920 copy of the *Daily Mail* (Continental edition), in which was set forth what Poincaré thought of the German evasion of the Allied (just) demand for reparations. The extremity of the shock brought him back to sanity. When he listened to one German after another who told him that if Germany had been arming it was because the

Entente Cordiale was stifling them by a tightening ring of alliances (to whom he had said that if the Entente Cordiale was stifling them by a tightening ring of alliances it was because Germany had been arming), who were convinced that we had started the war as we were convinced that they had done so, the thought struck him: 'Of course they must be convinced. When A is roused to a pitch where he will do B in, and take the risk of being done in by B in the doing, he is sincere in believing B to be in the wrong. This is the shady side of faith.' Frank looked to the Pastor to display some soothing impartiality, and gave him a lead. 'All nations are very much alike and equally unjust to foreigners,' Frank said. But to all such overtures the Pastor, who thought the world was all right, the church all right, and nothing wanted changing, replied: 'We Germans are well known to be over-indulgent to foreigners. Germany is too idealistic a people.'

'Patriotism,' said Frank, 'is like wine—a good thing when you haven't had too much of it.'

'You don't understand,' said the Frau Pastor. 'Only a German can understand what we feel about these things, only a German who has gone through what we have gone through and who knows what we know.'

There is a limit to an intelligent person's enjoyment of the irony of being regarded as an imbecile by fools. And it is soon reached. A new war was starting before the discords of the old have had time to resolve themselves, and, identifying a nation of sixty million people with the two who had displeased him, Frank felt that they deserved it and hoped that they would be beaten!

'And what ridiculous names these foreigners have!' remarked one of the Scottish old maids, when the Germans had left the table. 'That Viennese lady opposite—Frau von Endte! I don't know much German, but I know that much: that Ente means duck! It's as if she called herself: "Mrs. de Ducke!" '

Frank strolled away into the hills. The night was calm and benignant; the stars whispered; and all this rocky waste listened, moonlit and silent, to God. At every corner, a crucifix. Green lights and blue lights and red lights illumining the twisted naked body of Christ, with red blood flowing from the wounds. Yet, curiously enough, Christ's message had not been understood, he thought; and looking back at the bloody centuries which had followed on the crucifixion and at Christ's tortured body, so shamelessly paraded, Frank asked himself: had we Christians not perhaps mistaken the meaning, inferring all along that it was blood-letting that He meant and advocated to us. On consideration, Frank thought the world was well ripe for destruction.

Above and beyond, what peace! All desire abated, in the soft ablution of the moon. O Lust, where is thy sting, and Satiety thy victory?

A figure in the dark. 'Hello, is that you? Oh, Frau König! All my homages.'

Frau König, with a preoccupied air, took him down the mountain track into the thicket, the while saying: 'I don't deny. I don't deny how hard it is for a woman who has contracted certain habits in marriage suddenly to find herself without a man. Well, here I am. Here I am, I say! Here I am; you may have what you wish. But my condition'—she touched his wrist—'is that you are to take me out into society.'

'I do not wish it. I mean I do not wish what you wish me to wish. You make me feel good, Frau König, and that's the truth.'

'I do not understand you. I have gone as far as I can.'

'That's the truth. Do not go further.'

'But——'

How could he explain? How could he tell her that where unattractive women were concerned he was a prude and a puritan? For all morality, if we examine it more closely, is founded on aversion. It pleased him to recall to her an ideal of womanhood which she was in no mood to follow; of reticence and chastity, which he counselled her to practise. 'Not in abandon, but in restraint and self-discipline, Frau König,' he said, leading her out of the thicket into the open road, 'lies the hope of a sane and healthy mankind.'

'If,' she said, 'my fiancé does not come soon, I shall go mad.'

As they turned into the *pension* courtyard, they passed the apoplectic Baron's bungalow, who peeped through the window and, though it was evening, wished them: 'Good morning.' The Baron's knowledge of English must have been very slight, because every time Frank passed him in the morning, the Baron touched his cap and said: 'Good evening.' In the big barn, an

automatic barrel organ played excruciating music, and Herr
Kogl explained that it had been a first-class barrel organ till the
Italians—a nation, as all knew, of organ-grinders—spoilt it during their military occupation of the town by over-taxing its
musical capacity.

'How very inconsiderate!'

Several couples were dancing. Herbert, removing his waistcoat,
danced in his braces and shirt sleeves with Lina, the bare-legged
scullery maid, at a considerably accelerated pace, as if to show
them all what he could do. 'Our Herbert,' Herr Kogl pointed with
his chin towards him, 'once he starts dancing, outstrips them all.'
Frank stood and watched till it would be time for Lina to go up
to bed. Heavens of ecstasy, oceans of rapture awaited him. The
Kogls sat there as always: Herr Kogl; Herr Spatz, a fat, rough man
of the same proportions as the host himself; the policeman; the
policeman's wife, who was a waitress; and drank wine. The
policeman's little boy slipped in and out between their legs and
ran about all day long, and they christened him 'Quick-silver.'
Herr Kogl alone did not drink. The cook, a bewildered-looking
old woman, who was never seen about during the week, drank,
after good takings, on a Sunday night with Frau Kogl. Herr Kogl
watched them drink, but refused to participate. His maudlin eyes
were fixed on the dog, to whom he would talk for hours at a
stretch: 'Rags, you wretch! Rags, you immoral little bitch!'

'Nice old doggie, what?' Frau Kogl would remark.

Herr Kogl would shake his head. 'It's not a dog—*kein Hund,
sondern ein Skandal!*'

The dog was very old, toothless, and refused all food but
chocolate. The Frau Wachmann, the policeman's wife, a young
shrew, shouted and cursed at her husband, a shy, middle-aged,
upright man, because he would not at once go to bed with her,
but preferred of a Sunday evening to play cards with the others.
Herr Spatz thundered forth as he played: 'Two aces! Bang! Ha-a-a!—
Queen of Clubs! Bang! Bang!' with his fist, so that all the glasses
on the table jingled nervously. He had once spent nine months
in Turkey, and he looked, with his clean-shaven head and his
mouthful of glittering white teeth, himself like a Turk, and
behaved like one, or at least, as you would imagine 'The Turk' to
behave in his more lustful moments. Frau Kogl, drunk,

attempted to sing, but it came out very badly and dismally, and she stopped, ashamed of herself.

'To hell with Czecho-Slovakia!' Herr Spatz was saying to a relative who, thanks to the Treaty of Versailles, had become Czecho-Slovakian and now said he was proud of the great country. 'Great country!' roared Herr Spatz. 'I've lived nine months in Turkey: who can talk Czecho-Slovakian there? Answer me that!'

'Who will drive the van to town to-morrow morning, that is what I wish to know?' Herr Kogl interjected.

'Willi.'

'Hm!—Hm!' distrustfully from Herr Kogl.

'Why?' from Herr Spatz, whose son Willi happened to be.

Herr Kogl looked on the ground. 'Willi! Willi is not Herbert, that's why!'

At long last the clock on the Schloss tower struck half-past ten, and Herr Kogl was locking up. Frank paced his room up and down; every moment the door might open and Lina come in, and then——

From time to time, unable to stand the suspense, he would go out and wait for her in the corridor. Simultaneously, the door opposite would open, and the Pastor and Frau Pastor peep out, again and again, as if to put out their boots: but surely, Frank thought, they could not have so many boots to put out. Then, as he stood in the corridor, the adjacent door opened, and the Frau Professor peeped out to ask if her dachshund's coughing had not, perchance, disturbed his sleep. 'He has acute inflammation of the lungs,' she said, 'and I am very anxious to know what the specialist will say to-morrow morning.'

'I am very sorry,' Frank said, 'for you both.' And while he stood there assuring Frau Professor Koch of his complete sympathy, and the Frau Pastor peeped out of her room to put out another pair of boots, the bare-legged Lina slipped into his room.

He forgot everything, looked at her intently, grasped her eagerly, savagely, asked: 'Yes?'

'Why?' she parried.

'Because.'

'Because what?'

'Because—because we're young, and because life isn't for ever.'
She bent her look and was silent.

'Yes?'

'Yes.'

She had said it so quietly and convincingly that his soul was devastated by certitude. He was as certain of his reward as one is certain of money placed to the credit of one's current account, once receipt of it has been acknowledged by the bank. It would take place all right. It was indeed as though it had already taken place; and she seemed to him like some tedious acquaintance; he asked her tedious questions and, asking them, had not the patience to concentrate upon her tedious replies. 'Are both your parents alive?'

'Yes, both my parents are alive.'

'Have you any brothers or sisters?'

'Yes, two sisters and one brother.'

From outside came the sound of tears and choking. 'I suppose,' said Frank, 'that is the policeman's wife, by the sound of it.'

'No, it's he—the policeman.'

'What! Sobbing like that? Why?'

'She curses him dreadfully: that's why. It's the same every Sunday night because she wants him to go to bed, whereas he, poor chap, wants to sit out with the others and play cards. He's an upright, decent, quiet man; it's a shame the life she leads him!'

It did not interest him. The wind that bellied out his sails had suddenly ceased, and his soul flopped down like a flag on a flagstaff. He, she, and the world, seemed as flat as a pancake—as flat and as unprofitable.

'You—you—you!' she gasped. In this 'you' was all her being, her illusory love, her reunion with him, the dissolution, the loss of her 'I' in his 'you.' But he thought he had squeezed her leg and said: 'I beg your pardon? Did you say anything?'

She shook her head.

'That's all right, then.'

She had begun to look forward, and he went to sleep at once. She waited awhile, scanning his face with hatred. Then shook him by the shoulder. 'You *ninny!*' Then dressed herself and went out.

She was gone. Presently he sat up on the edge of the bed, his naked feet dangling down like a pendulum. He was drunk. It was significant that he was both spiritually and physically drunk at the same time, and he had just sufficient reason left him to comprehend and thoroughly appreciate the humour of this interesting coincidence.

Next morning he was woken by the conversation in the yard below his window. 'You were born in eighteen sixty-four, Herr Baron; I was born in eighteen sixty-six. I take it that I am two years younger than you—yes!'

'Kh-kh-khrr-rrr-khrrr!'

'Kh-kh-kh-khr-khrrr!'

'The Herr Baron complains to me that he is damned and done for, mattering as he is all over. But I say, *aber wo*! Herr Baron: what does it matter if you matter in a world of matter: it is all matter—spirit, flesh and all! Oh, yes!'

The Baron now was telling Herr Kogl of a brother who lived in Vienna and was professor of modern languages at Vienna University; and Herr Kogl at once retorted: 'My son lives in Bizirk IX and has to go to his studies in Bizirk V.'

'What does he do?'

'Studies at the Institute.'

'What institute?'

'The Hotel and Restaurant Institute. Why, Herbert can do any-thing!—Drive a car—stick a pig—wait at table. Wonderful boy! This—all this—is to be his. Ah! he will go a long way, our Herbert will, he will, when he finishes his studies at the Institute. And I intend to send him abroad for a year or two to pick up foreign languages, so that he secures all the benefit that we old folks can afford to give him.'

'Of course. Why not?' said the Baron, 'if you have the money to give him.'

'Ah, no!' exclaimed Herr Kogl. 'He must earn the money himself. I don't believe in extravagance, Herr Baron. "No," I tell Herbert: "you go abroad to France and England and serve your time there in the big hotels and earn every penny yourself as a waiter." That's the way to bring them up——youth,' he added tenderly.

He looked at his wife, who was coming down the steps towards him. Here was this woman with all her money and property; he came along and made it his, and gave her a son and made it his son's: more than ever his own. 'I was telling the Herr Baron,' he said, 'how when Herbert finishes his studies at the Institute and has been abroad in France and England he will, on coming back, devote himself to the development of the *pension* and alpine tourism generally by making use of the ties and influence he has established in France and England. Oh, yes!'

'That's all right,' said the old woman, 'but what are we to do about Herr Dickin? All the ladies are leaving. I don't know what to do. He will have to go, that's all.'

'He—is a—good—man,' Herr Kogl replied.

'What are we to do?'

Herr Kogl did not reply.

'Come on!' she cried. 'Don't stand there like a———'

'Shut up, will you!' he shouted formidably, and banged his fist on the table.

She quailed before the man with the strong will.

'I never bother; it is none of my business,' Frau Kogl began as Frank came downstairs. 'I attend to my own job and what with the prices of everything going up, I've got my work cut out. Meat, as you know, has gone up twenty per cent; vegetables, too. Fish is not to be had. To me it is all the same, you understand; I never bother about what other people do.' Her hands shot out awkwardly. In that gesture was all her weary dissatisfaction with people who make bother. 'I don't mind what you do upstairs. But I can't lose all my clients, you understand. The season is a slack one, and where will I get other guests? Meat, as I say, has gone up; vegetables gone up. Fish is not to be had in the neighbourhood, and they are all complaining now about you. But what can I do?' She shot out her hands. She must have acquired these gestures in the French convent in Alsace where she had been put by her mother.

And, indeed, there was trouble ahead. Lina's entry had been observed. The Frau Pastor had communicated it to the Frau Doktor Wirt, and the Frau Doktor Wirt, with the confirmation of the Frau Professor Koch, to the Frau Direktor Bödingen and Frau Nikulitsch, and the Frau Direktor Bödingen to the Frau Oberst von Kaisar, who complained to Frau von Endte. A commotion had been caused. Frank was suspect. Two elderly German women locked their doors at his approach and accused him of having tried to force his way into their bedrooms. When all complained and armed themselves against her, Frau Kogl could not decide. She scratched her head pensively. 'Yes,' she said, 'yes, I don't know what to do.' She looked old and ill with worry; even her housemaid's knee had taken a turn for the worse. 'I am afraid we must ask you to go.'

'With regret,' added Herr Kogl.

As for Lina, Herr Kogl made short shift of her. He merely bawled at her: 'Out you go, you slut!'

'If,' Frank reflected, 'I can't be anything better, let me at least be a hero.'

The little red car was prepared for him, and he got Lina to make a bundle of her things and get inside with him. It was a desultory morning and rain fell perfunctorily. 'You ugly young thing!' he thought, surveying her from his seat in the corner, as the car turned out of the courtyard past the Baron's bungalow (who peeped out of his window and, touching his cap, said 'Good evening!'), 'what the deuce am I to do with you now?'

'What sort of wage did you get?' he asked aloud.

She told him; and, on taking thought, he decided to run her down to his old friend Frau von Kestner; who afterwards wrote to him:

'I have ordered her to put on a longer skirt and wear stockings. She was embarrassing the postman each time he called with letters, as well as the policeman in the square. Now, I need hardly say, nobody takes any notice of her, because she really is not one little bit pretty.'

38

Tod Und Genesung

The tall lighted building, the abode of the *Daily*, the *Sunday*, the *Monday*, the *Evening*, the *Midday*, the *Pictorial* and the *Illustrated Runner*, loomed in the fog. Lord de Jones looked up from the pavement at the large lighted windows over the roof; behind which, he knew, the big spider sat in the midst of his web; and

Lord de Jones, entering, by appointment, did indeed feel as a fly
might feel if it had an appointment with a great big spider who
had expressed in unmistakable terms the wish to speak to it. He
went up in the historic lift and, arrived at the top, was ushered
into the presence of Lord Ottercove.

'Now where is that crop?' asked Lord Ottercove, without
greeting the visitor.

'Under the sod, I expect,' retorted de Jones.

'This mission of yours has cost me thousands in sealing-wax
alone to enable you to seal up all the craters. Stationers have
made fortunes out of me! And there is not a blade of grass anywhere; in fact, the termination of our mission has synchronized
with an unprecedented famine in Russia. And, damn them,
they're blaming me for it!'

'There is always a famine in Russia at one time or another
through causes, as is invariably urged, not connected with the
political faith of the government of the day.'

Lord Ottercove ignored this retort. 'The Foreign Secretary is
ringing me up all day long, and I refuse to see him; refuse to see
him, Chris, for, quite frankly, I wouldn't know what to say to
him. All that sealing-wax—and nothing to show for it. Shame!'

Lord Ottercove walked over to the sideboard and poured
himself some Perrier water into a glass. 'And there's that other
fellow,' he said, drinking.

'I know, the Prime Minister.'

'Yes. Joe's shouting himself hoarse about the bursting granaries,
the wheat springing up all over the globe—increased crop—the
end of international jealousies—the economic solution of
national rivalries! And you with all your untried genius cannot
raise a blade of grass anywhere to substantiate his speeches. He has
to rely on the dog stunt entirely, which, I frankly tell you so—is
not good enough. It's not good enough, Chris. Read this.'

Lord Ottercove handed him a copy of the *Evening Ensign*
containing the report of Lord Balfour's speech at the Carlton
Club, the burden of which was that the election in which the
Conservatives were defeated had been fought on an unreal issue,
against the advice of the experienced members of the party.

'An unreal issue, he says!' exclaimed Lord Ottercove.

'No more unreal than Gladstone's Turk.'

'An unreal issue! They've realized it at last and have decided to leave the dog stunt out of their party programme, and they are already winning all the by-elections, and we've not a friend anywhere except among sealing-wax manufacturers.'

'I'm sorry to hear it, Rex.'

'Now, I believe in Joe. He is my friend, and if a man is my friend I'll stick to him through thick and thin. But he must have increased crop if he is to go on shouting about it, and he's shouted about it so much that he can't go back on it now. You promised us two blades of grass to every one. Where are they? Where *are* they, I ask?' He looked at his visitor with the unrestrained ill-humour of a man who, being completely accustomed to things going well with him, suddenly discovers that they are going badly. 'You make my papers look ridiculous.'

'I'm sorry. I will make amends—look into the matter—enquire. It may be that the sealing-wax is defective. I promise to do what I can, Rex.'

'Promises! To hell with promises! It's meat we want. Meat, not promises!'

'True, we want meat. But all we can give you is cats' meat. Indeed, that is all you have ever had in the past.'

'Enough of your cynicism, Chris.'

'Now let me tell you, Rex, that I don't care two tuppenny damns about your crop. What I care about is the world. And that is no more.'

Lord Ottercove rose and leaned heavily first on one leg, then on the other. 'It's still there, Chris,' he said.

'Only for a week. I've disintegrated the atom.'

'Well?'

'Which means that all other atoms, at first slowly, then faster and faster, will follow suit, till not a rack is left behind.'

'The cloud-capped towers, the gorgeous palaces, the solemn temples, the great globe itself?'

'Yea, all which it inherit shall dissolve and, like this insubstantial pageant faded, leave not a rack behind. We are such stuff——'

'I know: as dreams are made on, and our little life is rounded with a sleep.' He turned away and bit his lip. 'Chris, I am vexed: bear with my weakness; my first-class brain is troubled. Be not disturbed with my infirmity. If you be pleased, retire to that sofa and there repose: a turn or two I'll walk, to still my beating mind.'

'I wish you peace.'

When he came back Lord Ottercove's face looked eager with hope. 'I don't believe you, Chris. You say you've done it?'

'A week ago. In Greece.'

'My Athens correspondent is silent about the matter.'

'Inevitably. He has disintegrated.'

'There is no sign of panic anywhere.'

'There is no panic because there is no way to communicate panic. No sound, no sight: a whole area vanishes invisibly, ceases to be there.'

'But what of the people in the adjoining area? Why don't they communicate or run away?'

'The people next to those just vanished, vanish next. They do not know that anything has vanished till they themselves vanish.'

'I see. It's a knowledge which is vouchsafed you at vanishing-point, so to speak.'

'Exactly.'

'But they must know if they find that a familiar house or square has vanished.'

'No: if it is not where they expect to find it, they naturally suppose that they are in error: that what they are looking for is probably round the other corner.'

'H'm, I see.'

There was a pause.

'Well, what have you to say, Rex?'

'Chris: I advise you against it.'

'Too late, too late! The world is fast unravelling, like a laddered silk stocking.'

'Shame! And quite a new world, barely 200,000,000 years old. It will do you no good, Chris.'

'If an employee of yours, Rex, came to ask you for a rise, I verily believe you would not say No, but: "I advise you against your suggesting the idea to me." And should he ask for a reason, you'd say: "I don't think it would do you any good." '

'I don't think this will. I don't think it will do any of us any good. Disintegrate. Ha! What an idea!'

'Why?'

'Well, look here, Chris, do you think it's considerate? Do you think it's altogether kind?'

'It's the very milk of human kindness to spare us all the horrors of this new war. You, Rex, must see this, for you are good at heart.'

'Yes. I want, Chris, to do good. There is no greater pleasure in the world than doing good. If you destroy the world, I wouldn't be able to go on doing good, now would I?'

'That, I admit, is hard on you.'

'It's hard on us both, Chris. I wouldn't be able to *do* good, and you wouldn't be able to *make* good. You would remain for ever a Genius of the Untried.'

'What! now that I *have* tried and succeeded?'

'I follow your argument. But believe me, Chris, it's defective. To destroy the world is not what I might call constructive work. I am rather tempted, if you follow my line of thought, to relegate it to the category of the destructive. It's negative, Chris. That's the word: negative.'

'Negative? Why, it's positively destroying itself with a vengeance, bolting away into nothing, overjoyed at the chance of release, bubbling over with sheer *joie de vivre!*'

'H'm.'

'And can you wonder? For millions of years the atom has been kept in harness. Round himself and round others like him, he was made to jump without cease or sense, as if to bite off his own tail. He hasn't known a holiday since the world began. And what was it all for? To convince crass fools that matter was solid!'

'Since you came in this evening, Chris, everything seems less solid.'

'Glad you are beginning to see light. I am looking forward to the time, which is not distant, when what now serves, inadequately, to distinguish the outward form of Baron Ottercove will be converted into the purest radiation. All matter, Rex, is a disease. It *is* "matter." When pools stagnate, or tissues decay, life springs to the surface, a pestilential vermin. It's a hitch somewhere in the atomic mechanism of the universe, a clotting of the blood, an imperfect interplay of atoms in the cosmic body which creates this fretting disease we call life. In the healthy regions of the universe the atoms change their make-up millions of times in a second and so are for ever dissociated and incapable of association and cannot degenerate into a condition in which decay breeds life.

Unscientific people or unimaginative scientists would say that what I have done is to "explode" the atom. Nonsense! Even "disintegrated" is hardly the word for it, for it is apt to mislead us on a vital point. What I've done is no more than what a watch-maker might do to a clock which has got clogged and is losing time: I've speeded up its electrons to the pitch at which the degenerated matter we call life regenerates itself into radiation and, for us, ceases to be. A mere question of revolution.'

'Revolution!' cried Lord Ottercove. 'I thought as much. You've let him loose, the atom! Relinquished your hold on him, when your betters were on the point of harnessing him to do all the world's labour.' Lord Ottercove suddenly jumped to his feet, a flush of anger suffusing his cheeks. 'Stop him, man!' he yelled. 'Stop him, quick!'

'Can't catch him now.'

'Run!' Lord Ottercove ran and opened the door.

'You'd need a greyhound to catch him: he has galloped off into not-being.'

'What's that?'

'Death.'

'Sheer idleness!' said Lord Ottercove. 'At a time when servants are scarce; when the human labourer has downed tools; when inertia like some horrible disease has laid low the human race; when all our hope was in the atom, you've released him, let him go to whirl senselessly in the void!'

'Far from it. There they have to dash round like fury to main-tain a high standard of death. For the moment they slacken their speed, sickness sets in and life.'

'That,' said Lord Ottercove, 'might frighten the bird-livered neurotics who are sick of life. I am sick with the healthy fear of death. I am all for keeping the atom in his place. All this talk of Beyond, a Future Life for the Atom—tell this to Sir Arthur Conan Doyle or to Sir Oliver Lodge, don't tell it to me! Sheer sabotage! Allow one atom to strike, and all the rest will follow suit. It's not fair to the public. Next thing they'll want the dole. The country, Chris—I mean the world—will not stand for it.'

'It's not work, Rex, but unhealthy conditions of work that the atoms object to in life. Over there they work harder and quicker, yet freely and joyfully, that we may all remain in the balmed and blessed state of death.'

'I see. The struggle for non-existence.'

'Exactly.'

'You are, I take it, a sort of Official Receiver winding up the affairs of the visible world.'

'No, a doctor who has released the circulation of the world which these many centuries have clogged at our end: and the patient is speedily recovering. When you and I and other sufferers cease to be, it will mean that the patient is once again in the pink of condition. By healing one atom I have healed the wound of the world.'

'Who are the wound?'

'All that which feels.'

'I feel the coming death, feel it deeply and painfully, Chris.'

'You must not feel: you must dry up.'

'Dry up yourself!' said Ottercove, ruffled.

'We're mere boils and pimples, Rex, who feel the hurt. When I have nursed the universe back to death, none of us shall feel any more.' De Jones was muttering something.

' What's that?' asked Ottercove.

'Just words. A German title has suggested itself to me as a caption for what I mean— "*Tod und Genesung*," which, in our own rotten tongue, might be translated into "Death and Recovery." Shakespeare says:

> ' "*My long sickness*
> *Of health and living now begins to mend,*
> *And nothing brings me all things.*" '

'Come, Chris. Don't make us all look asses in the eyes of your Maker.'

'Asses?'

'Asses.'

'I'm going,' said de Jones, 'not to my Maker—no: he is an usurper—but to my Unmaker! He is the true God.'

Lord Ottercove sat down dejectedly and stretched out his legs by the electric radiator. 'The world,' he began, 'is a heritage which has been committed into our keeping. It was not, I take it, put there to be unmade at will. It is not ours, Chris, to dispose of.'

'Oh, isn't it?'

'It isn't, Chris.'

'Whose is it, then?'

'Well, a considerable portion of it, measured in terms of property and money, happens to be mine.'

'Ah!'

'You smile at my alleged materialism. Unnecessarily, Chris! For it is only in the banks and company offices that this wealth—and it is much—is recorded in my name. I hold it as if it were in custody for...Providence (call it the Deity, Fate, Destiny, the Supreme Being, or the First Cause). We are but the stewards, the servants, as in the Parable of the Talents, from whom account of stewardship will be exacted by the master. I have increased my five talents by... I can't tell you how much. As for you, Chris, you've absconded with the one talent entrusted to you. Which is worse than in the parable. You wonder at my prosperity. It's faith, Chris, faith. Faith in money. "For unto every one that hath shall be given, and he shall have abundance: but from him that hath not shall be taken away even that which he hath." Wish I was a preacher, like my father. I'd be the Archbishop of Canterbury now. For I like the sound of my own voice. The first condition of good preaching, Chris.' Lord Ottercove sat still, wrapped in thought.

Then he roused himself from his reverie. 'Chris,' he said, 'how much do you want for it?'

'What for?'

'The visible world. I will buy it from you at your own price.'

'Do you care for it so much?'

'Not a damn!'

'What do you want it for?'

'For my friend Vernon Sprott. Like Gautier, he is one for whom the visible world exists. I take it that you could ensure its existence.'

'I might. I don't know.'

'How, Chris?'

'By reversing the process. By crippling the mechanism of the atom and reducing the electronic revolutions to a condition of slow decay in which alone life for us is possible.'

'Name your price.'

De Jones considered. 'It will be,' he said in the tone of a solicitor calculating costs, 'including all dues and charges, eighty million pounds sterling. Guineas, I mean.'

'Nothing doing. Good-bye to you.'

Lord de Jones turned round on the threshold. 'What will you do about it, Rex?'

'Have you arrested.'

'On what charge. There is no law against introducing the Kingdom of God into this country.'

'Sedition. Instigation of atoms to mutiny. Under Dora.'

'But why, Rex? Tell me why.'

Lord Ottercove was a long time in replying.

'I will not have humanity let down,' he said at last.

'You and your humanity!' Anger had made de Jones inarticulate. 'Running your secretaries off their feet. Putting the fear of God into your butlers. That last man you had has taken to drink, and is now in the last stage of *delirium tremens*. Gilbert has developed the St. Vitus' dance, waiting on you and your follies. What respect have you ever shown to the atom? When you look at a man you make all the atoms in him jump the wrong way. Then about this war. You've gone right back on your pacific scheme. Oh, these business brains! Oh, these strong, silent men! Curse and damn your breed!'

Lord Ottercove had walked over to the sideboard and was pouring himself some Perrier water into a glass. 'When you have done, please tell me,' he said, drinking.

De Jones was foaming at the mouth. 'You and your confrère across the road—newspaper proprietors! Bags of money! That's all you are!'

'And you're an empty bag of money!'

'Give the public what it wants. That's your line—the line of least resistance. But to write regeneratively is beyond your scope.'

'Regenerative degenerates!' bawled Ottercove. He bawled so loud that Gilbert came in to ask if his lordship wanted anything.

'Nothing from you.'

'Yes, m'lord.'

'Leave us alone.'

'Yes, m'lord.' Gilbert's eyes danced. His face twitched. His hands trembled.

'Get out! I mean both of you. I've had enough of you all!

Twitching drivelling imbeciles! Atom mongers! Flea trainers!'
Lord Ottercove seized one of the eight chairs placed round the
octagonal table and flung it at Viscount de Jones. When the Editor
of the *Evening Ensign* came in a moment later, Lord Ottercove
flung the second chair at him. Outside his door a queue of
secretaries, marshalled by Mrs. Hannibal and each nervously
scanning at her file of papers, awaited the Chief's summons.
Time was when Mrs. Hannibal alone centralized all Lord
Ottercove's activities. The traffic proved too much for a single
channel, and was accordingly decentralized, carried by a dozen
streams. A dozen secretarial maidens were always in attendance
in the anteroom, waiting for the signal to appear before the
Chief, who shouted from his chair: 'Forward, Miss Davis!' and
hurried her: 'Come on, come on!' And Miss Davis reported in a
flutter: 'We purchased sixteen bottles of Apollinaris, of which
you drank three; that leaves us thirteen.'

'Carry them forward. Forward, Miss Badmington!'

'The franc account shows a balance of seven francs, which I have
changed into pounds at the rate of one hundred and twenty-six
francs to the pound, making a total of one shilling and threepence.'

'Forward, Miss Harrison!' And so forth.

And now as they appeared in the doorway, Lord Ottercove
flung a chair at them, and they retired in disorder. This left him
with five chairs, including the one he was sitting on. He flung
the fourth chair at a literary aspirant whose dream was to contribute humorous articles to the *Daily Runner*, and the fifth chair
at a lady who wished to sell him tickets for a charity concert at
the Albert Hall, and having flung the sixth and the seventh chair
at some nondescripts who peeped through the door to see what
was happening, he remained seated in the eighth and only chair
in the room. Mrs. Hannibal came in with a fearless smile on her
face, the practised smile of a lion trainer whose first rule is to show
no fear of the lion for fear of encouraging the lion to behave in
a manner compatible with his nature.

Lord Ottercove looked at her affectionately. 'Do you admire
my moderation?'

She admired him, and this physical symbolism of his political
power, and the sincerity of his self-expression, and his freedom
from sham convention.

Lord Ottercove seized the receiver—Mrs. Hannibal thought, to speak to Scotland Yard. She was wrong. Lord Ottercove was telephoning to his editors. Here was real news! The end of all things: something not to be missed.

News, he thought, such as Lord Northcliffe would have appreciated at its true value! There was no jealousy in Lord Ottercove. He admired Lord Northcliffe, and though secretly he thought he himself had no peers among living newspaper proprietors, he suffered from an inferiority complex in the presence of Lord Beaverbrook. And so he was glad of the exclusive news. In the beginning there was the Word. And in the end, too. He was proud that it befell to the *Daily Runner* to write the Omega. 'I, Baron Ottercove of Ottercove hereby announce the end of the world.'

His principal editor, he was informed, was dining out. 'As ever! Just like him!' he muttered. 'Dining, while the paper—not to say the world—can go to hell.' For some minutes he sat alone in his vast roof office, full of a strange wonder at the imminence of the fate which confronted mankind. At last he had to believe it. He sat very still, while below the printing presses, with accustomed celerity, manufactured the tidings. Then a sudden foreboding overcame him. It was not so much that he feared the end for himself and his race: it was the uncertainty of it that gnawed at his nerves. The uncertainty of when and under what circumstances he might disintegrate. He stood by the enormous window with a wide view of London roofs, including that of St. Paul's, and sadness filled his soul. An indescribable sorrow for all mankind descended upon him. But as the minutes passed, the need for action braced his nerves. Hatless, he stepped into the lift, and passing the solitary commissionaire, dashed into the busy streets.

39

Where he went, he did not know. He walked on and on, his straggling hair blown by the wind, and feeling a little like King Lear on the heath, till, cutting across the Park to the Marble Arch, several open-air meetings beckoned to him as a sign and a portent.

Two hostile meetings, of Free Thinkers and devout Christians, were held side by side, the speakers abusing each other at intervals, as though, Lord Ottercove thought, God and the Day were not in sight! The Christian protagonist, pointing at the blackboard on which a hen and an egg had been sketched by him, questioned his audience: 'They talk of science, but what do they know? Can any of them tell me—can any of you here tell me who came first? The hen or the egg? Did the hen first make the egg, or did the egg first make the hen? Now, then, can any one here tell me, I ask ye? Can any of the science students tell me? Ye can't? Well, *I* can tell yer!—God made them both!' And he looked round triumphantly.

'They tell us—these Christian fellows,' shouted the Free Thinker, 'that Adam and Eve was sent to 'ell because Eve 'ad eaten an apple. Now here is an apple.' He held up an apple for all to see. 'Now, Ladies and Gentlemen, I ask ye: What is there in an apple? 'Ere! *And yet they tell us*—the Bible tells us—that Adam and Eve was sent to 'ell 'cause Eve'd eaten an apple! Now I ask ye, Ladies and Gentlemen, can ye believe such a silly thing?'

'Free Thinkers!' shouted the Christian protagonist, pointing derisively at his antagonist not five yards away. 'Free Thinkers!—Free *Stinkers* I call them!'

'Because they'd eaten an apple. Now here! Just look at it. Look at it! What is there, I ask, in an apple? And yet they tell us——'

Suddenly the wish to impart to this large gaping audience the momentous message came over Ottercove. It was the end of the visible world. In a few hours, perhaps in a few moments—at most in a week—they would have to face the Judgment. It was for him to break the news. What consolation had he to offer them? Call on their national pride in facing disaster calmly and stoically? Recall the serene joys of eternity? Dwell on the ultimate mercy of God? Or prophesy that there would be much weeping and gnashing of teeth?

Biblical language came readily to his lips: Lord Ottercove, though few knew it, was the greatest living authority on biblical texts. He knew the Bible from cover to cover and backwards: indeed, he could, at a pinch, recite it by heart under an anaesthetic.

'What does it profit a man,' he began in a loud robust voice, the crowds gathering round him, 'if he gain the whole world' (he paused as if to prolong the tension of the 'poser'; then added quietly): 'and lose his own soul? And why should it sadden a man if he lose the whole world' (Lord Ottercove paused), 'never having gained it?' He had the pleasurable sensation of discovering (alas, as the world was about to let him down) that he had the gift of a preacher and prophet, a gift that could hold and sway multitudes. 'Before I came here,' he went on, 'I sat in the dim light of my study, and I dreamed and meditated by the fire; and there came one of the seven angels, and he carried me away in the spirit to a great and high mountain and showed me that great city, the holy Jerusalem, descending out of heaven from God, having the glory of God, and her light was like unto a stone most precious, even'——Lord Ottercove stopped as if seeking the *mot juste*——'like a jasper stone,' he said, 'clear as crystal.'

The audience was writhing with excitement, but he stopped them with a movement of his hand, leaning forward over the stand and speaking almost in a whisper: 'And I saw a new heaven and a new earth: for the first heaven and the first earth were passed away; and there was no more sea.'

Once indeed he was taken aback by an interpellation: 'Why the dickens didn't you stop the man, man?' yelled a dingy figure from the crowd, when he had spoken of the adventist-scientist.

'He wouldn't stop!' returned Lord Ottercove. There was indeed no sort of good in stopping him, he hastened to add. Did they not know that an invention or discovery was at no time the monopoly of a single brain? What use indeed having this scientist arrested when his successor, whose hiding-place they could not know, was waiting to spring the mine?

But suddenly, as he spoke, a sort of mental cramp seized upon his brain, and he could not bring himself to utter another word. The harder he tried, the more did thought and words elude him.

He stood gazing at them with what seemed to him an inane smile, but so magnetic, so masterful, was his personality to the people around him that they stood fascinated, with their eyes glued on him, while he gazed back at them, in silence. Three minutes elapsed.

'Come on!' shouted a man from the crowd.

'Sir,' Lord Ottercove turned to him, 'will you be good enough to allow me to complete my prayer?'

At which the interlocutor relapsed into the obscurity whence he had emerged.

'Ladies and gentlemen!' said Lord Ottercove: 'I thank you for your kind attention.'

As he walked home, posters of his own newspapers informed him of the imminent dissolution of our planet. He groaned as he saw them. How bad! How unimaginative! Posters depressed him. Never a day, never an hour but that they would trot out some fresh disaster. A train derailed, liners colliding in the Channel, a steamer run aground in the fog, a bus toppled over, an airman lost in the Atlantic. Disaster, disaster, disaster! 'Disaster mongers!' he called them. How the public must be getting sick of it. Never good news. He'd have to change all that. And, suddenly, he remembered that he could not change it: disaster mongers had for ever triumphed.

At a street corner he bought a newspaper. 'End of the World' meetings, he read, were being held in various parts of London. People began to close their shops, and the excitement increased to such an extent that later troops were called out, and large forces of police appeared at the street corners, and the approach to Downing Street was barricaded, the Prime Minister having refused to receive deputations who, resenting his wait-and-see policy, were eager to compel him to do something *and do it now*. Riots broke out in the East End of London, led by persons of an irreligious disposition, desiring to have a last good run for their money, and men and women were committing suicide and going insane. There was a vast crowd in Trafalgar Square. The Bishop of London, it seemed, was addressing it. 'Nearer my God to Thee, nearer to Thee...' Voices, out of time, and tune, soared to the skies. A score of elderly virgins, earnest, spectacled ladies in white, sang with transport, invoking speedy transportation to

the Seat of Judgment to be first among the Brides of the Lamb.
'A scramble,' thought Ottercove. 'A queue before a first-night.
Wish I could be sure of my dramatic critic. Bright lad, Allan
Scoffer, might manage to get in.'

The Brides' white stood out luminously against the drab crowd.
'What a chance to make a corner in muslin,' Ottercove thought to
himself, 'to meet the sure demand for Ascension robes!' The
untimeliness of such an enterprise, in the face of timelessness
which would rob him of the fruits, damped his speculative ardour.
He had long since lost interest in making money, though the habit
persisted into middle life, and whenever now he sold a yacht or a
Venetian palace, or a country house in Scotland, he would pride
himself on a minimum profit of £5, as a private reassurance that
his old cunning had not left him.

He was like a veteran golfer who suddenly, during a quiet
walk in the country, borrows a club to show his friends the stuff
he is made of. 'Not lost the knack yet,' they say tonelessly.

He walked all the way home to Stonedge House and, unnoticed by his servants, sauntered sombrely into his ground-floor
sitting-room. His mood was sombre. He stood at the wide french
windows and looked out at the darkling park which stretched
before him, melting away into the mist, stood there, a little weary
and disenchanted. So this was the end. Good! He felt sorry for
the world, and for himself, and for the race robbed of the promise
of fulfilment. The imminent end of human life and, with it, of
his career on earth, threw him back upon a reminiscent mood.
He saw himself a boy way back in Ottercove, bright-eyed, eager,
wide awake, the visible world a glittering prize, a pear waiting to
be plucked. Well, he had plucked it. It had proved, however, more
than he really cared to chew; his appetite had waned as he par-
took of it. He had had his fill; and, perhaps—he had always kept
an open mind about these things, had always been awake to
otherworldly possibilities—perhaps there was room for his versatile talents beyond. He had always been keen, modest, ready to
learn the rules of the game—any game—to appreciate the
change in the nature of things, and always successful. Those oft-
quoted words with which his father once adorned his dreary
sermons, words whose beauty had arrested his attention, now
stood before him, cavernous with meaning: 'We shall not all

sleep, but we shall all be changed, in a moment, in the twinkling of an eye, at the last trump.'

Probably. His father—a curious man. No pliability of mind. No disinterested curiosity. Only a rigid belief in heaven and hell. Wrong! Life was pliable, generous and miraculous to a degree we could not even guess; it opened out suddenly, wondrously, as a flower overnight. To-day a caterpillar—to-morrow a butterfly. But we, dull, sodden ruffians ruminating over our existence, like cows chewing the cud, could not imagine a heaven other than of grass and water—greener grass and clearer water. Fools!

He paced up and down. A series of articles on the nature of immortality, for the *Sunday Runner*, commended themselves to his mind. A fitting counter-blast to the precocious spiritualism exploited by a rival group of newspapers. He would write them himself. It was wonderful how his mind was opening out, like a bed of flowers, all looking, straining to the sun. Intuitive orientation. Knew where the sun was; in fact, had always had a place in it. And God was just there, too, behind the sun. He felt that he would get on well with God, owing to his reasonableness, modesty, and readiness for transfiguration at short notice. He would not ask questions, but watch every movement of God's brow and anticipate His every mood.

Ah, well! he had faith. He would go on believing in a personal immortality till, with a poker, from behind, Providence would knock him dead.—A sinister afterthought; he brushed it aside. He stretched out his hands to the unseen: 'I am reasonable. Will not the reasonable from beyond the grave claim me?' Half forgotten feelings flooded his heart. He remembered his arrival in England back from his New Zealand tour, as the train rolled noisily over the bridge into the great metropolis, the witness of his crowning triumphs. He remembered a thrush outside his bedroom window way back in Ottercove in early boyhood. The trees seemed to stand still, as if waiting for something. These feelings, eternal essences of things, were they to be wasted? These anticipations, were they not to be fulfilled? They were pledges of something that was to be, had always been, existed now, as if round the corner but somehow out of reach. The quickness with which people disposed of dead bodies, the rapidity with which they resigned themselves to their loss, suggested that, at bottom, they thought it was all right. It was all right. *How* all right, he could not say, but all right it was.

'Time for bed.' He stretched out his arms to the ceiling and yawned. 'I am,' he said aloud, 'such as I am, and what I am—neither more nor less—for the universe to chew and digest and assign to the requisite uses.'

40

Lord de Jones had been in a hurry to cross over to the Continent, for there was no means at all of knowing how much of it had disintegrated to date. The uncertainty of the whole business appalled him. The stationmaster at Victoria might not be able to communicate with the *chef de la gare du Nord*. Yet he had no means of knowing whether this was because Paris-Nord (or, for that matter, Paris) had disintegrated, or whether it was because the number was engaged.

There was of course an aeroplane service for abroad, but people still clung to the *terra firma*—Lord de Jones thought, without good cause. Moreover, they were travelling with luggage—a good deal of luggage. It was indeed difficult to know how much luggage to take with one—Eva could not take enough—to last one to the end of one's days in time. The sight of passengers reclining in the easy luxury of the Pullmans, looking trim and hard, appalled him. They would not come back, he mused. Never come back from this last journey into space whither they were travelling *de luxe*, over viaducts, away, away, urbane materialists melting into air...

And on the French side, against all the easy felicity of the language, the sinuous tones of the restaurant-car attendant who sang out as he squeezed himself along the swaying corridors: '*Prière de prendre place pour le premier déjeuner!*', contrasting favourably with the brisk 'First luncheon!' of the British dining-car attendant, the incorrigible insularity of the English passengers who said they wanted to shut out, if possible, French passengers from the *coupé* (forgetting that they were travelling across France in a French train), stood out a black and reeking ghost of shame which made him think the world was doomed because it lacked all manners. In the night the train stood still, emitting long sighs at intervals; and his heart beat loud within him with foreboding.

Images passed through his mind, of a life *à la* Jean Jacques Rousseau, in which he must rely on his dexterity of arm and on nature's bounty. A hardened hunter he is, building her a hut. Eva with only furs from furry animals which he had hunted down for her to hide her nudeness. Primeval love and lust. Long days of bliss. But what is this? The roar of a lion. Bother! He must get up and see about it. He had been dozing, and opening his eyes, she was there indeed, not in the wilderness as yet, but facing him in the *coupé*, and smiling at him.

But what if it fail him? She, the child, no more than she could understand how, having undone one atom, he had automatically undone the world, had not the remotest comprehension of how he could now isolate a specific portion of it from destruction. Yet when he had, to illustrate the process, said to her that all he had to do was to vaccinate the hill they had selected as their future world, she said: 'Of course! How silly of me not to think of it myself!'

But even if it fail, then death. And what was death? A change of outlook. He remembered once crossing a wide river somewhere, and as he landed on the other side, straying into a bathing place where lots of naked people sat about on benches in the garden and on chairs in the adjoining restaurant, smoking, eating, chatting, listening to music—but with nothing on them. It was uncanny. And he thought that landing on the other side of death must be as strange: for everything seemed different, yet everything the same.

Dusk fell as the train raced across Austria, and sheaves of corn in the vast whirling fields looked like humans stealing away one by one in the twilight. 'Escaping,' he thought.

And, waking in the morning suddenly, they saw the mountains.

In the station square at Innsbruck, a fat German who looked like a pig waved his whip at his dog and threatened it: '*Ach, du Schweinhund!*'

'Disgraceful!' said Eva, and as she passed him, she gave him an icy look over her slim shoulder. It was a beautiful day in June.

They hired a victoria and drove, at first through the old mellow town with its cloistered streets, domes, turrets, and pinnacles; then by the side of the river, angry and turbulent. A faint hazy summer afternoon was drawing to its close, and as, at sundown, they came to a hanging bridge chained between rocks and the foaming green river rushing angrily under the horse's hoofs, Christopher's eyes filled with tears: the beauty of it all was more than he could bear.

And when, at the Pension Kogl, they came out on to their balconies, they were stunned with rapture by the view which opened out on to the mountain scenery. Below was the river, the passionate Inn, and the bridges, the funicular slowly climbing the mountain slope, and all around were pine trees, birches, roses, villas hidden in lanes lined with foliage; and at night when they walked by the river, where lanterns shone forth from between secretive trees, it was as if happiness, long dreamt and forgotten, awaited one round the corner.

41

That night Lord Ottercove slept at The Cottage, and the following night he spent in the country. It was not till he had got into bed on the third night and turned over on his left side that he was aware of the sound of rustling paper in his pyjama coat pocket, which, on inspection, proved to be a letter, a *billet-doux* from his Eva. She was, she wrote, with Christopher de Jones, who, as Rex probably knew, had gone off his chump and had disintegrated the world, which was unravelling rapidly of its own accord ('like a piece of crochet-work,' she wrote, 'if you know what I mean, whose first stitch he had undone'), and she had with difficulty persuaded him to isolate the top of a hill, which he said he could do by vaccinating it, so to speak, against the spreading corruption, to save her and himself, and she was now secretly indicating the exact location of that hill in the Austrian Alps whither he, Rex, should fly at once. He must not, however, bring anyone with him, as there would be very little to eat. '*I told Him I'd like to have you saved, but He won't hear of it. I am furious.*

I told him all the Truth that I have written to you. And He is Furious.
Never mind, darling, if I flirt with him perhaps He will not kill you.
Your loving wife,

'Eva.'

Lord Ottercove never weighed or reflected: he knew. Light came to him without intermediaries, direct from the Holy Ghost. He must save himself *and Vernon Sprott*. Vernon Sprott was, since the death of a late Prime Minister, his oldest friend, and friendship was to Ottercove a pure and sacred thing. In other departments of life he had displayed a versatile ability, but in friendship he was a genius. No coldness, lack of response, animosity, or even treachery could dull his friendship. If he once liked a man, nothing that that man might do to him would stop his liking him. Equally, he would stop at nothing if he could render even the smallest service to a friend. Lord Ottercove was said to have made the war in order to oblige a friend whose special gifts, he thought, would find their happiest expression in a war cabinet. His tenderness in the cause of friendship knew no bounds. And so, entering hatless into his chariot, he muttered the address of Mr. Vernon Sprott.

But when, his heart thumping within him, he dragged himself up to Vernon's study at the top of his house in Berkeley Square, Vernon Sprott was writing a novel. Vernon Sprott was invariably writing a novel. That was, according to the more esoteric critics, the special trouble with him. And the special trouble to-night was that Vernon Sprott would not stop writing the novel, hoping to finish, print, sell it, and retire on the proceeds before the world came to its final dissolution. Lord Ottercove beheld the broad industrious back of his friend, who made a slave of himself to keep afloat a large yacht, and said: 'Vernon, you're a writer of talent: but a merchant of genius.'

Vernon Sprott turned round on his chair. 'You, Rex,' he said, looking at him with critical thoughtfulness, 'who have cut such a figure in the visible world, why don't you now turn your mind to the invisible mystery of things and solve, say, the Riddle of the Universe?'

Lord Ottercove pondered silently awhile. 'I cannot solve it,' he said.

Mr. Vernon Sprott turned back to his desk.

Lord Ottercove looked at his friend with grave significance. He loved Vernon Sprott. All the music, all the poetry in the world was not so fine nor yet so pure as this devotion of the younger for the elder friend, and when he spoke of him his voice grew tender and tears came to his eyes. 'Vernon!' he said at last. 'I am going to save your life! For, you know, there's a divinity that shapes our ends, rough-hew them as we may. My chariot is at the door, and' (looking at his watch) 'we must fly.'

'Let me put the last stroke to my novel.'

'I advise you against it.'

'Why?'

'Vernon: it would do you no good.'

'But I must. No first-class artist——'

'Vernon: we must fly.'

Vernon Sprott, smoking a long fat cigar, followed Lord Ottercove critically into the chariot, which, cutting sharply round the corner, took wing, and clearing the roofs of the Berkeley Square houses, soared into the sky. Lord Ottercove and Mr. Vernon Sprott beheld for the last time the great city of London, which, viewed from this imposing height, looked as though it had been inadvertently dropped out of the back of a cart. An architectural effect that, though it was not premeditated, could hardly be called happy, thought Mr. Sprott. However. He puffed at his cigar. 'Your secretary and telephone operator gone ahead, I expect?'

'Yuh. Can't get on without them.'

They were now flying right into the dawn.

42

CASTOR AND POLLUX

Herr Kogl was in charge of the telephone and telegrams. He would come up and say to you with oracular pride:

'A—telegram—is—on—the—way—to—you.' He articulated slowly, as if appreciating the necessity of talking distinctly to foreigners.

'How do you know?' Lord de Jones asked him.

'I know,' said Herr Kogl, turning to go. But he came back at once and explained:

'They—have—telephoned—from—the—post—office—to—say—so.'

The telegram arrived an hour later. De Jones opened it and read:

'Lord Ottercove and Mr. Vernon Sprott arriving by chariot this evening. Reserve first-class accommodation.
                              Hannibal.'

In the afternoon while everybody was at tea—'*Jause*,' in the vernacular—Mrs. Hannibal and the telephone operator arrived in an aeroplane and installed themselves with the efficiency and celerity of a quartermaster. Mrs. Hannibal occupied the little reception room; the telephone operator, a graduate of the Royal College of Science, commandeered the telephone. Then, there being nothing for them to do till evening, they strolled down the hill into town to inspect the sights.

And Baby? She was not at the gate, nor at the bandstand, nor in the by-ways of the park. Since his demise from the Pension Kogl, Frank lived in town, often meeting Baby when she came down to Innsbruck. And here she was, as fresh as May, beckoning to him from across the flower-bespangled field. That laughing, slanting look in her eyes stirred something in his frame as though a bird had suddenly flown into him. He was joy, his body the cage. Soon joy would fly out; and he fretted and flurried trying to lock the door of the cage, losing his happiness in the anxiety of losing it. That piquant blend of childish innocence on her face with a suggestion of ripening womanhood about her form, so irresistible to men, was no less irresistible to Frank. They took the funicular up the mountain slope and continued the spiral ascent by foot, stopping now and then to look down at the town in the valley, when he would feel her lovely weight against him. They wound their way up the Schillerweg and stopped at a Gasthaus in the precincts of the Pension Kogl and had coffee and cakes amidst the beer and wine drinking peasants with goat beards like shaving brushes stuck in their coloured hats, and the women in Tyrolese peasant dress, taken in tightly at the waist and showing off their figures to advantage, and sat still and looked down into the green folds of the valley and up at the jagged summits of naked rock. She gave him a look that came straight from the soul. Her eyes were as if they had just been sad, had understood all, and now chose to see only the heavenly, sunny side of your being. And looking at her eyes, you too felt but the sunny side of yourself, and wanted to dance and prance in the sunshine that emanated from those eyes. Fowls, chickens, strutted all over the place, jumped on the chairs. The little serving maid, bare-legged, would call them: 'Chuck-chuck-chuck!'

They were screened from sight by a tree. He put his hand on her arm. Her look moistened. The sun, as if making a last effort, shone with a tragic brightness; then, unable to sustain the effort, diminished its light. The bare-legged maid had gone in. They kissed. When she came out she wore a pair of brown stockings: and they stopped kissing.

'Hello, hello!'

They turned round and saw Eva and Christopher de Jones. 'Wherever have you been?' Eva turned on to her cousin. 'We've been looking for you everywhere. Chris is anxious to begin.'

'There isn't any time to waste. It's coming our way now, spreading fast,' de Jones confirmed.

'Like creeping paralysis,' said Eva, 'and Chris is going to vaccinate this hill.' Then, turning impulsively to Frank:

'Let me see! Have you any hair left?' He quickly removed his hat. 'Oh, lots and lots!' she exclaimed.

'It's about the only thing I have.'

'It's time I did it,' said de Jones. 'Herr Kogl, can you oblige me with a little gasolene?'

'Yes, yes. We'll see if we can get any,' said Herr Kogl politely. 'Kindly follow me to the garage, and we shall see if we are lucky.'

Then in another tone: 'Hey there! Herbert! Any gasolene! Any gasolene, I said! Come on and get about it, quick! I'm waiting. I said: *waiting*!'

Christopher de Jones returned with a mysterious air. 'I have timed,' he said, 'the explosion for five-fifteen.'

'What explosion is this?' Frank said with enquiring charm.

'Oh, perfectly harmless in itself. But it will frighten away all the rest, and leave this mountain-top for our little party.'

'Is this discrimination not perhaps a little heartless?'

'Surplus; surplus. One must always get rid of the surplus.'

He took out his watch and held it in his palm. Three minutes elapsed.

There was a mild crash. Then several faces were thrust enquiringly out of the windows of the Pension Kogl. Next, the word 'earthquake' passed from mouth to mouth, and a thin stream of visitors trickled down the narrow mountain path into Innsbruck, which stretched below them, sunning itself in the valley. Herr Kogl, Frau Kogl, the policeman and the Frau Policeman with her quicksilver of a little boy, the apoplectic Baron, and some others, made light of Lord de Jones's warning and refused to budge.

They stood with Frank and Eva and Baby and de Jones in a group on the terrace and watched the other visitors trot down the hill: the Grand Duke, the Frau Professor with the dachshund, the Herr Pastor, the Frau Pastor, Herr and Frau Nikulitsch, the two Scottish old maids, Herr Spatz, Frau Spatz, and their son Willi, the Frau Doktor Wirt, the Frau Direktor Bödingen, the Frau Oberst von Kaisar, and Frau von Endte. There lived among others in the annexe of the Pension Kogl an effeminate-looking young artist from Vienna who was kept by a poor, consumptive German girl who paid for him and cooked his meals, whereas he, tired of her love, powdered his face and, adjusting his tie before the mirror, went to town every day to distract himself with her money. On the fatal day he, adjusting his tie, went to town and did not come back. And she, going down the hill to the grocer's to get him his supper, did likewise.

Frank remembered this afterwards. Now he stood between Eva and Chris and watched his erstwhile enemies from the *pension* go down, never to return. It was a warm Sunday afternoon. Far away, a train whistled, and then coiled below, like a serpent, on its long journey to Vienna. It will not reach Vienna, Frank thought, not in eternity! All the peasants, save for one old man, had already vanished down the hill. He drank his big mug to the bottom, smacking his lips. Having paid for the beer and lighted his pipe, he rose, and at once there came the sounds of his jolly accordion, as, with twinkling eye, he strode to his own happy tune out of the courtyard. Fresh and alert, he went down the road making his own music, till his long curved pipe, and his knapsack, and the plume in his hat, ducked by the hill, and only the jolly tune spoke of his fresh onward strides.

The sun had long ago set behind the hills. It was very still: the empty spell which hangs over the world before twilight.

'And what's that?' Baby exclaimed, pointing to an approaching dot in the sky. Eva peered at the clouds. An aeroplane was speeding towards them.

'It's the chariot,' said Frank.

'It's Rex! It's Rex!' she cried. 'Hurrah! it's Rex!'

They could see them now with the naked eye, Lord Ottercove and Mr. Vernon Sprott, seated side by side, puffing at their cigars.

One moment it seemed as if Lord Ottercove's winged chariot would land safely and gracefully in the courtyard of the Pension Kogl. The next, it looked as though it would do no such thing.

The two occupants of the chariot suddenly looked at each other. They were both, in their different ways, strong men, and said nothing. They were, they knew it, subject to immediate dissolution.

And there was method in it. First, Mr. Vernon Sprott began to disintegrate (his eighty-five volumes of fiction and belles-lettres in the British Museum having already preceded him). Mr. Sprott realized with his usual imperturbable objectivity that he, who had always been one for whom the visible world existed, was on the point of no longer existing for the visible world. Now Lord Ottercove also began to get diffuse. He was not aware of any pain or discomfort: he only felt that he was becoming less and less homogeneous. This master of a million voices yielded inaudibly to extinction, his last conscious feeling, one of sorrow not of anger, being a profound regret that Lord de Jones had not remained a Genius of the Untried. Soon their fabric melted into air, into thin air. Their insubstantial pageant faded and left no rack behind.

But in the growing twilight the tips of their cigars, fiery particles immune from dissolution, two beacons of light, two golden stars in the sky, twin brothers, Castor and Pollux, shone for ever and ever.

43

There was no sound at all, and nothing to see: something that had hitherto been ceased to be, like a dream on waking. Nothing crashed, nothing fell: no mist, not a whiff of steam. No gossamer. Things rolled up into nothing, as if they had vanished up their own sleeves. The world around seemed to be burning, silently, quickly, invisibly.

They stood round and watched intently. Would the vaccination prove adequate in neutralizing the creeping disease? Or would it overtake their little hill, reach them and consume them all? By the answer to this question Christopher de Jones must stand or fall. If he succeeds, how will they reward him? Foolish associations steal into their minds. 'Payment by results.' How long, how long! Will this ever end? Has it ended? Are they dead, and, in a sense, as good as before? 'Come, now,' said Christopher impatiently.

Gradually the hill detached itself and, as Baby and Herbert ran down the slope hand in hand to ascertain if they were clear of the contamination, floated away into space.

'A clean piece of work, what?' said de Jones, looking round at everybody for approbation. 'We're clear of the old earth.'

They all looked admiringly at the wizard.

'We've peeled right off the rotten crust of the world; the old planet's gone off to die by itself.'

'The whole of her fabric vanished by now?' asked Frank.

'Well, there may still be a piece of Asia left as we are talking. But it need concern us no longer.'

'I should hate to think, Chris,' Eva said, 'that you have not quite killed the earth and that she is suffering.'

'A matter of a day or so, that's all. The wound is mortal.'

They stared away into space. 'Look out!' he cried. 'We are floating away. No need for alarm. Merely changing our bearings in the firmament. The stars are looking at us inquisitively; that is because we are new-comers.'

They could not recognize their Chris, their gloomy, silent Chris. He was gay, excited, communicative; like a Cook's tourists' guide. 'Hold on!' he cried presently. 'We seem to be getting away somewhere, I don't quite know where.'

Away, away, away! To the sun, Frank thought, to be consumed in its light!

The movement increased in velocity. It seemed they were falling. Falling, falling, still falling; but falling upwards, not downwards. With indrawn breath they awaited the final impact which was to shatter them into space. Now, with a crash, they would fall on the moon.

Trembling, Eva came into Frank's arms. He held her close that he might drink her breath, commit her kiss into the keeping of his soul, forever lost in hers. For his identity, as it dissolved in the encroaching dusk, clung to his own self's dream in her soul mirrored. Was it the end? Shut in that vision! Now, Doom, devour them!... 'Ever, and again, and forever, thine.'

Yet the minutes passed and no blow came. When they had stood tensely and motionlessly for what seemed to them a decade, the velocity of their fall decreased perceptibly, and they came to a halt. The sky gradually cleared, and the sun flickered through the clouds. It looked as though it might be over.

Lord de Jones looked as nonplussed as the others. 'Apparently,' said he, 'the law of gravity is no object to God.'

'Yes,' Frank agreed, releasing Eva from his protective grasp, 'we are saved—if unscientifically saved.'

'God has shown,' remarked Herr Kogl, 'that whatever else He may be, He is no doctrinaire.'

'Apparently,' replied de Jones, still looking worried, 'our knowledge of astronomy is incomplete—if this sort of thing can happen.'

'There are more things in heaven and earth, Horatio, etcetera,' said Frank.

Herr Kogl looked at Frau Kogl. They smiled faintly at each other. They were pale, yet happy. But where was Herbert?

'Never mind Herbert. Where was Baby?' The question flashed through Eva's mind.

Steps were taken accordingly to satisfy the curiosity on both sides. Herbert and Baby had, it was remembered, run down the slope hand in hand to ascertain whether the hill was clear of the dissolving earth, before the hill had shot, like a bolt, into space;

and neither Herbert nor Baby could be traced any more. Lord de Jones advanced an interesting and plausible theory that Herbert and Baby, having thoughtlessly overstepped the line of demarkation, had rendered themselves subject to the chemical laws operating outside the area he had thoughtfully isolated by means of vaccination, and thus had shared the fate of all matter. While they were discussing the sensational disappearance of two of their number who should have been saved, the ground beneath them gave a jerk and then began to revolve, at first slowly, then faster and faster.

'Hold tight!' cried de Jones. The new globe was whirling with incredible rapidity on its own axis and, what was even more distressing, round the sun; which made it doubly difficult to keep one's feet. They were, thank God, for the most part of them, Londoners, accustomed to roughing it on the tops of omnibuses, and this sort of thing held no real peril for them. But twenty Austrian citizens, mountain folk who had lived away from urban surroundings, failed to keep their poise and were hurled into infinity to ascertain, but never to report, whether Einsteinian infinity was indeed boundless but finite (even though some of the victims had no scientific bias at all).

But all things come to an end sooner or later, as was remarked by some keen observer. Gradually the revolutions slowed down and then almost subsided: and there they were—behold! the new Jerusalem descending out of heaven from God, having the glory of God: and her light was like unto a stone most precious, even like a jasper stone, clear as crystal. And they saw a new heaven and a new earth: for the first heaven and the first earth were passed away: and there was no more sea.

'By God, John, you're right!' Frank exclaimed: 'as right as six-pence!'

'That was a narrow escape,' said Herr Kogl.

Lord de Jones sat down on the ground and stretched out his limbs and yawned. 'Ha!' he laughed.

'What is the joke, if I may ask?' Frank smiled enquiringly.

'Fifty years ago,' said de Jones, 'when the laws of science were absolute, this would have been impossible. But in this age of Relativity, nothing, thank God, is absolutely impossible!'

'Relatively speaking,' said Frank.

'I have always put God above mathematics,' said Herr Kogl.

'Either nature lacked science,' Frank said, 'or God knew a lot more. Our experience is decidedly novel and interesting.'

'As a matter of fact,' rejoined Lord de Jones, 'it all happened according to plan. Just as I thought. Nothing surprises me.'

He *hadn't* thought so. He was like a captain who in a storm mislaid his chart and instruments and, when the storm was over, pretended to take his bearings and said that they tallied with his intended course.

They were miraculously saved; and there was still a world. But what a world! A rounded mountain-top, peeled away and revolving very slowly by itself round the old sun.

And there, as before, stood the Pension Kogl. Nothing seemed to have happened to it; all the windows were whole. Here was the garden, the courtyard, the stables; and there the fields with the cows and sheep and horses grazing imperturbably as before. Was it a dream? Where was it? When was it?

And here was Herr Kogl standing on the doorstep puffing at his pipe; and there was Frau Kogl, agitated, throwing out her hands, probably saying, Frank thought, 'I don't know what to do!' to the policeman, who was mystified, though not disagreeably, by the disappearance of the young shrew who had been his wife. And in her agitation Frau Kogl seemed to be forgetting her own grief.

'The matter is simple,' de Jones was explaining. 'When our new little planet began to whirl like a merry-go-round, the Frau Policeman, having failed to clutch at a solid object, or clutching an object that was not solid (possibly her husband), was hurled like a stone outside the now negligible gravitation zone of this little earth of ours, and was attracted by the superior gravitation of the moon.'

'For one who has always whined for the moon,' said Herr Kogl, 'the transference must have its attraction.'

'The bump,' retorted de Jones, 'will have been fatal. But that is neither here nor there. All I ask you to note is that her death was due to natural causes.'

'Lucid, admirable,' said Frank, 'and entirely convincing!'

The apoplectic old Baron came up to say that he had just stumbled over the body of little Hans, the policeman's boy, and the company, sobered by recent apocalyptic events, slowly made for the spot. De Jones again assumed the initiative.

'Observe,' he said, 'an interesting phenomenon. The boy, too small and not used to transit either by omnibus or the Metropolitan Railways, had not developed the instinct of a strap-hanger, and if his ancestors had, indeed, ever had this instinct, it had been atrophied in him through long disuse. And thus he failed to clutch instinctively at the small bush that might have saved him, and was hurled instead into space. But, being light in body, he was not hurled far enough to reach the gravitation zone of the moon, but remained within the gravitation halo of this little planet, whose power of attraction, as you are aware, is so weak that when we raise our legs in walking we have some difficulty in touching ground again. We might be penny balloons on the day after their purchase when, no longer able to rise in the air, they do the next best thing. And so, observe, this infant's fall was not heavy; it did not maim or deform him: only knocked the life out of him. All in the natural order of phenomena.'

'Most interesting and instructive,' said Frank.

'Poor child,' said Eva. 'Poor Baby! Poor Herbert! I wish now, Christopher, you had never begun it.'

'You can't have,' retorted Christopher, 'a world-wide cata-clysm like this without a victim here and there, which is all in the day's work.'

'The number of your victims,' interjected Frank, 'is in the neighbourhood of one thousand, six hundred millions.'

'What!' Frau Kogl was appalled. 'That is not allowed! *Das gibt es nicht*! Herr Wachmann!' she called out to the policeman, 'will you have this gentleman arrested. He is the biggest murderer that ever lived!'

The policeman, a tin sword trailing at his side, looked from one to the other with an irresolute air.

'Come, come!' said Lord de Jones, patting him on the shoul-der, 'this is no longer your old Austria.'

'Now don't be a funk,' Frau Kogl egged him on, 'assert your authority, show what you can do.'

'I am the only policeman in the world, a poor, lonely man. How can I arrest anybody?'

'Come, come, don't you bother them,' Herr Kogl intervened. 'What is done is done and cannot be undone.'

But she would not listen to him. And even when he bawled at her, she did not quail, this time, before the man with the strong will; and he turned into the house with a shrug. 'Women,' he said tenderly.

'You're a fine policeman and no mistake,' Frau Kogl jeered, till even Lord de Jones himself felt sorry for the man.

'Leave the poor man alone, can't you?' he said. 'What has he done to you?'

'It's not what he but what you've done, sir. Killed Herbert, killed everybody. Everybody, everybody—absolutely everybody one can think of. And now with this funk of a policeman there will be no justice, no authority left in the world; no one to bring you to book.'

'That will do, Frau Kogl.'

'No, it *won't* do, sir. This is *my* pension, bought on my mother's hard savings she made in Alsace-Lorraine from where we spring, and as an Alsatian I am too proud to tolerate the presence of the murderer of the human race in my house.'

'Stop!' cried de Jones. 'Don't try my patience too far, woman! My nerves are on edge. I've had a very exceptional day. Do you know what you are saying? This is the new Jerusalem that you see, the home of pacifism. None of your Alsace-Lorraine now, I beg of you.'

'I came from there———'

'And you'll go that way, if you are not careful.'

'All this is mine.'

'Oh, is it? Let heaven be my judge.' He snatched the sword from the policeman and struck her on the head.

She collapsed in a heap.

The policeman walked away into the hills with a look which implied: 'I haven't seen it.'

Lord de Jones lit his pipe. Frank and Eva stood by, aghast. Christopher looked at them with a propitiating smile. 'I have slain,' he said, removing his pipe, 'this dragon of contention, this symbol of war and nationalism, I hope, for ever.'

'Cain!'

A cock crowed twice.

He started; then relaxed again. If the cock crowed twice to remind him that he had betrayed his ideal at least once, he was nevertheless mighty glad to know that there was a cock on the premises. He hoped there were hens, too.

'I have released,' he said, 'the spirit imprisoned in a foul house.'

'You're blaspheming.'

'It had to be done.'

'Oh, had it?'

'A hard thing, I admit, for a pacifist. But we must not sentimentalize if we are to survive; we must fight the peace as we fought the war!' There was silence.

'Even the cock is too sick with you to crow again,' said Frank.

The light sank: there was a long drop of rain, then another. It began to hail. The three of them turned in and stood at the window blurred with rain. The old woman's body lay out in the wet. Neither the hail nor rain could waken her. The earth was wrapped in a wet mist. And the spirit of God moved upon the face of the waters.

And Lord de Jones said, Let there be light: and there was no light. So he switched on the electric light: and he saw that it was quite good.

'You blooming fool, Christopher! You've upset all the seasons!' cried Eva. 'You've made a mess of the weather! It's neither day nor night, but heaven knows what! It should be summer now, and it is winter.'

'O Wind! If Winter comes, can Spring be far behind?'

He sank into a chair and picked up a periodical, a copy of the *New Statesman*, the last number. The very last! Eva opened the *Illustrated London News*, full of pictures of the *concours hippique* at the Olympia, and Frank strolled over to the piano and tried his hand at the 'Symphony of the New World,' when Herr Kogl came in from the dining-room.

'Bad weather, Herr Kogl, what?'

'*Das ist kein Wetter, sondern ein Skandal,*' and he adjusted the electric stove. 'Everyone can switch it out—I mean switch it on —whenever he likes, but you must on no account switch it out without telling Herbert——' He stopped, blubbered; then continued with a catch in his voice: 'because I mean then you release so much current that the dynamo goes off like mad and may go phut, and then anything may happen. Though I don't care what happens now that Herbert——' He gulped and turned away to the window. 'What's that?'

Next, he was in the courtyard by her side. He stood still, petrified. 'Anna!' he said. 'Anna!'

Lord de Jones rose with the *New Statesman* still in his hand, and went upstairs, 'To spare his feelings,' he said. 'Though I wish these people would realize that a certain modicum of suffering is unavoidable even in this New Jerusalem. However, we don't want scenes.'

Herr Kogl placed the body on chairs in the dining-room and came back into the lounge. Eva eyed him compassionately. 'What will you do to him?'

'Nothing,' he said, 'nothing. It is between him and his God, and I can do nothing.' Tears streamed down his cheeks. 'There are laws, delicately adjusted spiritual laws. We must not meddle, must not touch God's scales. If I did, what would happen? "Leave off!" God would say. "Away with your clumsy hands, you bull in a china shop! By taking the law into your own hands you have upset the delicate adjustment of my spiritual world. You have disturbed the balance, disarranged the symmetry. Now, instead of letting him, who has wrongfully taken, put it back by his own exertion of soul, I must let him off lest I upset the scales of my world by the wrong you have heaped on him. And who will square the original sin? It falls back on the whole of mankind, don't you see, young feller-me-lad?" That's how God would speak to me if, in my great ignorance, I presumed to take things into my own foolish hands.'

For a minute they said nothing, but looked out of doors, where the rain had stopped, at the dripping trees flooded with light.

'And she was a clever woman,' he said; 'she knew languages. Brought up in a convent on the border of France———' His face puckered: he sobbed.

When the others had gone, he stood alone in the doorway, gazed at the clouds and listened to the wind in the pines. He looked with despair for the night to cover his grief: and it was perpetual day.

44

FINNEGAN!
BEGIN AGAIN!

Lord de Jones, having, he deemed, ended his work, took a hot bath, sitting in which he reflected that while it had taken God six days to make the world, it took him only one day to unmake it. Yet he felt he also needed a rest. It was 6 a.m. when he dragged himself up to his room, dropped on his bed and fell asleep. He dreamt that he had been given a lot of work which he resented because he was tired, having gone to bed as late as 6 a.m. All night he dreamt that he had gone to bed at 6 a.m., and when he woke at noon he felt more tired than when he had gone to bed at 6 a.m.

Rising, he put on his trousers and fastened on his braces, and, not troubling to put on a coat, went out on to the balcony to look at the world: and he saw that it was good.

The earth was certainly small, but there was a cosiness, an intimacy about it now which it lacked when it boasted five continents. It was dear to him because it was the work of his own hands—in his private opinion, a masterpiece. It had been for him to make it as small as he deemed fit, and he had deemed its present size—which was ten miles in diameter—entirely appropriate.

> ' "*In small proportions we just beauty see;*
> *And in short measures life may perfect be*," '

he carolled hoarsely. 'Yes, Ben Jonson would have understood me!'

'Or,' Frank rejoined, stepping out on to his balcony, 'as Goethe said, "*In der Beschränkung zeigt sich erst der Meister.*" '

'Very true, very true.'

'But not too true to be good. One should have watched you. One should have known that somebody like you, with more science than sense, must attempt this sort of thing sooner or later.'

'You supply your own answer. Someone, if not me, then another, would have done the same thing. No idea, not one so obvious, ever comes to one mind alone. Thousands must have cherished it. Not for ever was mankind to be mocked.'

'And poor Rex,' said Eva, coming out on to her balcony. 'A few seconds, and he would have been with us last night.'

'And Vernon Sprott.'

'And Vernon Sprott.'

'Yes—I can picture Rex with us! He would have called for Mrs. Hannibal, and there wouldn't have been a Mrs. Hannibal. He would want to print newspapers, and there would be nothing to print newspapers with or on. He is better where he is.'

'Poor Rex. I *did* want him to be saved,' said Eva. She was in a loose dressing-gown. It had become more and more evident that she was expecting a baby— 'of the old world,' said Christopher de Jones regretfully.

'I know. He was a great lad. We shall never see the like of him again.'

'There was,' said Frank, 'nothing "tinny" or snobbish about him. He was a great, warm-hearted creature, sensitive, knowing, not rancorous, kind and unspoilt. What energy, what enthusiasm, what mobility of mind! And withal what magnanimity! He was, I think, the most magnanimous man I have ever met. If he caught you red-handed, plotting against his life and fortune, and you politely put away your pistol or poison with the words: "So sorry, Rex," he'd tell you: "Say no more about it! If it's money you want, why the hell don't you say so?" and, so as not to hurt your feelings by simply giving you a batch of Bank of England notes, he would appoint you Editor-in-chief of all his newspapers.'

'And then worry the life out of you, till you resigned your job of your own accord.'

'He was the big drum in the jazz band of our civilization, in which I was the ukulele. But he was a rare friend, and, characteristically, he died trying to save his friend's life. There was at least nothing jazz-like in that.'

All Ottercove's sympathetic qualities, unnoticed when he was alive, now stood out and called for notice. They stood up as a mute reproach to them and called up images of callous and ungrateful thoughts about a man now mute, felled in the fullness of his strength, prematurely disintegrated. He felt sore, badly hit by the loss. He was fond, he knew it now, of Ottercove. Never again would he behold the glint of those eyes. Never hear that robust voice.

'But why have been so half-hearted? Why not have finished off everything?' He looked grievously at Chris.

'That the race may survive.'

'*Must* it survive?'

'Of course.'

'Why "of course"?'

'To honour my name and my memory.'

'What a name! What a memory!'

'We must recuperate, start afresh. My descendants will breed and multiply, expand, develop trade, build fleets of aeroplanes and shops and factories. Ultimately we shall hope to open a new Bank of England.'

> '*There was a little man*
> *And his name was Finnegan;*
> *He grew whiskers on his chin again.*
> *The wind did blow and blew them in again.*
> *Poor old Patsy Finnegan.*
> *Finnegan!*
> *Begin again!*'

'And we shall. As Goethe said: "*Aller Anfang ist schwer.*" Glorious life! Glorious beginning!'

'But what is there, you fool, to begin from?'

'Don't call me a fool.'

'What is there that the race, if indeed it survives, can learn from? Where is there a picture, a book, a gramophone record to pass on to those who shall follow us? Nothing. Not even an "Outline of History"!'

'Wells? Ha!'

'We could do with Wells here. The earnest, regenerative Wells. Where is he now?'

'Wells?' De Jones adjusted his telescope and peered at the clouds. 'I am looking if that is him over there.'

'Let me look.' Frank looked and saw what looked like Mr. Wells floating, it seemed, only a few yards away, a compact, self-contained little figure, apparently immune from dissolution. 'I think,' Frank said, still peering, 'I can see Winston's hat.'

'I might have saved Shaw.'

They strained into the skies at a few dissociated splinters which may have been fragments of George Bernard Shaw.

> *'I stand in no awe*
> *Of George Bernard Shaw,'*

Christopher quoted.

'The attitude of the press and the reading public towards Shaw has been one protracted joke.'

'How so?'

'You see, when Shaw began he was not taken seriously but was treated as a joke. It was not till recently that he succeeded in being regarded as a serious artist.'

'But where is the joke?'

'That is the joke.'

'And do you see that blot on the face of the sky?'

'Let me look. Yes, I see.'

'That is Lord Birkenhead.'

'You are forgiven.'

'I am touched by your recognition. You were rather chary of it last night.'

' Well, Chris, you must admit that, near as you have come, you have not quite brought it off.'

'I suppose, like Jesus and Napoleon and Lenin, I shall be deemed a failure.'

'A splendid failure.'

'Not brought it off, as you say.'

'Not quite.'

> *'Well, well! Nor I nor any man that but man is*
> *With nothing shall be pleased till he be eased*
> *With being nothing.'*

The cook, who was never seen about in the week, and thus was not missed in the upheaval, came up to say that breakfast was served; and they all repaired downstairs, Eva placing Herr Kogl on her right (because he was old and had suffered), and Christopher, though he was a peer of England, on her left. De Jones did not like it. He had scattered his title about, but now he would take himself in hand. He would take care to leave his full history to his descendants, so that they should all know who their ancestor was. It occurred to him that possibly Adam himself was, had we been privileged to enquire more closely into his record, the ninth earl of something or other. 'I daresay,' he said aloud, 'it will tickle them no end to know that their founder was of the English aristocracy.'

'I am not sure,' said Frank, 'whether I should not contest your sovereignty. The last of the Romanovs having disintegrated (and even the last before so doing having relinquished his claim in my favour), I am by all accounts the Emperor and Autocrat of All the Russias, Tsar of Poland, and Grand Duke of Finland.'

'With no heir to the throne,' said Chris.

'That depends on my Queen Consort, who in the case of my death and no issue would succeed to the throne as Eva the Second.'

'Eva is my consort—already by the fact that she is bearing me a child.'

'My child?'

'Eva, whose child?'

'I don't know.'

'Strange not to know.'

'Don't you see, Chris, we must have children, little boys and girls, so that they may marry again and carry on the race.'

' What! Their own half-sisters! Eva, I am shocked.'

'Beggars can't be choosers.'

'Well, so long as they are good de Jones stock. Say what you like, there's something in having blue blood. I'm a believer in old families.'

'My mother,' Dickin proffered shyly, 'was an Adams.'

'Adams and Eva!'

'And we must hand down such knowledge as we possess, do you hear, Chris? We must put it down on paper—all we know and remember. There is Mrs. Hannibal's typewriter. Though we have no printing press, we can make carbon copies. When I was at Cambridge——'

'Were you at Cambridge?'

'Why?'

'It's a rare thing.'

'Why?'

'It's no more.'

'When I was at Cambridge I made a point of recording all I knew. Do you know any algebra?'

'I don't know any algebra. Leave me alone.'

'But poetry? Has anyone got any poetry? My God! There is no poetry.'

'Yes, darling, there is poetry.'

'Give it here. Let me have it, quick. Where is it?'

'I have some. Here, in my album.'

'Give it me. God! Not real poetry?'

'Yes, darling, very nice poetry. There in the middle. There.'

'Thanks.

> ' "*O Eva, O Eva,*
> *I love you so mighty,*
> *I wish my pyjama was*
> *Next to your nighty.*"

Thanks.'

'You can copy it out on the typewriter, darling, for all the boy and girl lovers after our time. I suppose they will be able to read English.'

'Yes,' said Chris. English, he laid down, was to be the only language of the new world, to perpetuate the traditions of the English-speaking world. On the other hand, to show his complete lack of racial prejudice, the daring unconventionality of his mind, he confessed, with a smile, that though he preferred to stick to the criminal law of England, in civic matters he was in favour of the Code Napoléon. He looked upon himself as holding the new world under a mandate from the British Empire; in fact he was himself in lineal descent from the Stuarts. He was in reality the trustee of the British Crown. 'Gentlemen,' he said: 'The King!'

'The King!'

The Baron and Herr Kogl, both of them confirmed anglophiles, did not protest.

After breakfast, they carried the body of Frau Kogl into the wood and buried her among the trees and flowers. Christopher, who presided, said a few unsentimental words over the open grave, the burden of which was that to understand everything was to forgive everything. After that he marched Herr Kogl away, the while enquiring in detail as to the number and condition of the cattle, the orchard, the poultry farm, the vegetable garden, and even the household utensils. 'I shall require from you,' he said, 'a regular account of these.' And when later he inspected the cattle, he said: 'I am anxious at all cost to prevent the outbreak of the foot-and-mouth disease. I shall hold you personally responsible.'

Herr Kogl, wondering sorrowfully what his poor Anna would have said to the noble lord's attitude to her own property, took it all in with good grace. His reputed strong will availed him but little, but his good sense a great deal; and when on returning home he addressed Lord de Jones as '*Il Duce*,' Lord de Jones appointed Herr Kogl Chief Intendant and Quartermaster-General with the acting rank of Minister of the Interior.

While *Il Duce* and his Quartermaster were discussing economy, Frank Dickin, after being appointed Poet Laureate of the New World, strolled away in search of inspiration. A thought struck him. He ambled on and, when he was well out of sight, dashed across to the archducal Schloss and hoisted his striped shirt, for want of a flag, according to the rules of the old world. And according to the rules of the old world, he looked about for something with which to defend the newly acquired possession, and felt that in so doing he was also performing an act of loyalty to the old world so ignominiously done in overnight. He waited for Lord de Jones to attack him with bombs and shrapnel and machine guns. And he reflected that if Lord de Jones did not attack him with bombs and machine guns, it was because Lord de Jones had no bombs and machine guns to attack him with.

It was odd, this feeling of proprietorship, in the face of universal dissolution. He had to tell himself again and again that this castle with the stately staircase, those long rows of red-gold rooms succeeding one another as in a picture gallery, the quadrangle and the park and the surrounding moat, the drawbridge and the water falling down the steep of the enshrouding hills, and not a soul around—were his and his alone. And when Eva visited him there that morning, he showed her round till she felt faint.

'Talking of castles,' she said, lying down on the archducal sofa, 'look: is it not sweet?'

And she displayed her garters with a castle worked in silk and bearing the inscription on the castle gate: 'For one only.'

'Chris gave me this on leaving London.' She moved about the room and fingered his things. 'What's this bottle, Ferdinand?'

'The beautiful crop you see on my head I owe to the regular use of this lotion, reinforced by sheer strength of will.'

'Where will you get a new bottle when this is used up?'

'Not in this world. It's a French make of pre-Dissolution days, with an excellent translation of the instructions for use. Read the label.'

'I see. "This very energical and excitative lotion for the hair whose it favours the growth and gives to the hair, sweetness strength. Mode of use: with a little sponge, washing plentifully the head during a week. Afterwards thrice in a week." Quite amusing.' She put it back. 'You have fine hair now.'

'It's the only thing I have left. And it wasn't there before.'

It seemed a shame that this fine crop of hair should survive in the teeth of a dissolving world. Survive? How survive?

'We had better go back to the *pension* for lunch now,' she said.

'Yes,' he agreed sourly. 'That is the annoying thing about large houses. All this luxury, and not a cook on the premises. What good owning a castle with a hundred and seventy rooms, and no servants? Spend all my days mopping the floors. Saw an automatic mopper in Tottenham Court Road the other day. Ought to have secured one. Lacked vision. Lacked faith.'

It would not always be so. He saw in the future unborn Dickins living in these lofty halls. A brilliant party. Bare-armed women. And his portrait looking down at them from the wall. His great granddaughter eloping with a de Jones youth. Romeo and Juliet. Family feud. Capulets and Montagues. Noble families. Hundred per cent. pre-Dissolution. Dreams, dreams, dreams...

The prospect of there being nothing to eat at first upset them all so much that they lost their appetite. But when they ascertained that there was a great deal to eat, they were so delighted that they began to drink heavily. While they were at lunch the cook came in to say that she had just come upon Frau König in the cellar, where she had evidently hidden herself since yesterday's sham earthquake and bore signs of being of unsound mind.

'Bring her forth,' commanded de Jones.

Frau König, dishevelled, and looking more than ever like a gipsy, was led into the room, whereupon Lord de Jones addressed her courteously but firmly. 'Your appearance,' he said, 'is both timely and opportune and, in the sociological sense, clearly an asset. The world has reached a stage at which immediate repopulation has become of paramount importance. We lack women, though we do not lack men. We have but two women and five men. I do not count the cook as a woman because she is clearly beyond the age of reproduction. The men, on the other hand, are all (I do not exempt even the older gentlemen, such as the Herr Baron and Herr Kogl) rare examples of virility coupled with a high sense of public duty.'

'Unfortunately,' said Frau König, 'my fiancé in Paris, having again failed in his examination at the University, it has set us back two years with our knitting factory. Otherwise——'

'Frau König, it's not knitting factories I am talking of, though we could do with one here at a later stage, when we have reproduced an adequate number of mill hands, which is the task we have in hand. And you have no right to shirk the call.'

'I don't understand. My fiancé is still in Paris——'

'Don't understand? Am I not making myself clear? Frau König, I cannot presume to know your opinion of our late educational system, and I know that in a purely scholastic sense it perhaps ranked below that of the late Continent. But we were taught at our English public schools something which was called "playing the game." Now is this, if I may ask you, "playing the game"?'

'But I desire nothing better. If my fiancé were here, of course. I'm quite ill waiting for him all these years, living on hope deferred.'

'Your fiancé! Your fiancé! What do I care for a fiancé who exists but in your memory?' De Jones grasped her by the wrist. 'Frau König,' he said, 'there is no room for thoughts of self. It's a question of repopulating this planet, at the shortest possible notice. Are you (I will not say patriotic, for patriotism, as such, has lost all meaning): are you mundic?'

'I am not averse,' said Frau König. 'In marriage one contracts certain habits. But,' she added, 'my condition is that you take me out into society.'

'But, good heavens!' Eva cried. 'Her offspring will be as mad as hatters!'

'Which may add a touch of genius to those who will follow. We have come near enough to the Kingdom of God: but have not quite tumbled to it. They, with a touch of genius, may go one further and clear up the mess after themselves, and themselves as well.'

'Better let me do what I can.'

'Now, Eva, don't be jealous. You can't, Lilith, do it all yourself. You will kill yourself.'

'I am willing to do my bit.'

'There must be no slacking, no half-heartedness,' cried Chris. 'Here we start anew!'

> '*There was a little man,*
> *And his name was Finnegan;*
> *He grew whiskers on his chin again.*
> *The wind did blow and blew them in again,*
> *Poor old Patsy Finnegan.*
> *Finnegan!*
> *Begin again!*'

'A message of courage and hope,' said de Jones. 'Our new mundic anthem.' Christopher had changed; he was 'another man,' as they say. He was like an artist who has just finished a picture, or a scholar who has completed a treatise. This his work had been the making of him. He was light-hearted, positively gay. Only the wrinkles round his mouth had deepened still more.

'Art thou man or devil?' Eva asked.

But he cried, jumping to his feet with a glass in his hand: 'Now all together, please:

> '*There was a little man,*
> *And his name was Finnegan*———'

The Baron and Herr Kogl, unable to contribute to the singing, since the Baron's knowledge of English was confined to saying good morning in the evening, and Herr Kogl's was nil, yet contrived to join in the chorus at the end, and shouted lustily with the others:

> '*Finnegan!*
> *Begin again!*'

45

In due course, that is exactly in the course of time prescribed by nature, and unaffected by changed meteorological conditions, Eva gave birth to a son, who, though both Frank Dickin and Christopher de Jones were anxious to claim his paternity, proved to be, on inspection, without the remotest shadow of a doubt, the second Baron Ottercove of Ottercove. And all day long he laughed to himself.

'That's all right,' said Christopher, on being admitted. 'But let him not expect too much of the new world. For we came crying hither: thou know'st the first time that we smell the air we waul and cry.'

'Alack! Alack the day!'

'When we are born, we cry that we are come to this (small) stage of fools.'

'What shall we call him?' asked his overjoyed mother. And many names were suggested.

'Rex Alexander,' by Eva herself, in undying memory of his illustrious father.

'Christopher,' by Lord de Jones, in honour of himself and Christopher Columbus, the explorer, and Christopher Morley, the American critic.

'Ferdinand,' by Ferdinand, and in honour of Ferdinand. 'Ex-King of Greece,' he explained when Lord de Jones frowned at him.

'Call him Adam,' suggested Herr Kogl. 'For he is the first-born of this new earth.'

'Yes, yes, Adam,' said Eva.

And he was called Adam. In honour of the late Miss Adams (which was Frank's mother's maiden name), as Frank liked to think fondly but on insufficient evidence.

Eva had become very competent. The Pension Kogl was transformed into a day and night nursery; the kitchen was used for drying the second Baron Ottercove's garments; and when the men argued as to whether their world could survive, she invariably cut short the discussion by saying: What mattered the world? It was the survival of baby that mattered.

'I wish,' she said, 'Pilling could have seen my baby.'

'Damn Pilling! Didn't you think of your mother when you were making your selection for your Noah's ark?'

'Well, darling, I thought she wouldn't be alone in all this. She would have all the other people with her. And Mummy always loved crowds.'

Chris looked away, ashamed. 'It was no use,' he said at last. 'It was a hopeless, incurable race. A perverted mentality. Nothing to be done with them. Even the best of them were beyond salvation. Take my aunt. An amiable old lady, yet cruel in her very kindness. During the last war, like most old ladies, she had been vehemently, almost indecently, anti-German. After the war, travelling about in Italy, and being the really nice old English lady that she was, she confessed to a feeling of shame at the snarling attitude of the *Continental Daily Mail*, while so many titled Germans were about. What she most quickly recovered was her interest in the imperial family of Germany, and she confessed a heartfelt sympathy for the ex-Kaiser. "Rather a fascinating man," she said, "and after all, he was the grandson of our own dear Queen Victoria, so we should-n't be too hard on him." The dear old lady! I can see her now as she walked beside me, stopping every few paces to recover her breath, but pretending she was doing so to bring home a point in our conversation: "Now isn't that remarkable!" or else to examine a bicycle propped up in front of a shop: "What an unusual bicy-cle!" or to read a poster: "Have you seen this?" She was a good woman, and the very stuff our race was made of. You might have thought that it would have profited by its mistakes and devised a working social order. But (as Goethe said about politics) men would not learn, and God did not seem to want it.'

'That is so, but, if anything, you have made things worse.'

'Hardly worse,' said de Jones. 'I have in my pocket a newspa-per fragment. Let me read it aloud so that you may realize what you have been saved from. Here it is. It is entitled "Royal Month of February," and it goes on: "Many famous hostesses have already come to town, and during the next few days will make the final preparations for their participation in the stately pageant in the House of Lords when the King opens Parliament in state to-morrow week. New Court gowns will be tried on in Mayfair, St. James's, and Belgravia, and priceless family jewels will be brought from the strong-rooms of historic banks." '

'Almighty God!' said Frank.

' "Among the weddings within the next week or two will be that of Major the Hon. Maurice Duff Glayton and Lady Ursula Blaming at St. Margaret's, Westminster. The Marquis of Lillings-worth's two charming daughters will be among the bridesmaids. Both bride and bridegroom are well known in the yachting world of Cowes." '

'Almighty God!'

' "The Marquis and Marchioness of Epping spent the week-end in town in Curzon Street. Lord and Lady Castle have come from Kent, Lady Walden de Munford from Paris, the Dowager Duchess of Hawke from Ireland, and the American Ambassador from the United States. The Countess of Buxham and her daughter are back again in Eaton Place." '

'God Almighty!' He wiped his brow with his handkerchief, and as he walked away he stopped every few paces and said: 'God Almighty! God Almighty!'

46

Elle avait appris dans sa jeunesse à caresser les phrases, au long col sinueux et démesuré, de Chopin, si libres, si flexibles, si tactiles, qui commencent par chercher et essayer leur place en dehors et bien loin de la direction de leur départ, bien loin du point où on avait pu espérer qu'atteindrait leur attouchement, et qui ne se jouent dans cet écart de fantaisie que pour revenir plus délibérément, d'un retour plus prémédité, avec plus de précision, comme sur un cristal qui résonnerait jusqu' à faire crier, vous frapper au coeur.—Proust.

He returned to his Schloss park, went down the gravel path into the hidden nooks where the waters dashing down from steep heights broke their fall in cool spray. All was as young as on that first untrodden morn. So Adam must have stood in the first-flush of Eden.

And suddenly he came upon her in the pine wood.

'Pale primrose.'

'Not here.'

'But yes. That you may bear me a child.'

'Yes, you—and Chris.'

He was overcome with tremulous anxiety that he might lose her, his one, his only woman. To hold her, if only for a moment, was to hold the beauty and the passion of a world no more. He thought of all the loving behind lighted windows, of meetings in leafy lanes and cloistered streets by moonlight, and sunny flower-blown glades—gone for ever. He tried to gather it all and impress it on these lips, these taut, supple fingers, these heaving young breasts... And they took of the fruit thereof, and did eat: and they heard the voice of the Lord God walking in the garden in the cool of the day.

'And do you remember,' she said, 'how we were lost on the hill?'

'I remember.'

'And how the storm came on, and how you held me, and how it rained and we ran to hide under the rock?'

'And you remember Count Kolberg?'

'Yes, that soppy-face! And how when he asked us out to dinner he sent in a long bill next day, charging up to Mummy our share of the meal, giving all the details:

> 3 rolls.
> 3 soups.
> 3 cutlets.
> 3 salads.
> potatoes—3 portions.
> 2 lemonades.
> 1 beer.

And that night he took us to the "München" he ordered champagne. But when it came to paying, he had no money and began to cry. And Mummy said to him very kindly: "But why, if you *knew* you hadn't any money, did you order champagne?" "Because all the others did," he said.'

'And what happened?'

'Oh, the waiter boxed his ears for him and kicked him out and called him names. It was very disagreeable for us.'

'How did he take it?'

'Not very badly. Sort of half playfully. "You don't know what I was going through in my inner soul," he said, when we were out of doors, "*Ach! Ai, ai, ai! Ai, ai ai!*" '

'Then it was we who were lost. Now it is the world. The poor world, with no lovers in it any more, save you and me. It seems we must love for the lot. Justify love. We shall not fail. We shall not fail.'

She looked wistful.

'Eva…honey love.'

'Yes.'

'I am unworthy. But God in His infinite love has brought all this about that we might come together again, you and I, Eva.'

'Darling,' she said, 'I don't believe it!'

'Nor do I, for that matter,' he said, pressing her to him, 'and I scarcely think that this was an end pursued by Chris.'

'The last thing that he intended.'

The sun subsided towards evening, and suddenly the landscape shone forth with a crystalline clearness, as though you had adjusted your binoculars to the required focus. Before them stretched a plain. No more horizons.

They stood up and walked on, lifting themselves from the ground with one foot and coming down in a leisurely curve with the other, as horses in a slow-motion picture clearing a fence.

'The gravitation,' he sniffed, 'is ludicrously weak.'

'It's only a small planet, darling,' she said, 'and hasn't much strength.'

'We walk as on air.'

'I don't mind it, darling. And we're in no great hurry.' The sun came out again, and, as they climbed up the steep ridge to the pine wood, shone through the trees with a dazzling whiteness such as only acetylene lamps can contrive. On the edge of the wood they halted; below was a lake surrounded by firs: a little lake, like a plum dipped in water. Sky, firs, hills, water, all was blue, each just a shade darker; all blue and motionless, as if still waiting for something. They stood still, their hearts thumping; till the sun sank and the first silver stars twinkled feebly in the sky.

'And don't you miss your dear Rex?'

'He was so strange and peculiar.'

'Yet I never met anyone who did not like him. It was his eagerness which fascinated one. I once arrived during a very agitated conversation between him and Vernon Sprott, who was pained by the alterations made by Ottercove in his last article, when Ottercove defended himself with spirit. "What's the good of being a newspaper proprietor," he said, "if you can't butt in occasionally?" There was a rare dash about him. It was a joy to dine with him; all the waiting service congregated round his table in the restaurants. Dinner over, he would step into the lift, a panting waiter getting in with him to present the bill, which Ottercove would sign without looking. "Don't they ever swindle you?" I once asked him. He looked at me earnestly. "Frank, I expect them to swindle me." This was great, if you like. But he would come out with better things, too. Once, in failing to please him with my definition of him, I suggested that my definition was not flattering enough, and he said: "Not a bit. If I only listened to flatteries, it wouldn't do my character any good, now would it? I wouldn't develop, would I?"'

'The darling,' said Eva. 'The little pet.'

'What made him greater than most men of action was that there was, side by side with his sense of his own abilities, an essential humility in him. It would have been the most natural thing in the world for one who had started literally with nothing, and rose to a share in the control, and an enlightened control, of the destiny of a great empire, himself surrounded on every side by awe-struck relatives and bowing sycophants, to grow bumptious and megalomaniacal, intolerant and overbearing. Not a sign of it in Ottercove! Instead, an enquiring charm, a readiness to listen and learn even from youths. The same bright-eyed mischievous boyishness at forty as at twenty, a touching eagerness to do worthwhile things, ever the man of the world equal to every situation, and yet, a sort of wayward kindness, an engaging modesty which left him unaware of what it was in him that made up his charm. And withal a public fearlessness, the sure touch of a genius in everything he did. I doubt if he was ever told his worth. We did not tell him. And now it is too late.'

He paused before he spoke again. 'For us who can remember him he is gentle, human, and kind. But to those who will follow us he will be just a star god, together with Sprott-Pollux, the two gods of material success! What I say is, If not Ottercove, then the cigar of Ottercove! May it shine for ever and ever.'

They kneeled down and bowed low, touching the earth with their brow. And in that attitude of holy prostration they remained a long time.

'Look,' he said, lifting his face from the ground and sitting back on his heels, 'there they are, Castor and Pollux, looking down on us through the clouds.' Eva, who, like a small girl in church, had followed all Frank's movements through her spread fingers while prostrate in prayer, uncouched as yet in the new ritual, now also sat back on her heels and looked up at the stars. 'Pollux once wrote something about somebody with the High Hand.'

'Yes. There he stands with raised hand; you feel as if the whole of the Five Towns were gazing down on us with quiet, benignant reproach. And next him is Castor. Even in life Castor never used more than one eye at a time: he closed one and put it all into the other. What an eye! All the fire of Zeus was in that eye; it could pierce through stone walls. He sees everything we do. There, read that look now. He seems to say: "You have disintegrated my thousand reporters: yet from here I see everything and report it all direct to my God." '

'Good God!' Eva turned to him, alarmed. 'Then he has seen how you have loved me a minute ago.'

'Castor was a reasonable being. His morality was pragmatic and rational. Look again at that eye of his. What does it say? Not "go and sin no more," but "sin and sin again till you have brought the population of the earth back to pre-Dissolution standard." Rex, you see, was always a man who believed in giving you another chance.'

Eva looked thoughtful.

'The curse of Eve is upon you, my girl!'

'What is that, darling?'

'I haven't got my Bible here—and I sadly fear we haven't a copy of it in this world—but I believe it is something to do with bringing forth children in pain and labour.'

'It is a pity,' she said, 'that we haven't brought with us any labour-saving devices.'

'Lacked foresight, lacked vision.'

'And you, darling, will have to work in the sweat of your brow.'

'Not I! My motto is: "Give us peace in our time, O Lord," and *après nous le déluge!*'

'They may do it yet. They may come to it yet. We must not lose faith.'

'No, we must not! We must not lose faith in the sense of mankind to wipe out mankind. But must wait, must be patient. That this idea may occur to one among millions of men, we must breed millions of men, till there emerges out of these masses the new Messiah, not a half-hearted devil like Chris who has let himself be tempted by this dew-eyed woman Eva, but a man who will at last administer the *coup de grâce*. And so, *allons, enfants de la patrie!* Breed, breed, breed!'

'There's only Frau König and me,' sighed Eva. 'The cook does not count.'

'Cook or no cook, we shall have to bring down the age of consent, or else to precipitate the age of puberty, to twelve. In twelve years nine months from to-day you and Frau König (for I have commended her to the bereaved policeman) will be able, all being well, to give birth to sixteen children, a total of thirty-two, of which two will come of age that day. Some of the children may die, and the Baron's may prove apoplectic. But the general outlook, if not rosy, yet enables me to look into the future with confidence.'

He sat down, and was lost in reverie. He saw the population of their little planet rising annually, by geometrical progression, till it was black with people, like a dish with cranberries, people packed like sardines: working in mills, the din of machines, roaring furnaces: producing, producing,—a sight fit to delight the eyes of the gods. And Sunday always spent in devotion, kneeling (for lack of other gods) before Castor and Pollux, while a priest in flowing robes held forth on the dignity, the nobility of hard work, winding up his oration with the new mundic anthem, and from a million throttles came one long roar:

> '*Finnegan!*
> *Begin again!*'

What a religion!

With a start, he detached himself from his reverie. 'The stars are getting more golden,' he said, rising, 'and the sky is a dark, deep blue.'

'And, darling, look at them, I mean the stars. We can see them everywhere, underneath as well as on top.'

'That is quite natural. The earth is a tiny ball and we can walk round it like flies.'

'But Castor and Pollux are on top.'

'Always were top dogs even in life.'

'See, darling, Castor and Pollux are now pure gold.'

'Not unnaturally, either. Look at that wood, secretive, leering. Hush! Hark!'

'Yes.'

'Listen:

> ' "*Die Rehlein beten zur Nacht:*
> *"Halb Ach!"*
> *Halb neun, halb zehn, halb elf, elf, zwölf,*
> *Die Rehlein beten zur Nacht,*
> *Sie falten die kleine Zehlein,*
> *Die Rehlein."* '

'Sweet. What makes you think in German?'

'I quote in the language of the country.'

'Which country?'

'Technically this is a piece of old Austria.'

'M'm! It makes you think. A piece of old Austria. But Australia gone, America gone, India, Russia, Paris, London, Vienna—all gone!'

'To kingdom come. Didn't Christ always warn us that it was at hand?'

'Nobody took any notice of Him, darling.'

'Till too late. But we shall muddle through. It is an English characteristic, to give the old country its due. Not because we are muddle-headed, but because no other race is clear-headed enough to perceive how muddled they are, except the Russians, who, having perceived the muddled nature of all life, have identified themselves with it for good.'

'There is the moon.'

'Yes, there she is.'

The moon swam out in all the fulness of her glory.

'Oh, do you remember that passage in "Hermann und Dorothea," as they go homeward by night, as we are doing now? How goes it!—

' *"Herrlich glänzte der Mond, der volle, vom Himmel herunter;*
Nacht war's, völlig bedeckt das letzte Schimmern der Sonne.
Und so lagen vor ihnen in Massen gegen einander
Lichter, hell wie der Tag, und Schatten dunkeler Nächte."

My memory is the only repository of poetry that we have with us. And nature, or what is left of it, the only promise of heaven. Look at those rocks,' he pointed. 'What serene dispassionate peace! They are death. They brood, but not darkly. They are pressing upon us: you and I have to bear their intolerable weight! The clouds sail above them, barely touching them, toppling over. They teach us that life is not what we do or think; that life is elsewhere, barely touching us, as those clouds.'

Somebody, probably Frau König, began to play Chopin, and the rippling waterfall of sound, marvellous and enchanting, filtered through the air; the strains pressed into the night and asked questions.

'O God of Love! How that woman plays. Her madness, resentment, then a cowed, shuddering awe, and overflowing tears of tenderness. They have summoned, you see, those other creatures, visitants from a world, certainly not ours. "Perhaps," says Proust, "we shall lose them, perhaps they will be obliterated, if we return to nothing in the dust. Perhaps it is not-being that is the true state, and all our dream of life is without existence; but, if so, we feel that it must be that these phrases of music, these conceptions which exist in relation to our dream, are nothing either. We shall perish, but we have for our hostages these divine captives who shall follow and share our fate. And death in their company is something less bitter, less inglorious, and perhaps even less certain." '

'It dawns.'

'It dawns. Home, darling, and to bed.'

They began the descent, as the sky grew threadbare, the moon paled, and a small peevish sun looked out, sleepy, red-eyed. Then a shaft of light licked a fugitive cloud. A cock cleared his throat in the yard below. The rich odour of mown grass and the rays on the ricks of straw bade them live. They blessed their fate, and that neither of them was to be hanged at dawn, that they had sufficient to eat and could go home and sleep in clean sheets upon feather beds.

47

It is Finished

Chor. Es ist vorbei.
Mephistopheles. Vorbei! ein dummes Wort.
     Warum vorbei?
                              —*Faust*, Teil II., Akt V.

Six weeks it rained without cease. Dark clouds ran on, as if there was still a scheme in the universe, even though this chip of a dead planet was discarded; dark, brooding, they ran, on and on. Never had they known such weather, except possibly in London.

They were sarcastic at the expense of Lord de Jones, who told them they had grown immodest in their expectations; that even in the New Jerusalem it was not always sunshine.

But lo! a shaft of sunlight. The wet valley glittered with gaiety; it spread to the hills, then the whole vault of heaven broke out into spontaneous sunlight. Soon they all cried out for mercy. Mercy! How hot! The sun pressed on, pressed on, pressed on.

It was—though the seasons played pranks—a midsummer's day, and—they thought—a Sunday, so warm and radiant that they brought out the table and chairs on to the terrace and lunched in the sight of the sun and the rocks. The cook, responding to the mood, expressed her personality in an exquisite meal of pre-Dissolution magnificence; and when Herr Kogl had filled their glasses, Lord de Jones rose and proposed the health of the King. The two ladies having retired, the five men addressed themselves to the usual business of imparting bawdy jokes, and Herr Kogl related how when he was in Wien and was told to buy a female fish he had ignorantly asked for a virgin fish. 'In Wien!' exclaimed the fishmonger, his eyes dilated with wonder. 'It's not to be had.'

'Ah, Wien! When as a youth I was doing my military service, we had to march through Wien, all along the Ring. There is no capital like Wien!—Not that I've seen other capitals.'

Capitals! It seemed a shame that they should have gone, capitals more magnificent than Vienna. But Herr Kogl, liberal on other topics, said that Vienna beat them all. Wien! Wien! His son Herbert had been to Wien—to the Hotel and Restaurant Institute. He had been getting on so well—when the blow came. It seemed a shame. Herr Kogl went into the house and came out with his son's certificate in his big, shaking red hands. 'Here it is. His college certificate.' He passed it reverently to Lord de Jones, and while the other read it, turned away his face. Two large beads rolled down his cheeks. Lord de Jones put on his glasses and read:

> Calligraphy——proficient;
> Arithmetic——good;
> Cooking——very satisfactory;
> Slaughtering——praiseworthy;
> Waiting at table——very good;
> Deportment——excellent;
> General conduct——excellent.

Herr Kogl turned round after an interval; hot tears streamed down his cheeks, as Lord de Jones handed him back the certificate. They all waited for Lord de Jones to say something. His mouth opened.

'Shall we join the ladies in the drawing-room?' he said.

But before they did so, Eva had come out with little Adam in her arms and sat on the *pension* steps, the second Baron Ottercove, a toothless radiance illuminating his whole countenance, on her lap. Herr Kogl sat by and tickled the baby's nose with a feather. 'Our only ray of sunshine, our little hope...' And he would look into these eyes basking in the sunshine, with wonderment and tenderness, and think and think. 'As for you, Rags,' he turned to the dog, at his feet, 'the outlook for caninity is black. Black.'

'I wish the Frau Professor's dachshund had been saved,'

remarked Lord de Jones. 'The canine race would have had a new start.'

'But the dachshund was no good, darling; he had weak lungs.'

'Still, beggars can't be choosers, as you said yourself, Eva.'

'And our Rags too is no good. Rags, you old bitch, you're no good, are you? No good! Poor old bitch! Poor old bitch!' Two large beads stood in Herr Kogl's eyes.

And, indeed, Rags was not much good to found a new canine race. She was blind and deaf with old age and lay in a corner all day. Only when you bent down to her and shouted very loudly in her ear: 'Scho—ko—lade!' she would turn over and twitch feebly with her forelegs, in reminiscent pleasure.

There were no more dogs. The Prime Minister had been vindicated.

'There was,' said Eva dreamily, 'a little tea-shop just off Jermyn Street, where you could get delicious ices.'

'Yes. The original sin was when man wrapped himself up in the visible world. The ultimate sin was when he shed it.'

'It may appear so to any one who has not been strong enough to shed his vices. But, for my part, I have given up smoking,' said Chris, 'for complete lack of tobacco.'

'How weak! Strength of will would lie in going on, in persisting in the face of unsurmountable difficulties.'

'But though I have nothing to reproach myself with,' continued de Jones, oblivious of Frank's interruption, 'I too have my memories of the old world, and in particular do I remember the Allied Victory march through Paris after the Great War as the troops passed under the Arc de Triomphe, ablaze with glory! A powerful emotion for a pacifist.'

Soldiers. Images drifted before Christopher. He saw ranks and ranks of them. Soldiers in scarlet uniform. Bayonets glistening in the sun. *His* soldiers, armed to the teeth, equipped with the latest weapons of war. Glorious manhood! Only waiting for the word of command to set off for the enemy. He saw other soldiers ready on the turrets of Frank's castle. His own lion-hearted warriors storming the castle, falling into the moat. He looked at Frank and wished that the jolly game were already beginning. 'Ah!' he moved restively.

'What is it, darling?' from Eva.

'One day, Frank,' he rubbed his hands anticipatingly, 'yours and mine shall measure their strength in battle. Wish I were alive to see the day!'

The Baron held up his glass: '*Der Tag!*'

De Jones sat pensive. 'It seems to me, as I sit here, a sedentary, useless man, that I can hear across the years the distant neighing of chargers, the sharpening of flints by the camp fire. Dangerous life! Glorious struggle! Give me Kipling or D. H. Lawrence. They'd understand this. My men advancing valiantly and capturing the forts of yon castle.'

'Nor, when they have captured it, Chris, let them rest. It is, remember, only a milestone on their road to further achievement. Let them go on capturing other castles, on and on, till they have had enough.' Frank's look grew reminiscent. 'When I joined up in the last war, there was a good deal of stealing— "pinching," they called it, going on amongst the troopers. What more natural and proper, you'd think, in a community of roughnecks. "But, nay!" says the Idealist in Man: "We stick bayonet blades into other men in the name of an Idea. Pinching from your comrade is subversive of ultimate efficiency in the business of stabbing your neighbour. It deflects attention, sows suspicion, where there should be love of one's own and hatred of others. The ideal is to eliminate dishonesty and to create a high standard of honour and mutual confidence among the troops so that they may devote their undivided attention to murdering the soldiers of another army (with an equally high moral standard). That is the aim. That is patriotism—serving the flag." '

'I agree,' said de Jones. 'We must not arm for aggression, but for defence alone. The best way to ensure peace is to be armed to the teeth.'

'I see.'

'The meek,' said Herr Kogl, 'shall inherit the earth.'

'None of that here, Herr Kogl,' protested de Jones. 'Maudlin mysticism! Quite the proper note to strike in a *fin de siècle* mood and period. But we're a new Finnegan-begin-again civilization, up-and-doing, straining every nerve that the race may survive. No room for mooners. It's men of action we want.'

'The Kingdom of Heaven is within you.

'Quite.'

'Peace within, love of those nearest to you, no desires, no regrets, only love, steady, translucent love of all living beings: what bliss could equal it? It fills your soul with peace, as beams of sun at eventide. A peace' —Herr Kogl's eyes filled with tears— 'that passeth all understanding. "Come unto me," He said, "all ye who labour and are heavy-laden, and I will give you rest: for my yoke is easy and my burden light."'

Frank jumped to his feet. 'Give me riches, give me women, each day a new one (unless I ask twice for the same one), give me food, wine—and I shall give no thought to the things of this world. But to renounce, to settle down when there is nothing—nothing...' He could not speak. He walked up and down.

Eva looked at de Jones very earnestly. 'You should never have done it,' she said.

But Herr Kogl smiled happily. 'What does it matter? What does it matter,' he asked, 'how we step over into eternity? We are shaken off this realm of matter one way or another.'

'Herr Kogl is a mystic—while there is wine in the cellar.' De Jones looked slyly at him. 'We've found you out!'

'Now I am dependent on spirits for my good temper—I might just as well make a clean breast of it. But not always shall I be so dependent. What matter old age and darkness? My watch,' he said. 'It still registers the revolutions of our little planet. Here it is. Its dial is phosphorescent. Now its face is dull and complacent; but take it into utter darkness and its face will illumine. So shall our souls, now bleak and obscure, illumine in the utter darkness of death.'

Herr Kogl looked at his friends. They did not hear angels; they felt not the utter glory of God. Only the baby smiled unendingly at God's world, smiled away all fear and concern into little ripples of light.

'But not a thing!' cried Frank. 'Where is there a book of poems, a scroll of music? Frau König,' he turned to her earnestly, 'you must teach Adam music when he grows up. You must teach him, Frau König, you must! Think: if this too goes——'

He jumped to his feet. 'But not a Shakespeare, not a Goethe, not a Raphael, not a Mozart——'

He wailed aloud. 'Oh! Oh! Oh!' He writhed on the damp ground. 'Oh! Oh! Oh!'

Eva looked on mournfully. 'The world—the poor world!'

'It's had a long run for its money,' muttered de Jones.

'And I never told it that I cared for it.'

'After life's fitful fever it sleeps well.'

The cook came in to say that she had prepared an egg dish for supper as she feared that the cows had caught the foot-and-mouth disease, and that they had better keep the sheep for wool, Frau König having told her of her projected plans for a knitting factory.

At this they all sat back, open-mouthed. The Baron shook his head. 'This intensifies the problem of survival,' he said gravely. But Lord de Jones jumped to his feet, his hand raised in challenge.

'Are—we—down-hearted?' he cried.

'No-o-o!' The echo of the cry resounded from the rocks. Frank was conspicuous by his silence.

'But how will Adam do now without milk!' Eva looked much concerned.

'He will have,' said de Jones, 'to fall back on the milk of human kindness. Frau König,' he turned to her, 'it will hence be incumbent on you to generate it. May your happiness consist therein! I will, for my part, endeavour to reproduce synthetic milk—or synthetic cows. Whichever comes easier. So tails up! keep smiling! and all the rest of it. Now all together, please:

> *"There was a little man,*
> *And his name was Finnegan."* '

They joined in the anthem.

'We shall survive!' finished de Jones. 'See if we don't! And little Adam will not be the last nor least to survive.'

Eva embraced him tighter. 'Oh, he must, oh, he must! for the sake of——'

'——of everything that's been.' Dear, dear earth! It was gone; suddenly, while nobody was looking. Even now Frank could not quite take it in. Slowly and doggedly man had been working, planning and thinking, cautiously, step by step, climbing the steep rocky path, the circle of light spreading before him larger and wider as he advanced to a knowledge of nature, a forefeeling of

God. Against heavy odds, divided against itself, mankind had struggled heroically; it had built temples and palaces, steamers and bridges and airplanes, mansions traversing the oceans and mansions traversing the air. A little more, and man would have conquered himself. But a morbid little mind had stolen the fire of Zeus and put back the clock. Egypt and India, Greece, Rome— had they laboured in vain? Had Europe created fortuitously? This is the end, he thought. And he mourned the earth, mourned all those millions who had once loved, suffered and died. Of course there had been misery, tribulations, hate, lies, sordid hours, and moments of pain. But there had been other moments. He remembered how fourteen of his friends had volunteered to be bled to save his mother's life. He wept at the thought of it. He remembered other hours. Holiday crowds. Gaily clad women. The briskness of mornings, the lassitude of nights. Dew on the roses. The chivalry of reconciliation, of respect, the dignity of moments.

And they had all died, died.

The sun set behind the hill and left the valley cold and unfriendly; only the tips of rocks still gleamed in the sun. Dark clouds, looking like furrows, ran on without cease; cold, bleak and unmeaning, they ran, on and on. A bird chirruped plaintively from a branch. Herr Kogl looked up.

'Bird, forlorn bird, you are surprised at the doom which has befallen our beautiful earth. You grieve, and I grieve with you. The oceans are finished—turned to air. These clouds, running furrows, shall still be passing, the sky will unveil its blue face and cover itself as before: but there will be no one to notice it. Not a soul!'

The baby smiled his dimpled, rippling smile, old, wise, and all-knowing. What did he smile at? Where did it come from? The smile of life winding through dark tunnels into light? Herr Kogl held out his finger at which Adam at once grabbed lustily. Was it for this that millions fought and toiled, and thought and felt? Was it for this that men went out 'over the top,' hung on barbed wires, bled on the cross? 'Little humanity,' he thought, 'is this all that is left of thy deeds and high hopes? Little humanity...' His face puckered. He turned away to the clouds chasing in the unmeaning, unmerciful vault; and wept.

THE END